Also by David McIlroy:

The Soulburn Talisman

THE SUBSTITUTE

David McIlroy

AMBER HILL

For those who tried to teach me.

some time ago

'Hey. Hey, buddy.'

A tapping on the glass.

'Hey. You can't park here.'

He stirred and looked towards the sound. The guy was right up close to the window. He wore a Seahawks cap, one of the old kind.

'You gotta move, unless you're buying gas. You buying gas?'

The man behind the wheel shook his head.

'Then move your car.'

He nodded and reached for the ignition; when the engine rumbled to life, the guy in the Seahawks cap walked back to the store entrance. The driver shifted gears and pulled out from under the gas station canopy into the rain without looking back.

It was late and the roads were slick. Traffic wouldn't be a problem tonight.

Traffic was the least of his worries.

Maurice looked at the shotgun nestled snugly into the passenger side of the car and thought it was funny, in some ways, how the guy at the gas station hadn't noticed it lying there. It was a big gun and he hadn't tried to hide it, so either Seahawks Cap Man hadn't seen it, or he just hadn't cared.

He also thought it was funny, in a different kind of way, that he'd never killed anything before in his life, intentionally or otherwise, and tonight he was going to jump straight to the big leagues, go from being a

MURDER VIRGIN

to, well, something else entirely.

Until not so long ago, he'd never even considered doing it. That's what he'd have told someone, if they'd asked. He was a rookie in the game when it came to even *planning* a kill (*a total novice, sir, green as they come, oh yes*) never mind actually *doing* it, actually pulling the trigger and snuffing out a life, right then and there. What kind of shit was that? That was for gangsters and drug dealers and guys who robbed their local 7-Elevens with their hoods pulled up. It wasn't for someone like him.

Maurice the Murder Virgin.

Tonight, though, things were different. Tonight it *was* for someone like him. *He* was different. He'd been different for a while now, he knew that much.

He knew it, and he was still scared shitless.

Driving east in the rain on I-90, somewhere between Moses Lake and Ritzville (he wasn't exactly sure anymore), he once again began to recite the details of his plan. He spoke each word carefully and deliberately, through gritted teeth: 'Go to the house, park on the street, leave the motor running...'

He inhaled as a car flashed by in the other direction.

'...walk to the door, knock on the door, wait for it to open...'

His knuckles bulged on the wheel. Hot sweat trickled down his forehead, pooling along his eyebrows.

'...when it opens, go inside, close the door, shoot twice. Make sure. Doubly sure. Then leave, and come home.' He cleared his throat. 'Go to the house, park on the street...'

No, Maurice Baxter the murder virgin had never killed anyone before. But tonight, he'd finally have his cherry popped. Yessir. Spectacularly and irrevocably *popped*.

Tonight, he was going to give his flower to Evelyn Sparrow. Both barrels of it, right in the face, if he got the chance. And he would do his best to make that chance happen.

Bang bang. Pop goes the cherry.

Up ahead, rain lashed down in driving sheets, turning the black surface of the highway slick and sharply reflective. The car wipers swished furiously across the windshield, beating in vain at the spray coming off the road. Maurice hunched over the wheel, leaning close to the glass - he was goggle-eyed, and any passing driver catching a glimpse of him might have assumed he was nervous and just trying to get a better look at the road. But he wasn't. He barely saw the road, or the rain, or his own strained, bulging knuckles.

He'd tried listening to the radio a few miles back, just to distract himself from thinking about what was ahead. But any station he'd tuned into was blaring stuff he'd never heard before, hopelessly repetitive "music" by artists more interested in their social media presence than writing halfway-decent lyrics. Just the same lines, over and over again. Incomprehensible trash. Maurice wasn't a big music buff by any means, but he still recognized real genius when he heard it - give him Hendrix or Berry ahead of these talentless hacks any day of the week.

After a few minutes of station hopping, he'd punched the 'off' dial and gone back to staring at the road in silence, listening to the sound of rain drumming on the car's metal body. Then, when even that got too much and his frayed mind started to turn in on itself, he'd stopped at that pokey little gas station for a breather and spaced out immediately, blocking one of the only working pumps.

And now, all he could do was recite the plan like some sort of comforting liturgy.

'... park on the street, walk to the door, knock on the door, wait for it to open...'

Another car flashed by, heading west. Outside, the rain-drenched landscape between towns was flat and empty, dotted here and there with growing puddles of muddy water. The road ahead of Maurice was nothing but a dark abyss glimpsed through smatterings of rain on the windshield, a blackness his headlights barely penetrated.

Headlights.

His wide and manic gaze flicked to the rear-view mirror. For the first time since passing through Moses Lake, there was another car on the road behind him.

Maurice Baxter's heart, which already thumped painfully against his breast-bone, began to beat faster. It was eleven-thirty at night. The roads had been pretty empty for a while - most sensible folks were tucked up in bed or heading that way; soon they'd snooze peacefully while rain pounded on the roofs of their houses and the wind whistled below the eaves. There weren't many people out tonight journeying along this little section of highway, unless they had somewhere particularly important to be. Or, unless they were cops.

What would he do if the police stopped him out here, in the dark of night during a rainstorm? What would a cop say when his flashlight beam lit on the double-barreled shotgun wedged down in the passenger side of Maurice's battered old Honda Civic?

Where are you headed tonight, sir?

Oh, not far. Just a ways down the road, you know?

Sure. And what's the purpose of your journey this evening?

Murder. Death. Blowing someone's head clean off her shoulders, all being well.

Well then, drive safe, sir. Take it easy on those roads.

Will do, officer.

Maurice watched the headlights draw nearer. They shimmered and blurred in the rain, sometimes appearing close, sometimes still far off. But they were gaining.

He swallowed hard, squeezing the wheel so tight it felt like his tendons would snap. He could feel the tires of his car struggling for purchase on the wet asphalt beneath him. It'd do no good to go off the road out here in the middle of nowhere, just because there happened to be someone behind him. They had every right to be on this stretch of highway, just as much as him. It was a free country.

He eased off on the accelerator. The needle dropped from sixty-five to sixty, then on down to fifty. Behind, the other car came closer and closer. He eased off more, slowing to forty-five. He dared go no slower, just in case it was a police car and he drew too much attention to himself. His eyes jumped from the rear-view mirror to the road ahead, and back. As the other car came up behind him, its headlights ballooned in Maurice's rear window, refracting off the rainwater and momentarily dazzling him. He shut his eyes, just for a second.

Then the headlights were gone from his rear view and the car was passing him, slipping by on the right. He caught a brief glimpse of a man wearing thick spectacles, lounging back in his seat. Then he was gone, motoring off into the distance. His taillights bloomed red in the dark, and then faded.

Maurice released the breath he'd unintentionally been holding. A shiver traveled up his spine and burst somewhere in his brain, and he began to laugh uncontrollably, thumping the steering wheel with sweaty hands. No cops, just some other driver. He probably had a gun on his passenger seat too, come to think of it. Why not? This was America, after all.

He pressed his trembling foot down on the accelerator again, speeding up to fifty, then sixty. He knew he was being an idiot, almost having a panic-attack because someone else was driving behind him late at night. If something as innocuous as that could knock him off kilter, how was he ever going to do what he'd come to do? He'd probably chicken out halfway up the driveway and bolt back to the car, or she'd open the door and he would...

But what if she didn't open the door? What if she wasn't even home right now? Or if she was, she might just decide to leave the door locked and chained, and call the police. He wouldn't be able to hide the fact he was carrying a big-ass shotgun, not if she happened to flip on the porch light and look out the window. He wasn't even wearing a long coat or something he could disguise it under. If she had even an ounce of sense, she'd just leave the door locked and wait for help to arrive, and that'd be the end of him.

No, not tonight. If he had to shoot the lock off the door, he'd get into that house. There was no going back, not now. And besides, if Evelyn was who he thought she was - who he *knew* she was - the sight of a gun wasn't going to faze her. He'd just have to be quick and decisive in the moment.

Bang bang, and back to the car.

He ran a hand down his face, trying to settle himself. His heart still bounced around inside his chest, but he was used to it now. From the moment he'd climbed into the car and jammed the gun securely between the passenger seat and the glove compartment, his pulse hadn't slowed. Maybe it was making up for the time it was about to lose. Maybe pretty soon, the 'ol ticker would be done for good.

It didn't matter. As long as he got to her first, anything that happened to him would be irrelevant. As long as he stopped her, and stopped her tonight.

He passed a sign for Ritzville but couldn't see how many miles were on it. The rain was coming down harder than ever. He swallowed again - his throat was bone dry. Not long now.

'Go to the house,' he said to himself, 'park on the street...'

His headlights caught raindrops exploding on the road ahead, glittering like diamonds.

'... walk to the door, knock on the door, wait for - '

'Where're you going, Maurice?'

His blood turned to ice in his veins, and for a solid three seconds, his heart simply stopped beating. His mouth hung open, frozen comically in mid-sentence. He willed himself to believe he hadn't heard it, that it had only been inside his head. It was an hallucination, delirium, his tired and brittle mind conjuring something in the dying minutes before his plan was to be enacted. It wasn't real.

'Maurice *Baxter*.'

His eyes turned first, grinding to the right in their sockets, pulling his head after them. He didn't want to look, but he was unable to stop himself.

She was sitting in the passenger seat, her hands folded casually in her lap. She wore a dress, plain and down to her shins, and flats on her feet. He saw these first. Then his eyes trailed up, following the point of her knees and up to the curve of her thighs. Her hands were white, so white. Her fingernails were purple and bloodless. His eyes kept going up her body, up and up, past her elbows and the small bulge of her bosom, tracing to her neckline and the first curls of her auburn hair.

Maurice tried to stop himself and found he couldn't. Time had slowed and he was no longer in control. His eyes kept drifting up, past her chin and mouth and nose and cheeks. And when they slipped into the line of her gaze it was like falling into a dark and bottomless hole in the earth, because where her eyes should have been, there was nothing but blackness.

There were no eyes in her skull.

'Hi, Maurice.'

The last part of his name came out in a long, snakelike hiss. His shoulders trembled madly, as though someone was trying to shake him from a dream. She grinned and her teeth were as white as her skin. Bone-white.

'Where're you going?' she asked again.

His jaw juddered, but somehow the words formed: 'You're not here. You're not real. This isn't happening.'

Evelyn threw back her head and laughed. It was a cackle, the sound of many crows cawing at once. Maurice felt his bladder loosening, ready to release.

'You're crazy, Maurice. Of *course* this is happening. I know what you're up to, you naughty boy. Yes I do.' She waggled a finger at him and he saw it was now just bone, without flesh. 'And you know what happens to naughty boys, don't you?'

He managed to tear his eyes away. His gaze fell on the shotgun next to her leg.

'Go ahead,' she said. Her voice rocketed upwards in pitch, becoming instantly shrill. '*You've already done it, anyway.*'

He looked up again. Her chest was now a gaping, bloodied hole, singed around the edges and still smoking. He could see the passenger seat through it.

'Good shot, Mo,' she cackled, her dead eye sockets growing large. Her grin became a hideous leer and her jaw seemed to elongate until it was over the wound in her chest where her breasts had been.

Her tongue lolled out and Maurice pissed the driver's seat.

'*What're you waiting for, Mo?*' she shrieked.

With a cry, he went for the gun with both hands. He actually got it up and turned towards her contorting white face before the car started to hydroplane on the road. The steering wheel spun and the Civic fishtailed, then went left, mounting the median. Maurice saw Evelyn grab the shotgun, laughing hysterically; it went off with an ear-splitting *boom*, shattering the passenger side window, spraying him with glass. She was still there, screaming laughter, a living corpse.

Then the car bounced over the reservation and flipped, rolling across the other lanes. The world became a tumbling kaleidoscope of screeching metal and flying glass. Maurice's head smacked off the steering wheel and the airbag slammed into his face, breaking his nose. His vision filled with red and swam in a haze. The car rolled again, maybe even twice, before coming to rest upside-down on the shoulder. Rain drummed on the underside; the engine hissed.

Maurice had no idea if he was alive or dead, but it didn't matter. Not really.

He'd failed. Evelyn's ghost had done her work.

He closed his eyes and sank into the dark.

Part one: Lou Jennings Gets THE FLU

one

18 days before Thanksgiving

Lou Jennings was getting sick.

It had come from nowhere, sneaking up during the last few classes of the day, unnoticed in the busyness of her teaching routine. First she'd felt fatigued (nothing new there, it was a Monday after all), then a banging headache had started (still reasonably normal for a Monday) and finally, just as her Grade Twelve class was winding down, the sore throat had arrived. And that was the kicker.

Flu.

It wasn't unusual for a high school teacher to pick something up around this time of year, especially when she had two young children of her own who were, at times, walking incubators of infection. November was early for flu, yes, but it'd been unseasonably cold and dry in October and the kids had been Trick or Treating all over the neighborhood just last week, so who knows? Maybe she'd handled a germ-covered Milky Way while helping them sort through the haul dumped from their little plastic pumpkins.

'Bye, Mrs Jennings,' said Darcy Keenan as she passed her desk.

'Bye, Darcy,' replied Lou with a smile. It vanished the instant she was alone in the classroom. She placed both hands on her desk, lowered her head and groaned.

The flu, already. It's barely winter.

Her head was banging. Lou eased herself into her chair and hoisted her bag into her lap. She rummaged through the untidy menagerie inside and came out with a small bottle of Tylenol. Her mug was empty - she'd have to swallow them dry.

As she unscrewed the top, Jeff Clarke sauntered into her room with a quick rap on the door frame, grinning in that annoyingly perky way of his. Jeff taught Geography, was obsessed with finely-roasted coffee and the places that served it, and currently lived alone in a pristine studio apartment across town. Lou had been at his place once for a Christmas party, and that was it. But he was a light and breezy presence in the teachers' lounge, which was more than she could say for some of her other colleagues.

'Another Monday down, huh?' he said.

'Looks like it. Your day good?'

'Superb. Had to confiscate a repeat offender's phone earlier - her parents'll probably be after me by tomorrow. Back in my day, the parents jumped to support the teacher, not the student.'

'In your "day"? What are you, thirty?'

'Twenty-nine.' Lou groaned and Jeff's grin widened. 'Can I borrow your stapler?'

'Yeah, but I'll need it back.'

'Sure.' She pulled open her top desk drawer; Jeff's eyes went to the Tylenol. 'You have a headache?'

'Pretty bad one, yup.'

'Sucks. Better lay off that Halloween candy next time.'

'You know me, I just can't resist those Reese's Pieces.' She handed him the stapler. 'Actually, I think I'm coming down with something.'

'Oh, really?'

Lou laughed and felt a quick stab of pain in her throat. 'I saw that.'

'Saw what?'

'That look, like you'd just been handed a block of pure anthrax. It's ok, I have some disinfectant in here as well if you want it.'

'It's not that...' Jeff started. His grin faltered. 'But it's not flu, is it? I've heard it's going around some.'

'Probably not,' she lied.

'Good. Want me to get you water for those pills?'

'No, I can take them dry. But thanks. Just bring back that stapler tomorrow, I had to buy it myself.'

'I will. Listen, feel better, ok?'

'Thanks Jeffrey.'

He made a face at the use of his full name - like a little boy, she thought - and headed for the door.

'You'll be fine by tomorrow,' he said. 'Just get a good night's sleep.'

'Will do.'

He left and Lou popped two Tylenol in her mouth. She swallowed hard, forcing them down her throat, grimacing at the unpleasant sensation.

Jeff was probably right, she'd be fine by tomorrow. She'd have to be - there was already a ton of grading to be done and lesson prep to finish. Tonight would be one of those "powering through" occasions. She'd make herself be fine, if she had to.

But as she rose to her feet and the room swam in front of her, she suddenly wasn't quite so sure.

She made her way through the emptying school building to the front entrance, throwing a quick wave to Beverley the receptionist. Beverley, phone to her ear, waved back amiably. A short while later, Lou was parked by the curb just down the road from the school. In the field adjacent to the sidewalk, her son was just finishing up with soccer practice.

Ben was a natural, she'd been told. He was nine - tall for his age and skinnier than she'd like, but he got that from his father - and had been playing since he was old enough to kick a ball. He was too scrawny for football and he couldn't swing a bat to save his life. He'd dipped his toe in a number of sports throughout his tender years and only one seemed to fit. Soccer was definitely Ben's game.

But as she caught sight of her son crossing the field towards her, the cold November breeze whipping leaves around his ankles, Lou knew right away that something was wrong.

She forced an easy expression as he opened the door, smiling warmly. As if to counter it, a sharp chill swept into the car and she suppressed a shiver.

'Hey honey,' she said, watching him.

Ben didn't make eye contact as he pulled the door shut.

'Hey, Mom.'

'How was practice?'

'Fine.'

His dark hair stuck out at crazy angles on his head. As he clipped his belt on, she saw he had muddy scuff marks on his arms and knees, and one below his left ear. Totally normal for soccer practice, especially this late in the year.

'Just fine?'

'Yeah. Can we go home?'

'Sure.'

She started the car and eased away from the curb. Warm air blew from the vents, mercifully heating the blood in her cold hands. She'd forgotten to bring gloves today. That ominous scratchy feeling at the back of her throat was becoming more pronounced by the minute.

Ben slouched in his seat, gazing out the window. His school and sports bags were jammed around his feet.

'What'd you do in practice today?' Lou asked casually.

He hesitated, fractionally, but she clocked it. 'Not much.'

'Not much? Well that sounds useful. Does the coach always teach you "not much" at practice? Maybe I should have a word with him - '

'We did shooting drills,' he said quickly.

'You score much?'

'Some. What's for dinner?'

'No idea, your Dad's in charge of it tonight. Probably chili again.'

'Aw, not chili...'

'You know it's his speciality.' *And he can't make a whole lot else.* 'What happened at practice?'

'I told you, just shooting drills. And we played a game at the end.'

'Did you score then, too?'

'It's not always about scoring, Mom.' There was reproach in his voice now. 'You have to defend as well. I was in defense today, at the end.'

Buildings blurred past on either side, gray and cold under the darkening November sky.

'Oh I see. How'd you defend?'

'Good. I'm good there, Coach says I know how to read the game. I made some great tackles.'

He was brightening now. 'Yeah?'

'Yeah, I won the ball every time. Then at the end, I tackled Ralph Nowak and kinda kicked his leg, here' - he pointed at his shin - 'and hurt him, I think, because he started crying. And Ralph said I did it on purpose, and Coach must have believed him because he said he might bench me for the next game.'

'Bench you?' She coughed once, unexpectedly.

'Yeah, but I didn't do it on purpose Mom, I *didn't*.' Now he was looking at her and she saw the insistence in his green eyes, so much like hers. 'It was just an accident. But Ralph said I was trying to hurt him because he's a Pole.'

'*What?*'

'Yeah, but that's not true. I would never - '

'I know you wouldn't. Did your coach bench you for the next game because of that? Did he think that's why you tackled him?'

'I... I don't know.'

Now he was looking down, and a quick glance over confirmed what she'd heard in his voice. There were tears brimming around his eyes.

'Hey now.' She reached over and took his hand, squeezed it. He didn't pull it away. 'I know you'd never do something like that, Ben. It's not in your nature. Besides, you're one eighth Polish on your Dad's side.'

'I am?'

'You are. Of course, that shouldn't be the only thing keeping you from doing something like that, should it?'

'No.'

'You just forget about it, ok? And if your coach or Ralph says anything again, you tell me right away and I'll handle it, got it?'

'Mom, I don't need you to handle it for me. I'm not a kid anymore.'

That startled her. She'd never heard him use the words "I don't need you" in a sentence before. She didn't like it. But all she said was, 'I know. But I'm here if you need backup.'

She drove on in silence for a few minutes. They'd be home soon.

'Much homework?' she asked, piercing the quiet.

'Yeah, too much.' He scowled. 'Math and English. It's only Monday.'

'You like Math.'

'It's easy.' He glanced at her hopefully. 'Can you help me with English?'

'That wouldn't be fair, would it?' Then she winked and he grinned for the first time since getting in the car. Out of the corner of her eye, she saw his grin falter.

'Mom, are you feeling ok?'

'Why, Benjamin?'

'You look awful.'

'Aw shucks, thanks son. You know how to make a girl feel special.'

He laughed. She caught a glimpse of herself in the rear view mirror and noticed then how pale her face was.

I do look awful.

'Ben, I want you to help your Dad with dinner tonight, ok?'

'Can I use the big knife?'

'Of course, hun. And then you can drive yourself to the emergency room so they can sew your thumb back on.'

'Eww, Mom! That's gross.'

She grinned and pulled into the driveway.

That evening, Lou sat at the kitchen table and graded papers. The dinner things had been cleared away and the dishwasher hummed reassuringly next to the sink. She could hear Ben in the living room, laughing at some TV show. She'd looked over his English homework and gently suggested a few improvements (resisting the urge to highlight the mistakes outright), and then he'd flown through his Math assignment in fifteen minutes. No sweat.

Above her head, a door closed and there were footfalls on the landing. Their little girl, Ruth, had called for them a couple of times already. She was four years old and increasingly concerned about the inexplicable something lurking under her bed at night. Ben had been the same at her age, but the boogeyman was no match for Daddy.

She listened as he entered the living room and took a sip of lukewarm tea, wincing as it slid over the inflamed flesh in her throat. She was achy and sluggish, and that was with another dose of Tylenol running through her veins. With a sigh, she circled the C+ and set the paper aside, reaching for the next one.

Derek came into the kitchen, an empty glass in his hand. He glanced at the pile of papers on the table as he went to the sink.

'Our girl's thirsty tonight,' he said, twisting the faucet.

'It's all that chili.'

He filled the glass and set it on the countertop. She felt his eyes on her and looked up. There was concern there.

'How do you feel, babe?'

'I've been better. Can you make more tea, please?' He took her mug and went to the kettle, flicking the switch.

'You've looked better.'

'I believe "awful" was the word your son used earlier.'

'He hasn't learned to sugarcoat the truth just yet.'

She threw him a look, then smiled. 'You men have to protect us ladies from our own delicate sensibilities, after all.' Suddenly, she started coughing explosively and had to push back from the table. He was at her side, rubbing her back.

'I think you should call in sick tomorrow, honey.'

'I... can't,' she managed in between coughs. 'Too much to do.'

She coughed several more times, so loud she was sure Ruth would call for them again. In the other room, Ben had lowered the volume on the TV.

'Mom?' he called. 'Are you alright?'

'I'm fine, sweetie,' she replied, lying again. 'You need to get ready for bed, ok?'

'I will soon...'

'You've got about two minutes, Ben,' said Derek. 'Then you better get ready.'

'Ok.' The volume on the TV went up again.

Derek frowned down at her, still rubbing her back. Behind the copper beard, she saw his mouth take on that familiar lopsided slant. His spectacles slipped down his nose and he pushed them back up.

'I'm serious,' he said, 'you don't look well.' He put his palm to her forehead - it was delightfully cool and her eyelids flickered involuntarily. 'You're burning up.'

'I'll be fine,' she replied. 'Just make me some tea. I'll finish these papers and come right to bed.'

Reluctantly, he went back to the kettle. She started into the next paper, but with some alarm, found that the words were out of focus. She rubbed her eyes and they became clear again, but it was enough.

'Leave it, Derek,' she said. 'You're right, I feel horrible. Take me to bed.'

'Now you're talking.'

'Really? Even now, when I'm like this?'

He took her in his lanky arms. She could smell his cologne, sweet and soothing. He met her gaze and held it. 'For you, I'd push through.'

She broke from his embrace and threw a couple of mock punches, which he batted away, laughing at his own joke. She smiled despite herself.

'I'll be up soon, jerk.'

He winked and strolled into the living room with Ruth's water. After some mild protestations, Ben allowed his father to usher him upstairs.

Lou headed for the door. Reaching for the switch, she cast a dismal look at the remaining papers on the table.

I'll do them before breakfast.

She flicked off the light.

Lou woke in the middle of the night from the midst of a fever dream. She'd been at the kitchen table again, surrounded on all sides by teetering piles of white paper, towering over her like skyscrapers. No matter how fast she graded, the piles never got any smaller - if anything, they only grew, closing in tight around her. The room became warm, then hot, and finally she realized with horror that the piles of paper had caught fire and she was trapped, with no way to escape. Flames leapt up the paper towers, creating pyres of searing heat. One by one they began to topple, covering her with sheaves of burning death that wrapped around her skin and set her on fire too...

Then she was awake, sitting up in bed next to her peacefully snoring husband. She really was burning up - her body radiated heat and every pore on her body churned out hot sweat, drenching her pajamas.

She swung herself out of bed and walked shakily to the bathroom. Her head was pounding and even in the dark, she could tell the room was spinning madly. She made it to the bathroom and switched on the mirror light, and almost gasped at her appearance.

Her face was slick with sweat and her green eyes seemed to pop from her skull. Her hair, jet black and only just beginning to lose some of its youthful luster in her thirty-fifth year, was a tangled mess matted to her head. The fever heat pulsing from her skin seemed to bounce off the walls of the bathroom, washing back over her in nauseating waves.

She twisted the cold water faucet and splashed her face several times until the heat dissipated slightly. That helped, and she was finally able to pull her thoughts together. She had the flu, a bad strain of it, and she needed to knock the fever back. She needed pills.

But as she started to open the medicine cabinet, her lungs seemed to erupt inside her and she exploded into a fit of painful coughing. Bent double, she pressed her hands tight to her mouth, desperate to avoid waking Derek and the kids. The coughing fit lasted for a solid minute and left her throat raw and throbbing.

Maybe she should wake Derek? He'd know what to do.

But then the coughing came back, threatening to make her wretch, and she knew she had to get downstairs, away from her sleeping family. She snatched a bottle from the medicine cabinet and staggered down the hall, suppressing her coughs as the world swam around her. Each step on the stairs seemed to drive a fresh wave of pain into her head. By the time she reached the ground floor, her face was once again lashed with sweat. She wanted to lie down then, right where she was by the front door, and not move for the rest of the night, because moving made it worse.

Get a hold of yourself, Lou. You're a big girl, you can handle this.

She forced her legs to move. Her fluffy polka-dot pajamas clung to her sweat-soaked skin and her joints ached, making each step towards the kitchen torturous. The house was cold inside, chilled by the November night, but it felt to her like the thermostat had been cranked up to eighty.

Have I ever had a flu this bad in my life?

Then she was in the kitchen, shuffling towards the sink. The paper pile was still on the table, silently mocking her. *You'll never grade us, Louise! And we've got reinforcements on the way! Surrender!*

She filled a glass, her hand trembling under the faucet, and uncapped the Naproxen. The little blue pills went down easily with the water. She leaned over the sink for a minute or so, fighting the powerful urge to wretch. The fever heat became chills and her body began to shake uncontrollably. She stood there in her bare feet, her pajamas glued to her body, shaking like an addict coming down.

After what felt like an hour (though it could have been just a couple of minutes, for all she knew), she shuffled through to the living room. Ruth's toys were still scattered on the rug by the cold fireplace and she stubbed her toe on one, swearing aloud. Up above, she imagined she heard someone stir, then become still again.

Can't make it back up there, she thought. *Can't do it.*

It didn't matter anyway - the choice was taken from her. As she neared the couch, a wave of dizziness swept her from head to toe. The edges of her vision began to gray out and it was all she could do to get herself onto the couch before she passed out. Then she did faint, just for a few moments. When she came to, hot with fever again, she hauled her lower half up onto the couch and pulled the blanket over herself.

And that was how Derek found her later that morning.

'Hun. Hey, hun.'

His hand on her forehead, cold and gentle.

'Mmmmm?'

'Lou, are you ok?'

She opened her eyes and found even that was painful, somehow. Derek was hunkered down by the couch, his face lined with concern. No, not just concern - shock.

'You don't look great, hun.'

She swallowed and winced as a dagger went through her throat. 'I... think I've got the flu.'

'I'd say so. What can I get you?'

'Water. What time is it?'

'Six-thirty.'

He stood, gunshots going off in his knees, and left the room. She stared at the ceiling, aglow with lamp light, and tried not to swallow again. The Naproxen had knocked back the fever, for now, but she doubted the war was won. Her nose was blocked up now, too.

Derek came back with a glass of water and helped her sit up. She drank half of it and stopped. He made her finish it before taking it gently from her weak hands.

'I'll get you something from the pharmacy before work,' he said. 'You'll need to start tackling it now.'

'I have... have to go to work,' she mumbled, a little delirious.

'I don't think so,' he replied with a grin, touching her forehead again. 'You're on fire, babe. You're not leaving this house today.'

'But the kids...'

'I'll take care of them, don't worry. Can you call Perry?'

'I'll... text him.'

He brought her phone over and went back to the kitchen to start breakfast. With considerable effort, she typed out a message to the school principal. It read: *'Morning. I've come down with a bad flu, really sick. I can't make it in today. So sorry about this. L.'*

Perry Martin had been principal of the school for two decades. He was a kind, slightly eccentric man in his late fifties whose wife had died of cancer three years ago. Lou had a good relationship with him and she knew what his response would be when he read the message.

Derek stuck his head round the door. 'Toast?'

'Please,' she croaked. 'Dry. And some tea?'

'Sure.'

He disappeared again. Lou sat up properly on the couch and groaned, long and low. It was cathartic and brought some momentary relief. But every bone and muscle in her body was aching - she felt like she'd gone ten rounds with Muhammad Ali. Worse still, she knew this would just be the beginning of it all.

Lou could count on one hand the number of times she'd been seriously sick in her lifetime. A couple of those had been flu, one prolonged bout of postnatal depression after Ben came along, and a week of measles as a child. They'd all been bad, in their own way. But this was surely the worst flu she'd ever experienced. So far, anyway.

From the landing, she heard a voice call uncertainly: 'Mommy? Daddy?'

'It's ok, Ruthie,' she tried to call back, but it came out in a weird gargle.

'I've got her,' said Derek, sweeping into the hall. Lou listened to the soft, deep tones of his voice as he reassured their daughter, followed by the sound of his footfalls going upstairs.

She smiled. This was Ruth's routine, awake shortly after six then in and out of sleep until seven. Ben wouldn't stir until closer to eight. The boy could sleep through a hurricane.

Her phone buzzed and she looked at the screen. The message from Perry was as she'd expected. She set it down and closed her eyes.

'*No problem, Lou. I'll send for the sub.*'

TWO

17 days before Thanksgiving

It was unseasonably warm that week in Amber Hill, Illinois. The cold and wet of the previous weekend gave way to sunshine and cloudless skies. Around town, people ditched their winter coats and heavy boots for wool sweaters and sneakers; school children, forced by parents to wear layers under their Halloween costumes, kicked and danced their way through piles of crunchy red and yellow leaves in t-shirts. By Thursday, temperatures peaked at a balmy sixty degrees and Mister Lee on Beechwood Avenue declared that Mother Nature had decided to skip winter altogether and jump right into spring, if his old hip was anything to go by. The normally depressing limbo period between the magical end of October and the early promising signs of Thanksgiving had been supplanted with a very late (and very welcome) Indian Summer.

It was a pleasant week in Amber Hill, many of its residents observed, very pleasant indeed. For some of them, it was the calm before the storm.

Lou Jennings missed nearly all of it - the week went by in a haze. She spent all of Tuesday on the couch dosed up on painkillers, working her way through a carton of orange juice and most of a box of tissues. Her throat felt like someone had spent the week scraping fall leaves off it with a rusty rake and her headache refused to budge an inch, no matter what she took. The Naproxen, however, did a fine job knocking her fever back, and she was lucid enough at least to watch some awful but easy daytime TV.

Derek wanted to stay with her. He'd offered to work from home, even suggested rescheduling an important client meeting that day, but she wouldn't let him. He took the kids off to school, promising to return later with antivirals and whatever else she wanted. Lou requested chocolate, and lots of it.

After lunch (successfully held down), her headache eased and she managed to finish grading the papers that had languished on the kitchen table. There were plenty of Bs, a few Cs, one unfortunate F, and several As. Her ninth grade class was currently halfway through *To Kill A Mockingbird* and Scout had just discovered Dill Harris under her bed, mistaking his arm for a reptilian intruder.

How does a snake feel?

Sort of rough. Cold. Dusty.

Lou had taught English at Amber Hill High for six years now, and this novel was still one of her favorites. Most kids liked it well enough.

She texted her spin instructor to let him know she couldn't make it that evening. The thought of trying to pedal one of those fixed-position bikes made her feel dizzy. Derek, Ben and Ruth arrived home mid-afternoon - Derek was able to get out a little early and planned to finish up some work after dinner, as he often did. Ruth had gone to their friend Debbie's after kindergarten. She spent a good ten minutes regaling Lou with stories about the imaginary creatures she and Debbie's daughter Sarah had captured in the sandbox that day. Lou listened patiently from across the room, suppressing the growing urge to cough. She didn't want to infect the rest of her family, but it'd be tough to avoid them for long in their small house.

She took the Tamiflu pills Derek had picked up on the way home and retired to the pull-out bed in the spare room. He woke her carrying a tray laden with chicken noodle soup, buttered crusty bread and a steaming mug of tea. There was a Hershey's bar on the side. She blew him a kiss, ate and fell asleep again.

By Wednesday she was beginning to feel better, but still not well enough to return to school and definitely still contagious. Alone in the house once again, she spent the day working on lesson plans for the following week and cleaning, though the draining effects of the flu only allowed her to do so much at a time. In between writing notes at the kitchen table and vacuuming the kids' bedrooms, she had to flop on the couch and chug juice while Gordon Ramsey did his darndest to save another failing Italian restaurant from self-inflicted closure.

Lou hated being unproductive. It was just in her nature to stay busy, and she found herself stressing about the classes she was missing, wondering if her students were keeping up with the tasks she'd left for them. The lesson plans for the week were there - all the sub had to do was work through them. Most subs did a great job, but there were the occasional ones who slacked off and allowed the kids to dictate the pace. She hoped her sub was the former type.

That afternoon, she texted her fellow English teacher Alain Doyle and asked how things were going. She didn't text Alain much because she saw him most days. He was one of those people whose friendly demeanor didn't translate well into text form.

'Hey Alain, how're things going? Sub doing ok? Still flu-ridden here but getting better. Hopefully back soon. L.'

Alain replied a few minutes later with: 'Things are good. Sub seems to be fine. Get well soon, Lou.'

Comprehensive, Alain.

She shot a text to another teacher, Julie Heller, her best friend at Amber Hill High. Julie taught French and Spanish.

'Hey Jules, you good? Hope you're surviving. Let me know if anything interesting is going on this week, I'm very bored. Flu's the worst. L.'

She'd barely set the phone down before Julie replied.

'Hey Lou, glad to hear you're still alive. When are you back? Not much happening here. Your sub's nice. See you at the game on Saturday, maybe?'

She coughed hard for a minute and had to gulp down a glass of water before typing her response.

'Still ticking for now! Hoping to be back on Friday. I'll try not to infect you. Glad the sub's ok. Maybe see you at the weekend - fingers crossed!'

Julie replied: 'Sentirse mejor.'

By Thursday, Lou did indeed feel a whole lot better. The antivirals were kicking the flu's ass and the rest was doing her good, though being alone all day was starting to drive her crazy. She called her mom in Mount Vernon and received a blow-by-blow report on her church's plans for their annual Thanksgiving lunch for the elderly, as well as which of those elderly folks were sick or dying, or had already died.

'And Mrs Easton... you remember Mrs Easton, from down the road? She used to work in the post office, and her son George is in the army? Well, she's got the cancer in her skin. I hear they caught it early, but she's seventy-four, so who knows? Margerie Thomas says her sister also had the skin cancer, and she was never right again. She lives near Springfield...'

And so it went.

She texted Perry Martin again towards the end of the school day, saying she might be well enough to come in on Friday. He replied two hours later, when Derek and the kids had already arrived home. She thought it was a little curt: *Leave it until Monday.*

'He's probably right,' Derek said over dinner, wrapping spaghetti around his fork. 'You're still contagious, and what harm would another day off do?'

'I know, but I hate leaving it so long. I feel... Ben, stop doing that... I think I feel fine now, mostly. My throat's a lot better and the fever's almost gone.'

'You still look tired.'

'I'd look tired anyway, I'm a teacher.'

He grinned. 'Try being an architect, then you'll know what tough work really is.'

'I'd love to. Sitting around drawing houses all day. Talk about a cushy job, huh?'

'Cushy!' Ruth echoed, then giggled at the sound of it - a new word for her. Lou reached over to wipe her mouth, and she squirmed away.

'How about you take tomorrow as a final rest day, just to recover completely?' Derek said. 'Then maybe you can come to the game on Saturday?'

Ben looked at her hopefully, spaghetti hanging from his mouth. He was still young enough to want her at his games. She knew that wouldn't last much longer.

'I'll be there,' she said. 'One more day sitting round on my butt and this ol' flu will be done.'

'Mommy said butt!' cried Ruth, and they all laughed together.

On Friday, the flu had one final throw of the dice. Lou's fever made a brief reappearance, chilling her one minute and boiling her alive the next, and she coughed like a twenty-a-day chain smoker. But by lunchtime, its last embers had burned themselves out and for the first time that week, she felt energized. With no more lesson plans to prepare or papers to grade, she spent the rest of the afternoon tidying away all remnants of her flu-fighting paraphernalia (she was a little disgusted at how many used tissues had piled up in the wastepaper basket), raking up leaves in the back garden (chilly, but the fresh air was rejuvenating) and preparing dinner.

That night, they lazed on the couch and watched a Pixar movie, munching on popcorn ("poopcorn", according to Ruth) and nachos. Ben went to bed already excited for Saturday's game. There'd been no more talk of Ralph Nowak or the soccer bench since Monday.

'I think I'll join you again tonight,' she informed Derek as they prepared for bed.

He rinsed toothpaste foam from his mouth and spat into the sink. 'Yeah?'

'Yeah. Feeling better now.'

'All the way better?' he asked with a sly grin, his hand on the small of her back. She knew he was kidding, she probably still looked terrible. But he was a man, after all.

'Maybe, tiger,' she replied, slinking to the bedroom.

But as soon as she climbed back into bed after three nights of self-imposed exile in the spare room, sleep took her, and that was the end of any monkey business.

At ten-thirty the next morning she sat on the bleachers by the soccer field, watching the game. It was a brisk but sunny Saturday. The bulk of the spectators (mostly parents) were wrapped up in coats and scarves. Lou clutched a travel mug of coffee in her hands, relishing the smell of it. Next to her, Derek bounced Ruth on one knee, trying to keep her occupied - Ruth wasn't much of a sports fan just yet.

Ben's coach had unfortunately made good on his promise. Their son was on the bench alongside two other boys, but he didn't seem in any way put-out. They yelled and cheered every kick of the ball as the Amber Hill Raiders took on the Bloomington Blues, chasing each other around the field like mad things. Lou wondered, not for the first time, how children always had so much energy by the end of the week.

'Take it easy, little Miss,' said Derek, wincing as Ruth clambered into a standing position in his lap. Her blonde curls fell about her face endearingly.

'I have to go to the bathroom,' Ruth announced abruptly, in the succinct way young children often announce things.

'We'll be right back,' said Derek, hoisting her into his arms.

'Get me a chili dog on your way,' Lou replied. 'With cheese. And an extra large chocolate milkshake.'

'Fries on the side, yeah?' he called back.

'Two portions.'

He laughed. She watched them go, smiling as Ruth tried to steal Derek's Chicago Bears cap. Other parents glanced her way, wondering if she might be serious.

The game was approaching half-time when Debbie appeared, plunking herself down in the seat next to her.

'Morning sunshine,' she said. 'How're you feeling now?'

Debbie Lathem lived nearby and often babysat Ruth. Lou met her at a Moms and Tots group a couple of years ago and they instantly hit it off. She didn't have many close friends in Amber Hill but Debbie would definitely have been at the top of the pile regardless. She was a single mom whose boyfriend had vamoosed when she became pregnant. Debbie said it was the best thing that could have happened, looking back on it - the guy was an idiot.

'Feeling good Debs, thanks,' said Lou. 'What're you doing here, anyway?'

'Nice to see you too!' Debbie said, feigning offense. 'I was passing by and thought you might've made it down. And here you are, right as rain. Playing hooky all week, eh?'

'You know me,' Lou grinned.

The half-time whistle blew and each team drifted back to the sidelines. Ben glanced up at her and she gave him a thumbs-up. He threw one back and went to join the team huddle.

'Your boy's getting big,' Debbie said.

'Gonna be tall, like Derek. But he has my brains.'

'How'd your sub get on?'

For some reason, the question took Lou by surprise. *How* had *the sub gotten on this week?* Alain hadn't revealed much in his clinically-brief text, and all Julie had to say was that she was "nice", and Julie thought everyone was nice. Lou didn't even know the sub's name.

'Fine, as far as I know. I haven't actually heard much from the school.'

'Do you think the kids like her more than you?'

She laughed. 'Probably.'

Did they?

'I'm kidding, I know those kids think you're great. She was probably fresh out of college and more scared of them than they were of her.'

'Or she was a total babe and hilarious and they all loved her.'

'Who cares if she was? She's gone now and the Boss Lady is back.'

'She could have had three heads and a tail - as long as she got them to work, I don't mind at all.' Lou sipped her coffee, watching the coach gesture animatedly on the sideline as the kids sucked on orange slices. It looked like Ben might be coming on for the second half. 'Thanks for looking after Ruth this week, Debs. Really appreciated it.'

'My pleasure, she's no trouble. Sarah always asks to see her anyway, I think they might be besties. Speaking of...'

Derek edged his way across to them, holding Ruth above the heads of still-seated parents. She was wearing his Bears cap now.

'Hey Debbie,' he said.

'Debbie!' Ruth cried. 'Where's Sarah?'

'Not here right now, sweetie,' Debbie said. Ruth looked crestfallen. 'But maybe your Mom can bring you over this week for a playdate?'

Lou nodded and Ruth lit up again. Derek swiveled the cap round on her head.

'It's amazing actually,' said Debbie, 'that the rest of you guys didn't get that flu.'

'I have the constitution of an olympic athlete, you see,' Derek replied. 'Plus I repeatedly spurned Lou's advances all week.'

'Yeah right!' she laughed. 'If I'd batted my eyelashes just once you'd have come running, my darling.'

'Uh oh, how do I extricate myself from this?' Debbie said, pretending to slide away from them.

'You can't, you're part of it now.' On the field, the kids were getting ready to start the second half. 'But you're right, it's amazing no-one else got it. I felt like a walking contagion.'

'These things can burn out pretty quickly,' said Debbie. 'And it probably came along at just the right time. You needed the rest.'

Down below, the referee blew his whistle and the teams drifted back onto the field. Ben was on now, playing in defense.

'I'll leave you guys to it, you've got some cheerleading to do.' Debbie stood. 'Give me a call to arrange that playdate, yeah?'

'Sure. Bye, Debs.'

The day grew colder as they watched the second half, cheering any time the ball was near Ben. He played well, putting in some good tackles. In the end the game was a tie, two goals apiece, and both teams meandered off the field in decent spirits.

Lou shivered, squinting up at the graying sky. 'It's getting chilly. Should we get her coat on?'

'No coat!' exclaimed Ruth, but Derek was already pulling it from the bag. Other parents were doing the same for their kids as they exited the bleachers.

'Let's go straight home,' Derek said, struggling Ruth into her coat. 'I don't want you getting a chill. We can pick something up for lunch.'

'Sounds good.'

They waited for Ben at the field entrance. He found them, muddied from head to toe but beaming, and they headed to the parking lot. Cars were already swinging out of spaces as parents tried to beat the traffic.

As Lou buckled Ruth in, Derek said, 'Hey, isn't that Julie from the school?'

Lou looked up. Julie was a few spaces down, chatting to another parent over the roof of her car.

'Julie!' Lou called amiably.

Julie turned and looked her way. Lou smiled and waved.

A frown creased Julie's forehead; she slowly raised her hand and waved back, her frown deepening. Then she ducked into her car.

What was that?

Lou got in and closed her door. She reached for her belt.

'That was Julie, right?' said Derek, starting the engine.

'Yeah,' said Lou. 'It was.'

'Mom, can we stop for ice-cream?' Ben said from the back seat.

'Ice-cream!' Ruth echoed.

'It's too early for that, Ben,' she replied, looking at him in the rear view mirror. 'How about popsicles?'

'Ok.'

'Popsicles!' cried Ruth.

They maneuvered their way out of the parking lot and onto the street. There was already a lot of traffic and Derek sighed. 'Think I'll need a popsicle too.'

Maybe she just didn't recognise me, Lou thought. *Maybe the flu's taken what was left of my youthful vitality.*

She smiled to herself, but it quickly faded. No, Julie would have recognised her right away, and probably would have come over to ask how she was.

That was a weird moment.

Lou rested an elbow on the rim of her window and watched the street go by. The sky was now scudded with dark clouds, threatening rain, and the first inklings of a headache sparked somewhere deep in her brain. Maybe she wasn't totally out of the woods just yet.

As they drove away from the soccer fields, she leant her head against the glass and closed her eyes, just for a moment. When she opened them again, she caught a brief glimpse of a woman by the side of the road, walking the other way. She had mousy brown hair and wore a wool jumper and a plain, knee-length skirt. Their eyes met for a second, and then she was gone.

That afternoon, Lou Jennings had the worst headache of her life.

Lou lay awake on Sunday night, staring at the ceiling. Derek snored gently next to her. It was a still night and she heard every car pass by on the main road.

Something was gnawing at her, some sense of wrongness. Her body had finally given the heave-ho to the flu, and the blistering headache that had arrived so suddenly yesterday had died out just as quickly after a couple of hours. Bodily, she now felt fine. Internally, however, some strange passenger was camped out in her subconscious, whispering away. Whispering that something was *wrong, wrong, wrong…*

Earlier that evening, she'd texted Principal Martin one more time, just to confirm she'd be back the next day. She hadn't heard from him since Thursday, which was unusual for Perry - they worked in a fairly small school and he liked to keep track of his teachers. When he didn't reply right away, she set her phone face down and told herself to forget about it for now, it was still the weekend and he had no obligation to respond. But she couldn't shake the strange passenger and that growing sense of disquiet eating at the back of her mind.

As she'd clambered into bed that night, she'd told Derek what had happened with Julie in the parking lot after the game.

'She probably just didn't recognize you in the moment,' he said as he undressed. 'You know what I mean. It happens.'

'Does it? You recognised her across the lot and you've only met her a few times. I see her almost every day.'

He shrugged. 'Maybe she had something on her mind and she was distracted.'

'Maybe.'

'Stop worrying,' he said, climbing into bed. 'You'll keep yourself up thinking about it.'

That was typical of a man, she thought, as if she could simply choose to stop worrying. She sighed then, pointedly, and he rolled over to face her.

'What?'

'Nothing.'

'Lou...'

She looked at him. He was handsome in the lamplight with his unshaven face and soft blue eyes. Those eyes drew her in, as they always did. He knew it and grinned, taking her hand under the covers.

'I know you hate being away for so long,' he said. 'But you needed the rest, and I'm glad you got it. You'll be fine tomorrow - just ease back in.'

'Teaching doesn't really work that way,' she replied, but a smile played at the corners of her mouth, and he saw it.

'Make it work for you,' he said, planting a kiss on her lips. When she didn't pull away he pressed harder, running a hand through her hair. She opened her eyes and saw him looking at her expectantly, and the kiss became a muffled giggle.

'Not tonight.'

'When?'

'Maybe tomorrow. Just let me get my energy back properly.'

'Sure thing. You'll need it, baby.'

She laughed as he rolled away to switch off his lamp.

And now here she was, watching the shadows play across the ceiling at three in the morning, knowing she had to be up for work in less than four hours. Her body begged for rest but her mind wouldn't let up. When Derek had gone to sleep, the strange passenger had started whispering again and the events of the past week, trivial as they'd seemed at the time, had begun looping in her head like a slideshow: the lack of communication from the school as the week went on, no contact at all from the substitute, the fact her family had somehow avoided the flu, the Julie episode after the game... and, for some reason, seeing that woman on the sidewalk, watching her as they'd driven by. Her eyes had been big and gray, and Lou felt like they were still on her now.

Another car drove by in the distance and sleep tugged at her eyelids, but still she remained awake, her fingers interlaced on her stomach, her breathing soft and rhythmic. Lou lay like that for a long time, replaying the slideshow, listening to the whispers.

Eventually, she rolled over to face Derek and allowed herself to drift. But when sleep finally arrived, the last image that passed through her mind was of her phone screen displaying Perry Martin's text response. She'd seen it just before switching off her lamp, and it unsettled her more than anything else.

The message read: '*Who is this?*'

THREE

11 days before Thanksgiving

'Mommy, mommy! Come find me!'

'Ruth, get out of the pantry,' Lou said, slipping Ben's lunch box into his bag. 'Derek, have you seen my pumps?'

'Pumps? Umm...'

'Never mind. Where's Ben? Ben!'

'He's brushing his teeth, I think.'

'Ben, hurry it up or you'll miss the bus.'

'I'm coming!'

She heard Ben pounding down the stairs. Derek appeared in the doorway, holding a pair of her shoes. 'Found them!'

'Those aren't pumps, darling. Ruth, you have five seconds to get out of there.'

'Mommy I was -'

'Five, four, three...'

She heard Ruth throw open the pantry door and scramble out. Ben sauntered into the living room, pulling on his coat. His cow lick stuck up at the back of his head - Lou resisted the urge to try to flatten it.

'Got your soccer gear?' she said, handing him his backpack.

'Yep, it's in the hall. Are you getting me after practice?'

'Sure am. Now get going.' She kissed him on the cheek before he could dodge away. He made a face but grinned. Derek ruffled his hair affectionately as he passed, making the cow lick worse.

'Debbie'll pick Ruth up after kindergarten again,' Lou said, handing Derek their daughter's Dora the Explorer backpack. 'Could you grab her on your way home?'

'No problem. You still feeling ok?'

'Never better, babe. Now you two mush or you'll be late.'

Derek and Ruth left, and Lou went back to the kitchen to fill her coffee thermos. She glanced at the clock on the wall - it was just before seven-thirty. If she left in the next few minutes, she'd be in her classroom by a quarter of eight, slightly earlier than usual. After an enforced four days off, the extra five or so minutes would settle her. Why she felt *so* unsettled, though, was still beyond her.

Who is this?

Perry must have been out of it last night, or maybe something was wrong with his phone and he'd lost her number. Or maybe he was playing some sort of prank. But that didn't seem much like Perry Martin, collector of antique coins and stamps.

Lou swept it from her mind and focused on her morning routine. She liked routine, drew comfort from it. She wondered if that was one of the reasons the last week had been so off-kilter for her. It didn't matter - today was a new day, a new Monday, and she'd kick it off in the usual way. She finished pouring her coffee and squeezed the thermos into the mesh pocket on the side of her backpack, then brushed her teeth (she always did this last) and left the house.

It was noticeably colder than last week and barely light. Above, the sky was blank, a featureless mass of cloud - the sun was shining somewhere, but she couldn't see it. On the radio, the morning DJs bantered back and forth about sport and mundane local news. Lou half-listened, her mind already on the day's classes as she guided her Toyota Corolla through Monday morning traffic. Tenth Grade were up first and that meant *Lord of the Flies*. Plenty to work with there. A bit of mob mentality to start the week.

Kill the pig. Cut her throat. Spill her blood.

It wasn't her favorite text to teach, but just to be back in the classroom again - to even be on the *way* to her classroom - was a relief. Four days of the flu had been more than enough. As much as the rest had done her good, routine and structure were better. Plus, she'd found she actually missed her students. Most of them, anyway.

Maybe she'd make good on her promise to Derek that night, too.

She was about a mile from the school and the radio guys were bantering about the weather when her car started listing to the right. Two seconds later, the tire pressure light started flashing.

Lou swore and pulled over to the side of the road. Fortunately she was still in a suburban area with street lights blazing, and a space was available to ease the car into. She killed the engine and got out to look.

The rear passenger-side tire was flat.

'Oh come on,' she muttered, casting a glance up the road in the direction of the school. She was so close, almost near enough to keep going on the flat. But she'd already made the decision for herself by stopping.

The tire was sunken all the way to the wheel, puddled beneath the car. It hadn't blown out but it mustn't have been far away. It had to be changed.

Great, thought Lou.

Zipping up her coat, she went to the trunk and took out the jack, then hauled the spare tire round to the sidewalk. A man passing by wearing earphones hesitated when he saw her crouch by the wheel, then carried on.

Lou propped the jack in the correct spot under the Corolla and started spinning the arm. She didn't need any help, though it probably wouldn't hurt. Her college boyfriend, the one she'd dated just before Derek, had once laughed at her when they'd gotten a flat on the way to the movies and she hadn't known how to change it. Then he'd had trouble getting the tire off and spent the rest of the evening in a foul mood, embarrassed, as though it'd somehow all been her fault. The relationship had run its course shortly after that. Lou had taught herself how to change a tire and had never asked Derek to do it for her, though he would have in a heartbeat and wouldn't have given her any grief for it.

She glanced at her watch. It was already quarter of eight and she'd only started.

Just great.

It took her another fifteen minutes to remove the flat tire and replace it with the spare. The flat wouldn't come off and she had to sit on the cold sidewalk and kick it until it loosened enough to detach. No-one stopped to help her. By the time she was getting back into the Toyota, it was after eight o'clock, the clouds were beginning to break up, and her hands were filthy with grease.

'Great, great, great,' she muttered through gritted teeth, starting the engine.

Her heart was racing as she pulled into the parking lot outside Amber Hill High. In her six years at the school, she'd never once been late to work. Sure, she'd taken a few days of sick leave here and there, but she was never late. And now, as she hurried from the car towards the red brick school building, not only was she late, but she'd missed homeroom and morning registration.

Lou climbed the steps to the main entrance, her pumps clocking on the smooth granite, and pulled open one of the glass doors. Her backpack caught on the other door as she went in and she swore again. Behind the glass window that opened into the school office, Beverley looked up, phone to her ear.

'Uh huh, uh huh,' she said, smiling pleasantly at Lou.

'I'm late, sorry!' Lou mouthed, hurrying past. She pushed through the interior doors and left the reception area, heading straight down the Languages hallway; she didn't see Beverley start to rise from her seat, one finger held questioningly in the air.

The hallway, now empty, was lined on both sides with lockers. Lou's footfalls echoed off the walls and ceiling as she passed them. She'd caught a glimpse of herself in the glass of the entrance door and knew she looked pretty disheveled - her face was flushed and her hair was everywhere - but she didn't care. She was here now, just a couple of minutes into the first class period. Behind closed doors, she could hear the familiar murmur of students not yet settled down to work. She saw that her own students, her Grade Tens, weren't waiting in the hallway.

Another teacher must have brought them in, she thought. *Probably Alain, he's right next door. I hope he isn't annoyed.*

She came to her classroom door and paused to catch her breath, smoothing her hair. On the other side, she could hear the drone of conversation and laughter. Lou inhaled, let it out slowly, and opened the door.

'So sorry, everyone,' she exclaimed, breezing inside. 'I had some car trouble this morning.'

Twenty-two heads swiveled in her direction. She threw them her customary beaming smile, genuinely glad to see them after nearly a week away. Faces instantly matched up with names: Bradley Hargreaves in the front row, Jessica Grant behind him, Thomas Joyce at the back. Sophie Wentworth, seated in a shaft of bright sunlight by the window, turned to look her way. She was frowning.

Many of them were.

'Hi,' came a voice from the corner, 'can I help you?'

Lou hadn't seen her. She was standing at the computer station, an open folder in her hands. Their eyes met, and for a moment, no-one spoke.

Lou realized she was still grinning stupidly, except now her mouth was also ajar, frozen in a rigor of surprise. She could feel student eyes shifting from her to the woman in the corner, and back to her again.

'Umm... sorry, I was late getting in today,' Lou said hoarsely. 'I'm Mrs Jennings.'

The woman in the corner turned fully towards her now, her gray eyes unblinking. Her light brown hair was tied up in a bun, making her appear older than she likely was. Lou thought she couldn't be more than twenty-five. She wore a beige sweater, long gray skirt and black flats.

Am I in the right room? Lou thought. But her cursory glance upon entering had told her that she was. It wasn't something she was liable to get wrong, was it?

'Hello, Mrs Jennings,' she said. Her voice was soft. 'I'm Miss Sparrow.'

'Miss... oh, you're the substitute teacher.' Relief flooded through Lou and she laughed. 'Of course, that makes sense. There must have been a misunderstanding with Per... with Principal Martin. I'm actually back today.'

A frown creased Miss Sparrow's forehead. 'Back?'

'Yes, I've been off sick. Sorry guys - ' She addressed the kids, who were still staring at her in silence, ' - I'm interrupting your class. Miss Sparrow, can I speak to you for a minute?'

'Sure. Everyone, open up to chapter six and start reading, please.'

Sighs and murmurs as the kids opened their books. Miss Sparrow closed the folder in her hands and crossed the room. Lou noted that she was short, probably at least two or three inches below her own modest five-eight. She smiled and motioned towards the door. 'After you.'

Lou led the way into the hall. Miss Sparrow closed the door and the kids instantly started talking.

'I'm very sorry about this,' said Lou, as warmly as she could muster. 'This has happened before, I think. Sometimes they forget to let the subs know the teacher's back. Sorry you've wasted your time coming in today, I know it's a real pain.'

Miss Sparrow's gray eyes fixed on her. Lou felt the beginnings of a headache starting somewhere in her brain. The other woman smiled, but when she spoke, it was with careful deliberation.

'Mrs Jennings,' she said, folding her arms. 'You'll have to forgive me, but I'm a little confused. You said something about a substitute teacher...'

'Yes.'

'Ok, and are you saying that's *you*? Because if so, I wasn't aware - '

'No, no,' Lou laughed, spreading her hands. 'Not me. I'm not the substitute, Miss Sparrow - you are.'

The words sounded ridiculous coming out of her mouth. Another door opened further down the hallway and there was a brief babble from inside. A student emerged, closing the door behind him. He glanced their way and headed for the bathrooms. The clapping of his footsteps on the tile floor bounced off the walls like ricocheted gunshots. He turned the corner and was gone.

The little crease in Miss Sparrow's brow had deepened. Up close, Lou could see she had bad skin, masked inexpertly with too much makeup. Something about her was horribly familiar. Had she met this woman before?

'What do you mean, *I* am?'

Lou hesitated, feeling heat rise up her neck. 'Aren't you the one Perry called in to cover me last week?'

'Last week?'

'Yes, I was off sick with the flu. Since Tuesday. But I'm back now.' Her explanation came out in little bursts. 'I contacted Per... Principal Martin... last night to let him know I was coming in again today. Someone should have told you. Like I said, I'm sorry no-one did.'

Miss Sparrow was staring at her now in open confusion, laced with something else. Lou knew her face had gone red, but she was powerless to stop it. Why was her heart beating so fast? Why did she feel like she'd been caught in a trap?

'Mrs Jennings,' said the mousy-haired stranger in front of her. She spoke slowly now, as though to a child. 'I'm really not sure who you are. If you're a substitute teacher, that's fine, we can get things cleared up right away' - Lou opened her mouth and closed it again, 'but this is my class.'

'It isn't,' Lou croaked.

'It is,' Miss Sparrow replied patiently. 'I teach English. I've taught here for several years, and this has always been my classroom. I'm afraid you're mistaken.'

Lou felt a wave of dizziness wash over her. What was happening here?

Perry's text again: '*Who is this?*'

'Is this a joke?'

'No, no joke. If it is, I'm not in on it. Maybe you should try reception? Beverley might be able to help you out, she's great. I should get back to - '

Lou drew herself together with a shake of her head. 'No, Miss Sparrow. There's been some mistake. I don't know what it is yet, but I'll find out. I'm not a substitute, I'm the English teacher here. I've been at this school for years. Those are my students in there, in my classroom...'

She trailed off. She'd been pointing at the door, and now she stared at where her finger was aimed and the dizziness grew stronger, stirring up nausea. When she'd left the room last Monday, a sign on the door had read 'Welcome to English!' and below it, 'Room 2, Mrs Jennings'. It was a customized thing she'd bought online a few years back, after her contract was made permanent. Just a little quirk, something to put her stamp on the role.

The sign still read 'Welcome to English!', but the second line was now 'Room 2, Miss Sparrow', with a little cartoon bird attached to the corner.

Lou moaned and the words swam out of focus. Down the hallway, the kid returned from the bathrooms and glanced their way again.

'Mrs Jennings...'

'No!' Lou snapped suddenly. She grabbed for the door handle.

'Hey, wait!'

Lou pushed open the door and went back into the room. Conversations faltered as the students turned to look at her again.

'Everyone,' she announced, crossing to the front desk (*her* desk), 'sorry for interrupting you again. This'll just take a second.'

'Mrs Jennings, please - '

'I really don't know what's going on here,' Lou continued. She was aware her voice was rising in pitch, and she was grinning again, like a maniac. 'If you're all playing a big prank, that's fine - ha ha, very funny, you got me. Your poker faces are top-notch, really they are. But honestly, it's been a rough morning and I'm just coming back from illness. I wish I had the energy to get on board, but I don't, not today. So if we could just wrap this up now and get back to work, that'd be great.'

They stared at her. One or two were smirking. At the back, Thomas Joyce whispered something to Natalie Tempo and she stifled a giggle.

'Mr Joyce,' said Lou automatically, 'something funny?'

The boy looked at her, his smile evaporating. 'How do you know my name?'

38

Lou just stood there, dumbstruck. The room seemed to close around her, the walls leaning in, walls covered in displays she'd made herself. Her displays, *her* room. All hers.

Wasn't it?

'Bradley,' said Miss Sparrow from the doorway. 'Could you go next door and get Mr Doyle, please?'

Bradley Hargreaves pushed back his chair and left the room. Lou tried to meet his gaze as he passed, but he wouldn't look at her.

'Guys, this is crazy,' she said, pleading now. Her heart was thumping so hard she thought it might burst from her chest. 'Please, can we just stop this?'

But they just continued to stare at her. She could see they were uncomfortable now, shifting in their seats. And there was something else there too, something she sensed in them, and the abrupt realization sent panic surging through her.

They were afraid.

Lou took a step back and her bag slipped off her shoulder. It hit the floor and her thermos fell out of the pocket. The cap opened as it struck the tiles and coffee spilled out.

'Oh shit!' she gasped, stooping to pick it up. 'Oh sorry, sorry.'

A couple of kids in the front row stood up as steaming brown liquid spread towards their desks. Lou fumbled the cap back onto the now-empty thermos and lifted her bag away from the coffee puddle.

'Someone get me some paper towels,' she cried. The kids looked towards Miss Sparrow, who nodded. Sophie Wentworth went to a cupboard below the windows as the smell of strong coffee filled the room. For some reason that Lou couldn't comprehend at the time, Sophie's simple act of obedience to another authority, of circumventing her, shoved her forcibly towards some internal tipping point, and she snapped.

'*Sophie!* I asked you to get it, you don't need her permission. *I'm* the teacher here!'

Sophie stared at her, wide-eyed and scared. Lou straightened up slowly, pushing back hard against a sudden urge to start laughing. It wouldn't be happy laughter, and she knew she wouldn't be able to stop once it started. Her backpack was a dead weight in her hands and the coffee pooled at her feet.

And then Alain Doyle was in the room.

'What's going on here?' he demanded, looking incredulously from the students to the coffee spill, to Lou.

'Alain!' she cried, abandoning all pretenses of teacher etiquette. 'Alain, please!'

Her fellow English teacher stared at her. Alain was pudgy and balding with horn-rimmed spectacles. Most of his students weren't especially fond of him - unless they were prodigies when it came to the English language, in which case they found him immensely helpful - but Lou had always liked him. Never moreso than in that moment.

Alain continued to stare, uncomprehending, for another few seconds. He looked at the students, who were frozen in their chairs. Then, to Lou's overwhelming relief, his face broke out in a smile and his tone changed.

'What seems to be the problem?' he asked pleasantly.

'Alain - ' Lou began, but Miss Sparrow cut across her. Her tone was almost apologetic.

'Mr Doyle, we have a visitor here today.'

'I see.'

'She's here without invitation, I'm afraid.'

'Ah.'

Lou took a breath to steady herself. Her legs had turned to tissue paper and it was all she could do to stay upright. Inside, however, a spark of anger was starting to kindle her resolve.

'Alain,' she said again, measured now. 'Something strange is going on here. I don't know what it is exactly... a joke, a misunderstanding, whatever. But it's stressing me out and, quite frankly, it's embarrassing me in front of my students. They're here to learn and we're wasting their time with this. So if you don't mind, I'd like an explanation as to why this woman is in my classroom, calling herself the teacher.'

At the word "woman", Miss Sparrow ducked her head and folded her arms tighter. She seemed smaller then, even timid. Lou felt the anger inside her grow hotter.

'I understand,' Alain said, the pleasant smile still painted on his face. 'And you're right, this is detrimental to the students' education. Why don't you and I go see Principal Martin? Perhaps we can straighten all this out. Miss Sparrow can look in on my class until I get back.'

He's pretending not to know me, Lou thought. *He wants to get me away from her.*

'Ok, let's do that.'

Alain nodded and turned to go out the door. She followed, ignoring Miss Sparrow, who had stepped back to let her pass. As she went, Lou said to the kids, 'I'm so sorry, guys - I'll see you soon', but none of them smiled back. Sophie Wentworth remained by the window, the roll of paper towels in her hands.

As soon as she left the room, Miss Sparrow closed the door behind her.

The hallways were still empty as she and Alain walked back to the reception area. Perry Martin's office was right next to the staff room. He'd be in there now.

'I'm so sorry, Alain,' said Lou, carrying her dripping, coffee-stained bag by the top handle. 'I really don't have a clue what's going on here.'

'It's ok,' he replied, still smiling. 'We'll get it all worked out.'

'I have no idea who that woman is, do you? Was she here last week?'

'She was...'

'And was she saying the same stuff then too? About having been the teacher for years? I'm not sure I like leaving her with the students, Alain. She could be dangerous for all we know.'

'Let's just get it all worked out,' he repeated.

It was at that moment she realized he was keeping a couple of feet away from her, and his arms, normally swinging freely, were rigid by his sides. They were almost at Perry's office.

'Alain,' she said, her throat dry. 'You know who I am, don't you?'

He glanced at her but didn't make eye contact.

'Let's just... see what Principal Martin thinks, shall we?'

Lou's stomach dropped. Her tissue-paper legs wobbled, threatening to send her sprawling onto the hallway floor. The unsettling sensation she'd experienced all week, that feeling of wrongness and disconnection, was manifesting itself right now, here in the school, with a co-worker who didn't seem to know who she was, or was pretending not to. Her strange passenger was now alive and well and running the show.

As they approached the Principal's office, the door opened and Beverley the receptionist came out. She was talking over her shoulder to Perry.

' - just went right by me, didn't have time to stop her. I was on the phone and only thought about it afterwards. She could be anywhere. I'm so sorry...'

'Never mind, Beverley,' Alain interjected. 'I believe I've found who you're looking for.'

What followed next were the strangest few minutes of Lou's life. She stood there in the reception area outside Perry's office while he, Alain and Beverley scrutinized her. Beverley, flustered and annoyed at a "visitor" entering the school without her permission, demanded to know who she was. Lou told them, and then told them again. The three exchanged skeptical glances, wordlessly relaying to one another what they actually thought of her story. Here she was, some stranger telling them she worked in the school, in the role occupied by someone else who they'd apparently known for years. The more Lou insisted, pleaded, laughed in self-conscious disbelief at what was happening, the further she seemed to push them.

Finally, Perry invited her into his office and dismissed the others - Alain was reluctant to leave, but eventually agreed to return to his classroom. Lou went in and sat down shakily in the chair opposite Perry's desk. The principal eased into his seat and steepled his fingers, surveying her with kindly blue eyes.

'Now, Mrs Jennings,' he began.

'Lou,' she said.

'Lou. How do you feel now?'

'I'm ok.'

'Would you like some tea?'

'No, thank you.'

'Alright. Lou, I hope you can appreciate my perspective in this matter, why I'm reluctant to accept your... account... of the situation. You caused a major disruption in one of my classrooms and probably frightened a few of our students, though I doubt they'd admit that themselves. I'd have every right to remove you from the premises, maybe even involve the police in the matter. Can you appreciate this?'

Lou stared at Perry Martin, her boss of the last six years. She remembered him getting a little tipsy at last year's Christmas party and belting out 'Sweet Caroline' on the karaoke machine.

'I can,' she said.

'Good. Now, you say you worked here previously, as a teacher of English?'

'Yes.'

'Was that in a temporary capacity, and perhaps I don't recall you? I'm afraid my memory isn't what it used to be.'

'No, it was full-time. I've been here for six years, as long as Julie Heller, the Languages teacher.'

She saw a ripple of uncertainty pass over Perry's face, then it was gone.

'Yes, Mrs Heller has been here for a while. Tell me, have you ever had children study at Amber Hill?'

'Not yet. They will in a few years.'

'Ok. And you have no other connections to the school that I should know about?'

'Beyond working here for the last six years? No, not really.'

Perry cleared his throat and shifted in his chair. The leather squeaked under his buttocks.

'So what would you like me to do, Mrs Jennings?'

'It's Lou,' she replied. 'I'd like you to tell me what's going on. I'd like to know who that woman is in my room, masquerading as the full-time English teacher. I'm concerned for my students and my fellow employees, and for myself, and I'd like you to do something about it, sir.'

Perry shifted again, clearly uncomfortable.

'Look, Lou, I really don't know what - '

Enough. I'm going for it.

'Perry, I know you,' she said, leaning forward. 'I've known you for years now. You helped me get started in this town and I'll always be in your debt for that. You've been at my house once, met my husband Derek a few times, and my kids as well. Ben and Ruth, you know them. You sent us a gift when Ruth was born. We're friends, Perry, not just colleagues. Friends.'

'Mrs Jennings, I - '

'I knew your wife,' she continued in a rush. 'Margaret. She liked gardening and Agatha Christie novels. We organized a couple of charity events together. That's how I got so into fundraising - she inspired me. She was kind and funny, like you. She got bowel cancer and died three years ago. I was at the funeral. It rained that day. Please. You know me.'

His face was locked somewhere between shock and confusion. She could see him searching her, could see the conflict behind his eyes. There was recognition in them, flickering, on the periphery. She reached out to take his hand.

'Perry.'

Then his face changed, darkening with anger. His cheeks flushed red and he stood up, knocking into his desk. A stack of papers toppled and skidded over its surface.

'Get out of here,' he said, his voice trembling.

'Perry, please...'

'Get out of my school!' he yelled suddenly, slamming a fist down on his desk. 'I don't know who you are. Get out, before I call the police!'

Startled, Lou got to her feet and went to the door. Perry stood on the other side of his desk, red-faced and seething, glaring at her until she left the room.

Lou could feel a lump pushing its way up her throat as she headed past Beverley in reception. She didn't look at the other woman but she felt her stare, cold and filled with warning - Beverley had the phone handset in her hand and her fingers were poised over the keys, ready to punch in 9-1-1.

The Corolla was parked at the far end of the lot (her usual bay was taken this morning) and with every step towards it, Lou felt the lump force its way closer and closer to the back of her mouth. *I'm going to cry*, she thought. *This is pathetic. I'm going to sob like a little girl. And then I'm going to start screaming.*

But when she eventually got in the car and slammed the door, it was laughter rather than sobbing that erupted from her. She gripped the wheel and laughed hysterically, suddenly not caring who heard her, until tears were streaming down her face. She wiped at them with the back of her hand, gasping for breath. Across the parking lot, Amber Hill High watched her silently in the cold morning sunshine.

'What the hell,' Lou breathed, drying her face with her sleeve. 'What the hell.'

She looked across at the school, half-expecting to see Perry and Beverley marching towards her, police sirens in the distance. But she was alone. Beyond the red brick walls of the school, students and teachers busied themselves with the first classes of the day, oblivious to what had just happened in Room 2.

Her classroom, *her* students.

'What the hell,' Lou said again.

What was she supposed to do now? More than anything, she wanted to gather herself and go straight back to Perry's office to talk it out. She deserved an explanation, and perhaps he deserved an apology from her. Maybe that would smooth things over and they could work out what was going on. Perry knew her, she was certain of that. They could figure it out.

But as she gazed across at his office window, just a silvery sheen in the morning light, she knew that going back in there right now would be a huge mistake. She'd seen Perry angry before, most often with misbehaving students, but it'd been a *forced* anger, a sort of performance for the benefit of others. What had transpired in his office just now was totally new to her. She'd witnessed a normally calm and gentle man become consumed with rage. She knew he'd call the police as soon as she set foot inside the building.

Letting out a shuddering breath, Lou pulled her phone from her pocket and called Derek. His face, rugged and handsome, flashed up on her screen as it dialed. She put it to her ear and waited, but after at least a dozen rings he still wasn't picking up. She canceled it, sent him a text saying '*Call me*', and set her phone down on the passenger seat.

So what now? She looked at the clock on the dash - it wasn't yet a quarter of nine. Should she wait here and see if anyone followed her outside? If Jules heard about it during the first break, would she come after her?

No, she wouldn't. She knew it now for sure - Julie Heller hadn't recognized her after the game on Saturday, hadn't known who she was. If she spoke to Jules or Jeff Clarke or any other staff members now, the reaction would be the same: *Who are you? How'd you get into the school?*

Somewhere deep down, Lou understood that something had been wrong all week. Yes, she had the flu, and at times she'd been crazed with fever and exhaustion. She'd spent most of the week alone in the house; no-one could have blamed her for not being able to think straight, for feeling that something wasn't right. But now, sitting in her car puffing little clouds of breath in the chill air, she understood: something had been *wrong* since her flu started, certainly since Tuesday morning. Since the sub had been called in.

Miss Sparrow.

Lou glanced at her coffee-stained backpack. She knew many of the subs who were called in to cover for teachers - Amber Hill wasn't a big town, and there were only so many people in it with teaching qualifications. If there *had* been a mixup with a sub, she might have expected to see old Mrs Ernest behind her desk, squinting at the teaching notes through her cataracts, or the newly-graduated and relatively-clueless Mr Johnson stuttering his way through the lesson as the mocking stares of older kids dared him to try teaching them.

She hadn't expected to see anyone at all, much less this bun-wearing twenty-something in her long skirt and sensible shoes. Her gray eyes were too large for her face, further exacerbating her mousy appearance; Lou had discerned no real curves under those plain clothes, no hips or breasts to write home about, no junk in the trunk. Not that she was anything special herself. She knew she was just being cruel, but why shouldn't she be? This woman was an intruder. Somehow she'd taken her classroom and her students and no-one seemed to know who she was, not even her colleagues, her friends. How was that possible? Something had been wrong last week, ever since Miss Sparrow entered Amber Hill High.

I teach English. I've taught here for several years, and this has always been my classroom. I'm afraid you're mistaken.

The headache that had been threatening in the school was now pulsing through her head. She felt terrible and it probably showed on her face. Lou turned the rear-view mirror towards herself and gasped - her right cheek was smeared with grease. She must have wiped her face without thinking after changing the tire.

Cursing, she rummaged in her bag for the Tylenol bottle. *Maybe I should sleep,* she thought. *I'm probably exhausted and I'm not thinking straight.*

She popped the Tylenol in her mouth and swallowed them dry, wincing.

Should she go straight to Derek's office and see him? It'd definitely make her feel better. Or would it just make things worse? She was already angry and embarrassed, and she may end up taking it out on him. The last thing she needed was an argument starting over this, and if he tried offering advice she knew she'd explode. Why did men always feel the need to advise rather than just *listen*?

She sighed and closed her eyes. She should try calling him again, or call someone at least. Either way, she knew she couldn't stay in the Amber Hill High parking lot much longer. Beverley was undoubtedly watching her through the reception window, phone ready in her hand like a sniper rifle. She had to leave.

Lou opened her eyes, blinking as they readjusted. She dropped the Tylenol bottle back in her bag, sighed, and twisted the rear-view mirror towards its proper position.

Miss Sparrow was sitting in the back seat.

Lou cried out breathlessly and recoiled. She twisted around and looked behind her.

The seat was empty.

She stared at the space where she'd seen the woman sitting. It was Ben's seat, on the passenger side. She was sure she'd seen her just then, grinning, watery gray eyes fixed on her own. She must have imagined it, but her heart was pounding hard nonetheless.

I need to talk to someone, Lou thought, and her voice was high with fright in her head.

She fumbled the key into the ignition and started the car.

Debbie Lathem was a copywriter and editor. She worked in a semi-freelance capacity for several news and magazine outlets across the county, writing articles, blog posts and website copy. She was a good writer and did well for herself.

As Lou neared Debbie's house, she began to worry her friend wouldn't be home. She knew Debbie often went to a coffee shop in the morning and spent a couple of hours on her laptop with her phone on silent. If she wasn't home, she could be hard to track down.

Fortunately, Debbie's car was in the drive as she pulled up. As Lou came up the walk to the house, she opened the front door and waved her in.

'Lou, what're you doing here? Shouldn't you be at school? What's on your face?'

Debbie made good strong coffee and they sat at her kitchen table. Birds chirped and twittered around the feeder in her little back garden as Lou recounted what had happened at the school. Debbie listened in silence, sipping coffee. When Lou finished with Miss Sparrow's appearance in the back seat, she set her mug down. Lou waited.

'You're feeling ok?' Debbie said. 'No more flu.'

'No. I'm fine now. It's not a fever talking, trust me.'

'And it definitely wasn't some sort of joke?'

'No way.'

Debbie took another sip of coffee, turning Lou's story over in her head. When she finally spoke, it was exactly what Lou needed to hear: 'I believe you.'

'You do? Really?'

'Of course,' said Debbie. 'It's too bat-shit crazy to make up.'

Lou laughed then. The sound of it was strange in her ears.

'I thought I was going insane,' she said. 'All the way over here, I kept wanting to turn around and drive back to the school, just to see if I'd imagined the whole thing. I pinched myself real hard on the arm in case I was dreaming, but it hurt like a mother.'

Debbie grinned. 'I can confirm you're awake.'

'What do I do, Debs?' Lou said, cradling her mug. 'I can't set foot in that school again or they'll call the police. You should have seen the look on Perry's face when I talked about his wife.'

'I think you did the right thing,' said Debbie, leaning back in her chair. 'I mean, that should have been enough to jolt him out of whatever funk he was in, right? Talking about his dead wife n'all.'

'Yeah.'

'It seems to me the worst thing you could do today would be to go anywhere near that school again. If it is some sort of stupid joke - a *really* stupid joke - someone there will call you and apologize. Probably Perry, or maybe even that Sparrow woman. It might've been her idea.'

'I'm not so sure...'

'Maybe not. But if it's not a joke and they're all experiencing some sort of mass hallucination or something, then you showing up again will just make things worse, and the police could end up on the scene.'

'Yeah.'

'So lay low for today, sugar. Go home and get some rest. I'll grab the girls from kindergarten as usual. Then you and Derek can talk it over tonight and decide your next steps. You may have to get a lawyer involved.'

'You think so?'

'I do. I mean, if some stranger's trying to take your job - '

'*Has* taken it...'

' - then you'll need to get serious. Get legal onto it and get her out of there as fast as possible. The longer she's there, the more difficult it'll be.'

'Squatter's rights, huh?'

'Something like that.' Debbie took a gulp of coffee. 'You said you knew something was off this past week?'

'Yeah, I did. I don't know what, exactly, but something was wrong. It felt like I *knew* she'd be there when I walked into that classroom, you know? Like I was doing something wrong just by being there, like I was the one intruding, not her.'

Debbie nodded and Lou shifted in her seat. Her headache was starting to ease.

'And I realized on the way here,' she continued, 'that I'd seen her before. It was after the game on Saturday, when we were driving home. I saw her on the sidewalk and she looked right at me. She held my gaze.' Lou shivered.

'Do you think she was following you?' Debbie asked slowly.

'Maybe,' Lou replied. 'Maybe *I* should follow *her*, see where she lives.'

'Not a bad idea.'

Lou looked at her. 'I was kidding.'

'Were you? It doesn't seem crazy, you know.'

'And what do I do when I find her house? Just walk up and knock the front door and say 'Hey Missy, how's about you give me my job back?', or something?'

This time Debbie laughed. Lou smiled, but a heaviness was settling over her again.

'I just don't know, Debs. I feel like an idiot.'

'You're not,' said Debbie, standing. Her chair scraped noisily on the linoleum. 'Now let me give the orders - go home and rest. Have a nap or something. You'll feel better. Then you can tackle this tomorrow.'

'I have to get Ben from practice.'

'So nap 'til then, ok?'

'Ok.'

She stood too and Debbie gave her a hug. Lou felt the sobbing-laugher sensation building in her again.

'I'll give you a call later, ok?' Debbie said.

'Sure. Thanks, Debs.'

'Anytime, Lou-Lou.'

She watched Ben trudge across the field towards her car. The November wind whipped at his hair and she noticed, as she had many times recently, how he was becoming more like Derek every day.

'How was practice?' she asked.

'Fine. Good.'

'Good.' He buckled up and she pulled away from the curb. 'Was it chilly out there?'

'Wasn't too bad. It was sunny. What's for dinner?'

She smiled. 'Chicken pie.'

'Awesome,' said her son, brightening.

Lou had decided to take Debbie's advice. After leaving her friend's house that morning, she'd gone home and slept. At first, she'd been able to do nothing but stare at the bedroom ceiling and listen to the sounds of the neighborhood outside as other people went about their day: cars swooshed by on the road, doors were opened and closed, dogs barked at everything, and a cold breeze whistled around the house.

Had it not been for the events at the school, she might have found it peaceful. Most parents would kill for a little alone time at home after the morning rush, with nothing to distract them. But of course, for the first half an hour or so, all she could do was replay in her mind what had happened earlier, over and over again: the confused, scared looks on the faces of her students; Miss Sparrow coming towards her across the room (was gliding a better word?); Perry's fist slamming down on his desk, his eyes bulging with fury. It still felt totally unreal, like she'd watched it all on a TV show.

I don't know who you are. Get out before I call the police.

She lay on the bed, turning it over in her mind. After relaying the story to Debbie and gauging her reaction, which she believed to be genuine and sympathetic, Lou had come to a few key decisions.

First, her confrontations in the school had definitely happened. She hadn't dreamt it all or had some sort of psychotic episode. It felt unreal, but it *was* real nonetheless - the coffee stains on her backpack attested to that, as did her lingering headache. Miss Sparrow had, in fact, ousted her from her position as English teacher at Amber Hill High, and her colleagues didn't seem to know who she was anymore. She had, in fact, been yelled at by Perry Martin and driven from the place she'd worked for the last six years.

Second, since the whole thing had happened in the real world, it must have a real-world basis. But that simply threw up a series of impossible-to-answer questions. Who was Miss Sparrow, if she wasn't the substitute of last week? If she *had* been the substitute, why did everyone else, including the students, believe she'd always been there? And why did no-one in the school remember who she was when Debbie had no problem recognizing her?

Looking at the situation analytically like that helped calm her nerves, and Lou felt weariness wash over her as the adrenaline ebbed away. She fell asleep, fully dressed on top of the bed covers, and woke up after lunchtime with a crick in her neck. Outside, the morning bank of cloud had dissipated and cold winter sunlight crept in around the edges of their blackout curtains. She tilted the digital clock face towards her - it was just after two.

Lou swung out of bed, groaning as her joints cracked, and undressed. She knew she had to wash up, had to cleanse herself of the remnants of that morning, which now seemed far-off and stranger than ever. She took a long shower, breathing in the steam slowly, then dressed and went downstairs. She made herself a sandwich, ate half of it, and threw the rest out. Then she worked at her backpack, scrubbing out the coffee stains as best she could. Derek still hadn't returned her call, and no-one else had messaged her.

With nothing else to occupy her, she gravitated to social media and spent more time than she'd have liked trawling for any sign of Miss Sparrow on the usual websites, but without a first name it was almost impossible to narrow the search. And besides, teachers rarely listed their full name in their profiles to avoid discovery by inquisitive students - she went by her middle name on her own accounts: Grace. Some students had still managed to find her, of course.

At quarter of four, she left the house and went to pick up Ben. The school rush had died down by then and the roads had been quieter than that morning. And now, as she drove them home with a fixed smile on her face, she thought ahead with some trepidation as to how she'd tell Derek about what had happened.

The moment arrived that evening as they were clearing the table. Ruth was in the living room watching post-dinner cartoons and Ben was upstairs, supposedly doing homework. Derek had come home around five after picking Ruth up from Debbie's - Lou had decided to keep her routine intact, as much for herself as for her daughter - and they'd hardly had a chance to chat before or during dinner. She'd skillfully dodged any questions about her day up until now.

It was Derek who created the opportunity. 'So your day was ok then?'

'Yeah, it was.'

'No more flu?'

'No, although I did have a headache. But it passed.'

'That's good.'

She finished scrubbing a pot, handed it to him to dry, and reached for another dish. She could see him watching her from the corner of his eye.

He knows, she thought.

'Oh, the car,' she said. 'I got a flat on the way to work.'

'Really?' He frowned, turning the pot over in his hands. 'That's annoying, those tires aren't that old. Were you ok?'

'Yeah, I got it changed myself. Made me late, though.'

'I'll bet.'

'I missed the first bell and homeroom,' Lou said, handing him another dish, 'but something weird happened. When I got to class, the substitute teacher from last week was there as well.'

'Why?'

'It was a mix-up, I think.' Then she stopped. The rest was on the tip of her tongue, straining to spill out. 'It's happened before -

and she said it was her classroom not mine and no-one knew who I was and I spilled coffee all over the floor and Alain brought me to the principal's office like a misbehaving child and I brought up Perry's dead wife and he went into meltdown and chased me out of the school and I didn't know what to do and you didn't answer your phone when I needed you

' - just some crossed wires.'

'Geez, sorry hon.'

A beat. 'It's ok. We got it worked out in the end.'

You idiot, she thought.

They made love that night. It was brief but good, and Derek promptly fell asleep as soon as they were done, leaving Lou staring at the ceiling once again.

Why hadn't she told him? Was she afraid he'd be angry with her, maybe blame her for the whole thing? Or maybe he just wouldn't have believed it. She barely believed it herself.

But she didn't think that was it. She knew Derek and knew how he reacted to news, good or bad. He was older than her by almost ten years and he never jumped the gun on anything. His response was always calm and measured, no matter what the situation. He would undoubtedly have talked it through and made her feel better about it.

Why hadn't she told him?

In all their time together she'd never been untruthful, not about anything serious. She told him everything, and she was sure he returned the favor.

So why had she lied?

Lou rolled onto her side, facing her husband in the dark. His breathing was slow and deep. She could feel his heat under the covers.

I was embarrassed, she thought. *I didn't want him to know I hadn't been able to handle it. I shouldn't have let Alain lead me from that classroom, and I should have stood up to Perry, made him remember who I was. I should have made him and Beverley and Julie and everyone else remember me, and then I should have thrown her out myself.*

Tomorrow.

She thought of Miss Sparrow and her cold gray eyes, and the anger bubbling deep inside burned off the last of her energy, and she fell asleep.

Four

10 days before Thanksgiving

Lou stared at her phone. It was just after nine on Tuesday morning. Tendrils of steam rose lazily from the coffee mug by her hand, and on the TV screen, Frasier Crane dispensed advice from his Seattle radio booth. Outside Lou's window, ugly gray rain clouds gathered over Amber Hill.

Come on, Jennings. Grow a pair.

She lifted the phone and hit 'Call', then canceled it again. She sighed, long and pained.

'Wimp.'

Derek and the kids had long-since left for work and school. Lou had played out her morning routine to perfection while they'd been there, even going so far as to prepare her ham and cheese sandwich for work, which was now in the refrigerator. She'd bustled around in her usual mom way, making a show of chiding Ben for almost missing the bus and chasing Ruth to the bathroom to brush her teeth. She made herself look busy in front of Derek so they had no time for anything beyond smalltalk. The less she spoke to him that morning, she reasoned, the less she'd have to lie.

Once they were gone, she did in fact get in the car and drive to school, arriving fifteen minutes earlier than usual. But rather than swing through the gates and into her normal space (which remained unoccupied), she parked across the street and switched off the Corolla's engine. From there, she watched students and teachers filter gradually through the entrance gates and on into the school building under a darkening canopy of cloud. She was able to pick out a few faces as they passed under still-burning streetlights. No-one noticed her.

Lou watched the entire student and teacher body of Amber Hill High arrive, including those dropped off by the convoy of yellow buses, all the way to the first bell at eight. Finally, the last morning stragglers jogged into the building and the exterior became still once again, with the exception of a few red and brown leaves skittering across the asphalt, swept by an invisible broom. Lights were on in classrooms; teachers had begun taking registration.

There'd been no sign of Miss Sparrow.

For a moment, Lou considered going inside herself. Maybe she'd enter her classroom and find Alain there, grumpily doing her roll call because no teacher had shown up, and she'd apologize, and he'd say 'No problem, Mrs Jennings, happy to do it', and she'd tell her class to open their books and begin the day, as she had a thousand other times. It'd all been a bad dream, she'd tell herself, and things would go back to normal.

But as crows began swooping down into the school parking lot from nearby trees to scavenge for any discarded on-the-go breakfasts, Lou told herself to remain where she was. She couldn't go inside, whether Miss Sparrow was there or not. As soon as Beverley (*Bev the Bouncer*, she thought grimly) saw her coming, she'd be on the horn to the police, and suddenly Lou would have to do a lot of explaining to Derek. Besides, the last person she wanted to run into right now was Perry - the man might actually go for her throat.

No, she'd have to bide her time. She needed more information before taking things further. She needed to have a plan, one that would end with Miss Sparrow's removal from the school, permanently.

Her stake-out complete, Lou started the engine again and pulled away from the curb. She drove back in the direction of their house but took a turn-off on the way, arriving at the local mechanic's around eight-fifteen. She left the car with Stevie to get the busted tire fixed (he'd worked on their vehicles for years and thankfully knew exactly who she was), then pulled her coat tight around her and walked home. It took around twenty minutes to get there, and by the time she arrived, the first drops of light rain were beginning to patter on the sidewalk.

She made coffee to warm herself, then opened her laptop and began scrolling through websites and blogs detailing what legal approaches she could take to rectify her situation. Most weren't particularly helpful because there was no precedent for job theft involving mass amnesia. Wearied, she closed the laptop and dumped it on the couch. Debbie was right - she'd have to call a lawyer.

But she had another call to make first.

'Come on, wimp,' she muttered.

She picked up her phone again, flicked open the contact for 'School Reception', hesitated only briefly, and hit 'Call'. She put the phone to her ear as it began to dial.

What do I say if she recognises me? Will she call the police?

She won't.

'Amber Hill High School, Beverley speaking.'

Lou cleared her throat - she hadn't realized it had gone dry. 'Yes, hello. I was wondering if I could speak to Mrs Jennings, please?'

A pause. 'Sorry, who?'

'The English teacher, Mrs Jennings? Louise Jennings.'

'I'm sorry, ma'am, there's no English teacher here by that name. Were you looking for Mr Doyle, maybe? Or Miss Sparrow?'

Lou's heart sank, though she wasn't really surprised. She thought quickly.

'Miss Sparrow,' she said, and the name tasted bitter on her tongue. 'Maybe that was it, actually. Has Miss Sparrow been at the school long?'

'Yes, quite some time. She's in class now but I can take a message if you like?'

'Um, a message...'

'Yes, I can have her call you back during her break. Are you a parent?'

'I, um... yes, I am -'

'Oh wait, here she comes now,' said Beverly chirpily. 'Just let me grab her. Oh, can I ask who's calling, by the way?'

Lou's eyes flicked to the television screen. 'Mrs Crane.'

'Thank you. One moment, please.'

All the moisture had gone from Lou's mouth. She stared at her coffee mug, her mind suddenly blank. What was she doing? What would this achieve? If they -

'Evelyn Sparrow.'

The voice met her ear, soft and polite, and an electric surge of panic spread through her skull. Her palm was slick with sweat.

56

'Yes,' Lou managed, keeping her tone light. 'Miss Sparrow... you're the English teacher?'

'I am. Are you someone's parent, Mrs Crane?'

Lou squeezed her eyes shut, trying to think.

'Yes, my son's transferring from another school soon... potentially transferring... and I wanted to ask about your curriculum there.'

'Oh, certainly,' Miss Sparrow replied. 'I'm very proud of the English courses we've developed here at Amber Hill High. I'd be more than happy to discuss it with you, Mrs Crane.'

The courses I *developed*, Lou thought, gritting her teeth.

'That'd be great.'

'Perhaps you'd like to call back later, after three? I'm in class all day but I hold office hours until four today. If you call anytime then, Beverley here will put you through.'

'Perfect, thank you.'

'You're most welcome,' Miss Sparrow said. Lou pictured her smiling sweetly on the other end of the line, and tasted bile. 'I look forward to our chat. Have a nice day.'

'You too,' said Lou, hanging up, 'you bitch.'

She tossed the phone aside and reached for her laptop again. At least she now had a full name to go on.

Lou trawled through the Illinois State Board of Education website for any mention of an Evelyn Sparrow but found nothing. Even if Evelyn had been a substitute teacher before last week, no official history of it existed. Lou also found no record of her own name on the website, but again, she hadn't really expected to.

She took a sip of coffee, gazing at the screen. Where else might Evelyn be online?

She decided to try social media again, now that she had her full name. It was a long shot, but what other option did she have? Practically everyone in the world had an online presence now, even if they were job-stealing imposters with bad fashion sense. Evelyn was surely the same.

Lou combed systematically through all of the major social media sites, searching for variants of the name on each one. She found a few Evelyn Sparrows (as well as some Eves and Emmas) but none of them were her, unless her appearance had drastically changed since the profiles were set up. Miss Sparrow wasn't on social media, it seemed.

With a sigh of frustration, Lou reached to close the laptop. Then she paused, her hand on top of the screen.

Of course.

She opened a new tab and brought up the Amber Hill High School website. It was a dated, late 90s-looking thing, badly in need of a revamp, but Perry Martin was in charge of it and could barely turn on his own computer. Lou navigated to the 'About' drop-down menu and clicked on the 'Staff' option.

She stared; her heart fluttered.

There she was.

The staff page featured separate bios for each employee at the school, neatly arranged in rectangular boxes with a headshot image and a sentence or two of personal detail. Evelyn's bio was halfway down the page, just below Alain's. It read:

Name: Miss E. Sparrow

Department: English

About: Miss Sparrow grew up in Mount Vernon, IL, gaining her Bachelor's Degree at the University of Chicago before going on to receive her Master's in Education. She joined the English department of Amber Hill High School in 2017 and has since become a valued member of our teaching staff, co-organising various extra-curricular and charitable events throughout each school year. Miss Sparrow loves to read and write poetry, and she's a White Sox fan - an Illinois girl through and through.

Evelyn Sparrow grinned at her from the headshot image in her bio box. Her hair was in a bun and she wore a beige cardigan, like an old woman.

Lou's fingers trembled above the laptop touchpad and she closed her fist. The corners of her mouth twitched in the beginning stages of what would either be an explosion of laughter or uncontrollable sobbing. Evelyn's gray eyes stared at her from within the screen, cold and mocking.

The bio was Lou's, almost word for word: she'd been raised in Mount Vermont by her elementary school teacher mother and accountant father, who was now deceased; she'd studied at the University of Chicago because she was too much of a home-bird to leave the state if she could help it; she read fiction constantly and wrote poetry occasionally, and she watched the White Sox play as often as possible. The only thing that was different about Evelyn's bio was the absence of Derek and the kids.

For now.

The thought came unbidden to Lou and she swiped it away with a frightened little gasp. She clicked through to the 'Gallery' page of the school website and scrolled down, and then the laughter started, because in every photo she'd previously been in, there was Evelyn, occupying the same exact space. There was Evelyn, standing next to Julie at the charity bake sale Lou had organized last month, beaming at the camera with a strawberry cheesecake displayed in her hands; there was Evelyn, laughing in the background with Jeff Clarke as Perry good-naturedly took place in the inaugural Field Day sack race in May; there was an emotional Evelyn, standing in her classroom with a small group of Grade Twelve students who'd just been accepted to English courses throughout the country.

Lou laughed. She laughed because she remembered baking that cheesecake at Julie's house, and how it had been the second attempt because the first hadn't set right and they'd had to throw it out. She laughed because Perry had face-planted in the grass seconds after that photo was taken and the other volunteer racers hadn't missed a beat as they hopped past him. Most of all, she laughed because she'd been incredibly proud of her students the day the last photo was taken, kids she'd worked with since starting at Amber Hill, the year group she'd journeyed with the longest. It'd been years of fatiguing work, staying up late to grade papers, providing support during emotional teenage breakdowns and then sharing in their jubilations, dealing with parents who were disgruntled one minute and super appreciative the next, swimming against the current in a relentless stream of good and bad times in a job that was both incredibly rewarding and mentally exhausting. That'd been time *she'd* put in. Not Miss Sparrow.

And yet there she was, in every photo Lou had once been part of, posing exactly as Lou had. She'd been replaced by a mousy-haired, frumpily-dressed copycat. Her six years at Amber Hill High had been erased in the space of a week. They'd all forgotten her; she may as well have never existed.

And so she laughed. She threw back her head and laughed, long and loud, not caring who heard her. Indeed, a man walking his dog that morning *did* hear her, and stopped briefly on the sidewalk outside to listen. He wondered for a moment or two if the woman inside was wailing in pain or despair and if he should do anything about it, and then he carried on down the street.

Lou laughed until tears streamed down her face and her breath came in ragged, aching gasps. The laptop slid off her knees and almost knocked over her coffee mug, and she kept laughing, on and on in hysteria and disbelief.

Debbie's fingers danced across her keyboard, *tap tap tap tap*, and the final sentence manifested on her computer screen. She leaned back and skimmed over what she'd just written, and then began to correct it. She was a compulsive editor, writing and rewriting every line at least twice, until it sounded perfect in her head. And when the entire article was done, she'd redraft it all over again.

Sarah and Ruth were on the couch in the den, absorbed in early afternoon cartoons, munching on apple slices. She'd picked them up from kindergarten as usual and they'd been enjoying TV time ever since. In a few minutes, she'd go in and turn it off, and they'd play inside until Derek arrived to get Ruth. It was too cold for them to play outside today - there wouldn't be many outdoor play times left this year.

Debbie brushed a strand of dark hair behind her ear and took another crack at the last paragraph of her article. It was a pre-paid copywriting job for a local company eager to boost their search-engine optimisation, the sort of thing she did regularly. Easy money for boring work.

As she deleted and typed and deleted again, her mind drifted once more to her earlier conversation with Lou. Her friend had called her up that morning in a terrible state, garbling down the phone about that Sparrow woman again, who she now knew was called Evelyn. Debbie had listened patiently, but she was worried. Lou had sounded manic.

'Do you want me to bring Ruth straight home?' she'd asked.

'No, no way,' Lou had replied, her voice wavering somewhere between another barking laugh and a tearful sob. 'She needs routine. Keep her with you, please. Away from me today, until I get myself together. I just need... some time here.'

'Lou, are you alright? I can come over - '

'No, don't. Not today. I'll be fine. Really. Thanks for getting Ruth.'

And then she'd hung up.

Debbie hadn't believed Lou's story, not at first. When she'd come over yesterday morning and relayed the whole crazy thing, Debbie had nodded along, asked questions, and listened. She was a good listener - it was what made her a good writer. But her initial reaction to Lou's account was one of skepticism (she'd gotten mixed up, somehow, and it was all just a misunderstanding) and then of deep concern (her best friend must have had some sort of psychotic episode, perhaps even a mild stroke or seizure), and she considered taking her to the hospital, by force if necessary.

However, the more Lou went over it and the more detailed the story became, the more Debbie realized she was telling the truth, or at least what she believed to be the truth. She'd never known her friend to lie - Lou was as level-headed and reliable as they came, and she was sharp as a tack. She wasn't displaying any signs of mental breakdown, either, beyond telling a very strange story that made no sense and yet was somehow fairly plausible. Perhaps there'd been some sort of mass hallucinatory event at the school while Lou had been off sick and everyone had, in fact, forgotten her. Maybe this Miss Sparrow was equally delusional, or she was simply taking advantage of the situation for as long as she could. Either way, her part in the whole thing couldn't be overlooked.

It was Lou's revelation about the school website and photo gallery that obliterated any of Debbie's lingering doubts. She'd visited the site and saw the images for herself. She knew Lou had been at those events, that the information in Miss Sparrow's bio belonged to her. Even if someone had hacked the site, changed the text and doctored the photos, someone else would surely have noticed. But she knew the images hadn't been altered - they were impossibly realistic. They were real photos of real events.

Debbie had been seriously disturbed by that.

And now, more so than ever, she couldn't get this intruding stranger out of her head. Maybe it was the investigatory journalist in her, the one she buried deep beneath all the boring copywriter bullshit. She had questions that needed answers, same as Lou. Who was Evelyn Sparrow? Was she a real teacher? How had she convinced all her colleagues and students that she'd always been at Amber Hill High, and Lou never had?

She had to know, in part to satisfy her own curiosity. She'd help Lou figure it out.

'Mommy, can we have more apples?' Sarah called from the den.

'Sure, honey,' she replied. Then she glanced at the clock, and something occurred to her. 'Actually girls, would you like a smoothie?'

Sarah and Ruth confirmed they would with a whoop of delight.

Debbie glanced at her watch. It was just after four.

Where are you?

She'd parked her Sedan across the street from the school, unwittingly in the exact same spot Lou's Corolla had occupied that morning. The girls were in the back seat, noisily slurping their smoothies through paper straws. They'd both chosen strawberry and banana.

'She wanted me to call back during her office hours,' Lou had said with a grim laugh. 'My office hours, really. Every Tuesday and Thursday until four.'

'Are you going to call her?' Debbie had asked.

'The hell I am!'

Debbie hadn't been able to resist. She knew Lou had been here earlier and wouldn't risk returning today, and she had to be at home when Ben got back from school to avoid arousing suspicion. But Derek wouldn't pick Ruth up until nearly five, so she had time to do some snooping on Lou's behalf. Assuming Miss Sparrow actually appeared, of course.

'Mommy, can we get ice-cream?'

'What do you think, Sarah?'

Sarah considered it. 'Yes?'

'No.'

They protested and she grinned despite herself. Sarah and Ruth were a funny pair - she suspected they'd be best friends for life.

Then she stiffened, her eyes on the school parking lot.

There you are.

Evelyn Sparrow crossed the lot to her car, a little silver Kia, parked in the corner bay. Debbie recognised her immediately from the school website gallery - plain clothes, long skirt, hair in a bun. She had an unfashionable leather bag slung over her shoulder and a couple of folders under one arm. Another teacher pulled out of his space and waved at her as he passed - she threw a furtive wave back, barely looking up.

This *is the imposter?* Debbie thought, watching as Evelyn got in her car and started the engine. *She looks like a scared fifties housewife. Lou could take her any day of the week.*

Debbie waited until Evelyn had turned out of the school gates before pulling away from the curb. She'd never tailed someone before and found she was rather excited by the idea of it. Evelyn was a slow driver too, which made the job a lot easier.

'Where are we going, Debbie?' Ruth asked, pink smoothie dribbling down her chin.

'Just taking the long way home, sweetie. Drink up.'

They drove across town. The school rush had finished and the end-of-the-working-day one hadn't yet begun, so the streets were reasonably quiet. She kept as far back from the Kia as possible, allowing another car to filter in between them to throw Evelyn off the scent.

Keep the Perp in sight, Detective, but don't let her make you.

Yessir. This ain't my first rodeo, sir.

They continued further west, heading for the suburbs. Storefronts and bars and filling stations gradually became townhouses and apartment blocks, and then they were right in the heart of Amber Hill's more recently-developed residential area, a neat and tidy middle-class section of town where hundreds of identical houses had sprung up over the last decade or so as the area became more prosperous. A Japanese company manufacturing components for kitchen appliances had opened a factory just outside the town limits in 2005, creating a veritable boom in the Amber Hill job market, and investors had been quick to buy up every available plot of land for suburban development. That development became two, then three interconnected developments, which were officially christened Amber Hill West in 2012. Debbie and the Jennings family lived on the other side of town, unofficially Amber Hill East, where the houses were older but less uniform, and groves of trees remained untouched between homes.

Debbie's fingers tightened on the wheel as the Kia wound its way deeper into the suburbs and the traffic separating them became lighter. She stayed as far back as possible, but she couldn't risk losing sight of the little silver car, not now. She licked her lips. If Evelyn glanced in her rear view mirror a couple of times in quick succession, she'd surely know she was being followed. And what then? A hurried getaway back to town?

Fortunately, if Evelyn had spotted her, she gave no indication she was going to stop. The Kia continued on, passing along rows of little white-washed houses with meticulously-trimmed gardens and minivans parked out front, under the gently-swaying boughs of oak trees stripped bare by the November chill, until Debbie had absolutely no idea where she was anymore. It was dark now and the streetlights were on; Evelyn's car passed in and out of shadow, its taillights watching Debbie's Sedan like a pair of monstrous red eyes.

Finally, at four-twenty, the Kia's blinker came on and Evelyn swung into a driveway up ahead. Debbie slowed to a stop by the curb, near the far end of the street.

'Where are we, mommy?' said Sarah, peering out the window.

'Still in town, sweetie,' Debbie replied absently, squinting through her windshield. 'Finished your smoothie?'

'Yeah. I don't want any more.'

'That's ok.'

Evelyn wasn't getting out of the car. Had she seen her? Was she watching her now?

'Mommy, I feel sick.'

'Me too,' said Ruth.

'You're ok, girls.'

Why was her heart beating so hard? Was it just adrenaline?

Then the door of the Kia swung open and Evelyn got out. Illuminated by the streetlights, Debbie watched her gather her things, bump the door shut with her hip and walk towards the house. She glanced in her wing mirror and pulled away from the curb.

Up ahead, Evelyn fumbled her key into the lock of her front door, pushed it open and slipped inside. Debbie sped up a little as the door closed.

'Mommy, can we go home now?'

'Sure, sweetie. We're going that way now.'

She slowed up as they approached the house. In the dim dusk light, she could see it was just as neat and picturesque as every other home on the street - climbing roses snaked over the front walls and solar-powered lights glowed among begonias in the garden. It was a nice little house, Debbie thought, probably a two-bedroom with a wood-burning stove in the living room and a paved yard out back. Perfect for a bachelorette, or a future spinster who already wore her hair in a tight bun.

Against her better judgment, she stopped in front of the house. The hall light was on, muted by the frosted glass in the front door. A red mailbox at the end of the driveway was emblazoned with the name *Sparrow* in white lettering.

She's been here a while, Debbie thought.

'Whose house is this?' said Ruth.

Debbie didn't answer. She had her phone out and was typing in the address, her heart still racing. They were on Oakland Avenue and Evelyn's house was number sixty-four.

'Mommy...' Sarah said, her characteristic time-to-go whine rising through the word.

'One sec, hon.'

Debbie finished writing out the message to Lou. It simply read: *'Evelyn's address: 64 Oakland Avenue, AHW. Only if you need it.'*

She was about to press Send when the porch light came on above Evelyn's front door. Swearing under her breath, she dropped the phone in her lap and accelerated. She drove stick and the Sedan lurched, threatening to stall. Then the clutch bit and they pulled away, the engine purring smoothly again.

Just before Evelyn's house was out of sight, Debbie glanced back and thought she saw the front door open. She stepped on the gas.

Derek picked Ruth up at ten past five, like clockwork. He noticed she was a little green around the gills and Debbie explained she'd taken them for a ride in the car after having smoothies, which hadn't been one of her better ideas, in hindsight. She didn't admit, however, that shortly after getting back from staking out Evelyn Sparrow, Sarah had hurled her smoothie all over the bathroom floor and Ruth, who'd thankfully been in the other room at the time, had come pretty close to doing the same. Debbie had given her a tall glass of water and sat her in front of the TV until her Dad arrived.

'How was kindergarten?' Derek asked as they drove home.

'It was fun. Today was painting. And afterwards, we followed someone home and Sarah said we were cops.'

Derek, assuming her story was still framed within the confines of the kindergarten schedule, just smiled and said, 'Sounds good. Cops and robbers was my favorite, too.'

They arrived home to find Ben kicking his soccer ball against the side of the house. Ruth ran to hug him, as she always did. Ben returned the hug half-heartedly and resumed kicking the ball. Ruth scurried off round the back of the house.

'Where's your Mom?' said Derek, locking the car.

'Making dinner, I think.'

'Got all your homework done?'

Ben made a face. 'Most of it. It's English, really boring.'

'Don't let your Mom, the English teacher, hear you say that.'

'I won't.' Derek ruffled his hair as he passed. 'Dad, is Mom ok?'

He stopped and looked at his son. Ben was often quiet and reserved, much like himself. He kept his cards close to his chest and they'd sort of become accustomed to that over the years. Ruth was different, outgoing and tilted more towards extroversion, like her mother. In that moment, the earnestness in Ben's voice gave him pause.

'What do you mean, son?'

Ben kicked the ball again; it rebounded off the brickwork back to his feet.

'She's... been a bit weird the last few days. Like she's not herself. You know?'

'I'm sure she's fine,' Derek said, continuing to watch Ben carefully. 'It's just a busy time for her, with the Thanksgiving festival coming up. She probably has that on her mind.'

'I guess.'

'Don't stay out here too long, ok? It's chilly.'

'I won't.'

He went round the rear of the house. They used the back door more often in fall and winter to avoid trailing mud into the hallway. In the sky above, rain clouds swelled, dark and fat. Derek noted that their back yard had been raked clear of leaves and wondered fleetingly when Lou'd had time to do it. Maybe she got Ben to handle it as one of his chores and he just didn't notice.

As he opened the back door, Ruth tumbled out in her puffer coat and charged down the garden with a gleeful yell. He watched her go for a moment, grinning.

I'm glad we have kids who like being outside, he thought.

'That you, hon?'

'Sure is.'

He went through the laundry room and into the kitchen. It was warm and steamy - two saucepans on the stove bubbled and the smell of boiling vegetables filled the air. His stomach gurgled in response.

Lou was at the counter with her back to him, chopping something. She wore a baggy hoodie and sweats, and he took a second to admire her curved figure. Then he came up behind her and slipped his arms round her waist, burying his face in her hair. It smelled a little fusty, but he didn't care.

'Hey, babe,' she said, continuing to chop carrots.

'Hello.' He held her tighter, pressing into her. 'Missed you today.'

'You did?'

'Yep. What're we having?'

'Boiled rabbit and oysters.'

'Yum. Goes great with carrots, I hear.'

He reached for a slice of carrot, then jerked his hand away as she brought the knife down playfully where he'd been reaching.

That was *playful, right?*

'Don't spoil your appetite,' she said. Then she twisted her head round and met his gaze. Her face was flushed and she almost looked breathless, like she'd just come in from a run, and her hair was uncharacteristically unkempt. In that moment, she appeared simultaneously younger and older than she'd seemed that morning before he left the house. She kissed him and said, 'How was work?'

'Just the usual,' he replied, letting her go. He went to the table and pulled out a chair. 'The project's slow going right now but we're getting there. What about you? How was school?'

As he sat down, he thought he saw her stiffen, just for a second.

'It was fine. Busy, you know?'

She finished chopping her carrot and reached for another. Derek fished his phone out of his pocket and skimmed the screen. He could hear Ben's soccer ball bouncing off the wall outside.

'What about the festival, how's that stuff going?'

'Like you, we're getting there. It's a big team effort, not just from the school. But it'll all come together.'

'Always does,' he said.

'Can you set out things for dinner?'

'Sure.'

He tossed his phone on the table with a clatter. Lou let out a startled yelp, and for a horrifying moment, he thought she'd chopped her own finger off. Then she rounded on him, the knife glinting in her hand.

'Shit, Derek!' she snapped. 'You scared the hell out of me. Don't *do* that.'

'Sorry, hon,' he replied sheepishly. 'Didn't mean to scare you.'

'I have a knife in my hand,' she said, then turned back to the chopping board. *She's been a bit weird the last few days. Like she's not herself.*

Derek rose and went to the cutlery drawer, watching Lou out of the corner of his eye. He'd seen something on her face in that moment, something he didn't like. Something bordering on rage. And for what?

He pulled open the drawer and started removing silverware.

'Mommy, where do monsters go during the day?' said Sarah.

Debbie, who'd been tucking the covers round her, hesitated.

'There are no monsters, darling.'

'Yes there are,' Sarah replied. She'd pulled the duvet tight round the lower half of her face and her words were muffled. 'They come out at night and do things. But in daytime they sleep. So where do they go?'

Debbie brushed a strand of loose hair back from her daughter's forehead.

'I don't believe in monsters,' she said gently. 'Do you?'

Sarah considered this for a moment. 'Yes. I think so.'

'Why?'

'Because Ruth says they're real. She's seen one.'

Debbie felt a stab of irritation. What was Ruth doing telling her that? She'd have to talk to Lou, or Derek. It wouldn't be long before a few throwaway comments about monsters became full-blown night terrors for both girls.

'I don't think she has, sweetie.'

'Yeah she has. She saw one in her room, two nights ago.'

Ok, this one needs talking out.

'Really? Well, what did this monster look like?'

'It was a girl, with big eyes. She was standing near the window, Ruth said. She waved at her but Ruth didn't wave back.'

'A girl?' *Probably her own reflection, or a doll.* 'That's strange, I thought monsters were supposed to be big and hairy and slimy.'

'No, Mommy, not all monsters,' said Sarah, matter-of-factly. Debbie grinned in the dim light. Somewhere down the street, a dog barked twice.

'It sounds like Ruth just had a bad dream,' she said. 'Don't you think?'

'Maybe.'

'And if it was a girl, she was probably just looking for her bed. I bet she's in bed now, sleeping. I'll bet she snores.'

Debbie made an obnoxious snoring sound and Sarah smiled.

'Don't, Mommy.'

She did it again, louder, and Sarah giggled. She reached for her face.

'Mommy you sound like a pig, stop it!'

Debbie switched to pig snorts - quite convincing ones, if she did say so herself - and snuffled round Sarah's neck. Her daughter squealed with laughter and threw her arms round her mother's shoulders. Debbie laughed too and hugged her back. She was so small and warm under the covers.

'Now, you go to sleep, little miss,' she said, tucking Sarah in again. 'You've got school in the morning.'

'I like school,' said Sarah, rolling on her side. She closed her eyes.

Hope that lasts forever.

'You go to sleep.'

Debbie leaned down to kiss her cheek. Suddenly, Sarah's eyes opened again and she looked up at her.

'You didn't tell me, Mommy,' she said. 'Where do monsters go in daytime?'

Debbie sighed. 'Sarah, there are no monsters.'

'But - '

'And if there were, I bet they'd stay far, far away from here most of the time. Especially during the day. Ok?'

'Ok.'

Debbie stood and the mattress on Sarah's little single bed sprang back into shape. It would soon be time to get her a new bed, Debbie thought. Probably by next summer.

She flicked off Sarah's bedside light and padded across to the door. Just before stepping out into the hall, a thought occurred to her. It came uninvited into her head and reached her mouth before she could stop it.

'Sarah,' she said softly. 'The girl Ruth saw in her room - was she old or young?'

For a few seconds, Sarah didn't reply and she thought she might have fallen asleep already. It would be a relief if she had - it was a foolish question to ask a four-year old at bedtime.

When Sarah did speak, Debbie barely heard her. 'Old. Like you.'

Debbie swallowed, trying to suppress the next question. But she couldn't stop it either.

'And what was her hair like?'

In the spill of yellow light from the hall, Sarah reached one hand behind her head and made a fist.

'It was like this.'

Debbie felt a cold chill rush through her bloodstream. She managed a choked swallow, bid her daughter goodnight and pulled the door over, leaving it slightly ajar.

Twenty minutes later, she crept back into the room to check the window was locked. Rain pattered like fingertips on the glass.

Lou bent to tie her laces and threw a glance at the clock. It was a quarter of eight.

'Derek, can you fill that water bottle for me?'

'Where is it?'

'By the sink. The big one.'

She heard the faucet turn on and shifted to her other foot. Her weekly spin class started at eight on the dot - she planned to be there at least five minutes early to get a bike near the back. She wanted to slip out at the end without having to talk to anyone, if she could. She straightened up and winced at the crinkle of pain in her lower back.

Getting old, she thought. *Or maybe it's more than that.*

Derek came into the living room and handed her the bottle, filled to the brim. She stuffed it into her bag and swung the strap over her shoulder.

'I'll be back just after nine,' she said. 'Make sure Ben's in bed by then.'

'I will.'

She kissed him lightly on the lips and turned to leave.

'Are you alright tonight?'

She slowed but didn't stop. 'Yeah I am, don't worry. Just feeling a bit stressed or something. This'll help, always does. I need the release.'

Derek normally seized on those comments with a suggestive joke. This time, however, he only said, 'Have fun, honey', and then she was out the door.

Lou's spin class was held at Amber Hill Community Center, just a short drive from their house. Stevie the mechanic had replaced her busted tire that afternoon, long before everyone had arrived home - thankfully, Derek hadn't asked anything more about it, so she'd been able to avoid throwing any direct lies his way for another few hours at least. But she knew that would come to a head soon enough.

It was the coldest evening of the month so far and rain was falling as she hurried through the automatic glass doors of the building, the November chill nipping through her leggings.

The community center foyer was bright and buzzing with activity. A group of middle-aged men were coming out of the sports hall, raucous and sweaty. One of them bounced a basketball on the foyer floor as they passed through the exit barrier to the right of the reception desk.

Lou approached the entry barrier on the left, took out her membership card and held it up to the scanner. The machine's electronic eye read the code on the card and *bleeped*. Lou pushed into the barrier, expecting it to swing open.

It didn't budge.

Frowning, she scanned her card again. The machine *bleeped*, and the barrier remained locked.

Lou went to the reception desk as the last of the basketballers exited the building. The lady on the other side of the desk, who she didn't recognise, smiled amiably across at her.

'Hi,' said Lou. 'My card isn't working.'

'Oh, that's strange,' said the receptionist. 'Did it work last time you were here?'

'Yeah.'

'And you're a member?'

Obviously.

'Yes. I'm here for the eight o'clock spin class with Trevor.'

'No problem, I can sign you in here. What's the name?'

'Lou Jennings.'

The receptionist's fingers clacked over her keyboard. Lou saw a wrinkle of puzzlement appear on her forehead.

'It might be under Louise Jennings,' she suggested.

'Ok, let's see.' More typing and clicking. The receptionist's frown deepened. 'I'm sorry, ma'am, I can't seem to find your name in our database.'

'I'm not sure how that's possible,' said Lou. A woman she recognised from her spin class passed through the barrier and disappeared down the corridor.

'Have you been coming here long?'

'About five years, yes.'

'Hmm, that's very strange.' She could see the receptionist deliberating internally over what to do. Lou knew the words 'I'll call the manager' were already on her lips.

'That's ok,' she said, thinking fast. 'I know what's happened - I might be in the database under my original surname, before I was married.' She forced the words. 'Try Sparrow.'

The receptionist typed. Her frown softened a little.

'There's a Sparrow here but it's under a different first name. I don't think it's you, ma'am.'

Lou smiled, resigned.

'She's signed up for the eight o'clock spin class, right? Is her name Evelyn?'

The receptionist looked at her. She didn't need to confirm it - Lou saw it on her face.

'Never mind,' said Lou, 'I've made a mistake.'

'Ma'am -'

She turned, her sneakers squeaking on the tile floor, and headed for the exit. In her peripheral vision, she caught sight of the clock on the wall. It was seven fifty-nine.

Suddenly, the dull sense of resignation inside her cracked apart and gave way to panic. Her heart, which had been gradually pumping faster since her card failed to scan, began to palpitate.

I'm going to run into her, she thought.

The glass doors slid open as she approached. She left the building and rushed out into the rain, almost knocking into one of the basketballers who'd stopped under the entrance porch for a smoke. She darted to the left, walking quickly towards her car.

Something made her stop. She turned and looked back.

Evelyn was walking towards the community center entrance. She was dressed in a gray sweater and black shorts, exposing skinny legs to the November rain. A gym bag was slung over one shoulder, and her hair was still in a bun.

Just as she reached the doors, she looked Lou's way. She grinned, and her hand came up in a wave. Lou felt something invisible slam into her through the rain and she rocked on her heels. Her heart seemed to miss a beat, as though it was being gripped in her chest and simply couldn't pump any more. Then Evelyn broke off her gaze and went inside, out of the rain.

Cold air surged into Lou's lungs and she gasped, slapping a hand to her chest. She could actually feel her heart beat through her sweats, moving under the fabric, now wet from the rain.

It's not just the school, she thought wildly. *It's not just my job, or my students, or the people I work with. It's everything. She's going to take everything until nothing's left at all.*

Lou staggered back to her car. Inside Amber Hill Community Center, Evelyn Sparrow scanned her membership card and the barrier swung open.

Derek stood outside the bathroom door, his head bowed against the wood, listening. Inside, hot water hissed from the shower head mounted on the wall. He couldn't hear Lou.

'You sure you're ok, hon?' Derek called.

No response.

'Hon?' he said again, reaching for the door handle.

'I'm fine,' she called back.

She sounded fine - breezy, even - but he knew she wasn't. Or he suspected, at least.

Rain had been pelting down when she'd arrived home shortly after nine. Ruth had bolted to the door to meet her but she was already up the stairs. By the time Derek had followed, she was in the bathroom with the shower running.

Normally, Lou's post-workout routine involved gulping down a protein smoothie and stretching out her muscles. She did both things in the kitchen and

Ruth, who was allowed to stay up later than usual on the evening of her spin class, would often try copying her movements, splaying her little legs as wide as she could, reaching to touch her toes. Those few minutes with Ruth were as much a part of Lou's routine as anything else, rain or shine.

So when Derek found her sodden gym hoodie on the floor of their bedroom, the alarm bells that had started ringing earlier before dinner kicked in again.

'Want me to make your smoothie?' he asked, just to have something to say. He needed to hear how her voice sounded.

'It's ok, I can do it.'

The shower continued to hiss.

'Ok, if you're sure...'

'I'm sure. See you downstairs.'

Derek stepped away from the door. He hesitated for a moment, grappling with the idea of just walking inside to check on her, then stooped to pick up her soaked hoodie. The word MAROONS was emblazoned on the back.

'See you downstairs,' he muttered, and left.

Inside the bathroom, Lou stood beneath the shower head, staring at the wall. She gripped an unopened bottle of shampoo in her hand. The water from the shower head was almost scalding hot on her back but she barely felt it.

After leaving the community center, she'd driven aimlessly around town in the rain, trying desperately to articulate her next step. She needed to respond quickly and decisively, to do *something* to counteract that woman. She couldn't just sit back and watch as Evelyn coiled her slimy tentacles around every aspect of her life, squeezing and squeezing until every ounce of Lou had been pushed out. She needed help. She needed people to believe her. Debbie understood, she hoped, but she needed more.

She had to tell Derek.

But as she'd driven up and down the slick streets of Amber Hill, her mind grew dull. It was as though her thought processes, normally sharp and earnest, simply wouldn't click into gear. She felt stupid, inebriated, slow. The only clear image her mind's eye would permit her to see was of Evelyn Sparrow, grinning and waving at her from the door of the community center. Soon, there was nothing but Evelyn's gray eyes and the beat of the wiper blades.

When Lou did finally stop the car, she found herself outside the school again. She got out, leaving her door wide open, and walked to the gates. The school janitor, Frank Orville, sealed them with a steel padlock every evening. Lou gripped the slippery bars and peered through the rain and darkness at the building where she'd worked for years, now just a black shape in the night. She stood that way for a long time, oblivious to anyone or anything else around her, cold rainwater saturating her clothes and hair and skin.

Lou remained that way, numb and untethered, until she got home. She didn't remember getting back in the car and driving to their street. She didn't remember pulling into the drive or going through the front door, or rushing upstairs and locking herself in the bathroom. Some small part of her was still sentient and wanted to spare her husband and children from seeing her that way. It wasn't until Ruth thumped on the bathroom door and demanded a bedtime story that she finally snapped back to reality.

As she reached for the shower faucet, she looked down and saw shampoo pooling round her feet. She'd squeezed every last drop from the bottle.

It was ten o'clock. Rain fell thick and heavy on Debbie's windshield as she drove across town, heading west. Outside, Amber Hill's stores were closed and the streets were clear.

Debbie had rang Candice Preston, her seventeen-year-old sitter, roughly an hour after putting Sarah to bed. Candice had been babysitting for her since Sarah was one. She was a nice, capable girl who seemed to be perpetually single (Debbie had never had to worry about her bringing anyone over), and unsurprisingly, she was free that evening.

'Sure, Debbie,' she'd said over the phone, music blaring in the background. 'I'll come over as soon as I can.'

'Thanks Candice. Your Mom won't mind you being out late on a school night?'

'Nah, she's not even here. She's just started a night shift at the hospital. I'll be back before she even gets home.'

Candice arrived just after nine-thirty, chugging up to the front drive in her battered old Ford, rain hammering on the car's steel body. Debbie ushered her through the front door and took her coat.

'Thanks again, Candice,' she said. 'I know it's short notice.'

'No problem at all,' Candice replied, shaking out her wet hair. Her face, pimply as ever, was flushed from the run between her car and the house. 'Where're you going?'

'I have to go see a friend,' Debbie said, shrugging into her own coat. 'I shouldn't be too long, but you have my number if you need anything. Sarah's asleep - if she wakes up, just get her a glass of water and she'll go down again easily.'

'Sure.'

'You know where everything is. Make yourself some cocoa. There's some left-over pie in the refrigerator, too.

'Thanks Debbie.'

Then she was out in the rain, running to her car. Candice watched her from the front door and waved as she pulled out of the drive. She was already in the refrigerator by the time Debbie reached the end of her street.

A car flashed by, spraying rainwater over her windshield. She kicked her wipers up a notch, leaning forward in her seat.

Why am I doing this? she thought. *What good will this do?*

After checking Sarah's window was securely locked, she'd gone down to the kitchen and started into the dishes, trying to distract herself from the niggling unease deep in her subconscious. She knew she was being stupid and paranoid. So what if Ruth thought she saw someone in her room? Little girls had super active imaginations. She'd probably seen something on TV and the image had planted itself in her dreams that night. Tomorrow at kindergarten, she'd tell Sarah she saw a tiger curled up at her feet, and the next night it'd be a clown with a shiny red nose. A woman with her hair in a bun was actually pretty tame, all things considered.

But the more Debbie tried to reason with herself, the louder the voice at the back of her mind became. *It was her,* it cried. *It was that woman. The substitute teacher. It was Evelyn in Ruth's room, and she'll be in Sarah's soon, too.*

Finally, she hadn't been able to stand it any longer. She'd gone back to Sarah's room and checked the window again, listening to her daughter breathe softly in the darkness. Then she'd called Candice.

'I'll just make sure she's home,' she said aloud, starting at the sound of her own voice in the car. 'I just need to see for myself.' Then she added, 'You're an idiot, Debbie. You're being a real idiot about this.'

Idiot or not, she was on her way.

She continued across town, leaving the glass-fronted stores and empty parking lots behind, weaving her way into the suburbs of Amber Hill West. Shops, bars, churches and apartments began blurring into houses, first the palatial homes of the upper class surrounded by manicured lawns and carefully-designed floral borders, then the uniform lines of development-block row houses and semis with their neat little front gardens and painted mailboxes.

As Debbie passed those houses, she tried to catch a glimpse of the happy families inside: husbands and wives, probably gathered round the warm glow of the fire with their kids, blissfully drinking in whatever mindless crap was on TV that night. She found she was jealous of them, of their carefree ignorance. She wished she could turn around and go back home to Sarah, and just forget all this. A spark of resentment towards Lou flickered briefly (*Why did she have to tell me about this woman?*) and then died. If it hadn't been Lou, it could just as easily have been someone else Debbie knew. It could even have been her. Either way, Evelyn Sparrow was in her town, and she had to know more about her. She'd go by her house again tonight, and tomorrow she'd call Lou and tell her what Ruth had said. Then they'd work out the next step together.

She was on Oakland Avenue now and her heart was pounding. The mailboxes went by, wet and glinting under the streetlights. She couldn't make out the names, but she didn't have to. She knew which one she was looking for.

Sparrow.

There were no lights on in Evelyn's house. It sat dormant in the rain, silent and unassuming, not connected to the other homes around it. Oakland Avenue was one of the few streets in the area boasting detached houses, Debbie noted, and wondered how a substitute teacher could have afforded it on her own.

The driveway was also empty. *She's not home,* Debbie thought, parked at the foot of her garden, and then immediately pictured Evelyn clambering through Sarah's window, grinning toothily, her eyes wide and opaquely white.

Screw it.

She shut off the engine and opened the Sedan door. Cold rain lashed at her face and she gasped. She closed the door and, after only a momentary pause, hurried up the walk to Evelyn's front door.

There was some shelter under the porch and she huddled there, gathering herself. Evelyn's front door was pale green and looked freshly painted. The numbers six and four in gleaming brass had been screwed onto the threshold, level with the little square pane of glass at head height. The fruity scent of honeysuckle, which had been carefully cultivated to grow up lattice panel trellises on either side of the porch, hung in the air.

She's not home, Debbie thought again, and knocked on the door.

No-one answered. Nothing stirred inside the house.

She's not here, Detective Lathem. Go home to your daughter.

Debbie turned to leave and the porch light came on above her head. Her blood ran cold and her legs locked in place. If she'd wanted to run in that moment, she couldn't have.

Behind her, the bolt slid back in the door and it swung open. Warm yellow light enveloped her. She could hear music playing, melding with the rainfall.

'Can I help you?'

Debbie made herself turn around and look Evelyn Sparrow full in the face. She stood in the doorway, dressed in a blue wool sweater and faded pink pajama bottoms. Fluffy pink slippers adorned her feet.

'Umm...' Debbie replied, completely thrown. Her eyes went involuntarily to the bun on the other woman's head.

Evelyn looked her up and down, her gray eyes large and watery. Her expression was a mixture of surprise and suspicion.

'I'm, uh, looking for someone,' Debbie said.

'Who?'

She made up a name. 'Candice Mead.'

Evelyn shook her head. 'Sorry, there's no-one here by that name.'

'Oh. Sorry.' Debbie blinked - she'd been transfixed by Evelyn's gaze. 'I must have gotten the address wrong. Sorry for disturbing you.'

She made a move to leave.

'Wait,' said Evelyn. Her tone was different now, gentler, tinged with concern. 'You're drenched - you must be freezing. Come inside for a minute and get warmed up.'

'I shouldn't,' Debbie started, 'I have to -'

But Evelyn already had her by the arm, leading her inside. She was powerless (*or unwilling?*) to resist. The door closed.

'Come on, I'll get you a towel.'

Evelyn led her from the hall into the living room. Inside, the house was toasty warm and smelled of cinnamon. Debbie was instantly transported to Christmas. It would be that time again soon.

'Here, sit down,' said Evelyn, ushering her into an armchair by the fire. Flames crackled soothingly, licking at the logs. 'Would you like some tea?'

'No, honestly, there's no need.'

'Nonsense,' replied Evelyn with a smile. 'It's no trouble at all. Give me a minute.'

Before Debbie could protest again, she swept from the room, leaving her alone. *I'm in her house. What the hell am I doing in her house?*

Debbie found she'd gone along with Evelyn despite knowing she shouldn't - despite *trying* to stop herself, on some internal level - and that scared her. She hadn't been dragged to the armchair so much as coaxed, like one might lead a horse by the bridle. And now here she was, warming herself by the fire, waiting to be served tea by some imposter trying to edge her best friend out of her job.

Isn't this what you wanted?

The words cooed softly in her mind and they weren't her own. She gripped the arms of the chair, straining against the voice. *Did* she want this? Did she really want to be here, inside Evelyn's house at night?

Maybe she did.

'Here you are.' Evelyn was beside her again, handing her a freshly-laundered towel. It was embroidered with pink roses. 'Tea's almost ready.'

Debbie watched her leave the room. She moved easily, hips swaying under the baggy pajamas, trailing a hand on the door frame of what must be the kitchen. She wasn't as awkward and timid as Lou had led her to believe. Still, it was difficult to look past that bun in her hair. Why did she still have it in now, after ten at night?

Debbie patted her face dry with the towel, marveling at how agreeable it felt against her skin, and got a good look at Evelyn's living room for the first time.

It was tastefully, if sparsely, decorated. The walls were papered with rose-print, the floor fitted with a deep red carpet; a two-seater couch and matching armchairs were arranged around the fireplace and framed photos of well-known American landmarks had been hung around the room. There were no photos of people.

Debbie found she could think more clearly without Evelyn in the room, whether she was imagining it or not. She tried to get her detective hat on again and searched for signs of foul play, twisting round in the chair to scan the whole room: a standing lamp in the corner; a leafy green anthurium near the window; a flatscreen TV and DVD player with a handful of movies stacked next to it. Everything in its place, clean and tidy. Like the exterior of the house, Evelyn's living room was picturesque. Sixty-four Oakland Avenue was like a showhouse.

The address.

It suddenly occurred to Debbie that she hadn't finished sending that text to Lou earlier. When Evelyn's porch light had come on, she'd dropped her phone and hadn't remembered the text message until now.

'Milk and sugar?' Evelyn called sweetly from the kitchen.

'Just a little milk, please,' Debbie replied, keeping her voice even.

She tugged her phone from her pocket and opened the message to Lou. She was right, it hadn't gone through earlier. Perhaps that was why Lou hadn't been in touch all afternoon. She pressed send and slipped the phone back in her pocket, just as Evelyn swept back into the room.

'Here we are,' she said, handing Debbie a mug of steaming tea.

'Thank you.'

Evelyn curled up in the other armchair, cradling her mug in her lap. She fixed Debbie with that gray stare again, but the welcoming smile remained on her lips.

'Looks like you're drying up nicely,' she observed.

Something about the use of the word "nicely" made Debbie feel like she was a porterhouse steak Evelyn was waiting patiently to eat, and she suppressed a shiver.

'I am - thanks for the towel. The fire's great.'

Evelyn looked at it and the flames danced in her eyes.

'It does the job,' she said. 'This little place gets cold from October onwards. I light the fire almost every day.'

Debbie nodded. Evelyn was watching her again, waiting. She decided to just go for it - they were in it now.

'Have you been in Amber Hill long?'

Evelyn's smile was unwavering. 'About six years. Been teaching at the school all that time.'

Exactly like Lou.

'And where were you before? Out of state?'

'Oh, no, I'm Illinois through-and-through. I grew up in Mount Vermont. I've never left the state, except to go on vacation, of course.'

Lou again.

'And you like it here?' Debbie asked hoarsely.

Evelyn's grin widened. 'I like it just fine. More every day, in fact.'

The living room suddenly seemed very warm. Much too warm. Debbie's hands were glued to the hot mug of tea which she'd yet to try. Was it even safe to drink?

'What about you?' Evelyn asked. 'Here I am, gabbing on about myself, and I haven't even gotten to know my houseguest. How long have you been in town?'

'All my life,' Debbie replied. 'Born and raised.'

'Wonderful.' Evelyn sipped her tea, her eyes never leaving Debbie's. 'Family?'

'My parents live on the other side of town. I'm divorced.'

'And you have a child?'

A child? It hadn't really been a question, had it?

'I have a little girl,' said Debbie evenly.

'That's nice.' Evelyn took another sip and Debbie knew she was about to ask Sarah's name, and that was too much. She quickly changed tact.

'What about you? Are you married?'

Evelyn swallowed and then laughed. It was a light and breezy laugh that came with practiced ease.

'No, unfortunately I'm still single. Always on the lookout for Mister Right, though.'

She winked then. Debbie smiled and looked down at her mug - it was the first time she'd broken Evelyn's gaze.

'That's funny,' she said casually. 'I'd heard the English teacher at the high school was married with a couple of kids. Must have gotten my wires crossed.'

She looked up and saw Evelyn's smile falter, just for a second. The fire crackled and spat next to them.

'I don't believe I mentioned which subject I teach,' Evelyn said, a little slower than before.

'Oh, you didn't,' said Debbie, 'but I know who you are.'

Evelyn stared, hard and searching, but Debbie refused to flinch away. Several seconds passed and neither of them spoke. Rain drummed rhythmically on the roof above them.

'You a sports fan?' Debbie asked abruptly, breaking the silence.

'To an extent, yes.'

'Follow any teams?'

'I like the White Sox.'

Of course you do.

'Me too,' Debbie said. 'It's hard to beat, isn't it? Those handsome guys running around in their uniforms.'

Evelyn nodded, still smiling.

'Who's your favorite player?' Debbie asked.

In truth, she didn't follow baseball, so the question was a major gamble. Evelyn could have said any name and she wouldn't have known for sure if it belonged to a real person. Fortunately, Evelyn didn't know that about her - for the first time that night, her smile disappeared altogether.

'I like them all,' she said, and there was an edge to her voice. 'Listen, Debbie - '

Had she told her her name?

' - it's been lovely to meet you, but I'm sure you have work in the morning. I myself have classes to teach, and still have a few papers to grade before tomorrow.'

'Of course.'

Debbie felt a surge of relief. She'd made it through a conversation with Miss Sparrow - she'd call Lou tomorrow and tell her what she'd found out. She'd be able to confirm everything for her. She sat forward, looking for a place to set her mug down.

'Unless you'd like to finish your tea first?'

'Oh no, it's ok. Thank you for making it, but - '

'Debbie,' said Evelyn, 'finish your tea.'

Something changed in the room. The fire ceased crackling; the rain stopped beating against the house. Evelyn's smile was back.

Debbie couldn't move. She'd been about to get up and now her legs seemed to be bolted in place, pinned to the armchair. The mug came to her lips and she felt hot tea slide down her throat. Evelyn's eyes were locked on hers again. She could see nothing else.

'Relax, Debbie.'

Debbie relaxed, sinking into the armchair. The room was hot now; sweat trickled down the small of her back. She tried to speak but her tongue stuck to the roof of her mouth. Evelyn's gray eyes were wide now, bulging, too large for her skull to contain.

'We're friends, right Debbie?'

Debbie nodded. Invisible pincers gripped the skin of her neck, moving her head for her. *How convenient*, she thought hysterically, and then all her own thoughts were gone.

'We've been friends for a long time, haven't we?'

Her tongue was loosened. 'Yes.'

'Best friends, right?'

'The best.'

Evelyn's eyes were everything. Her grin had extended beyond the bounds of her face.

'You should bring Sarah here, for a play date.'

Debbie's forehead tried to frown. 'You don't have kids.'

'All in good time,' Evelyn said. Then she laughed again, and this time it was a wild, screeching cackle that rose in pitch until Debbie's ears stung.

Evelyn's living room had closed in around them, engulfing them in heat and light and new smells that Debbie hadn't been aware of before. The mug of tea was a dead weight in her hands, pressing her into the armchair. Evelyn seemed to be inches from her face now. Her eyes were so huge that Debbie could no longer see past them in any direction. They filled her peripheral vision entirely.

'Stay here for a while, Debbie,' said Evelyn, as much in her head as in the room. 'We can talk about the good times. We've so many memories to share, you and I. We are best friends, after all.'

Debbie felt Evelyn's hand on her face, cupping her cheek. It was cold against her skin. Freezing, in fact. Corpse-like. And yet, something stirred inside her, deep down, a familiar but unwelcome heat. Evelyn's musk was in her nostrils, intoxicating, asphyxiating. Their faces were almost flat together, and with some distant and impotent alarm, Debbie realized Evelyn was actually on top of her on the armchair.

'You'll stay awhile, won't you?' Evelyn whispered. 'Best friends stick together. Then you'll bring Sarah by and we'll make more memories. We'll have so much fun, Debbie. There's no-one but me anymore.'

Then Debbie fell into Evelyn's eyes. The room swirled and blurred and dropped away, vanishing into suffocating blackness.

Debbie stepped out into the night air. It was cool and fresh on her face, and she grinned. Raindrops invaded the sheltered space, pattering on her head and shoulders.

'You're going to get soaked!' Evelyn cried, laughing. 'Here, take an umbrella.'

'My car's right there, don't worry,' said Debbie.

She turned back to her friend and opened her arms. Evelyn stepped under the porch and into the hug. Debbie squeezed her tight, then let go.

'Thanks again, I had fun.'

'Me too. It's good to blow off a little steam sometimes.'

'Yeah. But seriously, thanks for listening. I know I went on and on there. You must be tired of hearing it by now.'

'Don't be silly,' said Evelyn, shaking her head. Behind her, music still blared from the movie's closing credits. 'That's what I'm here for, right? You can tell me anything, Debs.'

'I know, and likewise.' She ran a hand through her hair. 'Geez, I don't know what I'd do without a friend in this town. Seriously.'

'You're far too hard on yourself. Go home to your daughter and let that babysitter get to bed. She'll have a hangover tomorrow from drinking all your booze.'

'Ha-ha,' Debbie pronounced, still grinning. 'Thanks Evie. I'll see you soon.'

'Next week, right? Playdate with Sarah?'

'You know it.'

Evelyn stepped back inside and Debbie jogged down the walk to her car. Rain tumbled down as she opened the door and slipped behind the wheel. Evelyn waved from her porch and went back into the house.

Debbie closed her door and jammed the key in the ignition. She felt good, relaxed and de-stressed. That's what a night hanging with Evie would do for anyone - she was the greatest listener, always had time for others.

'Damn babysitter, drinking all my booze,' she said and laughed heartily. She was already looking forward to next week. Sarah loved Evie - they'd have a great time, she was sure of it.

Debbie started the car, glanced back one last time at her best friend's house, and drove off down the street.

Robert Thornberg, known to many in Amber Hill as 'Bert Berg', came down Oakland Avenue in his 1994 Ford Capri just as Debbie pulled away from the curb outside Evie's house. Bert, who was seventy-two years old and had been plagued with insomnia for as long as he could remember, often took a drive around town late at night when the ol' Sandman had once again passed him by, and that evening had been no different. Bert had bundled himself into the car in his overcoat (still wearing pajamas underneath), lit a cigarette, and just started driving. He was a good driver, always had been - no piss-poor excuse for a rainstorm was going to put him off his nightly ritual, no sir - and he knew the town like the back of his wrinkled, liver-spotted hand. He'd drive, perhaps for as long as an hour, then he'd go home and sleep fitfully until dawn.

Bert's hearing wasn't great and his sense of smell had abandoned him long ago, but for an old insomniac with a penchant for watching TV in the dark, his eyesight was just fine. As he trundled along Oakland Avenue and passed the navy Sedan coming the other way, he easily picked out Debbie's beaming grin, bright and cheery at quarter after midnight, before she flashed by and disappeared into the rain.

Bert shimmied the cigarette stub to the other side of his mouth and blew out a puff of acrid smoke. He frowned and rubbed his knee, which always ached in wet weather. Debbie Lanthem wasn't someone he'd run into before - their paths had never crossed in all the years they'd each spent in Amber Hill, as far as he knew. She was just another resident out for a drive in the rain, exercising her basic human rights, just like him.

But it was strange, wasn't it, Bert thought, how a young woman like that was out here late at night, grinning away like she'd just heard the best joke in the world, with no-one else accompanying her. Stranger still was the fact that young woman had just walked out of a derelict house with no signs of life inside: the windows were boarded up, climbing weeds snaked over the exterior walls, the grass was knee-length in the garden; the For Sale sign, posted by one of Amber Hill's real estate companies many years ago, had been blown flat in a storm and was never re-erected. Various agents had discovered that selling a house with a basement that flooded every year without fail was a practically-impossible task.

Sixty-four was the only derelict house on Oakland Avenue, a black stain on an otherwise well-maintained and reputable neighborhood, and that young woman had just strolled out of it like it was nothing.

Bert chewed on that during the rest of his car ride that night, and over the days that followed, during which what little sleep he managed to get was punctuated with nightmares that ended with him snapping back to full consciousness in a cold sweat. He knew something wasn't right about it, about that woman being at that dead, abandoned house during the night. He even thought about driving past it again some night, just in case she was there, but the idea of it gave him the willies.

Old Bert Berg had seen Debbie Lanthem that night, clear as day, but he hadn't seen Evelyn Sparrow, watching him from between the rotted wooden two-by-fours nailed across the windows of her home.

He saw her in his dreams, though, and he was dead within the week.

Five

9 days before Thanksgiving

The rain finally stopped shortly before six on Wednesday morning. Lou felt like she heard every single drop hit the roof of their house.

Today was the day. She had to tell Derek the whole thing or she'd crack.

She played out the same pantomime show of the last two days, acting out her normal morning routine for her family's benefit: she rose early - exhausted after having not slept all night - and showered, then ate a quick oatmeal breakfast in her nighgown; Derek rolled out of bed at quarter of seven and staggered downstairs in his usual morning stupor while she began the process of waking Ben and Ruth (there were three stages to this - kids playing possum, kids fiercely resisting her calls to get out of bed, kids finally obeying and suddenly discovering they had energy to burn); while everyone else ate breakfast, she got dressed, did her hair, and set about practicing her "everything's totally normal" face before going back downstairs.

She was going to tell Derek everything, but not right before he went to work.

'Mommy! Mommy, can you see me?'

'Honey, please get out of there.'

Ruth sighed dramatically and came out of the pantry. In the living room, Ben watched TV with a glazed expression, his cereal spoon poised halfway to his mouth.

'Ben, hurry up,' she said, dropping his lunchbox into his bag. 'You're going to be late.'

'I'm not,' he said. The spoon finally made it to his mouth.

Derek came in through the back door and shivered.

'Trash is out,' he announced. 'It's freezing today. Guess our mild Fall's over already.'

'Make sure you wear your coat,' said Lou. 'The last thing we need is you getting sick as well.'

'Olympic athlete constitution, remember?'

'Still, bring your coat, tough guy.'

He kissed her on the cheek and went through to the living room. Her heart swelled with sadness and guilt. She should have told him already. It'd been too long.

Ben left for the bus a few minutes later, followed shortly by Derek and Ruth. Lou waved them off at the door (Derek had looked at her for just a second longer than usual and she knew then that *he knew*), and once they'd rounded the corner and were out of sight, she quickly undid her "work" hairdo, switched into her gym gear, and went for a run.

Exercise was one of her sure-fire solutions to the debilitations of stress. She hadn't gotten her usual fix at spin class the night before and her body now craved its habitual endorphin rush. She jogged a three-mile loop of the neighborhood, sucking the cleansing November air into her now flu-free lungs (she suspected she'd pay a price for it later, but in that moment she didn't care) before arriving back at her front door, her face pink and sheened with sweat. She checked her watch: twenty-six minutes. Not her worst.

She went back inside, splashed some water on her face (she'd shower again later), then went to the kitchen, poured herself a coffee, and sat down at the table.

The house was suddenly and completely empty, and in the silence that followed her family's departure, Lou found herself alone with nothing but her own thoughts. Almost immediately, those thoughts rolled over and engulfed her like a pyroclastic cloud.

Now what do I do?

Should I have told Derek this morning after all?

What will he say when I do tell him?

I wonder what Miss Sparrow's doing right now.

How could Perry and Jules and all the rest forget me?

This is all some sort of hallucination, isn't it? I'm having a nervous breakdown.

What the hell do I do now?

An image of Evelyn Sparrow in her gym gear, grinning at her from the community center entrance, swam into her mind's eye and she downed the rest of her coffee. Maybe vodka would have been better.

She laughed out loud and cringed at the hollow sound of it.

Debbie had texted her, hadn't she?

Lou pulled out her phone and opened Debbie's text. She'd read it late last night, just before attempting sleep. Evelyn's home address.

What can I do with that? she thought. Some part of her answered back: *Break in and claim squatter's rights. Say you've always been there. Say it's your house now.*

She laughed again, humorlessly now.

She's taken my job, Lou thought. *I'm sitting here in the kitchen when I should be on my way to work because some random woman has taken my job. I wasn't gone a full week.*

What else had she taken?

She pushed back her chair and went to the living room. Her laptop was charging in the corner. She flipped it open and her browser window flashed up automatically.

The school website still occupied one of her tabs. She skimmed it again, already resigned to what she knew she'd find. There was Evelyn in all the photos she'd been in previously. There was Evelyn on the staff page. Miss Sparrow, English teacher extraordinaire.

She jumped to the community center website and tried her login, which she'd used hundreds of times before to book her spin classes. Unsurprisingly, it no longer worked.

Username and password not recognised.

Bitch.

Lou paused, fingers hovering over the keys. What else?

This was serious stuff, wasn't it? It was identity theft, pure and simple.

Money. Finance.

She called up the website for her bank accounts and tried logging in. Her heart did a jig in her chest when the next screen took a few seconds to load. But it worked

- her details hadn't changed. There were her savings, all in order. Evelyn hadn't snatched those yet.

Lou spent the next thirty minutes trawling through every account bearing her name: banking, insurance, medical, email, online shopping, social media. Anything and everything requiring usernames and passwords. Every single one was as she'd left it, even her pension plan, which was directly linked to her job. She could access them all, apart from two.

Her community center login, and her library account.

Evelyn Sparrow had stolen her library card, and Lou knew no-one down there would recognise her now if she walked in. But it didn't matter. She still had access to the important stuff, and those she didn't have would just serve as evidence when she told Derek about it tonight.

She set the laptop down and texted Debbie: '*Good work, lady. How'd you find it? What's the plan now?*'

There was no immediate response, but it was still early in the day. If she didn't hear back by lunchtime she'd give her a call. Thank goodness she still had Debbie on her side - she'd be able to ratify everything if Derek didn't believe her.

He'd believe her.

She glanced at the clock - it was after eight-thirty. Homeroom was over and her Ninth Graders would be settling in for a morning of writing mechanics and composition. She pictured Toby Whitmore and Ramesh Das, her favorite "challenging" students, looking back at her with the glazed expressions of those who'd rather be shimmying up ropes in Phys Ed.

Something moved upstairs.

Lou froze.

There'd been a creak in the bedroom, just for a split second. It was an old house and it creaked all the time, but she knew the difference between sounds made by the wind and those made by a person. It'd sounded like a footstep.

Another creak, louder this time.

Lou was on her feet now, her back to the fireplace, the two doorways into the living room in her eye-line. She stared at the ceiling, listening intently, straining for another sound.

Silence.

She swallowed and found her throat had gone dry. 'Who's there?'

Nothing.

The house had been a bit of a fixer-upper when they'd bought it back in 2018. They'd rented an apartment for a year after moving to Amber Hill and then went all-in once Lou was made permanent at the school. Not that Derek's salary couldn't have supported them, of course, but they'd wanted to be sure before putting down their roots. And it was a good thing Derek made what he did - the house needed plenty of work, basement to attic, and they'd spent at least two years working at it, repairing and redecorating each room until the whole place was finally finished. Lou loved their house and never wanted to move again, no matter how much it groaned in high winds and froze up in winter time.

She loved their home and she knew it well, and right now, she was pretty sure someone was upstairs.

'Who's there?' she called again, stronger this time.

Still nothing.

'I'll call the cops.'

She waited for what felt like the longest time before making a move towards her phone on the coffee table.

Upstairs, someone strode across the floorboards.

Lou started to collapse, then regained her feet. She was frightened now, truly and completely frightened. She had to get out of the house. It would be madness to stay here with an intruder inside.

Was it Evelyn?

Her mind raced, grasping at whatever thin threads of logic it could find.

Some animal had gotten inside - a cat or a racoon - and it was rooting around for food or a way out.

But no, those footfalls had been made by someone wearing shoes. No animal.

It was Derek - he'd come home and gone upstairs, and like last night after spin class, she'd simply forgotten it had happened. Was that possible? Maybe.

She had to know. If it was Evelyn, she had to confront her. She'd check and then leave the house.

Lou left the living room, went to the bottom of the stairs and looked up towards the landing. A weak shaft of sunlight cut through the little window in the second floor hallway, catching motes of dust in the air; they spread and swirled, as though they'd just been disturbed.

Derek's umbrella, still damp from yesterday's rain, was propped against the coat rack. Lou lifted it gingerly - it was stupidly light - and started up the stairs.

The higher she climbed, the more she expected Evelyn to step into full view at the top of the stairs, gazing down at her with those cold, gray eyes. Blood pounded in her ears. She squeezed the umbrella tight in one hand, steadying herself on the banister with the other. Ben and Ruth grinned at her from school photos hung on the wall to her right. Somehow, the sight of their beautiful faces both unnerved her and strengthened her resolve.

She came to the top of the stairs, almost sick with fright now. There were no more creaks or footsteps. The house had fallen silent again.

Lou stepped onto the landing and looked both ways.

The hall was empty.

To her left were the family bathroom and the master bedroom; to her right, Ben and Ruth's bedrooms.

She went left first, edging down the hall with the umbrella held aloft in both hands like a sword. If someone stepped out of her bedroom now, they'd get a soft, damp smack in the face. Maybe she could go for their eyes with the pointed metal end?

'If you're up here,' she said, 'just come out.' She hesitated, then added: 'Evelyn.'

Nothing.

Lou pushed open the bedroom door. The bed itself was unmade, the duvet bunched untidily to one side. Derek's socks and underwear were on the floor; her damp running gear was near, but not quite in, the laundry hamper. The room faced south, so even on a November morning, it was bright and relatively warm once the blinds had been opened. Lou looked into the en suite bathroom and pulled open the wardrobes, but the room was empty.

Next.

She went to the family bathroom, checking behind the door and, for some reason, in the shower. The kids' toothbrushes still dripped in the cup next to the sink. Lou caught sight of herself in the mirror and quickly looked away.

Back in the hall, she paused to listen. The house creaked once, but it was a familiar, reassuring creak. There were no footfalls.

She was starting to feel foolish. Had she imagined the footsteps on the floor? Everything about yesterday evening had left her feeling pretty spooked. She was jumping at her own shadow right now.

'Last chance,' she called.

Her eyes flicked up to the attic door, but the pull-string was still flush to the ceiling. There was no way someone could have opened the trap, yanked the ladder down, climbed up there and closed it all behind them without making a ton of noise. Still, she shivered as she passed under it.

Ruth's bedroom was also empty. The sheets on her little bed were all askew and her Dora the Explorer duvet had been unceremoniously dumped on the floor. Most of her toys had been packed away (Ruth attempted that dutifully every evening before bed and had managed to get a good few into the toy box, with the rest still scattered on the floor); only her tired old teddy bear Mr Bubbles had been spared - he still lay sentinel at the foot of her bed, his button eyes gazing mournfully at the ceiling. Apart from a couple of colorful posters on her walls, Ruth's room was still quite sparse, but she was a young girl, barely more than a toddler really; Lou suspected that it would become a glittery pink bazaar of vivid imagination over the next few years.

She checked Ruth's little wardrobe and looked under her bed (didn't she do this every night?), but of course, found nothing. Outside, the maple tree in the neighbor's garden swayed in the morning breeze, its almost-bare boughs reaching towards Ruth's window. Lou lingered there a moment, staring at the tree, before going to Ben's room.

Ben was the polar opposite of Ruth when it came to tidiness. His bed was neatly made and all his things had been carefully put away so that the room hardly looked lived-in; his Xbox controllers were tucked away between the console and TV, and his games were stacked meticulously to one side. He was only allowed to play it at weekends and he often spent part of the week ahead arranging his gaming schedule. Lou didn't mind if he was up here a lot on Saturday and Sunday - he got plenty of outdoors time during the week, unlike a lot of other kids she knew of, who spent every waking moment online with a controller in their hands.

With the umbrella still in one hand, she scoured Ben's room and found nothing. No-one in his wardrobe or under his bed; no sign that his room had been disturbed at all.

She'd imagined it.

Lou sighed and went to Ben's window, which looked out over their backyard. The grass had a fresh covering of damp brown and yellow leaves but the raking-up period would be over soon - the trees were almost spent. One of Ben's older soccer balls sat discarded in the far corner of the garden, deflated and muddy. There were only a few practices left before the winter break.

Lou watched the neighbor's cat stalk across their yard and then went back to the hall.

She'd wasted enough time with this, creeping around the house like some paranoid buffoon because she thought Evelyn Sparrow had broken inside. No, Miss Sparrow was currently several miles away, teaching her class. She was -

Lou jumped as the landline rang. It was blaringly loud in the silence of the house.

There was a phone in their bedroom. She went down the hall, propped the umbrella by their door, and lifted the handset by Derek's side of the bed.

Was it Debbie responding to her text? Had Perry or Beverley suddenly remembered who she was, and wanted her back in to school?

Part of her expected it to be Evelyn.

'Hello?'

'Lou, is that you?'

'Mom.' Relief washed over her. 'Yes it's me. Are you ok?'

'Oh yes, dear,' her mother replied cheerily. 'I didn't think you'd be home though, I was just going to leave a message on your machine. Much easier than texting, I think. Why *are* you home, anyway?'

'I, uh, felt a little sick again today,' Lou said. She sat on the bed, facing the window.

'Oh no, dear. You aren't coming down with that flu again, are you? It's been going around here too. Your Aunt Jane, her chiropractor knows someone who had a nasty second bout of it, you know. *Terrible* stuff.'

And with that, the Mount Vernon report began.

Lou didn't mind, really. She lay on the bed and listened as Carol Williams filled her in on the various goings-on in her hometown. Most of it was news about people she barely knew or didn't know at all, and on another day she might have steered her Mom back to more relevant topics, such as her own grandchildren. But not today. Today, she was glad to hear a familiar voice.

Carol finally burned herself out thirty minutes later and hung up. Lou had almost nodded off on the bed but her Mom knew to pepper her monologues with questions to ensure her fellow conversationalist was actually listening, so she'd stayed awake. She felt different now. There was something grounding about mundane chats on the phone - it had calmed her, taken away that irrational fear from before. The house still creaked and groaned, but now she knew it was just the house.

She was resolved. Tonight, she'd sit down with Derek and tell him everything, and then together they'd make a plan to tackle it. Maybe once he knew, she'd be able to start telling other people not connected to the school. Not her Mom, though. She wouldn't understand.

Until then, she'd keep herself busy. No more thoughts of Evelyn Sparrow and whatever the hell was going on at Amber Hill High. Save that for tonight.

Lou went back downstairs, made a fresh cup of coffee, gave herself twenty minutes to relax in front of some mindless daytime television show, and then began to clean. She did the whole house, working her way from the kitchen to the living room, through to the den and the study, the small downstairs bathroom, and then back up to the bedrooms and family bathroom. In the midst of all that, she also put on a load of laundry, started a dishwasher cycle, paid a couple of bills online and raked a section of the garden - anything to keep herself busy and avoid thinking about school.

She considered going into town to pick up a few things, but something kept her from it. She didn't want to leave the house, just couldn't leave it...

What? Unguarded?

...in case those footsteps started up again on the second floor.

She remained at home all day, relentlessly cleaning and tidying, until Ben arrived back from school. He was tired and teenagery and didn't want to talk much, so she let him go without any interrogation. Mostly, though, she was afraid of him picking up on her own mounting anxiety about telling Derek that evening, and she didn't want to worry him.

Derek and Ruth got back after five and she knew straight away that something was wrong.

'How was your day, hon?' she asked, pecking him on the cheek.

'Not so bad,' he replied. 'Ruth, go wash up.'

Lou watched their daughter skip off to the bathroom. Derek went to the sink and started on his own hands.

'What's for dinner?'

'Pot roast - hope that's ok.'

He made a noise that suggested it was. She slid a hand over his back.

'You alright?'

Derek dried his hands on the towel and turned to her.

'Yeah, I think so. It's just... Debbie was a bit weird when I picked Ruth up.'

Lou's heart skipped a beat but she didn't allow it to show on her face.

'What do you mean, weird?'

'I don't know exactly. She was fine when I got there - the girls were playing and stuff, nothing unusual - but when we got to talking, she seemed like she was struggling to... place me, or something.'

Lou's heart was galloping now. She went to the stove, facing away from Derek. 'That *is* weird.'

'Yeah, it was. She knew who I was, I'm sure of that - I mean, she said "Hi, Derek" when she opened the door and asked how many houses I'd drawn today. You know, that old joke of hers.'

'Sure.'

'But as we were getting ready to leave, I asked if you guys were hanging out this weekend, like if you'd arranged a playdate for the girls. And I swear, Lou, I thought she was having a stroke for a second. She just looked at me blankly, like this, and didn't say anything. I asked if she was alright and she just shook her head, like she was trying to clear something out of it. She said she was fine, but I don't mind telling you, it freaked me out a bit.'

Lou had been stirring a pot of boiling vegetables as Derek talked, not really aware of what she was doing. She noticed she'd sloshed some water onto the stove and reached for a towel.

'Have you been talking to her today?' Derek said.

'No, not today.' She patted the stove dry and replaced the lid on the pot. 'Hon, I need to talk to you about - '

'Daddy!' Ruth cried, running back into the kitchen. 'I spilled stuff in the bathroom.'

Derek sighed. 'Tell me later, ok?'

'Ok.'

He followed Ruth to the bathroom. Lou turned back to the stove.

It's definitely happening now, anyway.

The four of them ate dinner (Ruth had to be enticed with the promise of dessert, but she got there in the end) and swapped stories about their day. For Ben, this mostly involved regurgitating any new information he'd taken on board in class and stolidly avoiding any reveals in his personal life - gone were the days when their little boy would readily divulge which girl he had a crush on that week, or who had risen to the top of his best friend rankings (this used to change on a weekly basis, too). Ruth's stories, on the other hand, were almost entirely centered on the games she'd played, the imagination-fuelled scenarios she'd concocted, and the roles she'd taken on in each.

'Today, *I* was the princess and *Ella* was the dragon. And Noah was the soldier who saved me. And he had a sword, like this.' Ruth did a pretty good swordplay imitation with her fork. 'And we ran away but Ella caught us, and then *I* was the dragon...'

Lou nodded and smiled, genuinely enthused by her daughter's stories, but the anticipation of her impending conversation with Derek weighed heavily on her throughout. She noticed he didn't enquire much about her day. He was waiting to hear the truth.

After they'd finished their dessert of peaches and vanilla ice-cream, Lou sent Ben off to finish his homework and Derek aimed Ruth at the TV in the living room. They now had a small window for discussion before bedtime routines began. Lou decided now was the time - she didn't want to have this conversation right before going to sleep.

She gently closed the kitchen door and joined Derek by the sink. He handed her a plate with sudsy hands and she began to dry. He started on the next one, waiting.

She allowed a few moments of silence to pass before saying, 'I haven't been to work in three days.'

Derek continued to scrub at the plate.

'Why's that?'

Lou took a deep breath and began to tell him everything. She started slowly, choosing each word with care, unsure of how much he'd interrupt along the way. But he didn't interject, just nodded or occasionally lingered on some dishware to show he was considering what she was saying.

She'd rehearsed her story all day but it still came out of her in awkward, apologetic splurges, as though she was making it up on the spot. It sounded crazy, of course, and she was sure Derek thought so too. But the more she told, the easier it came: she recounted how her colleagues had seemed to forget who she was before she even set foot back in the school; she told him about her horrible, embarrassing experience on Monday morning in front of her class, and how Perry had practically chased her from the school building; she explained about the school website and her community center account, and how Evelyn had taken her place there as well.

When she came to the end and told him about today's imagined upstairs intruder, she realized tears had been silently rolling down her cheeks the whole time, and wiped at her face. Derek saw her do it, set down the scrubbing brush and put his arms around her, and she cried into his shoulder, digging her fingers into his back. They stood that way for a long time, her body convulsing with muffled sobs. In the next room, Ruth stared obliviously at the TV screen.

Once the tears dried up, she released him, sniffing. She reached across the counter and tore a sheet of kitchen paper from the roll. He grinned a little as she blew her nose.

'Don't,' she said breathlessly, smiling despite herself. 'I must look terrible.'

'Nope,' he replied. Now he was leaning on the counter next to the sink, watching her. 'So that's what happened, huh?'

She nodded.

'I knew something was up.'

'I know you did.'

'Why'd you hide it from me? I could've helped. I *will* help.'

'I know. I'm sorry.' She crumpled up the damp paper and tossed it in the trash. 'It just all felt so... unreal, you know? It's like I've been stuck in a really bad, confusing dream and I didn't think you'd believe me.' She looked at him now. 'Do you?'

'Do I what?'

'Do you believe me?'

She could see his jaw working behind the copper beard. He was, quite literally, chewing on the next words coming out of his mouth.

He doesn't believe me, she thought, aghast.

The kitchen door opened and Ruth walked in.

'Mommy,' she said, rubbing her eyes. 'Can I have some water?'

'Sure, baby.'

Lou filled a tumbler halfway and handed it to her. Ruth stood in the kitchen, gulping it.

'Go finish your show, honey,' said Derek. He followed her to the door and closed it behind her.

'Derek,' Lou said. Her voice was flat.

He kept his back to her for a moment before turning.

'If you'd told me that story - '

Story!

' - before this afternoon, then no, I'm not sure I would have believed it. You have to admit, Lou, it does sound pretty crazy. There's bound to be some sort of rational explanation, something we're missing.'

She didn't reply.

'But you said you talked to Debbie about it,' he continued, slower now. 'You said she believed you, and she got that Sparrow woman's address somehow.'

'I can show you the text - '

He held up a hand. She knew then he was suppressing something. Probably anger at not being told all this before now.

'Debbie was really weird today, Lou,' he said. 'I mean *really* weird. I've never seen her like that before. Maybe I downplayed it a little earlier, but I have to admit, it scared me. I didn't like that Ruth had been with her today. And now, after hearing your side of things, I think I know what it was that scared me. And even saying it now, it sounds so wrong, but...'

He stared hard at the floor, frowning. She waited, holding her breath.

'I think Debbie only started acting the way she was,' he said, 'after I mentioned you. That was when she got really strange and spaced out. I think it was because she didn't recognize your name. She didn't know who you were. And then she could no longer place me. In hindsight, I think if I'd been there much longer, I might've thought I was some stranger trying to take Sarah and could have called the cops or something.'

She could see it on his face now. It was becoming real to him, too.

'So I don't have a clue what's going on, Lou. But I don't disbelieve what you've told me, because I may have seen part of it firsthand earlier. Unless this is all some sort of really weird and unfunny game you and Debbie are playing.'

'It's not.' She gasped the words.

'Then I'm going to that school tomorrow,' Derek said, crossing the kitchen to where she was. 'I'll call in sick in the morning, and then I'll go down there and talk to Perry. And this Sparrow woman, if I have to.'

'No, not her,' Lou said, taking his hands. They were still a little sudsy from the dishes. 'I don't want her getting inside your head, like she's done to me. Just Perry, ok? He knows you, he'll talk to you.'

Derek nodded. She could see fire burning in his eyes. He was mad now, really mad, but not at her.

'We'll work all this out, hon,' she said, cupping his face. 'I'm sorry I couldn't do it on my own.'

'Why would you have to?' he said. 'That's why I'm here. We're a team.'

She kissed him. He drew her in and kissed her back, long and fierce.

Ruth went down easily that night - Lou and Derek's kitchen conversation pushed back her bedtime by at least twenty minutes and she was asleep before Lou had finished reading her story. It was a good one about pirates and talking fish. Ruth requested it at least once a week.

Ben was also reading when Lou went in to say goodnight. Despite being less inclined towards the Arts than they knew Ruth would eventually be, he could always get into a good middle grade fiction, and he was starting to dip his toe in more young adult stuff above his reading level.

He was thoroughly engrossed in some space adventure he'd grabbed during their last family visit to the mall and didn't notice Lou in the doorway. She watched him in silence for a moment - her boy. How much longer would he be a kid?

'Hey.'

He looked up, then went back to his book. 'Let me finish this chapter.'

'That's ok.' She went in and kissed his forehead. 'Night, son.'

'Night, Mom.'

Derek was already in bed when she came in. He was on his phone, scrolling through some website.

'What're you doing?' she asked, getting undressed.

'Looking at the school website again,' he replied. He shook his head and sighed. 'I still can't believe it. It's really screwing with me.'

'Welcome to my world.'

'I just can't figure out how she's doing it. Are the images photoshopped? How did she get them on the website? Who gave her access?'

'I don't know, hon,' Lou said wearily. 'Trust me, this is all I've been thinking about for the last few days.'

100

She slipped into bed beside him. He set his phone to one side.

'I'm sorry, Lou,' he said. 'Sorry I didn't help.'

'How could you? I didn't tell you about it.'

'I know. I wish you had, but... I know now, anyway.' He put an arm round her and she nestled into him. 'I don't know what's going on, but I'll damn sure find out tomorrow.'

'Do you want me to go with you?'

He considered it.

'No, I don't think you should. Not into the school itself, anyway. Maybe wait in the car until I'm done, in case I need you. Hopefully it's all just some big misunderstanding.'

Lou was silent for a moment. She had one hand on Derek's chest and she could feel his heart beating.

'Derek, what if it's not?'

'Not what?'

'A misunderstanding.' She swallowed. 'What if this woman - Evelyn - is doing something in there? Something to make everyone think what she wants them to think.'

'What, like brainwashing?'

'Maybe. She could be hypnotizing them, or something. It's not impossible. I've heard of people being hypnotized en masse before.'

'But the whole school?' Derek said. 'All the teachers and students? And the community center, and you said the library?'

'Yeah, I know. It's scary. *She* scares me.' She held him close. 'I don't know what it is. There's something about that woman that isn't... human.'

Derek didn't respond, but she could feel his heart beat become more pronounced.

Thump, thump, thump, thump.

'When she talked to me in the school, I really felt like something else was going on. It was like she was looking *past* my eyes, reading me. Just for a few seconds. She's small and weedy-looking, but some part of me was preparing to be attacked, like she was about to lunge at me and bite my throat.'

'Lou...'

'And when she saw me at the community center and did her little wave, I felt like a lobster in a tank and she was picking me out as her main course.'

'Lou, seriously.'

She giggled then, as much in fear as amusement at the ridiculousness of it all. Derek brushed her hair back from her forehead. She knew she was trembling a little in his arms.

'We'll go there tomorrow,' he said, 'after Ruth's been dropped off. And we'll pick her up from kindergarten ourselves this time.'

'Yes.'

'We'll go to the school,' he repeated, 'and I'll talk to Perry, and you can wait in the car. One way or another, we'll get some answers. And if we have to get the police or lawyers involved, we will.'

'Thank you.' She kissed his cheek.

'Any time,' he said. 'No-one gets to eat my wife.'

'But you?'

He grinned and reached across to flick his lamp off.

They dozed off that way, tangled up in each others' arms. Sometime during the night, Derek rolled away in his sleep and began to snore intermittently. Lou tried to follow suit but found that once again, she was unable to sleep.

She twisted her neck back and glanced at the digital face of her alarm clock, squinting into the green light. It was quarter after midnight.

She sighed and rolled back to face Derek again. It was chilly in their room but he was warm beneath the covers. She stayed close to him, listening to the rhythmic sound of his breathing. For the first time since last week, she felt something like peace.

Tomorrow, she thought. *Tomorrow we'll start taking my life back. I'm not alone anymore. I have Derek, and Debbie, and probably a host of other people who still recognize my face.*

I'll start taking it all back.

Tomorrow.

She closed her eyes. The rise and fall of Derek's breathing became the only sound, and then even it began to fade as she sank into sleep. Their bedroom fell away into a quiet darkness and the first flickerings of her dream reel began drifting into focus.

The house. Ruth's room. Ben's room, everything in place. The tree by Ruth's window. The view down into the neighbor's yard, where Fall leaves rustled over the stiff November grass.

Silence. Deep darkness. The safety of sleep.

Something else.

Lou opened her eyes. She'd been snapped awake. Something was wrong.

In the darkness of their bedroom, illuminated only by the weak green glow of her alarm clock, she could see the black outline of Derek's form next to her. He was still breathing softly, fast asleep. He always fell asleep right away, and it was always deep.

Her eyes went to the bedroom door. It was wide open as usual, a dark, unoccupied rectangle on the other side of the room. The door to their en suite bathroom was closed. Their bedroom was still and silent.

Lou was suddenly keenly aware of that silence. It lay heavy around her, pregnant with anticipation. Was it normally this quiet? Shouldn't there be some sound, like the wind in the eaves or a car passing in the street?

She shifted under the covers, just an inch closer to Derek, as much to create some sound in the room as anything else. Her pillow felt over-warm and moist against her cheek and she realized she was sweating. The room was chilly and she was burning up under the covers.

Stop it, she said to herself, gripping the duvet. *Stop doing this. Go to sleep.*

She closed her eyes again and willed herself to sleep, but just like that, she knew it was useless. Because something was wrong. Something was out of place in their bedroom and it wasn't allowing her to go.

And then she felt it - almost imperceptible at first: a prickle on the back of her neck. Her hair had fallen to one side and her skin was exposed, and now she felt gooseflesh appear there. The room was cold, but the air tickling the back of her neck was colder, and it sent electric tremors of fright shooting up and down her spine.

It wasn't just cold air on her neck.

It was breath.

Lou screwed her eyes tight. She squeezed the duvet so hard in her hand that it hurt. Next to her, Derek slept on in the darkness.

There's nothing there, she thought. *You're being a child. This is what children do.*

Of course there was nothing there. Her over-hyped mind was fixating on an imagined presence, much like Ruth and the "monsters" under her bed, and the fight-or-flight instinct was pounding adrenaline through her veins, keeping her awake.

She was being dumb. She had to see for herself, just to put her mind at ease. Then she could sleep. She needed her rest - they had a tough day ahead.

Just get it over with. Rip the band-aid off.

Lou rolled over and looked.

Her eyes automatically went to her alarm clock and she registered the time as twenty after twelve. Only five minutes since she'd last looked. She started to think about how it'd seemed so much longer, how time always dragged when you couldn't sleep, and then she saw Evelyn crouched by her bed, halfway in the light cast by the alarm clock's green digits, halfway in shadow. Lou stared back at her dully, not reacting, not really processing. She was just there, down on her haunches, leaning in close. Just a few inches from Lou's face.

Then Evelyn smiled and Lou understood she was real. Her mouth fell open in a silent scream, but her body had seized up in a rigor mortis of terror and no sound came out. She was locked in place, stricken, unable to move.

And this woman was in her room.

But she wasn't a woman, was she? Lou gazed unblinking into those eyes, blazing in the shadows, and saw no humanity there. Not anymore. She'd been fooled last time, in the school. Evelyn's gray irises had faded away, and now there were only two bulging whites with a soulless black pupil in each. Her smile pulled wider, too wide for her face, and an invisible icy hand closed around Lou's heart. She wanted to scream, to wake Derek, to wake everyone in town, but a fear more pure and terrible than any she'd ever experienced in her life had pinned her to the bed.

Evelyn's bony white finger came up and pressed to her pursed lips. Lou could see she was trembling in anticipation, radiating a kind of gleefulness. Then she cupped her hand around her mouth in a conspiratorial way and leaned still closer, as though to share a secret. Lou could smell her choking musk.

'Wakey wakey,' Evelyn Sparrow whispered, and the sound of her voice dragged furrows of gooseflesh down Lou's back and made her want to scream until her lungs exploded.

Evelyn grinned with teeth now (or were they fangs?), baring them like a wolf.

'I know what you're up to,' she said. 'You have a plan now, don't you? You're a naughty girl, Louise. Yes you are.'

Lou stared back, unable to reply. She'd begun to shake all over with fright.

Evelyn giggled, covering her mouth like a little girl. The sound she made was a horrible titter. It was unworldly and evil.

'Don't you know it's useless, Louise?' Evelyn continued. Her voice was deepening, becoming raspier. 'It's all gone. I've taken it, it's mine. Everything outside of this house, your whole world.'

Her pupils were gone now - her eyes were completely white.

'It's mine and I'm not giving it back. I've taken everything.'

That grin again. Those teeth.

'Well, *almost* everything.'

Lou's insides crawled. She could feel every single one of her organs.

'Let's see, who's left?' said Evelyn, counting off on her skeletal fingers. 'There's Derek, but I'm saving him for last. There's your mother down in Mount Vernon - oh how I'll enjoy that one...'

No no no please no

'...and of course, there's little Ben and Ruth, right down the hall. And gosh, I'm here now, so why not?'

Evelyn rose to her feet. Lou saw she was wearing a long white nightdress that came down to her ankles. She couldn't see her feet in the darkness.

'Back in a flash, Louise,' she cooed.

Lou watched, still locked in place and streaming tears now, as Evelyn walked silently around to the foot of the bed. As she went, she seemed to grow taller and thinner, her limbs and torso elongating, her hair snaking down her back, until her scalp brushed the ceiling and her frame occupied most of the available space in the room. She was no longer looking at Lou - she wasn't interested in her anymore.

She was going for the kids.

Evelyn reached the door and now she was so tall she had to stoop beneath the frame. Under the wispy white dress her body was grotesquely slender, with no flesh on it now. Lou heard her footfalls on the hall floor - bone clicking on wood.

And suddenly, she could move again.

She wrenched herself out of the bed, throwing back the covers. The scream that had been trapped in her throat pulsed and gurgled and then surged upwards into her mouth, and when it came out, the sound of it filled the whole world.

'NOOOOOO! STOP! KIDS!'

She staggered towards the door. As she came around the foot of the bed, her pinky toe crunched on the wooden leg of the frame. The pain was excruciating but she didn't slow.

'RUTH! BEN!'

Derek stirred in the bed. She barely heard him mutter her name before she stumbled out into the hall.

What happened next passed in a fleeting blur for Lou. She was in the hallway, lurching forward, limping theatrically on her injured foot. She had the impression Evelyn had just passed out of sight into one of the rooms, had just caught a glimpse of the tail of her dress. The nightlight, fitted halfway down the hall for Ruth if she had to go to the bathroom during the night, flicked on automatically as Lou approached. It hadn't activated when Evelyn passed by.

'Ruth,' Lou croaked, taking another drunken step towards her daughter's open door. Somewhere in the background of her consciousness, she heard Derek call her name. She was at the top of the stairs now, near Ruth's door. Evelyn was in there, she knew it, crouched by her daughter's bed, bony fingers reaching for her face in the darkness -

'Louise.'

The voice came from behind her - not Derek's voice.

Lou saw herself from without, turning on the spot. She heard the sweat-slicked soles of her feet squeak on the wooden hallway floor. The nightlight, plugged into a low socket, threw spidery black shadows up the walls.

Evelyn was behind her, right behind her, grinning and insane, her eyes popping out of a face that was now barely more than a skull with translucent skin stretched over it. Her hair, now free of its bun, was a wild tangle that filled the space around her head and consumed all of Lou's peripheral vision. Evelyn opened her mouth and her tongue rolled out, a slippery gray thrashing thing, and her mad screaming cackle pierced the night and shattered what was left of Lou's idyllic, rational reality.

She reached for the end of the banister, which muscle memory told her should be there, but it wasn't. Her hand flailed at thin air and she overbalanced; she felt her body tip towards the stairs and gasped in vague surprise at what was about to happen. She saw Evelyn step out of reach, her head thrown back in a howl of laughter, and then she went.

Lou tumbled down the stairs. For a brief moment she was airborne and the second floor hall swung away. Her lips had just enough time to form the word 'Oh' before her shoulder came down on one of the wooden steps and electric pain shot through her nervous system, and then she was rolling, over and over, grabbing in vain at the balusters as they flashed by in the dark. The pain and the shock of it were all she knew. Halfway down her back twisted unnaturally and her left leg bent under her, and that action seemed to propel her faster and more violently towards the foot of the stairs. Her head hit the wall near the bottom and actually punched a hole in the plaster, and something snapped in her torso with an audible *crack* that sounded like a stick breaking over someone's knee, and then her body thumped onto the ground floor hallway and she lay still.

Unconsciousness rushed in on her as she stared at the ceiling. Stars danced and popped in her vision and a constant ringing sound drowned out Derek's cries as he stumbled down the stairs after her. She wondered dreamily if her back was broken.

Derek was over her now, yelling her name, but she barely heard it. Her head flopped to one side and she looked up the stairs, and there was little Ruth, staring down at her with enormously wide eyes, and Ben was at her side now, mouthing the word 'Mom' over and over as Derek shouted for them to stay there. Evelyn stood behind them, smiling, her hand on the top of Ruth's head.

And then there was nothing but black.

SIX

8 days before Thanksgiving

'Mister Jennings?'

'Yes.'

'Good morning, I'm Doctor Randal. No, don't get up, you look exhausted. Have you been here all night?'

'I have, yes.'

'Then stay there. Your wife's tests came back just now and it's good news. Or at least, it's better news than it could have been.'

'That's... good.'

'Yes. The x-ray confirmed that she's broken two ribs, but the suspected fracture in her wrist turned out to be just a severe sprain. We'll strap her up tight and she should be right as rain in no time. Other than that, the knocks she took to her back, neck and shoulder will bruise and hurt for a while, but those can be managed with a round of painkillers.'

'And her head?'

'She received a concussion, nothing more. There was no fracture to the skull or bleeding inside, thankfully. We'll keep her here for a few days, but she should be home in time for the holidays. She'll need plenty of TLC and I suspect you'll be the one preparing the turkey this year.'

'Of course, yes. That's great news.'

'It could certainly have been much worse, given the nature of the fall. She was very fortunate not to have broken her neck.

'Yeah.'

'Are you alright, Mister Jennings?'

'Yes, I... I think so. It's just shock, I think. Scared the hell out of me, you know?'

'Understandably.'

'She was just... screaming, at the top of her lungs. I think she was having a bad dream. She was already going down the stairs before I could reach her.'

'Easily done. Many people sleepwalk their way up and down staircases on a regular basis - by the law of averages, some of them will trip and fall, I'm afraid.'

'That's just it, though. I came out of our bedroom into the hall and it was dark, but I saw her. I saw how she went. That's what scared me so much. That's why I wasn't able to grab her - my legs were... rooted.'

'You mustn't blame yourself, Mister Jennings.'

'No, you don't understand. I didn't get to her because I froze, and I froze because of the way she went. Because she didn't just trip and fall down the stairs. It looked to me like she *threw* herself down them.'

Lou had been in a dream. It was a bad one, the kind you think you'll never be able to leave, where one imagined scenario bleeds seamlessly into the next and the only constant is the thing that's chasing you. She'd been pursued through the empty dark corridors of the school where her clapping footfalls rebounded off the lockers and low ceiling, and then down Main Street, where the thing raced along behind her, its feet pounding on the sidewalk as it drew ever closer. She caught glimpses of herself in store windows as she passed and barely recognised the crazed, middle-aged woman staring wild-eyed back at her. Then she was running towards the town hall, crossing the grassy leaf-strewn lawn in front of it where, weather-permitting, the Thanksgiving festival would soon take place. The building loomed over her as she mounted the steps to the entrance - above, the sky was a swirling mass of black clouds.

In the dream, she slammed bodily into the doors of the town hall and her shoulder crunched with exquisite pain, but her momentum carried her inside. The thing was right behind her. She staggered into the darkened lobby, yelling for help now, but found that she was instead in the upstairs hallway of their home. The town hall entrance had become her bedroom doorway and she was stumbling, out-of-control, towards the top of the stairs. Derek and the kids were there, just out of reach, watching calmly as she twisted at the top step and grabbed for the banister, but it was too late. In the dream, the world tilted upwards and she fell again, and the last thing she saw was Evelyn at the top of the stairs, dressed once again in her unfashionable teaching outfit with her hair tied up in a bun. She held a bloodied knife in one hand; with the other, she gripped the severed head of a sow by its wrinkled pink scalp.

Kill the pig cut her throat

Lou fell into darkness, her insides rushing upwards,

SPILL HER BLOOD

She screamed herself awake and a nurse had her by the arms.

'It's ok, Mrs Jennings. You're ok. Easy, now.'

Lou thrashed until the scream had left her, then lay still.

'That's it. Easy, now.'

Spill her blood

'Where... where...'

'You're in the hospital, Mrs Jennings,' said the nurse. 'Amber Hill General. It's Thursday.'

Lou looked at her. She had graying curly hair and dry skin; bifocals perched precariously on the end of her nose, which was long and hooked.

She looks like a cartoon witch.

'You were having a nightmare,' explained the witch-nurse, 'but it's over now.'

'No, it isn't.'

The nurse hesitated, then stepped back and adjusted her lavender-colored uniform.

'The doctor will be around to see you soon. He may be able to prescribe something for -'

'Where's Derek?'

'He's not here right now but we'll let him know you're awake. Your mother's just gone to the bathroom though, she should be back in a minute.'

'My Mom's here?'

'She is. I'll see if I can find her. Just a sec.'

The nurse breezed from the room. For the first time since waking, Lou took in her surroundings: she was in one of the few private rooms in Amber Hill General, a small and under-funded hospital servicing too many towns in too large an area; the ceiling was paneled white but one of the LED lights was on the verge of burning out and there was a dark spot in the corner that looked like damp. A dog-eared paperback lay on the arm of a chair to her right. Opposite her bed, a TV screen mounted on the wall broadcast the local six o'clock news in muted silence. According to the headline, a boy in Amber Hill was missing. Lou knew his name, even recognised his face when it flashed up next to the news anchor, but somehow that recognition didn't connect with her reality right now.

Her eyes fell to her own body. She expected to see her legs encased in plaster and suspended by pulleys, but all she saw were the familiar curves of her frame under the white bedclothes. Her left wrist was strapped up tight, however, and when she leaned forward she felt a stab of pain in her middle. She sank back into the pillow and stared at the ceiling again.

She was alive and in one piece. Or she assumed as much, anyway - surely the nurse would have told her otherwise if it'd been the case.

A shadow in the doorway. She turned her head to look, half-expecting to see Evelyn Sparrow again.

Her mother was there instead, clutching a paper cup of coffee in one hand. Her face crumpled a little when Lou met her gaze.

'Oh, Louise,' she said, shuffling into the room.

Carol Williams was sixty-three and plagued with arthritis, particularly in her knees, so her journey from the doorway to Lou's bedside was a slow and painful one. Her husband George - Lou's father - had been ten years her senior and died of a stroke while cleaning out the gutters (the fall from the ladder had killed him, really). He'd never met Ruth and Ben barely remembered him.

Lou reached her good hand towards Carol. She took it and gave it a squeeze, then eased into her chair with a sigh.

'That blasted coffee machine couldn't be further from here if it tried,' said Carol. She took a sip from her cup, grimaced, and set it on the bedside table. 'Hardly worth the effort, either.'

'The nurse said you were in the bathroom.'

'I was headed that way but it's even further than the coffee machine. I can wait.'

Lou smiled. 'It's good to see you, Mom. You didn't have to come all the way up here.'

'Nonsense,' said Carol. 'You're my only child, what else was I going to do? I hopped in the car this morning and got here by lunchtime. Damn near had a heart attack when that husband of yours told me what happened.'

Carol rarely referred to Derek by his name. He was always "your husband", or some variation of it. Lou knew she liked him, though. It was just her way.

'I'm alright,' said Lou.

'You're lucky, is what you are. You could've broken your back falling down those stairs. I *told* you you need to carpet that hallway, it's too slippy.'

'Mom...'

'And what were you doing anyway, wandering around there in the dark? Don't you have a bathroom right next to your bedroom?'

'I had a bad dream. I think I was sleep-walking.'

Carol took another sip of coffee. 'You never slept-walked at home, Louise. I've certainly heard you *talk* in your sleep, but never walk about. Your husband said you were screaming. I think the kids were a bit shaken by it all.'

Lou rubbed her eyes. 'How are they? Have they been here?'

'No, not yet. It would've been too much for them, seeing you lying there with your head wrapped up.'

Lou reached up and patted her head. Sure enough, there was a thick bandage wrapped around it - she hadn't noticed it at all. How many painkillers was she on?

'Just a concussion,' said Carol. 'But you had a cut, I think, so they had to wrap it up. Should be off soon.'

Now it was Carol's turn to rub her eyes. Lou took her hand again.

'You're tired, Mom. How long have you been here?'

'Oh, not long. A few hours, I think. Once your husband's here I'll go back to your house - Ruth and I are going to make cookies.' She smiled and Lou saw every one of her sixty-three years on her face. 'I'm glad you're ok, Louise.'

'Me too, Mom.'

The news anchor finished his segment and the weatherman took over.

'Don't let Ruth keep you up late, ok?' said Lou. 'She always pushes her luck.'

'I know she does,' Carol replied, pulling her book towards her. 'That girl thinks she has me round her little finger, just like you.'

Lou responded with a weak chuckle.

'Has Debbie been here?'

'Debbie?'

'You know. She looks after Ruth sometimes.'

'Oh, her. No, I don't think so. Do you want me to call her?'

'No, that's ok. Just read your book.'

'You sure?' asked Carol, already opening it.

'Yeah. Give me a nudge when Derek gets here.'

'I will.'

Lou closed her eyes and wondered when, and how, Evelyn had gotten to Debbie.

Derek got back to the hospital an hour after Lou woke up. He brought Ben and Ruth along to see their Mom - Lou discovered she was desperately glad about that.

Ruth stared bug-eyed at her bandaged head.

'Did they take out your brains, Mommy?' she asked. All three adults laughed.

'No, honey,' Lou replied, stroking her daughter's hair with her uninjured hand. 'They left plenty in there. Ben, c'mere.'

Ben drifted over to her side. He looked pale.

'You ok?' she said. He nodded, but she knew he wasn't. He was that bit older than Ruth and had a better grasp of the implications of her fall, or of what could have potentially happened, at least.

'I'm alright, Ben. You don't need to worry. I'll be back home in no time.'

She could tell he was straining to hold back tears - she had to give him an out.

'Hon,' she said to Derek, 'have you got a couple of bucks?'

'Sure.'

'Can you loan it to Ben and Ruth so they can grab me a snack from the vending machine? I need something sweet.'

Derek fished the cash from his pocket and pushed it into Ben's hand.

'You guys go pick me out something nice, ok?' she said. 'I'll split it with you.'

'Ok, Mommy,' said Ruth, grabbing her brother's hand. 'Come on, Ben!'

Ben, who would normally have snatched his hand away from his little sister's grasp, allowed her to lead him from the room. Lou watched them all the way, her heart aching. When they were gone, she turned to Carol.

'Keep an eye on Ben when you get home, yeah?'

'I will,' she replied. 'He'll be fine once he has a cookie or two in him.'

Lou smiled and looked at Derek. 'Are you ok?'

Like Ben, he nodded; like Ben, his face was strained with suppressed emotion.

'So what's the damage?' Lou asked. 'How beat up am I?'

Derek relayed to her what Doctor Randal had told him. She listened in silence, feeling every injury he described. It wasn't as bad as she'd feared.

'They want to keep you here for a few days, just to be sure,' Derek said. 'But otherwise, it sounds like you dodged a bullet.'

'Sure doesn't feel like it.'

'It could've been worse, dear,' said Carol. 'Let's all be thankful it wasn't.'

Lou felt a flicker of resentment at that.

Thankful? Some demonic thing posing as a woman tried to kill me. Thankful Isn't the word I'd use right now.

Derek was watching her closely, reading her. She turned to Carol again.

'Mom, could you check on the kids? Maybe those vending machines aren't as easy to find as I remember.'

'Of course, dear.'

Carol shuffled from the room. Derek took her seat. He picked up her paperback, glanced at the blurb, tossed it on the bedside table.

'Honey -'

'Tell me what happened,' he said.

Lou held his gaze. It bore right through her.

'I had a nightmare.'

'No you didn't. I heard you. You were wide awake.'

She looked away. The TV screen was now showing a rerun of *Friends*. She'd seen the episode a hundred times.

'What scared you so bad?' Derek said. 'Did you see something? Was it her?'

Lou opened her mouth and closed it again. Her head was beginning to hurt.

'Just tell me once, hon,' he said, softer now, 'and I'll believe you.'

She saw the look in his eyes and knew he would. She told him everything, as quickly as possible. She didn't want Carol or the kids hearing anything.

When she was done, he only nodded. But his jaw was firmly set and she could see that fire in his eyes again, just like on Wednesday night before they'd gone to bed. She knew what he was about to say before the words left his mouth.

'Derek -'

'I'm going there tomorrow.'

114

Lou's lip trembled and she bit down on it. 'I don't want her to... I dunno...'

'What? Get me?' He snorted laughter and shifted in the chair. 'Shit, Lou. I need to talk to this woman. I need to talk to Perry. You just fell down the stairs and almost broke your neck. You're lucky it wasn't anything more serious. I'm going to find out what's going on.'

She took his hand. It was hot and damp with sweat.

'Just... look after the kids, ok?' she said.

'Yeah.'

'I mean it, Derek. Watch them. Don't let them go anywhere alone. And get Mom to pick them up from school tomorrow, not Debbie.'

He frowned for a moment, then understanding dawned on his face.

'You think...'

'I don't know, but I don't want to take the chance. If she calls you, just make up some excuse. Mom's visiting for the week so she can do it - it's not even a lie. Just keep them all safe until I get home.'

'I will.' He leaned over and kissed her forehead below the bandage. 'Don't worry.'

Carol came back with the kids a few minutes later. Ruth presented Lou with both a Butterfinger and a Three Musketeers bar. She dutifully split each in half and let them choose their favorite, then said her goodbyes, reassuring them that she'd be home in a couple of days. Carol gave her a kiss on the cheek and the three of them left.

'I'll be back tomorrow,' Derek said after a little while. 'Give me a call if you need anything, alright?'

'You do the same,' she replied, cupping his face in her hand. 'Better start learning how to cook a turkey, too.'

'I'll let Carol handle that one.'

She grinned and kissed him. He lingered, scanning the room.

'I'll be fine, honey,' she said. 'Go home and eat cookies with our children.'

'We'll bring you one tomorrow.'

'Make it three.'

Derek went home. Lou unmuted the TV and watched until the nurse returned with a fresh dose of painkillers.

Amber Hill General was a small hospital that nonetheless bustled with activity all night long. The door to Lou's room was ajar, spilling a sliver of light across her lower half. She lay on her back (the broken ribs prevented her from rolling onto her side, the position she preferred) and listened to the constant yet comforting sounds of night-shift orderlies, nurses and on-call doctors walking the corridors and murmuring conversation. She occasionally heard a bout of hushed laughter or the clang of some medical instrument; somewhere down the hall, a machine beeped and blooped rhythmically. Lou took in every sound with her eyes closed, unable to fall asleep but too weary to watch TV or read - Carol had left her paperback behind and Lou had managed to skim a chapter before the gushy romantic nonsense had gotten too much for her. She couldn't sleep and she didn't want any more drugs in her system, for tonight anyway.

The truth was, her mind simply wouldn't allow her to drop off. She could still picture Evelyn's crazed, inhuman face behind her eyelids and she was terrified it would be there again if she only turned her head and looked. Fear had pinned her to the mattress at home, and now her injuries prevented her from leaving her new bed, at least without causing her extreme pain first. One way or the other, Evelyn had her immobilized.

And what had happened to Debbie? Lou hadn't heard anything from her since Tuesday, and what Derek had said about her yesterday was deeply unsettling. How had Evelyn managed to get to her? Was it really that easy?

In the semi-darkness of her room, Lou shuddered. She hated the thought of Derek going to the school alone tomorrow. He'd taken the rest of the week off after her fall and planned to work from home next week when she got back. He was a good man, patient and rational, so he might stand up to Evelyn and those in the school she'd turned (*is that the right word for it?*) better than she had. Let's face it, she probably hadn't handled the whole thing very well and now Evelyn had her claws firmly embedded in multiple aspects of her life.

And what exactly was her goal? She'd taken Lou's place as English teacher at Amber Hill High, along with her spot in her spin class and had, more than likely, usurped her role as Debbie's best friend. What did she want? Why was she doing it?

I've taken it, it's mine. Everything outside of this house, your whole world.

Lou gripped the bedsheets with her good hand, recalling Evelyn's words.

It's mine and I'm not giving it back. I've taken everything.'

Well, almost *everything.*

Lou opened her eyes and looked.

She was alone in the room.

Derek's fingers clenched round the wheel of the Corolla. He stared at the road ahead, black in the November night, not really seeing it.

He was present in body only.

Lou had looked good when he left the hospital - better, anyway. She'd smiled and joked and brushed off his concern towards the end of his visit, playing down what had happened the previous night. Acting like it was no big deal, in that way of hers.

She'd only fallen down the stairs in the dark, screaming all the way. No big deal.

Derek had taken her car to the hospital purely out of convenience. It had more gas in it than his Ford and it'd been at the end of the drive already. She'd told him about the busted tire and, afterwards, how she'd initially planned to hide it from him if he hadn't noticed. Just a minor note in the song of her deception.

He batted the thought away - it was unfair. What she'd been through, everything she'd told him... if it'd been him, he would've gone crazy by now. How she was still smiling and joking and playing strong for him and the kids and Carol was beyond his comprehension. But he knew it was just part of the act. His wife was strong, but he knew her limits.

The car smelled of her, too. He swallowed down a lump in his throat.

An odd mixture of sorrow and rage bubbled away steadily inside him, buried deep beneath the practicalities of his husbandly duties. The whole situation was still a mystery to him, as confusing as it was infuriating. But the impossible problem at the core of it was all that mattered, really, no matter how much the thought of it enraged him: someone had taken it upon themselves to ruin his wife's life in a way that didn't make sense, and it had pushed her to a place where she had almost done serious damage (or worse) to herself, within their own home, with their kids watching. He wanted nothing more than to go straight to the cops and tell them everything, or to find this Sparrow woman himself and tell her to get the hell out of Amber Hill. But would the police believe him? Or would they, like so many others, simply not know who Lou was?

The traffic light up ahead went red and Derek eased to a stop. It was eight-thirty and the roads were already quiet. He waited, chewing on his lip.

I mean it, Derek. Watch them. Don't let them go anywhere alone. And get Mom to pick them up from school tomorrow, not Debbie.

Debbie. Lou's best friend in town. He'd thought about texting her after he'd called Carol, just to let her know what had happened. But he knew he wouldn't be able to bear it when her response came back with something like '*I'm sorry, I'm not sure who you're talking about*' or just '*Who is this?*', as Perry had responded to Lou. She'd shown him the messages and he'd hardly been able to believe it. It was now well beyond the limit of what was appropriate for a joke - it was, at best, mass delusion or hypnosis; at worst, well, who knew?

He glanced at the passenger seat, where his phone lay face-down, then at the side pockets in the door, packed with Lou's CD cases and shopping receipts. She still used CDs in this day and age.

The storage space below the radio and AC dials was stuffed with empty candy wrappers and tissues, and there were more in the side pocket of the driver's door, along with a scrunched-up water bottle. His wife kept a clean house, but all the rules went out the window when it came to her car. What he wouldn't give just to have her home -

Beep.

The driver behind him was laying on the horn. Derek glanced up - the light was green.

He held up an apologetic hand and accelerated, heading for home.

The first thing that hit him when he walked through the front door was the sweet aroma of fresh baking. Carol had kept her word - there was a stack of golden chocolate chip cookies in the kitchen. Ordinarily, he wouldn't have been able to resist grabbing one, and he *was* a little hungry. But tonight, the smell of them made his stomach turn and his head was starting to hurt. He checked the back door was locked, flicked off the light and went upstairs.

Ruth was in bed and Carol was sitting on a chair next to her with an open book in her lap. The bedside lamp was still on. Carol's chin was on her chest, and for an absurdly horrible moment Derek wondered if she was dead. He put a hand on her shoulder and she jerked awake.

'Wha... oh, it's you,' she said.

He nodded and put a finger to his lips. She looked over at Ruth, breathing softly, and closed the book.

'Go on to bed,' Derek whispered, 'I'll tuck her in.'

'Ok. You get some rest, too.'

She patted his arm and shuffled out of the room.

Derek leaned over and kissed Ruth's cheek, then pulled her duvet up to her chin. She stirred but didn't wake. He switched off her light and went to look in on Ben. He was also fast asleep, sprawled out beneath the covers.

The light under Carol's door was already off when Derek passed it. He went to his and Lou's bedroom, got undressed and stepped into the shower. He stood under the hot stream of water for a long time before starting to wash. His headache was growing worse.

Ten minutes after he'd finished and had toweled off, he was on the couch in the living room, wearily watching football highlights from last weekend. The Bears were set to play the Packers on Thanksgiving - he wasn't hopeful but he'd watch it anyway. Lou would be home by then and things would be better.

He rubbed his temple. His head was beginning to throb. *Stress-induced*, he thought, and went to the medicine cupboard in the kitchen. They kept all their medication high up, well out of Ruth's reach. Ben was sensible enough to ask them first before taking anything.

He rummaged through the cupboard but found nothing. No painkillers. *Dammit.*

He went back to the couch and flicked through the channels, but his headache was becoming more painful by the minute. He knew he wouldn't be able to sleep tonight if it carried on like that. It would help if he was well-rested before going into the school tomorrow.

He glanced at the clock - it was a quarter of ten. The gas station was still open.

Derek pulled on his shoes, grabbed his coat and left the house.

The nearest gas station was a two-minute drive away. Normally he would have walked the distance rather than drive, but it was beginning to feel like hornets were building a hive inside his skull. Real angry hornets, looking for a way out.

He pulled into a parking bay outside the station. Mercifully, the lights were still on and they hadn't started pulling down the shutters yet. The place also served as a convenience store - it was closer than the nearest supermarket and Derek often stopped in on his way home from work to grab some milk, or whatever it was they'd run out of that day. They were always running out of something. The gas was a little on the expensive side, though - he normally fuelled up on the other side of town, near the freeway turnoff.

Jamming his hands in his pockets, he walked towards the entrance. An external loudspeaker blasted 'Smooth Criminal' by Michael Jackson; it echoed tinnily around the forecourt and Derek hummed along to the chorus. He paused to let an elderly woman leave the store before passing through the sliding doors.

It was over-bright inside and he shielded his eyes for a second. The abrupt change in light made his headache rebound with fresh ferocity. He passed a display stand of cut-price sunglasses and headed for the drug section of the store, throwing a nod towards the greasy-haired kid behind the counter who was clearly watching videos on his phone.

There was only one bottle of Tylenol left on the shelf. Derek snagged it and started for the counter, but he knew right away that his head would be cracking in two by the time he got home. There was a point of no return with headaches and he was dancing on the line. He had to get these pills into him right away.

He veered up the seasonal aisle towards the refrigerators at the rear of the store. The shelves were stacked with Thanksgiving decorations: paper turkeys, pilgrim hats, the works. The holidays were the last thing on his mind, though - he just needed something to chug the pills. A bottle of Gatorade or Coke would do the trick. He couldn't swallow medication dry. Lou could, but he'd never been able to do it.

He wondered how she was right now. Was she asleep? Were they keeping her nicely doped up on painkillers?

Someone's watching me.

Derek paused next to the hair products. He examined the shampoos for a moment, then cast a glance back down the aisle towards the entrance. A man had stood there just a second ago, and he was sure he'd been staring at him. He caught the tail-end of his coat disappearing around the end of the aisle.

What now? he thought.

Grab a drink and get out of here.

He went to the refrigerator and pulled open the glass door, hurrying now. He lifted a bottle of Cool Blue Gatorade from the shelf. As the door swung shut, he glanced behind him again. He still couldn't see the guy.

He turned in the direction of the counter and walked straight into someone. The Tylenol fell from his hand and bounced on the tiled floor.

'Oh, sorry!' he said, stepping back.

'No no, my fault.'

It was a woman. She was shorter than him, bundled up in a winter coat with a faux fur-lined hood.

'Let me get that,' she said.

'No, don't worry,' he replied.

They both stooped for the bottle and she dropped a can of peas, which immediately started rolling away. He intercepted it.

She laughed. 'This is getting comical.'

Derek grinned, momentarily forgetting the pain in his head, and rolled the can back to her. She gathered it into her arms with her other items and stood. He rose, his back cracking.

'Thanks,' she said, a little breathlessly.

Her hair had fallen around her face in wavy strands. It was light brown with suggestions of blonde luster. Part of it was still tied up at the back of her head. Her cheeks were flushed pink, probably from the cold outside, Derek thought. She smiled, broad and bright.

'No problem,' he said.

He met her eyes. They were blue-gray and alive with youthful vigor.

'I'm such a klutz. I bump into someone at least once every time I'm out in public. Seriously, every time.'

She brushed hair back from her face and her coat fell open. Underneath, she wore a short navy dress with white polka dots, wool tights and ankle boots. Derek wondered why anyone would wear something like that in the middle of November, but it wasn't his first thought. His first thought was about what her milky-white skin looked like under that dress, about how her breasts threatened to spill out of it, about how blood was rushing south faster than it had in a long time and his head no longer seemed to hurt at all.

Lou.

He had to get home, away from here.

His eyes returned to her face. He'd only glanced down for a second - half a second, even - but she'd seen it. Her coat was still open.

'No, uh... don't worry,' he said again. 'We've all done it.'

She laughed again, a sing-song note crackling with electricity. Derek felt a smile break out on his own face, unbidden. It wasn't all he felt. He couldn't stop it.

'Got a headache?' the woman asked, nodding at the Tylenol.

He looked at the bottle in his hand.

'Yeah, I um... I did. It's not so bad now, I guess.'

Did I have a headache? Is that why I came here?

'You just need a good night's sleep, Derek.'

Why's it so important that I get rid of this headache?

'Yeah, you're right.'

Derek.

'Wait,' he said sluggishly. 'Do I know you?'

She was still smiling, and now her eyes seemed huge to him. Huge glassy orbs of blue and gray. He could swim in them, if he wanted.

'Sure you do,' she said. 'We've known each other for a long time, haven't we, Derek?'

'We, uh...'

'We know each other very well indeed, Derek.'

Deeerrrreeeck

He was hard now, throbbing. Quicker than he'd been in years. She was all curves and smooth skin and moist pink lips, beckoning him. His blood thundered through his veins.

I could swim in those eyes.

'Do you want me to come home with you, Derek?' she asked.

He opened his mouth to answer.

With a crash, the sunglasses display stand near the door toppled over, scattering frames across the floor. Derek's head jerked in the direction of the sound. He caught a glimpse of someone going out the door, tugging up a hood as he went.

'Hey!' cried the kid behind the counter. 'Mister! You can't just...'

The doors were already sliding shut again.

'Jerk-off!' yelled the kid, coming round the counter.

As Derek watched it all happen, groggy and dull like he'd just woken up, the pain began to seep into his skull again. He turned back to the woman.

'Listen...'

But she was already walking away down another aisle, her boots clocking on the tiles. The bundle of items that had been in her arms were on the floor by the refrigerators.

She passed the kid as he came round the counter, stepping over the scattered sunglasses. Then she was out the door and gone into the night.

'Thanks for your help, lady,' the kid muttered, righting the display stand. More frames dropped to the floor and he swore.

Derek put a hand to his head. A wave of dizziness had just slammed into him like a bus. He had to get home right away.

As he walked to the counter, he wondered disconnectedly who that woman had been. She seemed to know him, but he didn't recognise her at all. He also wasn't aware that he still had an erection, a big stonking one like an anti-aircraft missile, until he went to his pocket for his debit card, and by then the kid had seen it.

Derek left the gas station red-faced and confused. He didn't know it, but he'd just met Evelyn Sparrow and had narrowly avoided falling under her spell - another few seconds and they'd have been walking arm-in-arm to his car - but it didn't matter. Not really.

She'd done her work. The seed was planted. Derek was on a one-way street and there was no place to turn, no way to back out. His fate was sealed.

And from that moment on, so was Lou's.

The nurse checked on her in the morning and said nothing about the dark rings under her eyes. She just smiled and pushed back the curtains, flooding the room with sunlight.

'Looks like rain for later,' she announced cheerily. 'What would you like for breakfast, Mrs Jennings?'

Lou ate dry toast and a banana, then sipped on the hospital's putrid coffee for the rest of the morning while she waited for Derek to come back. Her eyes were constantly drawn to the clock on the wall.

Seven-fifteen. Ben would head for the bus in a few minutes. He probably wasn't close to being ready, as usual.

Seven-twenty-five. Ben was gone. Derek and Ruth would be on their way out the door. Her Mom would spend the day in the house, probably cleaning it from top to bottom. She'd pick Ruth up from kindergarten.

Seven-forty-five. Ruth had just been dropped off. Derek was en route to the school rather than the office.

Lou drained the last of her cold coffee. Her neck was stiff and sore.

Seven-fifty-five. Derek would be at the school. She pictured him swinging into a parking spot and stepping out of the car.

Lou flicked on the TV again and watched the morning talk show. The hosts were interviewing some guy from Alaska who'd been attacked by a grizzly while fishing. Lou registered that he'd escaped by swimming across an ice-cold river and throwing rocks at the pursuing bear from the bank, but that was all she managed.

It was after eight. Derek was probably waiting at reception to speak to Perry. Or maybe he'd marched straight to Evelyn's classroom... no, *her* classroom... to confront her directly. That didn't seem like him, but then again, nothing about this situation was producing a particularly Derek-like response in her normally calm and logical husband. Maybe he'd even take a swing at her.

Lou grinned to herself. It was a grin that meant nothing.

She knew the Sparrow woman was dangerous, if she was a woman at all. She didn't believe she'd imagined Evelyn in her room on Wednesday night. It was no dream or stress-induced hallucination - it had been all too real. She'd been there, even if no-one else had seen her.

She wasn't crazy.

The how and why of it didn't matter either, did it? Her husband was in the same building as Evelyn and could very well end up talking to her within the hour. That inescapable, frightening fact was *all* that mattered right now.

Nothing else -

'All done with your coffee?'

The nurse was back, cheery smile still plastered on her face. She came round to the side of the bed and began gathering up Lou's breakfast dishes.

'Awful stuff, I know,' she said, setting the coffee cup back on the breakfast tray. 'Sorry we can't do better.'

'It's ok. It does the job.'

The nurse smiled and lifted the tray. 'Want me to leave the table there?'

'Yeah, it's fine. Will the doctor be back later?'

'Yes, he'll do his rounds later this morning. You're looking a lot better today, Mrs Jennings. I'd say you'll be out of here very soon.'

'I hope you're right.'

The nurse turned to leave and caught sight of the TV. The talk show had given way to the local news. Lou had turned the volume down but the headline was clear enough: HIGH SCHOOL STUDENT STILL MISSING.

'Oh dear,' the nurse commented, 'they still haven't found that poor boy. Terrible. His parents must be so worried.'

An image of the missing boy flashed up in a sidebar next to the news anchor. He was square-faced with cropped dark hair and he grinned toothily in the photo, the red of the Amber Hill football jersey just visible above the bottom of the image. He looked more like a college student than a twelfth-grader.

Lou frowned. Did she know that boy? His face was familiar but her mind was still foggy from the concussion.

'Just disappeared overnight,' said the nurse, still standing with the breakfast tray in her hands. 'I can't imagine what his poor family must be feeling right now. That poor, poor boy.'

'He's probably just off somewhere with his friends,' said Lou. 'You know what kids are like. They don't tell their parents anything.'

The nurse looked at her over her hooked nose.

'Oh no, dear, that's not it at all. Kids in this town don't just run off all willy-nilly with their friends, you know. Not in this town. Not in Amber Hill.'

Lou shifted against the pillows. 'What do you mean?'

The nurse studied her for a moment.

'You're not from here, are you? Originally, I mean.'

'No, we moved here a few years ago.'

'I thought so.' The nurse - *why doesn't she have a name tag?* - turned to face Lou. 'Most people from out of town don't know much about the history of this place. Don't know how they could, either - it's not something the folks in charge shout from the rooftops. This town's won county awards over the years, you see:

125

Best Kept Town, Best Family Town, etcetera. If you've blown in from up-state, you won't have heard much of anything that isn't glowingly positive.'

Lou nodded. She supposed that was all accurate enough, though she didn't like being called a "blow-in" after six years living here.

'To cut a long story short,' continued Nurse No-Tag, 'kids went missing here more than once over the years. Three or four in total, I think. Something like that. It hasn't happened for a while, mind you, but people don't forget things like that in a hurry. Especially parents.'

She looked at the TV again - the report had moved on from the missing boy.

'There was never any rhyme or reason to it, no pattern or anything. The kids and families weren't connected in any real way, other than the fact they lived here. They just went missing and no-one ever saw them again. Three happened in my lifetime, but the one I remember best was Susan Stinne. She was around my age at the time, maybe a couple years older. She went camping in the woods with some friends, just outside town, up near Fair Creek. Do you know it?'

'Yes,' Lou said. 'We've taken our own kids a few times. She went missing there?'

'Near there, yes. There's a campsite a little ways up the river. It's all clearly marked, perfectly safe. Families like yours use it all the time. There was nothing suspicious or sinister about any of it, either. Her friends just woke up the next morning and she wasn't in her sleeping bag. She hadn't taken anything, not even her shoes. She was just gone.'

'And they never found any trace of her?'

'Nothing. I remember the police searching those woods for days, even weeks. Practically every family in Amber Hill had someone up there tramping through the trees, shouting her name. Even the sniffer dogs couldn't catch a scent. There was nothing left of her, not a single hair, as far as anyone could tell. Her folks never quite gave up and her mother ended up going a bit mad. I think she was institutionalized about a year after it happened.'

The nurse cleared her throat.

'Those vanishings got all kinds of rumors and stories circulating round town. It's funny how that sort've thing happens, isn't it? People started saying there was something in those woods. They said there was a witch living up there, that she had a little house somewhere further out, and every once in a while she would come to town in disguise to buy bits and pieces she couldn't get for herself. "Eyes peeled for the witch", they'd say.'

'Bizarre,' said Lou in a flat voice. A tension had crept into the room; it thickened the air.

'That's one word for it,' the nurse said, laughing weakly. She shook her head, as though trying to clear something out of it. 'I never saw a witch, but those stories were enough to keep kids from camping in the woods very often after that. A few still went out, of course, just to say they'd done it. But they always came home shit-scared - excuse my language - saying they'd heard things in the night. And when another child went missing about ten years later, they stopped going altogether. There was a real sense of evil in town when those disappearances happened. Everyone felt it. Absolutely everyone.'

The nurse looked at her then and Lou saw it in her eyes.

'Sorry, Mrs Jennings,' she said, 'I shouldn't be saying all this, especially to you.'

'No, you don't - '

'It's just that seeing that on the news about that poor boy, it's brought it all back again. I remember how I felt, how we all felt, when that last child went missing back then. You think you've moved on and then it just comes back, exactly like before. I've heard folks round town talking about it again, saying the witch is back, that the woods aren't safe anymore and kids shouldn't be out at night. I don't believe there was ever any witch, never have, but I don't mind telling you, Mrs Jennings, I've got that same, dark feeling again, just like I had all those years ago. There's something evil in this town that hasn't been here for a long time.'

The nurse stopped, as if in mid-thought. Her mouth worked through a couple of silent words, and then she laughed abruptly.

'But listen to me, talking your ear off about all this nonsense. I'm sure this is the last thing you need to hear.'

'No, it's good to know, I suppose,' said Lou, forcing a smile.

The nurse returned it. 'I'll be back in a bit, ok? Just give me a buzz if you need anything else.'

'Sure.'

She left the room. Lou immediately reached for her phone and called Derek.

He didn't pick up.

As early morning faded, the hospital came to life beyond the doorway to Lou's room. Nursing staff and orderlies came and went; white-coated doctors breezed along the hallway, checking in on patients. The ambient hum-thrum-beep-clack of Amber Hill General's internal workings hung in the air.

Lou's doctor, an older gentleman surnamed Randal, stopped by around ten and perused her chart before declaring (as the nurse had already done) that she was "looking a lot better today", and then promptly exited stage-left before she could ask any real questions.

In truth, she only had one question, and she doubted Doctor Randal could answer it: where was her husband?

She'd held off calling Derek again as long as she could, telling herself there was no point, that he'd be in a meeting with Perry, or maybe even with Miss Sparrow the substitute, now teacher of English Literature at Amber Hill High. Add possible child-knapping witch to her CV, while you're at it. Derek couldn't pick up because his phone was on silent in his pocket. He'd call her when he was done.

But he didn't call. Eight became nine, and nine marched on towards ten, and by the time Doctor Randal appeared, Lou had called Derek seven times without reply. She may have looked better to the Doc, but inside, she was screaming bloody murder from the bottom of a black pit and the headache her painkillers were supposed to suppress was gradually creeping back to the fore.

In fact, all of her injuries were beginning to become more painful, whether it was a case of the physiological protection provided by her lingering shock wearing off, or the medication losing its potency. Her broken ribs and sprained wrist ached constantly, and every time she sat up, a wave of dizziness forced her straight back down.

She needed Derek, or her Mom, or anyone at all who still knew her properly. The dial needle was doing its best to swing from Stoic Determination towards Self-Pity and Panic. If she allowed that to happen, she knew she was liable to start sobbing uncontrollably, and then they'd have to sedate her, and she didn't want to be sedated if Derek needed her. It was all bubbling just below the surface now.

At twenty after ten, she called her Mom. Carol picked up after the third ring and Lou almost wept when she heard her voice.

'Mom, are you ok?'

'Yes dear, of course. The children are at school and I'm just doing some cleaning. Is everything alright? I'm planning to visit after lunch.'

'I'm fine. Have you seen Derek?'

'Not since this morning, no. Why do you ask?'

Lou's stomach began to churn. She was going to be sick.

'Did he say where he was going?'

'To the school, I think. To speak to the principal.'

'Do you know if he went?'

'I'm sure he did, Louise. He could still be there, I suppose, couldn't he? They've probably got it all straightened out by now.'

'Listen, Mom, I need you to do something for me,' Lou said. Her uninjured hand was shaking and she knew the rest of her body would soon follow suit. 'I want you to call me if Derek comes home, ok? Right away.'

'Yes dear, of course. What - '

'If he hasn't come home by noon at the latest, I want you to call the police.'

'The police? Why would I do that? They'll - '

'I *need* you to do it, Mom. Ok? Please.'

There was a pause on the other end of the line.

'Louise, are you sure you're ok? Calling the police seems a bit... extreme, don't you think?'

'No, not at all.' Now Lou was shaking all over. She closed her eyes - the dizziness was coming back again. 'You *have* to do this, Mom. For the kids. If Derek isn't back by noon, call the police and tell them he's missing. Tell them to go to the school and check there first.'

'Louise - '

'I haven't told you everything, Mom, I'm sorry. I will, as soon as I can. Just... just promise me you'll tell them to check the school. And also give them an address, they'll need to look there too. It's, uh... it's over on the west side of town, in the - '

'Mrs Jennings?'

Lou opened her eyes. The room swam into focus and she saw the nurse standing by the door.

'You have a visitor, Mrs Jennings.'

The nurse stepped out of the room and someone else stepped in. Someone in a night-dress with long, tangled hair snaking down her back. Someone with translucent skin stretched thinly over pale bones and eyes that were full white with no irises or pupils or soul in them. Evelyn grinned and her smile stretched beyond the natural boundaries of her face and Lou felt the scream surge upwards towards the back of her mouth.

But it caught there and she didn't scream, because it wasn't Evelyn.

Derek stood in the doorway, arms by his sides. In his right hand was a bunch of flowers. Pansies and chrysanthemums from the hospital gift shop.

Lou made a choking sound and managed to gasp out his name.

Derek's eyes turned towards her. He had the kind of look on his face that you get when you enter a room and forget what you came in for.

'Derek,' Lou said again.

He stared. She saw the beginnings of a frown on his brow.

Why's he just standing there? Why's he just staring at me like an idiot?

'Derek,' she repeated a third time, stronger now. 'Honey, come here.'

He did, ambling into the room with the bouquet in his hand.

'Louise?' Carol's voice in her ear. 'Is Derek there now?'

'He is, Mom. I'll call you back, ok?'

'Ok. Are you sure - '

Lou dropped the phone and reached to take Derek's free hand. He let her. His skin was cold, like he'd had his hand in a bucket of ice. Up close, she saw he was very pale.

'It's good to see you, honey,' she said, straining every sinew to smile up at him.

He looked back at her. The frown was there now. She could see every wrinkle on his face, every gray hair in his copper beard. The cogs were turning, the internal mechanisms activated, working hard, working through the problem, pressing towards the solution.

Come on, she thought, squeezing his cold hand. *Come on. You know me. You know me. Just tell me. Say it. Please!*

His mouth opened, closed, opened again.

'It's good to see you, too...' he said.

The word formed, evaporated, formed again. And then, the circuits came together.

'...Lou.'

She sighed, long and slow. She could see the comprehension on his face now. The frown went away.

'Lou,' he said again, cementing her name. 'Lou, honey.'

He leaned down into her embrace. She held him for a long time, her face buried in his neck, ignoring the pain in her own. She didn't cry - there'd be time for that later.

She released him and he sat down in the chair next to her bed.

'They're lovely,' she said, nodding at the flowers.

He looked down at them, as though he'd just realized they were in his hand.

'Oh, yeah. I got them... in the gift shop, on my way in.' He handed them to her. 'I think I did, anyway.'

He touched his temple.

'Shit, Lou,' he said. 'I barely remember coming here.'

'It's ok, hon.'

'I got in the car and drove here, and I stopped to buy those flowers, and I got on the elevator and came up to this floor. I knew which floor you were on, and which room was yours.'

'That's good.' Under the bedsheets, she was trembling and couldn't stop. 'Derek, did you go to the school?'

He stared at her again and she could almost feel the heat emanating from his brain as it worked for the answer.

'I... yes, I did.'

'And what happened? Did you talk to Perry?'

'Perry.' He ran a hand through his hair. 'No, he wasn't there today. He was away... at some conference, or something. I didn't see him.'

'What about her?' Lou asked, leaning towards him. 'Did you talk to *her*?'

'Her.' He was parroting back her words now, struggling to compute the questions. 'No, I didn't see her either. I only spoke to the receptionist...'

'Beverley.'

'Beverley. She said I should go back next week, I'd be able to see them both then.'

'Did she know who you were, Derek?'

He nodded. 'Yes, she did. She called me Mister Jennings. She knew me.'

'That's good,' Lou said. She realized she was crushing the stems of the flowers in her hand and set them next to the bed. 'That's all fine. I'm glad you're ok.'

She squeezed his hand, gentler now. He squeezed back and smiled weakly.

'My head hurts, Lou.'

'Mine too,' she said. She'd meant to follow that with a laugh but it hadn't come. 'Can you stay here a while?'

'Of course.'

Derek stayed the rest of the morning. He got a coffee from the machine and sat by her bed. Lou asked about Ben and Ruth and Carol. Derek said the kids were fine, just missing her. He said Carol was helping out loads but he'd be glad to have her home again. By the time lunch rolled around, they'd both loosened up and were chatting at an almost-normal level.

As noon approached, they heard the orderlies rattling along the hallway with the lunch cart.

'Go home,' Lou said, patting Derek's arm. 'Mom will be here soon. Get some rest before you go to pick the kids up.'

'Are you sure?' he replied, rubbing his eyes. 'I can stay longer if you want.'

'I'm sure. Go home and have a nap or something. I'll be fine.'

He stood and kissed her on the lips. His beard bristled her cheek and she warmed inside.

'I'll be back tomorrow, ok?'

'See you then, babe.'

She released his hand and watched him go. Next to her bed, the flowers had already begun to wilt.

Derek left Lou's room and walked back down the corridor towards the elevators. He was tired now, more tired than he should be, maybe. But Lou was ok, and that was the main thing.

A twentysomething orderly passed with the lunch cart. He caught the smell of bacon and his stomach growled. Maybe he'd have bacon when he got home.

Bacon and eggs. Why not?

The elevator doors slid open and Derek stepped inside. He had no idea he'd just lied to his wife. He was a puppet on a string now, barely in command of his own thoughts and actions. The few hours he'd spent that morning wandering around town in a daze had seemed pleasant enough at the time. He'd gotten nowhere near the school at any point.

As the elevator doors closed and the car started to descend, his final weakening thoughts of Lou began to break down and fade out into the hollow nothingness that now occupied his mind. He was transitioning from Derek Jennings, loving husband and family man, into a blank canvas, ready for painting.

That was Friday. By Sunday, Derek had completely forgotten who Lou was.

seven

3 days before Thanksgiving

Rain pattered softly on the glass. It had been drizzling all morning; the drizzle had become fine rain by midday, and as the afternoon wore on, the droplets splattering against Lou's window had become thicker. The sky outside was blackening over with ominous clouds.

It was Monday, just a few days before Thanksgiving. Someone had hung a paper turkey wearing a pilgrim hat on the inside of her door. A speech bubble protruding from its beak read 'Gobble Gobble, Happy Holidays!' in bubble letters.

Lou hadn't seen Derek since Friday, when he'd told her he'd be back the next day. Carol had arrived shortly after lunch and stayed until four o'clock. She'd knitted and talked about which of her friends were ill, and which of those were most likely to die before the end of the year. Lou had listened contentedly - she'd been doped up on painkillers at that stage and Derek had still been replying to her texts. She read those texts now.

Lou, two-fifteen: '*Hey honey, how're you feeling now? Did you get a chance to nap? It was good to see you earlier. Can't wait to get home.*'

Derek, two-thirty: '*Hey hon. I feel ok, didn't get any sleep. Just picked Ruth up from school. She says she misses you.*'

Lou, two-thirty-three: '*Go to bed early tonight, ok? Tell her I miss her too. Call me later.*'

Lou, five-twenty: '*Hey hon, Mom says you're making dinner tonight - try not to burn the house down! Just kidding. Kids ok?*'

Derek, six-thirty: '*Hey. Yeah, we had Indian, just stuff from the jar. Kids are great.*'

Lou, six-thirty-two: '*That's good. Call me when they're in bed and we'll talk. I miss you.*'

Lou, eight-ten: '*Hey hon, call soon if you can, I'm pretty tired.*'

Lou, nine: '*You must've fallen asleep. I'll see you tomorrow, honey. Sweet dreams.*'

She stopped reading after that, when the texts and phone calls continued to go unanswered. By Saturday, she'd known Derek wasn't going to respond and didn't try contacting him again. She was scared by then, really scared. She didn't want to receive the same '*Who is this?*' reply Perry had sent during the week she had the flu. That would've finished her off. There was always a chance Derek had simply forgotten to reply.

But she was still scared.

Carol stopped responding by Saturday as well. She wasn't great with texts, and when Lou rang that morning to check what time they were coming to visit, she'd sounded confused. Lou had casually ended the conversation, set her phone to one side and screamed into her pillow.

Doctor Randal had come by a few hours later and told her they wanted to keep her for one more night, just to make sure the concussion was healing up properly. They removed the bandage from her head - fortunately, she hadn't needed stitches for the wound. Randal was still a little concerned about her potential memory loss (Lou stuck rigidly to her claim that she didn't remember getting out of bed, wandering into the hall and falling down the stairs) and ran through some questions to check her cognitive functions. Satisfied with her answers, he said it was likely she'd be discharged on Sunday.

Lou had smiled back and said that was great news. She knew no-one was coming for her.

Sure enough, Sunday morning came and went without any sign of her husband or mother. The nursing staff tried calling her home number several times without response. One of them joked that the family had left on vacation without her. Lou smiled at that too. She'd gotten good at it.

135

She spent the rest of Sunday weeping intermittently in her room. She made sure the nurses didn't catch her, she didn't want any more medication or comforting words. When she didn't cry, she slept. By Sunday night, she was all wept and slept out.

The hospital staff tried calling her home again on Monday morning, but by then, Lou had already decided what she was going to do.

After dinner was done and her tray had been taken away, she got out of bed and started to dress herself. Derek had brought a bag of her stuff on Thursday so she'd be ready to leave as soon as the doctors gave the all-clear. She pulled on jeans, a t-shirt and a sweater. It was a clumsy, painful process with her sprained wrist and damaged ribs, and when she bent to pull on her shoes, a wave of dizziness threatened to knock her out. She sat on the edge of the bed for a couple of minutes until it passed, breathing slowly, then downed two Tylenol pills she'd been saving and called a cab.

It was shockingly easy to sneak out of the hospital. The staff on her ward were still busy with the post-dinner cleanup and no-one noticed her walk down the hallway and board the elevator. There was no-one in the lobby area when she passed through, no-one at the reception desk. No-one tried to stop her leaving.

The rain was hammering down by the time the taxi pulled up outside the main entrance. Lou got in the back seat, gritting her teeth against the sharp pain in her torso. She gave the driver her home address and they left Amber Hill General behind, silent and glowing in the wet night.

Inside, the taxi smelled of cigarettes and stale sweat. The seats, once smooth leather, were now scuffed and faded. Lou didn't care, though - she was just glad to be out of the hospital, her prison for the last few days. She didn't even care how her body felt. Her head was heavy on her shoulders and her ribs ached, but the Tylenol was knocking back most of the pain. None of it mattered.

She watched Amber Hill sweep by in the night. The roads were emptying now as the post-work rush wound down. The asphalt was drenched with rain.

She'd be home in just a few minutes, back to her little house on the east side of town, where children played in the street on bright evenings and starlings nested in the trees above the sidewalk. Her home. The place where she lived.

The place where *she* lived.

The cab pulled up outside her house. The driver asked if she had a coat, because that rain was really coming down and she'd catch a cold if she wasn't careful - it was going around, you know? She said she'd be fine, paid him cash from her purse and got out.

She stood beneath the trees at the end of the drive, where there was some shelter. All the windows were dark. There were no cars in the drive. No-one was home.

She started up the walk to the house, shivering as the rain met her scalp and neck.

Here was Ben's soccer ball, poking out from the begonias by the path.

Here was Ruth's pink bicycle, kept erect by its training wheels, its wet metal frame catching the streetlight.

Her kids' things.

She mounted the steps to the front porch. Someone would see her, a neighbor maybe, but she didn't care. Maybe they'd recognize her, maybe they wouldn't. It didn't matter now.

She stopped at the front door, her hair now sodden, and stared at the handle. Would she have changed the locks?

Probably.

Lou bent, grimacing, and lifted the flower pot by the door. The spare key was still there, as it had always been. She picked it up, slotted it in and gave it a turn. The door unlocked with a *click*.

She went inside and closed the door behind her. Rainwater dripped from her clothes and hair, pooling at her feet. The house was dark, empty and cold.

Lou's eyes went involuntarily to the bottom of the stairs, the last place she remembered being before waking up in the hospital. There was no sign of damage to the wall where she'd *thunked* her head. Her gaze traveled up the steps, lingered just below the top, then went to the landing.

Empty, too.

She was shaking now, not just from the cold. She went down the hall and through to the living room.

Signs her family had been here recently: one of Ben's school textbooks on the couch; Ruth's Lego set near the TV; a half-full mug of tea by the chair in the corner.

But there were differences.

There were two throw pillows on the couch that hadn't been there before. They were embroidered with pink roses. In fact, there was a bunch of fresh pink roses in a vase by the window. Big, beautiful, vibrant roses. In November.

Lou also noticed a scent in the room. Something sweet and homely that she couldn't put her finger on. It made her want to wretch.

Starting to get dizzy, she went to the mantel above the fireplace and looked at the framed photos arranged there. She already knew what she'd see before the images swam into focus in the dim light.

There was Derek and the kids by the lake two summers ago. He cradled Ruth in one arm, the other wrapped around Ben's shoulders. All three were laughing, happy and tanned after a carefree week in the sun. A neighboring friend on vacation had taken that photo. Lou had been standing behind Ben, leaning on Derek's shoulder, also laughing.

Except now it was Evelyn.

There she was, wearing Lou's yellow summer dress, beaming at the camera. Lou couldn't tell for sure, but it looked like her hair was up.

Trembling, she choked down an hysterical laugh and looked at the next picture.

It was one of Carol with a much younger Ben on her lap. She was reading to him. His eyes were big, full of wonder. In the background, Evelyn watched on, her blue-gray eyes full of love and contentment.

A third picture. Lou and Derek on their wedding day, standing under the orange leaves of an oak tree on a September afternoon. But it wasn't Lou in that white dress with her arms around Derek.

She could hardly bring herself to look at the fourth and final photograph on the mantel, but she did it anyway. No sense in stopping now, the knife was already in. Give it a twist.

Evelyn sat propped up in a hospital bed at Amber Hill General. Her hair was tied back; she was flushed but glowing with happiness. She cradled baby Ruth in her arms while Ben gazed down in wonder at his new little sister. In the photo, Evelyn was saying something to Ben. Lou knew what it was - she'd said it, after all.

'You're a big brother now, Ben. You'll take good care of her, won't you?'

'I will, Mommy.'

Lou clapped both hands to her mouth to stop that hysterical laugh from screaming out into the silent house.

I've gone mad, she thought, staggering across the living room. *I've lost my mind. This isn't happening. None of this is real.*

She floated into the kitchen, leaving a trail of moisture in her wake. They might see her wet footprints on the carpet when they came home. She didn't care.

Like the living room, the kitchen was gray and near-silent, disturbed only by rainfall on the window. How many times had Lou stood in this little kitchen in the early hours of the morning, lulling Ben or Ruth back to sleep on her shoulder, gazing bleary-eyed at the dark shapes of the trees at the foot of the garden? How often had she cooked meals in here, graded papers at the kitchen table, talked or laughed or spatted with her husband about some mundane issue neither of them could remember the next day?

This was her kitchen. This was *her house.*

She drifted to the sink. It was still half-full of sudsy water, now cold and unmoving. Something protruded from it. Something black and familiar.

Lou slipped her good hand into the water and drew out the kitchen knife. It caught the moonlight from the window and flashed, sharp and slick.

She stared at it. How good it would feel to plunge that blade deep into Evelyn's heart. She'd stick it in, pull it back out, and stab again. And again. And again.

The handle of the knife was warm and wet in her hand. She squeezed it hard, savoring the feel of it.

Yes, she could do it. She knew she could.

Kill the pig. Cut her throat. Spill her blood.

She stirred now, excited by the image. Evelyn on the floor, red with her own blood. She'd gasp for breath, drowning in fluid. Lou would put the knife into her again and leave it this time. She'd stand and look down at her and laugh at the sight of the black plastic handle rising and falling with the rhythm of her labored breathing, slowing now, always slowing.

Then the laugh did come, and if anyone had walked into the Jennings' kitchen at that moment, they may well have agreed with Lou that she was going insane. She stood there by the sink, dripping water on the linoleum, kitchen knife wavering unsteadily in her trembling hand, and the laugh tittered out of her at first, eerie and child-like in the dark, before swelling towards the same lunatic gales of breathless hysteria from last time, ricocheting off the tiled walls, draining the room of oxygen, filling it with madness.

Lou laughed and trembled where she stood. She laughed until tears streamed down her face, and if she hadn't stopped to draw breath, she may not have heard the key turning in the front door.

The laughter cut off in an instant. Her body stopped shaking and went rigid. She became motionless, unbreathing, a statue in the dark.

She heard the front door open. Voices in the hall, muffled by rain on the window.

Lou turned on the spot. She couldn't be here, couldn't be in this house - they wouldn't know who she was.

She'd frighten the kids.

She went for the back door, then stopped. Derek often came round the back after he'd parked the car in the garage. She and the kids would jump out before he reversed in. She might meet him at the corner.

The light was on in the hall now. Footsteps on the wooden floor. At least two people. One of them spoke and the other chuckled in response.

What the hell am I doing here? Lou thought, her mind sluggish with panic. Then, the other part of her, answering: *This is my house. I live here. I don't have to leave.*

The living room light came on and she did the only thing she could think of.

She moved quickly across the linoleum floor to the pantry (three paces got her there), opened the doors and slipped inside. It was madness, total stupidity. She'd just trapped herself - there was no way out now without being seen.

Lou, you idiot.

She pulled the doors closed exactly two seconds before Derek and Evelyn walked into the kitchen.

The ceiling light flickered on. Behind the shutters, Lou put her hand to her mouth and almost stabbed herself in the face with the knife she was still clutching.

'Sheez, it's really coming down out there,' Derek said, crossing to the window. He was in light gray chinos and a navy blazer, and his hair was matted to his head. 'This jacket's soaked through already.'

'Should've brought an umbrella, babe. I did say, you know.'

Lou stared at Evelyn. She looked almost completely different from their first encounter in the school. Like Derek, her hair was wet and unkempt from getting caught in the rain, but the bun was gone - she now wore it loose and flowing, and despite having darkened with dampness, it had taken on a lustrous, auburn sheen and curled where it fell about her bare shoulders. She wore a figure-hugging red dress that accentuated every youthful curve on her body; her long alabaster legs, once hidden beneath an ugly ankle-length skirt, now glistened under the kitchen light. She was flushed and breathless and strikingly beautiful.

'I don't remember that,' said Derek, grinning.

Evelyn went to him, her red heels clicking on the floor.

'Funny the things you do and don't remember, Mr Jennings,' she purred. Bile stirred in Lou's stomach. The plastic of the knife handle was hot in her palm.

Derek shrugged out of his jacket. 'Kids'll be home soon. Hope they didn't give your mom any trouble.'

'Mom can handle them.' Evelyn put her arms around Derek's neck. 'Besides, who cares? When was the last time we had a meal out, just the two of us?'

'Far too long.'

Derek tossed his jacket at one of the kitchen chairs. Evelyn kissed him and his hands went to her hips, and then down to her ass. Lou desperately wanted to look away but found she couldn't. She was just an animal now, trapped in the light.

Evelyn uttered a little groan of pleasure and pressed into Derek.

'There he is,' she said.

Then she began to kiss him hungrily, working at his shirt. He kissed her back and gripped her buttocks through the thin material of her dress, and Lou suddenly discovered that she couldn't move a muscle. She was locked in place again, just as she had been when Evelyn appeared beside her bed. Her body was frozen, rigid, rooted to the floor of the pantry.

She wanted nothing more than to scream her lungs out and smash through the doors and fling herself at Evelyn. She wanted to haul the monstrous witch off her husband and bury the knife in the tight flesh of her abdomen, again and again until her insides were on the outside, and then keep going. But it wasn't possible. All she could do was watch with her eyelids pinned open as Evelyn mounted Derek and he carried her to the table, and for what seemed like an eternity, thrust into her over and over while she laughed and cried out and clawed at his back, and the table creaked beneath them, and when Evelyn looked across the kitchen and met her gaze through the narrow slats of the pantry door, grinning triumphantly between gasps, Lou knew it was all for her benefit, and she begged for death.

But death never came. Derek and Evelyn only stopped when a car horn sounded outside and, cursing, Derek pulled his pants back up.

'Kids are home,' Evelyn breathed, sliding off the table.

'Perfect timing,' Derek growled, snatching his shirt off the floor. 'They couldn't have stayed away for a bit longer?'

'To be continued when they're asleep.'

Tears ran down Lou's face, as much from her eyes drying out and shrieking for relief as her husband's words about their children. The children he loved.

'Why'd your mother bring them back already?'

Evelyn helped him do up the last of his buttons.

'It's ok,' she cooed softly, her fingers dancing across his chest. 'We have all the time in the world, my love.'

Derek sighed, but she had his attention again. He was back under her spell.

'Go and see if Mom needs help. I'll... tidy up here.'

'Alright.'

She kissed him lightly on the cheek. He lingered for a moment then turned and went out the back door. Before it swung shut, Lou heard Ruth cry 'Daddy, Daddy!', and then it was silent again.

Evelyn stood there, smiling at the closed door. The moment seemed to hang in time, detached from the other moments that preceded it. Lou wondered vaguely if she had, in fact, died, and she'd been left with this final image to torment her in the afterlife. Could hell be much worse, really?

But Evelyn did turn. Her head swiveled towards the pantry, then her body followed. She walked slowly - so painfully slowly - across the kitchen, smiling all the while, until she was just inches from Lou's face on the other side of the door. Her eyes were electric blue without a trace of gray.

Lou stared into them. She could do nothing else.

Evelyn spoke, cool and clear, and all other sounds evaporated from the world.

'Get out of my house and don't come back. If you do, I'll kill them all. Starting with the little girl.'

Then she winked, and went out the back door. She left it ajar and Lou heard Ruth say 'Mommy! What happened to your hair?', followed by Carol's laughter.

Control flooded back into Lou's body and she jammed her eyes shut. The pain was sharp and raw, and she wanted nothing more than to stay where she was until it passed, but there was no time.

She stepped out of the pantry, closed the doors behind her and walked out of the kitchen, passing through the living room to the hall. She hesitated at the door,

142

but only briefly. When Ben's voice came through from the kitchen, she opened the door and went outside, easing it shut behind her.

It was done. Finished.

Evelyn had won. She'd taken everything. There was nothing left for Lou now, and if she came back again, her family would die.

Her family who'd forgotten she'd ever existed.

Lou Jennings walked away from her house. She was numb to the rain, numb to the cold, barely aware of her surroundings. She'd been hollowed-out, emptied of everything. She was Lou Jennings, but equally, she wasn't. She'd been replaced, like a piece in a jigsaw puzzle - the picture was now complete and she wasn't part of it anymore.

She paused at the sidewalk and looked back at the house. She knew it would be the final time.

Derek stood by the window. He had his back to her. Ruth was on his shoulders, giggling and thrashing. Next to them, Evelyn stood with an arm round Ben, animatedly telling Carol about their night out. Carol beamed - she was delighted to be there with her beautiful daughter and her family. Evelyn, her only daughter. Her Evie.

Lou watched them until they left the living room and the light went out. She looked down at the knife in her hand, glinting in the rain.

She dropped it on the sidewalk and walked off into the night.

PART TWO: Jason Rennor Gets Detention

EIGHT

10 days before Thanksgiving

Jason Rennor broke his nose on November 14. It was a Monday, the day Lou Jennings first met Evelyn Sparrow in Room 2 of Amber Hill High. Jason wasn't in the room that morning, but he heard all about it later (word travels fast round a small town school): some lady marched into the Tenth Grade English class and had some sort of nervous breakdown, right there in front of everyone. Everyone agreed it'd been totally bizarre and a great way to start the week. Best of all, most of the teachers seemed to have been really disturbed by it, especially Principal Martin, who'd spent the rest of the day holed up in his office.

Jason wasn't in the room that morning because he didn't take English anymore - he'd dropped it the first chance he got. If there was one subject he didn't like, it was English. Well, most parts of it, anyway. All those books by dead authors that no-one cared about, all that reading and analysis. And poetry! What a load of garbage. No, English was for suckers, in his opinion, and Jason was quite certain he was no sucker. He was sixteen years old and in eleventh grade, a Junior barrelling towards the end of his academic career, and he knew by now exactly what he was good at, and what he wasn't. English was in the latter category. Always had been.

Of course, if Jason was telling you this himself, he'd be sure to tack a disclaimer on to the end, something along the lines of: 'Don't get me wrong, I don't hate *school*, nothing like that. I just don't have much need for most of what goes on in here, you know? What's the point in learning another language when you don't plan on leaving the good ol' U-S-of-A anytime soon? And who needs geography? Or history? And why would anyone *ever* need English?'. Those subjects, Jason would tell you, were for suckers.

What Jason *did* like about school, however (probably the only thing other than teenage girls in tight jeans and tops showing just the right amount of midriff), was Shop class. Shop was great. Shop was where you worked with your hands and learned real-life skills and got things done. It was where he learned how to use a hand plane properly, and how to cut the perfect miter joint, and to rewire a plug so it doesn't blow the fuse when you flip the switch.

Shop was for people who wanted to do something practical with their lives. It was for people who wanted to get a job, a *useful* job, and make some money, enough to buy a nice car and a big TV and maybe a house someday, one that you could fix up yourself because you'd have the skills. You got all that from the Shop.

And Shop was where Jason broke his nose.

You see, Jason Rennor was one of those students (one of those *people*, really) who tended to fade into the background in any given situation. He got straight Bs or Cs in class, often depending on how much reading was involved in the subject - his grades weren't good or bad enough to draw much attention from teachers, so he usually sailed under the radar when the time came to hand out test results or discuss his progress with parents ('Jason does fine, he doesn't give me any problems - if he continues to apply himself in class, I'm sure he'll achieve *all that's expected of him* come the end of the year'); his homework, unexceptional though it was, always came in on time, and he was usually capable of answering a question when called upon, on those rare occasions when he was selected (teachers always honed in on the students they suspected weren't listening, or went inexorably to those they knew would have the right answer, just for a taste of the sweet reassurance that *someone* understood). If Jason got the grades for college, fine, he might consider going; if not, that was fine, too.

He was also one of those people who had a pinky finger in every pie - he could talk sports smack with the jocks, weigh in on comic books with the nerds (he even had a pretty good handle on the interconnectedness of comic book movies and why DC was actually better than Marvel), and could even throw a little charm towards the girls, most of whom didn't find him remarkably attractive or repulsive either way, and never discussed him amongst themselves afterwards, or really thought much about him at all. They were rubber, he was glue.

Jason Rennor was everywhere, and he was nowhere. If you went to Amber Hill High, you'd probably recognise him, and you may even know his name, but that'd be about it. Just another kid in the crowd, doing his best to get by.

So when Rick Anderson went for Curtis Lawrence in Shop on that Monday morning, he didn't see Jason's intervention coming at all. In fact, he hadn't even been aware of Jason's presence in the room until that moment.

Curtis Lawrence was a pimply-faced, weedy kid with coke-bottle glasses who just seemed to rub everyone up the wrong way, no matter what he said or did. He had a nasally voice that always made him sound like he had a cold, and he *always* stood too close when talking to you. You know the type: just an inch or two inside the Personal Space Boundary, but it was enough. Guys wanted to smack him, girls wanted to run for the nearest exit. Curtis either wasn't aware of it or just didn't care. Curtis was just being Curtis.

Rick Anderson was a whole different ball game. He was a big guy, two-hundred and fifteen pounds of mostly muscle, with a chiseled jaw that put the fathers of his fellow students to shame. He played linebacker for the Amber Hill Trojans and spent more time in the gym than he did doing homework. He was big and mean and definitely a few beers short of a six-pack; he was also good-looking in a basic sort of way that was nothing to write home about, but most girls in the school were afraid of him and would have tentatively declined his advance, if he'd made them.

Rick wasn't interested in high school girls, though. Deep down, Rick wasn't really sure who or what he was interested in. He just knew he hated school and most of the dipshits in it, and he couldn't wait to get out. In that respect, he and Jason were on the same wavelength, except Jason wasn't just so inclined towards pounding on any kid who looked at him sideways. Jason just wanted to get by, remember.

So when pimply-faced Curtis Lawrence stumbled into Rick's crosshairs that morning in Shop and said what he said to him, words only he and Rick heard that were never repeated to Principal Martin later, the fabled red mist descended and a little sliver of hell broke loose. Rick had Curtis by the collar in seconds and would have closed his other gorilla hand around his throat and hoisted him off the floor if Jason hadn't stepped between them. He wasn't particularly strong, especially compared to Rick "The Rock" Anderson (a title Rick had given himself that wasn't quite catching on), and he was never really sure *why* he actually did it, but when he shoved the other boy in his meaty shoulder, it caught him completely by surprise. Rick's right ankle snagged on his left one and he off-balanced, staggering backwards into one of the ancient Shop workbenches, scattering pencils and notebooks and screwdrivers, and upending one of the rickety stools constructed by another Shop class many years prior. Every eye was on Rick as he tumbled, except for Mr Mansford the Shop teacher, who was in his storeroom at the time playing Words with Friends on his phone. Everyone saw Jason push Rick, and they saw the bigger teenager crash backwards into the bench; everyone heard the little yelp of surprise Curtis let out as Rick, still clutching his collar, momentarily dragged him forward; and everyone winced simultaneously as Curtis's flailing left elbow crunched into Jason's nose, sending a spurt of bright red blood shooting across the room into Tara Eldrid's long, recently-conditioned blonde hair. It was Tara's scream that finally alerted Mr Mansford to the situation.

'What's going on here?' yelled the mustachioed old man, hurrying back into the room. 'Tara, why are you... is that blood?'

Mr Mansford had been a Shop teacher at Amber Hill High for over twenty years. In that time, he'd seen his fair share of students pick up little wounds, usually cuts of various lengths and depths, some of which later required stitches. It's always been the fault of the students, of course - they hadn't been listening when he delivered the safety briefing, or they'd been messing around with tools and had gotten themselves injured. Yes, Mr Mansford had seen plenty of blood spilled in his classroom over the years (once he'd even watched as the tip of someone's thumb went skittering across the floor) and he'd always responded in exactly the same way.

As Tara Eldrid shrieked and Jason Rennor tried in vain to keep his own blood inside his nose, Mr Mansford's legs turned to jelly and he went into a dead faint, wilting to the floor like a dehydrated rose on a hot summer's day.

Jason had never broken anything before, not so much as a little toe. He had no idea how badly his schnoz was damaged until the school nurse stuffed a cotton wad up his left nostril to stop the bleeding and he screamed in her face. Turns out, the nurse didn't know his nose was broken, either.

After that, it was off to the hospital for Jason. By lunchtime he was perched on the edge of a bed in the Emergency Department while a nervous intern doctor examined him. Each poke and prod was explosively painful and he had to grit his teeth hard to keep from crying out every time.

'Oh yes, it's broken,' announced the intern. 'Definitely broken.'

I could've told you that, thought Jason.

The intern went on poking and prodding while he spoke: 'It doesn't look like it'll require surgery, though, which is good. I'll get a second opinion from Dr Randal, just to make sure. And we'll deal with that laceration before you go. Do you have ice packs at home?'

Jason's mother, a sallow-skinned lady aged forty-four who burned through about as many cigarettes each day, nodded. Her fingers twitched under her folded arms, desperately eager to cradle a smoke.

'That's good. We'll give you something to manage the pain, Jason. You're going to have two sensational black eyes by the end of the day.'

The intern wasn't wrong.

Dr Randal, who would meet Lou Jennings later that week, gave Jason a quick once-over and confirmed his broken nose wouldn't require surgery but may need some readjustment in a fortnight's time. His assessment complete, Randal swept off down the hall and left the intern to slap a glorified Band-Aid on Jason's nose and insert fresh plugs up each nostril to stem the flow of blood before discharging him. Jason left the hospital with his mother, who lit up the second they were out the door.

By that evening, Jason's nose had swollen to twice its normal size (he'd quickly learned not to touch it) and had turned a dark shade of red. The medication he'd been prescribed numbed the pain down considerably, enough for him to remove the plugs that afternoon, but black rings had already begun to settle around his eyes. While the Jennings family enjoyed their chicken pie across town and Lou grappled internally with the truth about her day, Jason stared at his battered face in the mirror and wondered how his new look would be received tomorrow.

The general reaction was pretty much as he'd expected it to be.

'Nice nose, Rennor.'

'Walk into the doorframe again, Rennor?'

149

'What the hell happened to your face, Jason?'

'Heard Curtis Lawrence sucker-punched you, Rennor. That true?'

He did not, however, anticipate the first words from his homeroom teacher that morning, which he delivered without looking up from his desk: 'You're in detention today, Mr Rennor.'

'What?'

'After school, in here. You can let your mom know at break.'

Other students were filing in now, chatting noisily.

'Why am I in detention? I didn't do anything.'

'That's not what I heard,' replied Mr Clarke. He glanced up and his eyes widened. 'Holy sh- ...yikes, Jason. He really got you.'

'Yeah, I know.'

'Well, either way, Mister Mansford says you started the whole thing by knocking over Rick Anderson, so you still have to serve some time. Mister Anderson will be here too, so that'll be fun.'

Mr Mansford wasn't there, and then he was unconscious.

'Great. What about Curtis?'

'He's off sick, apparently, otherwise he'd join you both. Grab your seat.'

The school day came and went. Jason called his mother during break and told her the good news. She asked him to walk home if he could and went back to her TV show.

His nose continued to ache, though the ice pack had taken the swelling down a good bit. The rings around his eyes had darkened to the extent he looked like he was wearing eye shadow makeup, which several of his peers gleefully pointed out. For once, Jason Rennor was getting noticed.

Most annoyingly of all (other than the fact he was due to be punished for rescuing Curtis Lawrence, who seemed to have gotten away scot free), he discovered his nose produced a high-pitched whistle sound when he tried breathing through it, which only drew more unwanted attention from his classmates; by lunch, he'd resorted to breathing solely through his mouth, giving him an overheated-dog vibe. The only upside to the whole thing was his newfound inability to smell, a saving grace on chili day in the cafeteria.

After the final bell, Jason went to the bathroom and popped a couple more of his prescribed pills, washing them down with tap water, then made his way back through the jostling hallways to Mr Clarke's room. There, he found three other students already taking their seats: some freshman he didn't know, Natalie Tempo from the grade below him, and Rick Anderson.

Rick glowered at him, dumping his heavy frame into a chair.

Natalie tittered behind her hand. 'Curtis Lawrence did *that* to you?'

'His elbow did, yeah,' Jason replied, sitting.

'It's an improvement,' said Rick. The big jock clenched and unclenched his fists; the kid at the back of the room watched him warily. 'You should've stayed out of it, Rennor.'

'Kept you from going to prison though, right?' Jason said. 'Pretty sure you were about to kill him. You're welcome.'

Jason saw the cogs turning in Rick's big square head as he tried to work out whether he'd been complimented or insulted. He must have decided he liked the idea that another student might think him capable of murder, because he didn't respond. And before anyone else could speak or Natalie could utter that annoying giggle again, their detention supervisor walked into the room and closed the door, cutting off the end-of-day din from the hallway.

'Hello, everyone.'

Miss Sparrow unshouldered her purse and set it down behind the desk. She straightened up and scanned the room with gray-blue eyes.

'Mister Clarke had to rush off so I'll be covering you today.'

Jason had never been taught by Miss Sparrow - Mr Doyle had been his English teacher, and was probably one of the main reasons he'd gone cold on the subject. He was a pleasant and friendly man, but he could turn even the most avid student off the text he was teaching.

'Look deep into the words used here, Mister Rennor,' he'd drone. 'What do they say to *you*? What are *you* getting from them?'

Hell if I know, Mr Doyle.

He'd heard Miss Sparrow was different. Some kids said she was fun, or at least, she didn't bore the pants off you, which was better than nothing in Amber Hill High. Still, it didn't really matter right now, did it? Right now, she was just their detention supervisor.

And Rick, predictably, was going to make the most of that.

'Miss Sparrow,' he said, sticking his hand theatrically in the air. 'Can I go to the bathroom?'

'No, Mister Anderson. You just got here.'

'But Miss Sparrow, what if I have an accident?'

Natalie giggled again. The freshman at the back grinned, unnoticed.

Miss Sparrow, who'd been leafing through her notes while Rick spoke and hadn't actually looked up at him, did so now. She smiled sweetly, but Jason thought the quality of her eyes didn't match up with her expression. There was something different in them.

'If you have an accident, Mister Anderson,' she said, 'you can sit in it, right there, until four o'clock. It won't bother me either way. How about you open up that book and start some work, hmm?"

Rick's hand, which had remained suspended in the air for comic effect, came down slowly. He shifted in his seat and muttered something under his breath. Miss Sparrow ignored it and finished arranging her notes.

'That goes for all of you,' she added in a sing-song voice. 'Start working, now.'

They did, and for a while the only sound in the room was the scratching of pens on paper and an occasional sigh of displeasure from Rick or Natalie. The freshman kept quiet - it was probably his first time in detention.

Jason's nose ached dully beneath the Band Aid, even with the painkillers running through his system. He'd long since given up trying to breathe through it (its whistling would be even more conspicuous now), and his constantly-open mouth was dry as a bone.

Stupid Curtis Lawrence and his stupid, bony elbow.

He tried to focus on the detention work set for him but couldn't muster enough interest. There was no point, really - he knew they'd barely glance at it. This wasn't his first rodeo. He knew detention was more about the time served than the work completed.

Beyond the classroom windows, he could hear other students laughing their way across the school grounds as they headed home or to their extra-curriculars. Rick was missing football practice right now - Jason knew that would royally piss off both him and his coaches, and Mr Mansford would have gotten a hard time in the teachers' lounge for keeping a star player from practice. Fair play to Mr Mansford, Jason thought.

He wondered how the work was going in Shop right now. Several older students, himself included, had volunteered to help with preparations for the Thanksgiving festival, an Amber Hill tradition for which most of the town would turn out in nine days' time. In the run-up to it, the square in front of the town hall would be transformed: colored lights strung between trees; pumpkins and fake leaves in orange and red and yellow carefully arranged around the lawn; big inflatable turkeys wearing pilgrim hats (for the kids, of course) and oversized lanterns strategically set out on plinths; dozens of stalls lining the perimeter of the lawn from which townspeople would sell homemade jams, chutneys, cakes, candy, bread, and even cheese, with all the proceeds donated to this year's chosen charity, the Little Hearts Clinic for terminally ill children, the only institution of its kind in the county.

And at the head of it all, positioned right in front of the town hall itself, would be the festival stage, garlanded in more of those fake Fall leaves and colored lights. There, the mayor would cheerily hand out various "awards" to the lucky Amber Hill residents voted for by their peers (that is, those with the most friends and largest families), and everyone would clap and cheer good-naturedly and wish one another a Happy Thanksgiving ahead of the actual holiday, and then leave to finish basting their turkeys and peel their potatoes. That's when the stress that'd been simmering below the surface all week would start to boil over and the panic would begin: what would the easily-offended Aunt Josephine say if the cranberry sauce wasn't to her liking again this year and no-one went out of their way to do anything about it? Who was going to keep an eye on Grandpa George, who so enjoyed his pre-dinner sherry and would be well past tipsy by the time the game started if no-one hid the bottle?

Jason didn't like Thanksgiving, hadn't ever since his Dad ran out on them when he was nine, but when Mr Mansford had called on volunteers to help build the festival stage, he'd jumped at the chance. Building the stage meant good solid time spent in Shop, during school and for an hour every day afterwards, working with his hands. That was his comfort zone. That's where he felt right.

He should be there now, not sitting in this Geography classroom surrounded by maps and graphics depicting climate cycles, with Rick Anderson scratching his balls under the table next to him.

Stupid, asshole Curtis Lawrence.

'Miss Sparrow.'

Rick's hand was in the air again. Miss Sparrow glanced up from her notes, that same sweet smile on her face again.

'Yes?'

'Can I go to the bathroom now?'

153

Rick was putting on a voice. He was playing a part in some show only he found funny. Well, him and Natalie, anyway. Her hand was over her mouth, barely disguising her grin.

Miss Sparrow turned her head (had Jason ever seen her without that bun in her hair?) and looked at the clock above the board, then back at Rick.

'Still another thirty minutes to go, Mister Anderson.'

'But Miss...'

'No buts, Mister - '

'You shouldn't talk about our butts, Miss Sparrow,' Rick said. 'People might think something's up.'

The room went instantly silent. Behind her hand, Natalie's mouth hung open. Jason realized he was holding his breath and let it out slowly as Miss Sparrow set her pen down on the desk, her eyes fixed on Rick.

Her eyes seemed bigger than they'd been before.

'And what might they think, Mister Anderson?' she said, and the change in her tone made all the flesh on Jason's back slither up to his neck.

Rick, who was either a complete idiot or had decided he may as well go all-in, leant back in his chair and flashed his winning smile.

'They might think you've got a crush on us, Miss Sparrow,' he replied jovially. 'Well, not him' - he thumbed at Jason - 'but me, anyway. Or Natalie. I don't know what you like best.'

The freshman at the back made a small sound that might have been a stifled gasp.

Jason's breath caught in his chest again as he watched red seep into Miss Sparrow's cheeks, creeping up from beneath the neck of her unfashionable blouse. Her eyes had seemed larger before, and now they were bulging. Her lips were parted, and even from halfway down the room, Jason could see the sinews around her mouth working, as if she was struggling to keep it from flying open, from screaming at Rick, whose winning smile was still locked in place.

And then, something happened to her. It was as if her internal needle had been hammering on the far-right of the gauge and then simply swung back to the left, all the way to zero. Her eyes, which for a moment Jason was sure had swollen to the size of golf balls (and had her irises always been so vividly... blue?), seemed to shrink back to their normal size and become rather watery; she carefully folded her arms across herself, and Jason had the distinct impression she'd pulled back, become smaller, somehow.

When she spoke, the ice was gone. She was softer now, timid, no longer assured. Her voice sounded like it might crack.

'My personal life is none of your business, Mister Anderson...'

Were those tears? Was she actually going to cry?

'...and if you make comments like that again, I'll have to get Principal Martin.'

'He's gone home,' said Rick, who was no more afraid of Perry Martin than a wolf was afraid of a rabbit. In that moment, Jason hated him.

'Then I'll speak to him tomorrow,' replied Miss Sparrow, and now her voice *was* cracking and her gray eyes were rimmed with tears. 'You can use the bathroom when we're done at four, ok?'

Rick studied her, and Jason saw what was going through his head. He was making a decision, something that couldn't have been easy for someone as blatantly stupid and callous as him. He was the wolf and he could smell blood. He had his prey right where he wanted her - she was alone and no help was coming, and she'd asked him a question that needed answering. With the right words, he could finish her off, here and now. It wouldn't be the first time he'd done it to a teacher.

Rick Anderson weighed up the choice, clenching and unclenching his fists. Jason's nose had begun to ache again and the vague awareness of his own pain seemed to snap him out of his stupor. He opened his mouth to speak.

Rick got there first. 'That's ok, Miss Sparrow,' he said. 'I'll wait.'

He'd chosen mercy, for once. For now.

Jason saw a flash of what might have been relief on Miss Sparrow's face, just for a split second, immediately replaced with something else, something... blank. It was as though a veil, briefly lifted, had been pulled back down in a hurry.

'Good,' she said. The sweet smile was back; it was sickly, like too much liquorice. 'All of you, keep going.'

The remainder of Tuesday detention passed without incident. Rick said nothing more, but that winning smile continued to tug at the corners of his mouth. Natalie was also suppressing the urge to grin, and not doing a very good job of it. Neither they nor Jason noticed how Miss Sparrow's eyes flicked towards them time and again, and how the sinewy muscles of her jaw continued to flex beneath her alabaster skin.

Jason did his best to focus on the legal pad under his pen, but his mind constantly went back to the unfinished wooden stage currently propped up on blocks in the storage area of the Shop rooms. Isaac Gonzalez and Ste Summer had probably been working on it since the final bell, hacking at it in that clumsy way of theirs. They were older than him, seniors, but Jason was far better with his hands, at least when it came to woodwork. He hoped to hell they hadn't wrecked the damn thing.

His nose was now completely sealed off (even the whistling had stopped) and he had to breathe entirely through his mouth. The freshman at the back of the room, hormones coming out the gills, had a significant case of BO, one that had been intensifying gradually throughout the hour in the enclosed space of Mr Clarke's room; Rick and Natalie had noticed long ago, and Rick was on the verge of going back there to thump the kid and tell him to take a shower, right now, but Jason was blissfully unaware. He couldn't smell for shit.

So when the clock finally hit four and Miss Sparrow announced they could pack up and go, only Jason noticed something was amiss. The others were pre-occupied with escaping that musty, stale stench, but not Jason. Something else had struck him as odd; he couldn't put his finger on it. Afterwards, he would compare it to the unsettling feeling you might get when you return home and suspect someone else has been in your house, or even in your room. Everything looks essentially the same as you left it, but there's an awareness there now, a surety that you've had an unwelcome guest. You don't know how you know, but you do.

It happened for Jason as he was heading for the door, passing up the aisle between desks behind Natalie, who was muttering cruel things to herself about the freshman (he'd made a quick exit to avoid Rick). Natalie was an attractive girl, if a little dim, and on another day Jason would have gladly checked out her ass all the way to the door.

But as he approached the front of the room, bag over one shoulder, his eyes went instead to the teacher's desk. Because in that moment, something connected in his brain, something about what Miss Sparrow had been doing during deten-tion. She'd been busy with her notebook throughout the past hour, her notebook that now lay open on Mr Clarke's desk, and as he walked by, he was unable to stop himself from leaning towards it.

Quick as a flash, Miss Sparrow snapped it shut.

'See you tomorrow, Mister Rennor,' she said, smiling with teeth.

'See you then,' he replied, and walked out of the room.

As he turned down the corridor after Rick and Natalie, a shiver started at the base of his spine and began working its way up. Jason didn't know why he'd wanted to see what was in that notebook; he had no idea what had caused the feeling of wrongness he'd experienced as he left the room, or why it had come upon him so suddenly. It was as if he'd been on the verge of waking from a deep sleep and the dream he'd been in hadn't quite ended.

He did know one thing, though. He was pretty sure of it.

Miss Sparrow hadn't been writing in her notebook. She hadn't written a single word throughout the last hour.

She'd been sketching.

That night, Jason did dream.

He was walking through the school, heading for Shop class. The hallways were full of other students at first; he didn't recognize them, but he definitely knew who they were, as was so often the case in his dreams. He had to step nimbly to one side to avoid being shouldered out of the way on several occasions. Even in his subconscious, Jason was just another kid in the background.

As he drew nearer to Shop, the bustling mass of students thinned. He caught a glimpse of Rick pounding some kid (maybe the freshman, he couldn't be sure), and he passed Ste Summer going the other way with a stack of two-by-fours under his arm. His footfalls clapped on the tiles, louder and louder, until they were the only sound in the hallway.

He stopped. Suddenly, he realized he was nowhere near the Shop rooms. In fact, he didn't recognize the hallway he was now in.

He turned on the spot, and as he did, the lights went out. The hallway became shadow, all still and silent. There were no other teachers, no other students. Jason knew he was now alone in the school.

And something was coming. He could hear it, shuffling quickly along the hallway in the darkness. The closer it got, the faster its approach became.

He started to run the other way. His footfalls were still so loud and he cursed himself for it, but it didn't matter now. The thing following him knew exactly where he was. It was right on his tail, shuffling after him, always in the shadows.

He was going full pelt now, sprinting down the hallway, blood hammering in his ears. The thing easily kept pace, growing closer. It made another sound now, too - he could hear it breathing, rasping hungrily behind him, animal-like and evil. He knew what would happen if it caught him.

Doors, up ahead. Light on the other side.

Jason ran. He ran with his arms outstretched, tripping over himself in his desperation to escape the school and the thing chasing him. If he could only reach the doors.

He got there. His fingertips touched them, then his hands, and then he slammed bodily into them. The doors shook on their hinges, and gave a little.

And stayed closed.

Jason bounced off them like a ragdoll. The thought actually occurred to him in his dream that it must have looked funny, how he rebounded off those locked double doors and went sprawling backwards onto the floor. If anyone else had been there to see it happen, maybe they would have thought that too.

But it didn't matter now, because the thing was on him. It was a black mass of shadow and heat, swirling above him, tangling his arms in its hair and flesh; he tried to beat at it but he only became more ensnared. It was on his face. He could feel its hot breath but he couldn't smell it, because even in the dream, his nose was still broken.

In the shadows, he saw teeth and a slobbering, snake-like tongue.

And then it had him by the shoulders and he was sliding backwards, faster and faster, away from the doors and into the darkness. He screamed and thrashed his legs, but the thing had him. It was taking him back there, away into the black of the school, to the place he knew it lived.

And there, it would tear him apart.

Jason woke up. He hadn't been screaming. In fact, he couldn't move at all.

He kept his eyes jammed shut until the feeling passed, tangled in his sweat-soaked bed sheets. He didn't open his eyes for an hour.

When he found he could move again, he switched on his lamp and left it that way until morning.

NINE

8 days before Thanksgiving

'Nice nose you got there, Rennor. Did you - '

'Shut the hell up, Todd.'

Todd Radetzky slunk away, chagrinned. It was just after homeroom on Wednesday morning and Jason had no time for jokes. He hadn't slept a wink and the black rings around his eyes had darkened further.

The central hallway of the school, the setting for his horror-show dream, was now filled with students rifling through their lockers. Jason was at his, hunting for a history textbook he'd forgotten to bring home yesterday. He'd been in a hurry to leave the building after detention and hadn't begun to look at his homework, which was due tomorrow. Probably more detention, then.

Mr Clarke had reminded him in homeroom that he had one more session after school, and then his time would be served. Rick Anderson would be in until Friday; Curtis Lawrence. coincidentally, was still "too sick" to come to school. He'd be right as rain next week, no doubt.

Jason closed his locker and started making his way through the dispersing crowd towards the history rooms. As usual, he was largely ignored, though his busted nose drew a few stares. It was still black and swollen, and he still couldn't smell a damn thing.

'Hey, Jason.'

Isaac Gonzalez appeared at his side.

'Hey, man.'

'Are you around later?'

Jason knew "later" meant the after-school Shop session, during which Isaac and Ste would continue butchering the Thanksgiving festival stage.

'Not today. Detention again.'

'Geez,' said Isaac. They rounded the corner. 'We could really do with some help - Mansford says the thing isn't level, but it is. And he's worried about the old trapdoor in the middle, even though we sealed it up.'

The trapdoor had been built into the stage for a middle school production of the Nativity three years ago. Rather than have the angel Gabriel lowered from the ceiling when delivering the good news of great joy to the shepherds, the director had opted instead to have him rise from the floor, shrouded in white smoke from a bucket of dry ice beneath the stage. That had been all well and good, and it had certainly saved some time and money (winches and pulleys were well beyond the school's meager budget, it turned out), until some members of the audience pointed out that Gabriel was arriving on scene from precisely the wrong direction, and there were no Glad Tidings to be had from down *there*. The trapdoor hadn't been used since.

'It's sealed,' Jason replied, nasally. He scratched his nose and winced. 'I'll be back tomorrow. We'll get it done.'

'Sure. See ya.'

Isaac sidled off.

Give it a rest, Mansford, Jason thought. *It's just a stage. People in this town act like the Thanksgiving festival's the be-all. Load of bull, is what it is.*

He glanced up and felt a fresh stab of pain in his nose.

Miss Sparrow was coming down the hallway towards him. She was deep in discussion with Mrs Heller, who taught French and Spanish. Mrs Heller appeared to be tickled about something and was giggling like a schoolgirl. Jason had been at the school long enough to know both teachers were good friends. He'd always hated language classes, but he didn't mind Mrs Heller. He didn't especially mind any of his teachers, because none of them minded him, for the most part.

Mrs Heller saw him coming and nodded. 'Morning, Jason.'

'Morning,' he replied, returning the nod.

Miss Sparrow made eye contact as she passed but said nothing. The teachers resumed their conversation and continued down the hallway in the other direction.

Jason walked a few paces then frowned, slowing. He looked back over his shoulder.

Just yesterday, Miss Sparrow had shown up at Mr Clarke's room in a long, plain skirt and the kind of blouse Jason had seen his grandmother wear not so long ago. Today, she was in a fitted dress embroidered with pink roses, one that ended just above the knee, and wore leather ankle boots, which seemed to give the impression that she was taller, and...

What? Attractive?

He'd never thought of any of his teachers in that way before, mostly because they were (in Jason's eyes) middle-aged, often with kids of their own, and constantly eclipsed by hundreds of teenage girls, many of whom were well worth the distraction.

Still, he thought absently, *Miss Sparrow has nice legs. Who knew?*

He reached the door of the history room and filtered inside with his classmates.

Miss Sparrow didn't cross Jason's mind again that day until he walked into Mr Clarke's room just after the final bell and saw Sophie Wentworth seated glumly at a desk by the window.

'You?' he said, genuinely surprised.

Sophie glanced his way and nodded, then frowned. He'd seen that expression on plenty of faces during his time at Amber Hill High and he knew what it meant.

'Jason Rennor,' he said. 'I'm in the year above you.'

'Oh, yeah. Sorry.'

Yeah, you and everyone else. She'd forget his name by next week, but that was ok. Why should he care? No big deal.

Sophie Wentworth was a Sophomore. She had a pretty face, short blonde hair and bright green eyes, but unfortunately for her (and for her social standing in the life of the school), she was also overweight. Not very overweight, mind you, not by any real stretch. She was just overweight enough to ensure the eyes of Amber

Hill's male cohorts didn't linger on her very long as they sought out their next eligible mate. Jason would be lying if he claimed he was any different, but he didn't feel bad about it. It was just the way things were.

Again, no big deal.

'Where's Natalie?' he asked. The smelly freshman was gone and Rick was yet to arrive, if he was coming at all.

'I think she's done,' said Sophie, flipping through her textbook. 'Or she just decided not to show up.'

'Sounds about right.' He sat down at the same desk he'd occupied the day before, at the other side of the room. 'Where's Mr Clarke?'

'Don't know.'

A good thirty seconds passed, during which time neither of them spoke; the cacophony of sound from the hallway and beyond the classroom windows made by students leaving school for the day was enough. When it began to die down, Jason cleared his throat and ventured another question, the answer to which he was at least semi-interested to know.

'So what happened on Monday?'

Sophie frowned again, then understood. She set her pen down.

'You heard about it?'

'Sort of.'

'It was really weird,' she said, shifting in her seat. 'We were in English, just after homeroom, and this woman burst in and started saying stuff to us. Acting like she knew us, that sort've thing. Miss Sparrow took her into the hallway, but then she came back again and flipped out. And she spilled coffee all over the floor.'

'Weird,' Jason agreed. It was the story he'd heard from someone else.

'Yeah. Mr Doyle came and took her away, and I heard she flipped out again with Principal Martin. Someone said they were going to call the cops.

'The weirdest thing though,' Sophie continued, leaning a little in his direction now, 'was how Miss Sparrow acted after she was gone.'

'What do you mean?'

Sophie's bright green eyes were alive now - Jason could tell she didn't get the chance to share gossip like this very often. With boys, anyway.

'Well, she'd been normal before the woman came in, pretty quiet and stuff, like she usually is. I've had her since Ninth Grade and she's always been like that, you know? She's kinda... reserved, traditional.'

And she dresses like an old woman, Jason thought, before remembering how she'd looked walking away from him earlier, and the image of her smooth, pale legs momentarily took center stage. Then Sophie's voice filtered back in and the welcome image dissolved.

'... heard some people say she's strange, but I've always thought she was nice. She's a good teacher. Anyway, she's normally quiet and calm, but after that woman was gone, she became sort of... excited. Like, hyped-up, or something. She started talking really fast and laughing a lot, and we didn't get much done in the end. I've never seen her that way, have you?'

'I've never had her.'

'Oh, right. Well, it was all really weird. And she's been in a great mood ever since.'

Jason thought about how Miss Sparrow had been yesterday during detention. She hadn't *seemed* like she was in a great mood, but then again, he didn't have much context to compare it to.

And the notebook. What was it about that notebook?

'What's up, Rennor?'

Jason started to turn his head, but Rick's beefy thigh had already bashed into him. He was jolted sideways and almost fell out of his chair, just about regaining his balance at the last second. The big linebacker chuckled to himself, pleased to have caught Jason off guard this time. Sophie ducked her head as Rick ambled to a desk in the middle of the room and collapsed into the chair behind it.

'No Curtis again, huh?'

Jason didn't reply. Rick grinned.

'I'm sorry, Rennor,' he said, 'did I hurt you just now?'

Fuck off Rick, Jason thought, and was about to toss another zinger his way, one that would probably have gotten his nose broken all over again, but was cut short as Miss Sparrow strode into the room again and closed the door.

'Afternoon,' she said. 'Sorry I'm late.'

Jason and Sophie mumbled their replies. Rick said nothing.

She definitely looks different today.

'Mr Clarke's unavailable again and he's asked me to cover you.' The English teacher glanced around the room with blue-gray eyes. She met Jason's gaze and held it for a moment, as if trying to discern something about him, and then began rummaging through her purse.

'How's that nose of yours, Mister Rennor?'

'Still broken, Miss Sparrow.'

She smiled crookedly but didn't look up.

'Sorry to hear that. Also sorry to see you here, Sophie.'

Sophie Wentworth's face flushed bright red and she seemed to sink even lower in her chair. If she could have fitted under her desk, Jason thought, she may well have scrambled under there.

'Sorry, Miss Sparrow. I - '

'No need to say sorry to *me*, Sophie,' Miss Sparrow cut in with the breezy air of someone who'd been apologized to a thousand times before. 'I'm sure you've learned your lesson, haven't you?'

'Yes.'

'There you go. Anyway, you've all got work to do, and so do I, so let's get to it.'

She slipped behind Mr Clarke's desk and, as Jason watched, took out the notebook again; she laid it in front of her, closed. All of her movements were fluid, assured and, again, just a little different than yesterday.

Jason started writing, but barely saw his words as they appeared beneath the tip of his pen. As the minutes ticked by, he kept one eye on Miss Sparrow, who busied herself with her own work and wasn't paying attention to them at all. But she *had* noticed his nose, which was indeed still broken, though it hurt less today. Occasionally he'd forgotten himself during the day and sniffed, and received a sharp, painful reminder for his trouble. But other than that, and the fact he couldn't smell anything, it wasn't so bad.

Why had she mentioned it, though? Was she just being nice, like Sophie said she was?

And what was it about that damn notebook?

Something's not right.

Jason's pen lowered to the page and stayed there. He watched Miss Sparrow openly now, studying her. He didn't care if she noticed. He was drawn to her by some inexplicable force and it wasn't allowing him to look away. It wasn't necessarily attraction, though he was palpably aware of how much better she looked today (what color had her hair been yesterday, exactly?) and how she seemed more at ease, maybe even de-stressed, as if she'd just returned from a week-long spa vacation in the Bahamas.

The thing drawing him in was that sense of wrongness again. He looked at her the way you might have looked at a Spot The Difference cartoon strip as a kid: here she was, painted into a familiar scene, surrounded by familiar items in an environment long-established by the relentless progression of time and regularity, and some aspect of it all was simply... out of place. It was right there, so close - he just couldn't articulate what it was. Or rather, perhaps he could, and didn't really want to, because whatever it was, it was unsettling him more with each passing minute.

His nose was beginning to throb - he'd forgotten to take more painkillers before detention.

'Miss Sparrow?'

Rick's hand was in the air.

Here we go, Jason thought, and felt himself snap some way out of the hoodoo around Miss Sparrow. *What's it gonna be this time, Rick? Need to pee again? Can't hold it in? Just can't sit there for five minutes without having another go at the teacher?*

'Yes, Mr Anderson?'

Jason could see Rick in his peripheral vision, sitting there in the middle of the room with his big dumb hand in the air like he was in elementary school. He didn't mind his teachers, and he didn't care one way or the other about most of his peers, but Rick Anderson was a dick.

When Rick the dick didn't reply, Jason looked his way. He saw Sophie was doing the same thing.

Rick was just sitting there, motionless, with his hand still up. He was staring at Miss Sparrow with his mouth slightly ajar. Jason hadn't thought it was possible for him to look any stupider until that moment.

'Mr Anderson?' enquired Miss Sparrow.

Finally, Rick's mouth began to move again and he replied, 'I, um... nothing, Miss Sparrow.'

'Nothing?'

'No.' Rick sounded like he was sleep-talking. He seemed to remember his hand was still up, and lowered it.

'Good. Get back to work, then.'

Rick did, and did so in a sort of daze. But Jason didn't. Jason didn't write another useful word for the rest of that day. He couldn't have, even if he'd wanted to.

Because in the split second when he'd glanced at Miss Sparrow to catch her reaction to Rick's very un-Rick-like response, he'd seen something. It'd been lightning fast, so fast his eye hadn't quite picked it up in full, and when he blinked it was gone. Later, he'd wonder if he'd seen it at all, or if his mind had merely been playing its usual tricks on him; he'd even reason with himself that what he thought he'd seen couldn't possibly have been real, and by the next day, he'd have done a fair job of convincing himself it hadn't happened at all.

But during that miniscule passage of time in Wednesday detention, in the same moment Lou Jennings was obsessively cleaning her house to avoid thinking about the footsteps on the upstairs floorboards, what Jason had seen was enough to freeze his heart dead in his chest.

When he'd looked back towards Mr Clarke's desk, something had been sitting in the spot Miss Sparrow had occupied seconds before. It was not something Jason had ever seen before, and it wasn't something he'd ever wish to see again. He wouldn't wish that on his worst enemy. The thing's arms lay casually on the desk, adjacent to the notebook, and its black, membranous wings were fanned out behind it, obscuring the board; its head, barely more than a skull, jutted forward on the end of a neck draped with dead, gray, ropey skin. A jaw that was almost the length of the skull to which it was attached hung just above the surface of the desk, and a repulsive, throbbing tongue slobbered around its translucent gray lips. It had no eyes, just empty, black holes in its face.

It was there, and then it wasn't.

Miss Sparrow smiled at Rick, and then she turned her blue-gray eyes on Jason. He hadn't disguised his reaction, hadn't had time to, and she saw it. Her smile faltered, and then vanished. She stared at him, plain and unassuming Miss Sparrow with the bun in her hair, marginally more attractive than yesterday in her rose-patterned dress, with her pale, dainty hands on the notebook; she stared at him, and she saw it, and by the time he broke her gaze and wrenched his eyes away, she knew.

And just like that, someone at Amber Hill High was finally paying attention to Jason Rennor.

Rick Anderson had been having a great day, right up until the moment he raised his hand in Wednesday detention.

It was mild and mostly dry that November, which was good news for football practice (Rick was no pussy, but no-one liked getting tackled into rock-hard frozen ground, did they?) and as a bonus, it frustrated his father, a man who loved nothing more than to toss his eldest son a snow shovel and tell him to 'Get out there and don't come in until you can't feel your hands'. Rick's old man was a piece of work.

He'd also managed to "persuade" a bespectacled ninth-grader to write his social studies paper on the collapse of the Soviet Union (who cares about *that* shit?), and he'd successfully groped Kat Taylor in the lunchroom in front of everyone. She'd slapped him pretty hard and he'd kept on smiling; the guys loved it, and he knew some of the girls did, too. Rick felt it was important that the guys saw - he needed them to see.

All in all, it was a great day, and Rick had no idea it was to be his last.

He'd arrived at detention with a spring in his step and almost managed to knock that weed Rennor out of his chair, and when the Sparrow dyke walked into the room instead of Mr Clarke, Rick thought his ship had come in. Clarke was a tough old sonofabitch and he'd never been able to get a rise out of him, but the droopy little English teacher was another matter. He'd almost cracked her yesterday and held off at the last second. He wouldn't pass up the opportunity again.

Rick Anderson knew no better way to get his jollies.

He waited until she sat down - it was always best to let them get comfortable, first - before raising his hand. He'd start off with another bathroom request and see where that led. There'd be no work done here today, no way. This time, when she gave him that look all teachers did, the one that says 'Please, Rick... please let me off this time', he'd smash it right back her way, right into her boring, forgettable face. He'd already decided - he wouldn't stop this time until he'd made her cry.

Jollies.

'Miss SParrow?' he said. Out of the corner of his eye, he saw the blonde girl by the window turn her head. She and Rennor were getting front row seats today, the lucky bastards.

The Sparrow woman had been writing something. Rick watched, revving himself up inside, engines purring and ready to roar, as she set down her pen.

Here we go, he'd thought.

She looked up.

'Yes, Mr Anderson?'

Rick had once been hit in the face with the pigskin from three yards in training, when he hadn't been wearing a helmet. He was about to set off on a sprint and it'd stopped him dead in his tracks, almost knocking him over, which was saying something for a guy as big as him.

When Miss Sparrow said his name, he felt like that failed button hook pass had caught him again, right in the kisser. Whatever ingenious quip had been in his head disappeared without a trace.

'Mr Anderson?'

'I, um... nothing, Miss Sparrow.'

'Nothing?'

'No.'

But there *was* something. It wasn't the something Jason had seen in that moment, which had him pinned rigidly to his chair a few feet to Rick's right. It was entirely disparate, and had an altogether different effect on Rick.

When the teacher said his name that afternoon, Rick felt as though he'd seen her for the first time, as if he'd never laid eyes on her before now. He felt like he'd seen a *woman* for the first time, in fact. All those dipshit teenage girls hiding under layers of makeup and celebrity-endorsed perfumes could go jump down a hole, couldn't they? Rick didn't need them any more. He didn't need anyone. Rick had seen what he really wanted, and she was sitting just a few yards away in Mr Clarke's classroom.

Part of his mind - the rational part that was still hanging on back there in the dark recesses of his consciousness but would soon be obliterated forever - tried to tug him back to where he'd been before. This was Miss Sparrow, the nervous waif of a woman he'd almost brought to tears yesterday with a few choice words; he'd never spared her so much as a glance before now. And why should he, with the way she dressed and everything? Why should he, Rick "the Rock" Anderson, who could have any girl he really wanted, want this woman?

But he did. Suddenly and completely, he did.

'Good,' she was saying now, 'get back to work, then.'

Her eyes were bright (so *bright*) and he found he couldn't look away until she broke the gaze herself and looked at Jason; when she did, he experienced a seismic, blinding rage like he'd never felt before. It surged through him

DON'T LOOK AT HIM LOOK AT ME ONLY ME NO-ONE WANTS YOU LIKE I DO

and it was all he could do to keep himself from picking up his chair, walking the few steps to where Jason sat and smashing it over his head. He had to grip the edges of his desk until the feeling passed, and he almost bit clean through his own tongue before it did.

Rick didn't remember what happened during the remainder of detention that day. He sat there in a muddling haze of desire and barely-contained madness, trying to look at his notes, his desk, the floor, the ceiling, anything other than *her*, because every time he did, his brain was flooded with a fresh wave of testosterone and dopamine, and he sank deeper into that red cloud of lust and confusion. Rick didn't know it, but he was caught in a trap - he couldn't have left Mr Clarke's classroom that day if he'd tried.

So when four o'clock came and Miss Sparrow told them they were free to go, Rick didn't move. Sophie Wentworth left first, offering a pleasant (and largely apologetic) goodbye to her teacher, who sent it right back with a smile; Jason Rennor followed, and said nothing. Miss Sparrow watched him leave, all the way out the door, then shifted her gaze back to Rick.

'Aren't you leaving, Mr Anderson?'

Rick gawked back at her like a goldfish observing a hungry cat from inside his bowl.

Miss Sparrow smiled again, different now. It wasn't the smile she'd offered Sophie, who had already succumbed to her charms in another sense long ago. To Sophie, Evelyn Sparrow was just a teacher she liked (probably her favorite teacher, if she *really* thought about it), one who'd taught her dozens and dozens of times already, which was, of course, not true at all.

The smile she reserved for Rick was just like the one Ka flashed at Mowgli up in the animated jungle trees all those years ago. It was the smile of anticipation a predator might flash when closing in on its prey.

'How nice of you to stay behind, Rick,' she said in a voice as smooth as silk. 'How nice indeed. You sit tight, now.'

She rose from behind the desk and walked over to the door. Rick gaped at her, transfixed; he was trembling now, his bloodstream overflowing with hormones. Any bodily control he might have retained before was all but gone.

Evelyn closed the door. She produced a key from somewhere and turned it in the lock. Rick was unaware of any of it. He saw nothing but the outline of her body under her rose-embroidered dress.

The blinds on Mr Clarke's windows were tilted upwards, just enough to stop any passers-by from seeing what went on inside the classroom, unless they pressed their face to the glass. Frank Orville, the school janitor, would walk by those windows in a few minutes' time, notice the lights were still on inside, and carry on his merry way without giving it a second thought. If those teachers were dumb enough to leave their lights on all night, that was their problem, not his. Let them take the flack, if it came to it.

Rick remained in his seat as Evie approached. His mouth remained wide open, and his fingers still clung to the edges of his desk. Just as Debbie Lathem (who would tell you Evelyn Sparrow was her absolute *best* friend in the world, if you asked) had been unable to resist Evie's command to "relax" and Derek Jennings had almost invited her home that night in the gas station when she put the suggestion to him, the final vestiges of hope had faded for Rick the moment Evie told him to "sit tight" at his desk. He was a big guy, and he could probably have muscled past her to the door, otherwise.

But right now, there were no thoughts of escape in his mind. There was nothing in his mind at all.

Evie was at his desk now. Her fingertips trailed on his right hand. They were stone cold.

'You gave me a hard time yesterday, Mister Anderson,' she said, looking down at him. 'I didn't like that. Not one bit.'

His head tilted back, a dead weight on the end of his neck.

'I... I... I'm sorry, Miss Sparrow.'

She grinned crookedly, amused.

'Are you, Rick?'

'Y-yes. I'm sorry, M-miss.'

Her fingertips traced his hand again, then gently nudged it aside. It flopped down by the side of his chair, limp and useless. She slid one hip onto the desk. Beneath it, Rick's teenage erection almost ripped a hole in his pants.

'M-m-miss - '

'So formal, Rick,' she cooed, strands of lustrous brown hair framing her face. The bun was still there, but it was coming loose. 'I think we're past all that now, don't you?'

He nodded, somehow.

'Call me Evie.'

Saliva ran down his chin and dripped onto his sweater. Her grin widened.

'Tell me, Rick,' she continued. 'Do you get detention a lot?'

'Y-y-yes.'

'So you must do a lot of bad things round here, right?'

'Y-yes, Miss Sparrow.'

'Evie,' she corrected, tapping him on the nose. Her touch almost made him pass out but something was keeping him conscious, almost against his will.

Her leg dangled playfully next to the desk. She was leaning across him now.

'What's the worst thing you've ever done in this school, Ricky?'

Ricky. Mom calls me Ricky.

'I... I...broke some windows once.'

She tossed her head back and laughed. Her bosom bounced beneath her dress, just inches from his face.

'You broke some windows,' she cried, still laughing. 'Oh how cute, little Ricky.'

Don't call me that. The voice spoke up from the back of his mind, where a tiny sliver of his sanity still remained. *Don't call me that. I need help. Someone help -*

'Listen, Rick,' Evie said, snuffing it out. She was close now, closer than any woman had ever been to him - Rick, for all his bombastic swagger, had only ever been with girls his own age, and even then, they'd been few and far between. Evie went on: 'I know what you want. I know you very well indeed. You want to prove yourself, don't you, Rick?'

Riiiiiiick

'You want to show them all what you're really made of, don't you?' she said, prodding his chest. 'You're no slouch, are you, little Ricky? You're no homo.'

Rick's eyelids, which had fluttered drunkenly since she perched on his desk, now flew open. His breath caught halfway up his windpipe.

Evie grinned, and Rick saw that her smile was much too wide for her face.

'See, I know all about you, Rick,' she said. He imagined he could hear another voice now, speaking just behind hers. Some deeper intonation. 'I know what you *really* want, Rick. I know EVERYTHING.'

The room was beginning to spin. Rick was dimly aware it had become ferociously hot; his skin was slick with sweat.

'So here's your chance.'

Evie slipped off the desk into his lap. His penis rammed against her firm hip and she giggled, but the sound of it wasn't pleasant. Suddenly, Rick was utterly terrified.

'Whadya say, little Ricky?' Her eyes were huge and pale - her irises were shrinking away to nothing. She draped an arm around his neck; her other hand traveled down his chest, heading south. 'Are you up to it? Can you prove your manliness, right here on this desk? Can you make this DYKE SCREAM?'

She pushed her breasts against him. His beefy, cumbersome hands were on her now, sliding over and under her dress, guided by invisible strings. The room was an inferno but her body was ice cold.

Her lips, full and succulent, trembled just beyond his reach. She was boiling over with anticipation, but it wasn't like his. She didn't care about the hand clenching her breast, had no interest in the throbbing male organ under her thigh. None of that mattered to her.

'Do you want me, Rick?' She breathed the words into his open mouth. 'Do you? Am I all you *ever wanted?*'

He just about managed it. 'Yes.'

'Good.'

Rick went for her mouth, but he never got there.

As he leaned forward, finally and irrevocably consumed, Evelyn Sparrow revealed her true form to him.

In that moment, what Rick saw was, in every sense, entirely more complete than what Jason had seen. It was more than Lou Jennings would see later that night. Much, much more. It was pure, unfiltered, and undiluted by all the trappings of humanity. It was Evie as she really was, right there in that searing hot classroom, her woman mask cast aside, mere inches from his face.

Rick looked deep into the place Evelyn's eyes should have been. His brain was unable to comprehend what it was shown, and it simply shut down. His heart beat one final time, and that was it.

Rick Anderson was never seen again.

Frank Orville, as it turns out, did go back later to check on the lights in Mr Clarke's room. Teacher's fault or not, he knew *he* would be the one to take the fall the next morning if that pissant Perry Martin happened to notice they were on when he arrived (the damn fool sometimes showed up to work early, much earlier than was necessary; Frank was sure he was trying to catch him in the act of doing something, though the hell if he knew what it was). He'd been janitor at the school long before Perry was cutting his teeth as a rookie first-year teacher upstate, and he had a feeling he'd still be janitor long after Perry had moved on to pastures new. Janitors, in Frank's view, were the only enduring aspect of any half-decent school.

The lights inside Mr Clarke's room had most assuredly been on when Frank passed by in the afternoon semi-dark with his ancient, rusty rake propped against one shoulder, but when he arrived at the geography room less than ten minutes later, he found the door locked with no light emitting from the half-inch gap along the bottom, through which a chill draught often reached the ankles of the students inside during the day. Whoever had been here was now long gone.

'Shitfire,' muttered Frank.

He made to leave, then hesitated.

Had he just heard something move inside the room?

The sound was nearly imperceptible, and maybe he'd imagined it. It'd sounded like the scraping of a chair leg on the tile floor.

Frank tried the handle again. The door was locked.

He knew he could open it in two seconds using one of the dozens of keys strung on his keyring, and his other hand automatically gravitated towards his belt to retrieve it. But something held him back; his dry, wrinkled fingers, covered in partially-healed hacks, hovered just above his keys.

Frank cleared his throat and said 'Hello?', and the sound of his own voice echoing in the empty hallway almost made him jump.

What was wrong with him? He'd been in this school alone thousands of times before, often in the dark, and not once had he ever been remotely concerned about anything other than getting The Job done so he could get his ass home as soon as possible, where a cold brewski would be calling his name from the refrigerator. Why was he now, after nearly three decades as janitor at Amber Hill High, beginning to feel... unnerved...

frightened

... because of some barely audible sound in an empty classroom.

It was childish, is what it was. He was acting like a damn fool, just an old man scared of his own shadow, when -

He heard the sound again and quickly let go of the door handle.

'Shit. Fire,' he whispered.

On another day, Frank Orville might have snatched up his keys and flung open the door; he would have searched that classroom from top to bottom, pulling open every cupboard and even checking the store room, which every teacher locked before leaving for the day. If some kids had snuck their way back inside, he'd find them, and boy would there be hell to pay. Shit, even if he came across a bloated, hungry rat (which had happened on more than one occasion), he'd beat the damn thing to death without a second thought.

Frank was no pussy.

But that afternoon, he made the snap decision to let sleeping dogs lie, just this once. He was pretty sure... no, he was *certain*, in fact... that he'd imagined it altogether. There'd been no sounds from inside - nothing had scraped across the floor. The lights were off, the door was locked, the room was empty.

Frank walked away from the geography classroom door, patting the set of keys in his pocket, making them jingle.

As he turned the corner into the central hallway of the school, his pace began to quicken.

That night, Evie paid a visit to the Jennings household.

Her business with Rick - that witless, snot-nosed boy who'd dared insult her the day before - had given her just the little kick she'd needed. Nothing energized you like vengeance, after all. Oh, how that stupid child had feared her in his final moments. The look in his eyes when she'd thrown off her weak and limiting human guise... it had been *delicious*.

And now, it was Lou's turn.

The feeble-minded creature had told her husband. In keeping with her nature as a mortal animal, she'd pulled a loved one into her mess. They always did. Evie only chose those with loved ones, and they always, *always* got them involved. *Invite friends and family to receive a discount on your next purchase. Spread the word; get everybody signed up.*

She'd expected Lou to tell Derek, and she obliged in her predictably human way. She'd already told Debbie, hadn't she? Debbie had been easy, in the end: the fox hadn't needed to break into the henhouse - the hen had come straight to the den with her feathers already plucked and her neck halfway broken.

Evie had watched Lou that night just as she'd watched her every night for the past week, growing steadily stronger, more alive. She watched her with the kind of appreciation a hunter might have for the majestic forest stag before he pulls the trigger and mounts its head on his living room wall above the fireplace. She'd watched them all, even the kids, drinking them in each night; in her presence, they'd dreamed, and their dreams had been dark.

Lou would have had more of those dark dreams if Evie had let her sleep, but that time had passed. Things were motoring on and Lou needed a nudge to catch up. Besides, having Derek march into school the next day and cause a fuss just wouldn't do. He needed a little reminder of where his priorities should lie.

Of course, Evie hadn't necessarily *intended* for Lou to fall down the stairs and smack her head off the wall at the bottom - that was all just a delicious coincidence. A simple scare would have sufficed, just enough for her to understand what was at stake if she got too bold in her truth-telling. Children always made the best trump cards; parents became very compliant when Evie started dangling the knife over their kids.

Still, the silly woman had tripped and tumbled down the stairs, concussing herself in the process, and just like that, Evie regained full authority over the situation. The spanner had been yanked out of the machine; the clouds had cleared, the stars had realigned.

It was only a matter of time now, and then she'd be done. She'd get what she needed from Lou, and that would be that. Done and dusted.

Amber Hill, it's been a blast.

There was just the small matter of that other boy, the quiet one with the broken nose. Evie hadn't liked the way he'd been looking at her that day. People rarely looked at her the way he had, and if they did, they weren't around for much longer.

No, that boy required her attention.

She'd pay him a visit soon, too.

Ten

7 days before Thanksgiving

Jason pushed his taco salad around the plate with his fork. The lunchroom was noisy and Ste was practically shouting in his ear, but he barely heard what he said.

'... and I'm telling you, his completion percentage is off the *charts* this season. And it's getting better with every game. Seventy-eight percent against the Vikings, man. That's consistency that takes you straight to the play-offs. Maybe all the way, you know?'

Joe Carabine laughed and *thwacked* a hand down on the table.

'The Super Bowl? Are you kidding me? The only way they're going to the Super Bowl is if their de-fence' (Joe liked to put special emphasis on the dee when arguing about football) 'suddenly gets good, and that's not happening. They blew the draft, and now they're four to six. Maybe next year, Ste.'

Joe continued chuckling as he shoved a turkey and onion sub into his mouth, spraying crumbs over his tray. The sandwich stank to high heaven, but Jason couldn't smell it. His nose was healing and the bruising had begun to fade, but he was still breathing almost entirely through his mouth. He wondered if he'd ever be able to smell anything again.

'I keep forgetting how little you know about sports,' Ste said to Joe, and Joe flipped him the bird.

Ste and Joe were two of the guys Jason hung around with most at school. They were his friends, he supposed, as long as you were only interested in shallow smack-talk about sports, movies and girls. Most of the time, Jason was ok with that.

That day, however, he had other things on his mind. Confusing, terrifying things.

After leaving detention yesterday, he'd hurried home, forced down his dinner, barely spoke to his mother (not that she noticed), and spent the rest of the evening in his room. He jammed on his headphones, blasted some vintage Linkin Park as loud as his ears would allow, and played video games until his eyes hurt.

Anything - absolutely anything - to drive that image out of his mind.

He did a fairly good job of convincing himself it wasn't real, that he'd just imagined it. It'd lasted no longer than a half-second, after all; his brain had simply been playing tricks on him to distract from the numbing boredom of detention. Yes, there was something weird about that woman, he'd picked up on that as soon as she walked through the door. But that thing he saw, whatever it was... that had been nothing more than a figment, a composite image conjured from hours of binged horror movies and gaming. Of *course* those elements would eventually combine and produce a nightmarish thing like that in his mind's eye, right in the middle of the day. It was simple psychology, wasn't it?

Sure it was.

And yet, after he'd switched off his lamp that night, he didn't open his eyes once. Not once.

Even when he was certain something was moving slowly across his carpet, feet dragging, breath rasping, he refused to look.

When his alarm went off the next morning, he'd snapped awake in an instant and scanned his small bedroom - empty. It was still dark, but the simple knowledge that the night had passed without incident was enough. Once again, that rational, disbelieving part of him began its soothing discourse on why he'd really seen nothing at all in detention yesterday, that he needed to cut back on his late-night streaming, didn't he know he was practically an adult now and he needed to start thinking about his future, not imagining monsters where monsters didn't exist?

He didn't look too closely at the carpet, though. If he had, he might have seen the faint imprints next to his bed where something had stood watching him in the dead of night.

Jason walked to school that morning. It added on an extra fifteen minutes to his journey, but he didn't care. He just wanted to get out of the house, away from that confined, shadowy space. His mother had been put down for an early shift at the supermarket and was gone when he got up. She'd scrawled a note on the magnetic board attached to the refrigerator with a reminder she'd pick him up from school after detention.

Detention.

The thought of it now terrified him, no matter how hard he tried to reason away that image of the black, winged thing behind Mr Clarke's desk. In all truth, that hadn't even been the worst aspect of it, strange as it might sound - the worst thing, ladies and gents, had been the way Miss Sparrow had looked at him afterwards. He'd watched a rapid succession of emotions track across her face: curiosity, then understanding, and finally, resolution. She knew that he knew, and the awareness of that fact filled him with sucking, cold dread.

As he'd walked to school that morning, his boots clocking on the sidewalk under the still-lit streetlights while Lou Jennings lay unconscious in Amber Hill General, an icy November chill had plucked at his hair and ears, and he'd pulled his coat tighter around him. Houses on either side of the street were decorated for Thanksgiving: wreaths hung on doors and fat orange pumpkins stood guard on steps. The whole town would gather for the festival next week, and for a brief time, the cold of November would be forgotten.

Jason shivered.

How was he going to make it through detention if *she* was there again? Would she fix him with another penetrating stare before her bat-like wings ripped from the back of her dress and she swooped across the room, fangs bared, screaming with hellish bloodlust? He actually smirked at that, then jumped as a school bus went by with a bunch of fifth-graders banging on the glass. It was more likely, he thought, that big Rick Anderson would keep Miss Sparrow busy again. He hadn't been on form yesterday, but he would surely make up for it later. Yes, Jason thought, that should get him out of Miss Sparrow's crosshairs for the time being, at least.

But when homeroom rolled around, Mr Clarke had some surprising good news for him.

'Mr Mansford wants you back in Shop after school,' he said, without looking up from the register. 'You'll do your last detention there.'

Excellent, Jason thought.

'That's fine,' he'd said.

And now, sitting in the crowded lunchroom with Ste and Joe, he was beginning to feel like things were getting back to normal. That was, however, until he saw Curtis Lawrence stand up from a table by the door, scratching at his pimple-ridden chin.

'What's Curtis doing back here?' he said. 'Thought he was lying low to avoid Rick?'

'Curtis?' said Ste.

'Yeah.' Jason nodded in his direction. 'He'll be in detention now with Rick, right?'

'He would be,' Ste said, 'if Rick was here.'

'What? He's not here?'

Ste grinned. 'Yeah. Where've you been, Rennor?'

'Rick didn't come home last night, apparently,' said Joe through another mouthful of bread and turkey. 'His parents can't find him anywhere. Think the police are involved now and everything.'

'The police?'

'Yeah. Heard his dad was pissed about having to call them but his mommy was real worried. Who knew Rick the Dick had a mommy who loves him?'

Ste sniggered.

Jason grinned. Inside, he felt as though a breeze block had just dropped into his stomach.

Aren't you leaving, Mister Anderson?

He'd heard her say it as he walked away from the room. He'd been in a hurry to leave - a damn *big* hurry - and hadn't stopped to look back, or even paused to think about it. And he hadn't seen Rick leave the school.

His parents can't find him anywhere.

It didn't mean anything really, he told himself. Rick was the kind of guy who cared so little about his education (and his parents) that he'd ride off into the sunset with some friends without a second thought. He'd probably been out drinking and was now passed out on someone's bedroom floor, or he'd shacked up with some poor, misguided girl and now she couldn't shake him. He'd turn up soon, probably had already.

Rick wasn't any of Jason's concern, and yet, of course, it was impossible for him to avoid connecting the dots. If he forgot about Logic and its partner in crime Reason, just for a second, it was all spread out before him, right there, like the easily-understood drawings in a child's picturebook: Rick had gone out of his way to piss off Miss Sparrow; Miss Sparrow wasn't Miss Sparrow at all, and was quite possibly not even human; Miss Sparrow had got Rick alone, and now Rick was missing. *And they all lived happily ever after. The End.*

Suddenly, Jason began to wonder if he might be going crazy.

'If Rick shows up later,' Joe was saying, 'Curtis is dead.'

'Big whoop,' said Ste, gathering up his tray. 'Nobody likes Curtis. I gotta take a leak, see you losers later.'

Jason waited until Ste was gone before asking Joe if he'd noticed anything weird around the school lately.

'Whadya mean?' Joe replied. 'Like Curtis busting your nose and you getting detention for it?'

'No,' said Jason, thinking, *Well, yeah, what the hell was that all about?* 'I mean, with the teachers. It's like something's going on with them, you know? Have you noticed?'

Joe turned the question over, chewing on the last of his sub.

'Don't think so,' he said. 'Teachers are just weird, aren't they? Although... yeah, maybe they've been a bit jittery this week, if anything. Probably because of that lady on Monday, right?'

'Yeah, in Miss Sparrow's class.'

'Yeah.'

'What about her?' Jason watched Joe's expression carefully. 'What do you think of her?'

Joe cocked an eyebrow. 'Why all the questions, Jas? This is the most I've heard you speak without being spoken to since middle school.'

'Just tell me. What do you think of her? Have you noticed anything... different?'

'Well, I've sure as shit *noticed* her, if that's what you mean?' said Joe with a goofy grin. 'I mean, she's hot, isn't she? She's the only good-looking teacher in this school and I'm pretty sure she's not much older than us. I'll bet...' He shook his head, eyes glazing. '... I'll bet she's wild in bed.'

Jason sighed - Joe was gone. Poor, horny Joe Carabine.

He picked up his tray and left the table.

Sophie Wentworth had a free period after lunch and decided to spend it in the library, as always. The library was her safe haven, a welcome place of quiet retreat from the busyness of the school day. It was also usually empty, or mostly empty, so she'd get a break from the behind-hand whispers and sniggering for at least thirty minutes. High school could be hell when you didn't look perfectly social media-ready every second of the day, as far too many of the girls (and guys) often did.

Sophie didn't care what they thought. Not really. That's what she told herself, at least.

The school library was really nothing more than a nook connected to the study hall, a square space occupied by two mobile bookshelves on either side of a long, narrow reading table beneath a row of dusty glove lights. The three walls of the room were also shelved and mostly stocked with books, but a lack of public funding meant many lost or stolen texts hadn't been replaced over the years, and as a result, there were plenty of empty spaces needing filled.

Sophie was alone in the library. Footfalls and hushed conversations drifted her way from study hall, where a dozen or so students pretended to work. Maybe some of them actually were - wouldn't that be a turn-up for the books? The school librarian, who was also the study hall supervisor, did her best to *shush* when she could.

Another student had abandoned their books at the reading table, which was bathed in the yellow hue of the globe lights; they probably wouldn't be back. Sophie moved to the other side of the left-hand mobile shelf, trailing her fingers along the spines of the books there.

She'd volunteered to help with the Thanksgiving festival next week, manning one of the stalls selling homemade preserves and chutneys. She knew she'd have to chit-chat with a lot of people during the course of the afternoon and evening, people who would smile and nod and secretly judge her for her weight and choice not to wear makeup to a public event, and she'd have to smile and nod back, knowing full well what they thought of her. That would take a lot out of her, and she'd need time and space to recover afterwards.

She knew no better way to do that than by diving into the pages of a good book.

Sophie consumed books. She'd often finish a fairly substantial novel in less than a week, which was saying something for a fourteen-year-old also loaded with copious amounts of homework. She'd read anything and everything in any genre, though her favorite was dystopian science fiction. Reading was Sophie Wentworth's first great love, and would remain so long after her second great love came along seven years later, a young man who didn't care one jot about her weight or aversion to makeup, a man who would marry her within six months of their first chance encounter on the quad at Johns Hopkins and would remain by her side some fifty-four years thereafter.

Yes, a good book was often the perfect antidote for the debilitating disease teenage life often was.

Sophie's fingers found the text she was looking for and worked it free of the shelf. She flipped the book over and skimmed the blurb, unaware she was no longer alone in that quiet corner of the school library.

'Hello, Sophie.'

She jolted on the spot and almost dropped the book she'd been holding.

Miss Sparrow stood next to her, smiling sweetly in the shadow of the mobile shelving unit. Sophie hadn't heard her come into the library, even though the floors were wooden and it was practically impossible to move around without making them creak.

How long had she been standing there?

'Hello, Miss Sparrow.'

'Studying hard?' said Miss Sparrow, and Sophie wasn't sure in that moment if the smile accompanying the question was supposed to be warm or inquisitorial.

'Um, sort of.'

Her teacher's eyes went to the book in her hands.

'Oh, that's a good one. You'll like it.'

'I hope so, Miss Sparrow.'

Miss Sparrow smiled again, and this time Sophie was sure of the warmth behind it.

'Sophie, can you do something for me?'

'Yes.'

'Just a little favor. It won't take long.'

'Sure.'

'Are you free now?'

'Yes, Miss Sparrow.'

That smile again. 'Perfect.' Miss Sparrow took a step closer, as if she intended to share a secret. Sophie, with whom secrets were rarely shared, leaned in to hear it. 'I need you to go to Mr Albee's biology room and get someone for me. He should be there now.'

'Sure,' said Sophie amiably. 'Who?'

'Jason Rennor.'

Sophie nodded. She knew Jason - they'd been in detention together just yesterday.

The remembrance of it, and the fact Miss Sparrow had overseen her time there, made her flush red, but the teacher didn't seem to notice.

'Good.' Miss Sparrow nodded along with Sophie, who found herself wondering how the woman's eyes could be so intensely blue in that poorly-lit corner of the library; the thought vanished as soon as it had appeared. 'Tell Mr Albee that I need to see Jason in my room right away, ok?'

'Yes, Miss Sparrow.'

'Mr Albee won't mind.'

Sophie was still leaning towards those eyes. *Those blue, blue eyes.*

'No, Miss Sparrow.'

'Excellent,' said Miss Sparrow. 'Thank you, Sophie. I really appreciate it.'

'It's no problem, Miss Sparrow.'

'How did you find detention yesterday? You can't have been there too often.'

The flush deepened and drew Sophie a half-step back to full consciousness.

'Um... no, Miss Sparrow. It was my first time there.'

'And how did you find it?'

Strange question...

'It was fine, I guess.'

'Nothing unusual about it? Nothing you remember as being... odd?'

Sophie frowned and drew another step back in her mind.

'No, Miss Sparrow, I - '

'Ok then,' said Miss Sparrow, placing a hand on Sophie's shoulder. Immediately, Sophie was sure she was just being silly: Miss Sparrow was her favorite teacher, after all, and she'd be happy to help her out. No questions needed, so none would be asked.

'Go get him now, ok Sophie? Tell him to come see me.'

'Yes, Miss Sparrow.'

Miss Sparrow smiled again, and was gone.

Sophie blinked. She hadn't seen her leave, but then again, she was feeling a little woozy. Maybe, after she'd passed the message on to Jason, she'd sit down for a while in study hall. Yes, a quick rest before Spanish class would do her the world of good.

She replaced the book on the shelf and left the library. She didn't know, and would never know, that Miss Sparrow had never been there at all.

Jason was slouched over a textbook in Biology class (another subject for suckers) when a girl knocked on the door. It wasn't exactly quiet at the time - Mr Albee was preparing to dissect a frog (students weren't allowed to do it anymore and had to observe instead, which was astoundingly boring) and had largely forgotten about the twenty-three teenagers in the room - so Sophie Wentworth had to repeat her question with more gusto.

'Is Jason Rennor here?'

Jason glanced across the room at the sound of his name. Mr Albee sighed and looked up from his dead amphibian. 'Yes, why?'

'Miss Sparrow wants to see him.'

'Lucky bastard,' muttered Casey Jackson next to him.

'Jason,' called Mr Albee, already returning to his frog. 'Make it quick, please?'

Jason rose slowly to his feet and made his way across the room. He went as he normally would, in what his mother referred to as a "walking slouch", with his head down and feet dragging a little, but inside, his heart was pinballing around his chest cavity.

This is it, his internal voice practically screamed. *She knows, and now she's going to get it out of you. Or*, he thought, *maybe she just suspects, and she's going to make sure. And when she's sure, then whatever's happened to Rick is going to happen to you as well.*

He followed Sophie out the door and closed it behind him. When he started talking, what he said came out far too fast.

'Sophie, what did she say? When she asked you to come get me, what did she say? Did she say why?'

Sophie Wentworth looked at him like he'd just sprouted another head.

'No, she didn't say why. She just needs to see you right away.'

Right away.

Jason swallowed. He looked past Sophie up the science hallway, which was now quiet and empty. He could just make out faint voices from behind the classroom doors that lined the corridor, muffled as though he were hearing them from under water.

'Anyway,' said Sophie, stepping back, 'I should get going.'

'Wait,' Jason said sharply. He'd made a move to grab her by the arm and sheepishly withdrew his hand when surprise (and fear, he thought) registered on her face. 'Sophie, did she seem... strange to you, at all?'

'What do you mean?'

'Did she say anything weird? Or did she look weird?'

Had he asked Sophie that question just prior to Miss Sparrow laying a hand on her shoulder in the library, a hand that pulsated with a darkness neither of them could ever hope to understand (and why would they have wanted to?), she might have considered it, and might perhaps even have agreed that yes, now that you mention it, she *had* been a little strange, and I *had* been unsettled by the expression of earnest hunger on her face, and I wished someone else had been in that corner of the library with us. But the veil had been well and truly pulled across Sophie's eyes, and instead, what she heard come from Jason's mouth was simply a slight against her favorite teacher, the one who'd always been kind to her, the one who'd nurtured her love of literature and made her feel like she could, in fact, be *someone* someday, not just Sophie Wentworth, the pudgy girl in ninth grade.

'Geez, Jason,' she said, as coldly as she could muster, looking pointedly at his black, swollen nose rather than his eyes. 'You don't have to be mean about it. No, she wasn't strange or weird in any way. Just go see her, ok? I gotta go.'

Sophie turned on her heel and walked off in the direction of study hall.

Jason stood outside Mr Albee's room, watching her go until she'd rounded the corner, and when she was finally out of sight, he suddenly felt horribly alone in the hallway, one that had never seemed so long, dark or empty.

He had a decision to make.

Miss Sparrow would have dispatched Sophie to get him a few minutes ago at most (unless Sophie had taken the scenic route or made a stop-off along the way, which he doubted), and would expect him to arrive at her room in a similar time frame. He had, by his estimation, less than five minutes to get there - Amber Hill High wasn't a big school, and even though the science and languages departments were on opposite ends of the building, he could easily walk between them in that time. They were over halfway through the post-lunch class block by now, so if he arrived at Miss Sparrow's room in the five-or-so minutes it took to get there, he could potentially be in her company for almost twenty minutes, assuming she didn't have a class to teach.

Twenty minutes alone with her.

That was far too long.

Jason wanted nothing more than to turn and walk straight back into Mr Albee's classroom, but what would that achieve? Even a distracted Mr Albee would question why he was back so soon, and may even send him off again. And even if he got away with it and managed to remain in the biology classroom, Miss Sparrow would probably just send for him again during his next class.

He was walking now, slowly, thinking on his feet.

What if he didn't go see her at all? He could just go somewhere else, kill some time until the end of class and then go back to biology. But no, same outcome, right? She'd just find a way to get him again. He would only be delaying the inevitable.

He had to bite the bullet.

But he didn't have to bite it for longer than was necessary.

He went round the same corner Sophie had turned and approached the school's central hall, where each main department hallway - Science and Math, Languages, Social Sciences, and Arts - converged. Double doors to his left led into the reception area, through which Lou had rushed past Beverley in blissful ignorance just a few days ago.

Jason turned right, into the Languages corridor. His boots clocked on the floor, echoing around him. He had the distinct impression he was now inside a cave, moving further into its cavernous depths, away from the safety of the well-lit central hall. Indeed, the Languages corridor now seemed genuinely darker than the rest of the school. Or was that just his imagination?

He was halfway down the corridor, passing the French and Spanish classrooms, when he came to the bathrooms. There were two here, one on either side of the hallway; unlike the more substantial toilet areas next to the study hall and the gymnasium, these were nothing more than single-person spaces, with an external door leading to a small square room with a hand basin, which in turn led into a solitary toilet cubicle. These were the "bathrooms" teachers expected language students to visit when they asked to go during class, but most (Jason included) walked right by them and headed for the main bathrooms, just to kill a bit more time.

Kill more time.

Jason ducked into the boys' bathroom and locked the door. He hesitated, then went into the toilet cubicle itself and bolted the second, internal door. He sat down on the lid of the toilet and, oblivious to the sharp odor of urine hanging in the air, waited.

She couldn't question him if he said he'd needed to go on the way. For all she knew, he had a bad case of the squirts and couldn't hold it any longer. What was she going to do, check the cubicle for evidence of recent bowel movements?

You should have seen it, Miss. It was coming out of me like you wouldn't believe.

He pushed back his sweater sleeve and read his watch: he'd reached the bath-room in record-slow time from Mr Albee's room, but there were still fifteen minutes to eat up.

Oh well, he thought, *better start wasting time.*

He folded his arms, leaned against the cubicle wall and closed his eyes.

He almost did fall asleep, and was only jolted back to full consciousness when someone tried the external door: the sound of the handle jiggling, followed by footsteps moving away down the corridor. Whoever it was had given up pretty quickly, and was undoubtedly now en route to the main bathrooms.

Jason looked at his watch again. Thirteen minutes had passed.

That was enough.

He stood, unlocked the cubicle door and went to the hand basin. There was a small, grimy mirror above it. He looked into it and a messy-haired seven-teen-year-old stared back at him.

'This is it,' he whispered.

He had a brief flash of inspiration and, soaking his hands, patted water on his forehead and cheeks. Then he dried his hands and left the bathroom, making the final left turn into the short English hallway.

The doors to the English classrooms, which belonged to Miss Sparrow and Mr Doyle, were halfway down the corridor, just a few feet apart. Each room was a mirror of the other; separated by small adjacent store rooms which each teacher could enter via a doorway next to their board. Mr Doyle's door was closed, and it was clear from the sounds on the other side of it that he was teaching a class. Miss Sparrow's door was wide open, and her room was silent.

Jason stopped before going inside, just out of sight.

He swallowed hard. Why was he so nervous? No, not nervous. Afraid. Why was he so *afraid* to go into her classroom?

Then, from inside: 'Come on in, Mr Rennor.'

He almost laughed aloud, because there was no way she could have known it was him standing there. Unless...

UNLESS

Unless the thing he suspected about her, that he perhaps already knew but couldn't admit to himself, was true.

He went to the doorway and stopped there.

'You wanted to see me?'

Miss Sparrow was seated behind her desk, and Jason wasn't at all surprised to see the notebook in front of her. She closed it over and folded her hands.

'You took your time getting here, Jason,' she said. 'I sent Sophie to get you quite a while ago.'

He swallowed again, purposefully making it visible.

'I know,' he said, 'I'm sorry. Mr Albee was dissecting a frog and I felt kinda sick, so I stopped in the bathroom. I thought I might throw up.' He touched his forehead, still damp from the water. 'But I didn't.'

And the Oscar goes to...

She held his gaze, unblinking. He couldn't read her expression.

'Come in and take a seat.'

'I think I'll stand, Miss.'

'If you're not feeling well, Jason, you should sit.'

Come in and sit.

He heard the words in his mind. Not his words.

Suppressing a shudder, he leaned against the door frame and replied, 'All the same, I'd rather stand, Miss, if that's ok.'

And there's no way you're shutting this door.

Now she was really staring at him, staring *through* him, and he was keenly aware of how infrequently she was blinking. In fact, had she blinked at all since he'd come to her door?

Then, that sickly sweet smile appeared, the one she'd used on Sophie in detention.

'Of course that's ok,' she said. Her voice was different now - it was laced with something new. 'Stand there, if you must.'

She pushed back her chair and stood gracefully. He saw that, once again, she was wearing a figure-hugging dress - green this time - patterned with flowers. She straightened her back and her bosom rose prominently. Her eyes were electric blue with no hint of gray.

'I suppose you're wondering why I called you here, Mr Rennor.'

'Um, yeah.'

'It's about Mr Anderson,' she said, and his heart leapt to the back of his mouth. She was coming round the desk now, hips swaying with that same easy grace. Under that dress, every curve her body possessed wasn't just visible, it was amplified. 'I assume you've heard he hasn't shown up to school today?'

'Yeah.'

'He was due to be in detention again later, but apparently his parents don't know where he is. Isn't that *awful*?'

Jason wiped his fingers across his brow again. 'It is, yeah.'

'Tell me, Jason,' she said. 'Do you know where Mister Anderson might be?'

She perched on the edge of her desk and crossed her legs. Jason kept his gaze fixed in the general direction of her head but avoided making eye contact.

'No, I don't.'

'You haven't seen him at all since yesterday?'

'No.'

'You and Rick don't... hang out?'

'No. We're not really friends, Miss.'

'I see.' She looked down at her nails, which were perfectly manicured and gleaming with red polish. It was the first time she'd broken his gaze, and it was a relief. 'I thought as much, to be honest. You didn't seem to get along.'

'Not really, no.'

Where's this going? How much longer until the bell rings?

'I just wondered,' she said, her eyes on him again, 'because as one of the last people to see him, I thought you might have an idea of where he's gone. Perhaps you saw him after detention? Maybe you could help the police with their investigation?'

Right.

'No, Miss,' he said, crossing his arms. 'I don't know where he went.' And then, deciding to take a risk and test her, he added: 'And I think you saw him last, right?'

For the briefest of seconds, her face changed, and he thought he saw that gray-skinned, eyeless thing again, its mouth a gaping chasm below its skull-like head. Then it was her again, and she was smiling.

'Mister Anderson left immediately after you did. I'd say we both saw him last. Now, are you sure you didn't see where he went?'

Jason kept his arms folded and held her gaze, but it was getting more and more difficult. Her eyes seemed to grow larger with each thumping beat of his heart. Something invisible was pressing at him, grasping loosely at his mind, searching for a way inside. He could practically feel her bony fingers creeping over the soft, pink tissue of his brain, and when she spoke again, he knew what was happening.

'Are you certain, Jason?'

Jaaaaaaaaasssssson

She was trying to hypnotize him.

And, for whatever reason, it wasn't working.

'I'm certain,' he said.

She stopped smiling.

'That's interesting.' She started to stand again, and as she did, he suddenly became terribly sure of two things:

Miss Sparrow wasn't who she said she was.

And the distance between them was far too short.

'Listen to me, Jason,' she said, taking a step forward. Something about her was unraveling, as though she was about to come loose and break into her component parts right before his eyes. She was, he thought, beginning to *change* right in front of him.

He tried to take a step back and found he couldn't.

Something inside him was screaming.

'Listen, Jason,' she repeated, and now she was grinning again, and that grin was much too wide and low, and the blue in her eyes was fading fast. 'Listen. There's something I want to show -

The bell rang.

Jason's legs came free and he stepped back out of the room, just as Mr Doyle's door flew open and students began pouring out. The hallways immediately filled with noise.

Miss Sparrow was herself again - a pretty, smiling woman in a green dress wearing her hair in a perfect bun - and yet she wasn't. And he knew now, for sure.

'I better go, Miss,' he said, already turning away.

'See you soon, Jason,' she said.

He was almost running by the time he reached the central hallway, and now he really did feel like he might throw up.

Later that afternoon, Jason spent his last period of assigned detention in Shop class with Isaac Gonzalez and Ste Summer. Neither Isaac nor Ste were there for punishment - they, like Jason, simply enjoyed what went on in Mr Mansford's Shop class, where you worked with your hands, fixing things up or creating all new things from scratch. Plus, staying behind after school counted towards your extra-curricular credits, whether you would need them for your college application or not. Isaac and Ste would not; Jason was still on the fence.

Mr Mansford was also there that afternoon, overseeing the finishing touches to the Thanksgiving festival stage. It was almost twenty feet wide and ten feet deep, and had to be disassembled before it could be transported by trailer to the town hall lawn, where it would act as the festival focal-point next Wednesday, on the evening before Turkey Day.

Jason arrived in Shop shortly after three and stayed until after four. He spent the full hour working on the stage, combing over (and repairing) what Isaac and Ste had been doing throughout the week, while they sanded it down. The Shop space smelt of sawdust and grease; it was like a drug to Jason, who allowed his mind to dial down and let his hands do the talking. The whole thing was a welcome distraction from what had gone before that day.

Mr Mansford - who Jason suspected felt a little guilty for landing him in detention since Tuesday - was full of praise for their work.

'Excellent, boys,' he beamed, circling the stage, hands on hips. 'She's looking good, sturdier than ever. Should even hold the weight of that fat mayor of ours.'

Guffawing at that, he drifted back towards the store room.

Isaac unplugged the sander and started coiling up the lead.

'Man, I'll be glad when this festival's over so we can get back to actual Shop stuff in here,' he said. 'This woodwork is real basic shit.'

'Yeah,' agreed Ste, tugging off his work gloves. 'And it's boring as hell. Look at this thing.' He kicked one of the stage's supporting legs; Jason was pleased to see it didn't wobble at all - it'd been wobbling when he'd arrived that day. 'I'm back on metalwork next week, I don't care what Mansford says.'

'We have to paint it tomorrow,' said Jason.

'Screw that, let the art department guys do it.' Mr Mansford was back in the room and heading their way. 'Hey, it's after four. I'm outta here.'

'Me too,' added Isaac.

'See you guys,' said Jason, peering under the stage at the struts he'd removed, realigned and refitted over the last hour (the reason the stage no longer wobbled). 'I'm just gonna check this one last time.'

'Let's go Isaac,' said Ste, 'before Jason starts making love to this thing.'

Jason gave them the one-finger salute. Snickering, they grabbed their bags and headed for the door, throwing a wave at Mr Mansford. The old Shop teacher waved back and came up to Jason, who was still on his haunches.

'Fine job, Jason.'

'Thanks, sir.'

Mr Mansford produced a small spirit level from his pocket and placed it on the edge of the stage. The bubble bounced from left to right, then steadied dead in the center.

'Fine work indeed,' he chuckled.

Jason straightened up and his knee joints cracked.

'Careful, son,' said Mansford, putting the spirit level back in his pocket. 'Someone your age shouldn't make noises like that when they stand.'

Jason grinned. 'Old before my time, sir.'

'How's your schnoz now?'

'What?'

Mr Mansford pointed at his face. 'Your nose, son. How is it?'

'Oh,' said Jason, unconsciously touching the bandage below his eyes. 'It's getting there, I think. Still can't really smell anything.'

'Shame. Must have hurt like the dickens.'

'Like the dickens,' Jason repeated, smirking.

The old man didn't notice. 'I hope it heals up soon. And, for what it's worth' - Mr Mansford's face began to redden, and Jason suddenly realized he was embarrassed - 'I'm sorry the whole incident landed you in detention. It was my fault, really. I wasn't in the room at the time, so I had to, um, punish you all equally, if you understand.'

'Sure.'

'Still, I heard you had Miss Sparrow as monitor, at least,' he said in an all's-well-that-ends-well sort of way. 'Awfully nice person, I'm sure you'll agree. And she's done so much for the school lately. You don't know the half of it, Jason.'

'Yes,' Jason replied. 'She's nice.'

And she's something else, he thought. *Something else, entirely.*

Jason sat at his desk that evening, staring at the blank page on his computer screen on which he hoped his geography assignment would soon materialize.

Outline key developments in Federal Governmental attitude and response to climate change since the start of the twentieth century.

He typed five words - 'Climate change in America is' - and closed his laptop with a sigh. Even if he cared about geography (or global warming), there was no way he could possibly focus on this assignment tonight. Hell, he was only *doing* the work in the hope that it might occupy his mind for a while - it wasn't even due until next week.

There was plenty of time for that.

The TV blared downstairs. His Mom was watching some reality cooking show with the volume up way too loud, as usual. And yet, he knew she'd simultaneously be on the phone to one of her spinster friends from Book Club, which was really just a collection of single women in their forties who loved to smoke indoors and share trash gossip and not read very many books. She'd watch her show, have a final smoke on the porch (she'd cut back recently - the last smoke of the night was now just one cigarette instead of three, savored like a hot meal after a long walk outdoors), and then she'd be off to bed. She'd rap on his door on the way past and call 'G'night, son', and he wouldn't hear from her again until breakfast time.

He knew he should sleep, but as heavy as his eyelids were, his brain simply wouldn't wind down for the night. He wasn't the only one, either - across town, Derek Jennings was on his way to the gas station to buy painkillers and accidentally meet Evelyn Sparrow.

Jason opened the laptop, read the assignment title, and closed the screen again.

He stood and stretched. His joints cracked like pistol shots and he thought of Mr Mansford in the Shop classroom.

Awfully nice person, I'm sure you'll agree.

'Awfully,' said Jason aloud, and shivered at the sound of his own voice. Downstairs, the TV went off; he heard his Mom pattering across the living room to the kitchen. She'd have her smoke and then she'd come upstairs to use their only bathroom.

He glanced down one last time at the closed laptop on his desk and thought, *forget it*. Pacing his room restlessly, he cycled through each of his social media feeds and found there was nothing there worth reading. Was there ever? If the news wasn't fake, it was just plain boring.

His mind began to drift inexorably back to his... what... problem? Dilemma? Paranoia-induced delusion? He'd contemplated simply not going to school the next day, just feigning illness and staying at home until Friday passed and he'd be free for the weekend. Judy would never know anything about it. No harm done.

But he knew that wouldn't work. It would only delay the inevitable. His not showing up to school would just act as confirmation that he knew something about her, something he shouldn't, and then she'd come for him. He might have imagined the whole thing, or it could be entirely real. Next time he came face to face with Miss Sparrow, he suspected there would be no room for doubt. He had to play along, at least for the time being.

Nothing to see here, Miss. Just ol' Jason Rennor going about his day like everyone else.

He'd also given fairly serious consideration to actually *telling* his mother everything, from that first day in detention until his last who-blinks-first conversation with Miss Sparrow. Just spill the beans. What's the worst that could happen?

'Hey, Mom?' he'd venture.

'Yeah, honey?' she'd reply.

'I think my teacher's some sort of monster and she's kidnapped Rick Anderson, or something, and I'm pretty sure she's going to kill me. Can I skip school today? Maybe call the police?'

'Sure you can, honey. But first, let's take a ride to the county mental institution and see if they've got a nice bed to strap you into, ok?'

'Ok.'

He couldn't tell anyone. They'd either think he was crazy (maybe he was) or, if they *did* believe him, then they could be in danger, too.

Did he really believe he was in danger?

He was about to plug his phone into the charger for the night when something occurred to him, something he hadn't tried yet.

He opened his search app and, after a moment's hesitation, typed: *Monsters disguised as women.* Bizarrely, the app suggested the sentence before he'd finished writing it.

A list of creatures came up, some of which he recognized right away: Banshee; Siren; Wendigo. Vampire, obviously.

He clicked the link and the full webpage opened up. Now there were images under each heading depicting the creatures themselves. Naturally, they were all horrific - disfigured faces, dead eyes, fangs dripping with blood. Nothing he hadn't seen before on TV or in video games.

He scrolled, skimming the descriptions of each one. Then he stopped. One of the images caught his eye. He read the title above it.

Succubus.

The image depicted a beautiful woman with flowing dark hair and glowing red eyes. Two curved horns protruded from her forehead, just below the hairline, and her skin was alabaster white. She was scantily dressed in a scarlet robe that barely concealed the curves of her voluptuous body. Two enormous, bat-like wings extended out from behind her back, and a long, arrow-ended tail snaked around her bare legs.

Jason studied the picture for a moment, particularly the wings, then scrolled down to the text description beneath it, which read:

"The Succubus, usually depicted as an attractive woman, is variously described in folklore as a monster, demon or supernatural creature that appears in sexually-appealing forms in order to seduce men with the intention of draining their vitality. Literary interpretations suggest Succubi often approach and engage with their victims through erotic dreams, after which the victim is likely to experience diminished health, and may even die. Contemporary depictions of the Succubus are usually of beautiful, seductive women wielding dark magical powers, but traditionally, they were considered to be hideously-deformed winged entities with decaying features, ferocious talons, and a wanton disdain for the lives of mortal beings."

There was more, but he'd had enough. He swiped the webpage closed and tossed the phone onto his bed.

'Bad idea,' he muttered to himself.

Leaving his room, he walked the few paces to the bathroom and locked the door. The bathroom was small and always smelled a little damp; it was tiled floor to ceiling in a faded peach that must have been fashionable in the early eighties, and more often than not, the toilet didn't flush unless you really cranked the lever. But it was the only room in the house where he could be alone, if only for a few minutes.

He peed, listening to the sound of the porch door sliding open directly below him (cold, wind, rain or shine, Judy Rennor would have her smoke), then set about brushing his teeth. He had good teeth, one of the few features of his face he actually liked. Unlike many of his classmates, he'd never worn a retainer.

He cupped a few handfuls of water into his mouth, spat a gob of excess toothpaste into the sink basin, rinsed his brush and looked in the mirror. His dark hair was a greasy tangle against his forehead, which was sheened with sweat.

Sweat, in November? It was about forty degrees outside tonight, and it wasn't a whole lot warmer inside the house.

Jason studied himself in the mirror: his skin was peppered with pimples, which had gathered around the left side of his chin like an ugly little pink army about to invade his mouth by the corners. He liked his teeth, but he hated his skin. It'd always given him trouble, even before puberty hit and his hormone production went into overdrive. And now here he was, beaded with sweat on a cold November evening, with unkempt, matted hair, too-large ears, and a swollen, black, broken nose barely hidden under a graying Band-Aid. He looked at himself hard, and as always, he didn't especially like the gawky teenager staring back at him.

'What's with the sweat?' he muttered, ducking his head towards the basin.

hideously-deformed winged entities with decaying features, ferocious talons, and a wanton disdain for the lives of mortal beings

He twisted the faucet, filled his cupped hands with cold water and splashed it over his face, running wet fingers through his hair. He did it again, then, eyes half-closed, shut the water off and snatched the towel from the rail by the sink. He rubbed his face dry, aware that it smelled vaguely of smoke.

And then, with complete suddenness and total surety, and with the towel still covering his face, Jason knew she was standing behind him in the dank, peach-coloured Rennor family bathroom, and his heart was instantly gripped with icy terror.

Jaaaason

Shaking, he lowered the smokey towel from his face and let it rest on the edge of the sink basin. He didn't raise his eyes to the mirror, because he knew what he'd see. He'd see her standing right behind him, close enough for her chin to rest on his shoulder, and she'd look like she did in detention yesterday. She'd be her *true* self.

hideously-deformed winged entity

Look at me, Jason

Head still down, he reached across and, barely seeing what his fumbling hand was doing, unlocked the bathroom door and pulled it open with a creak of old hinges. The hallway was dark and empty. Keeping his back towards the shower with its plastic translucent curtain (his skin was absolutely *crawling* now), he left the bathroom, walked quickly to his bedroom, and closed the door. He didn't look back once.

Heart pounding and fresh sweat beading on his forehead, he stood there with his back to the door. He couldn't hear his Mom downstairs, but that was normal. She was smoking silently in blissful ignorance on the porch.

He closed his eyes and concentrated on steadying his breathing.

'Stop it,' he whispered to himself. 'Stop. Moron. You're making up stuff that isn't there. You're... projecting what you just read on that website. You need to jus-'

'-ssson...'

The whisper came from the other side of the door and he leapt away from it like it was red hot.

That had been real.

Hadn't it?

He was really frightened now, panting like an animal, flexing his fingers where he stood. His bedroom, always his sanctuary throughout childhood, now felt like a cardboard box, and he was the mouse trapped inside it.

From the other side of the door came a tittering of laughter, and then the voice again, soft and venomous: 'Jaaason...'

Without thinking, he said, 'No!', and was once again startled to hear his own voice reverberate in the room.

That giggle again, very faint.

'Go away,' Jason said. Then, louder: 'Go the *fuck away*.'

Silence.

He held his breath, his hands balled into fists, staring bug-eyed at the door. He was shaking again, not just with fear. His terror had suddenly become infused with rage.

And he was amazed to find himself thinking that, in the movies, this was the point where the door would suddenly burst open, still barely on its hinges, and the monster (*succubus*) would charge into the room and lunge at him, all teeth and claws, screaming in hellish fury. He'd swing one of those fists of his but it wouldn't do any good, and mere seconds later, he'd be strewn across the room in random chunks of bloodied flesh and torn clothes while Judy Rennor sucked on her cigarette and watched the moon rise over the woods on the edge of town.

wanton disdain for the lives of mortal beings

The door didn't burst open, however. There was no sound at all, and that was almost worse.

Screwing up his courage, Jason stepped forward and flung open the door.

The hallway was empty, and across the way, the bathroom was too. The light was still on in there.

Whether he'd imagined the whole thing or not, it didn't matter. Miss Sparrow wasn't here.

Succubus

Jason closed his door.

Down below, Judy Rennor finished her smoke and flicked the smoldering stub onto the paved backyard.

Sophie Wentworth woke up outside.

She was standing under a tree in her purple nightgown and slippers, and her first thought was, *Why am I in the garden?*

Then the fog behind her eyes cleared, and she saw that she was not, in fact, in her back garden beneath the big yew tree she often read under in summertime, but was on the sidewalk of a suburban street she didn't recognise, bathed in yellow from the nearest streetlight.

Where am I?

She looked up and down the street. Aside from a few parked cars it was empty, and none of the houses had their lights on. A chill breeze scattered leaves across the asphalt and whipped at her bare ankles; she shivered, drawing her gown tight around her large frame.

Where am I? she thought again.

A dog barked somewhere in the distance. Sophie turned on the spot, her heart racing now. She was alone on the street in what appeared to be the middle of the night, and she had no idea how she'd gotten there.

She looked up at the tree she was standing under, following the thick old boughs to where they branched from a trunk in the lawn next to her. It was a small detached house, neatly kept with a pale green front door bordered with trellises. The number sixty-four was emblazoned in brass on the threshold. Like the other houses on the street, this one was dark and silent.

Sophie frowned, staring at the house. She knew she'd never seen it before, and yet, it was *more* than familiar, as though she'd been inside many times, had dinner there, even slept there. Whose house was it?

Had Sophie been more widely awake, and had the red mailbox at the end of the drive not been hidden in shadow, she would have known exactly whose house it was. But all she cared about in that moment was getting home, away from this place she didn't recognize, and yet did.

Still shivering, Sophie Wentworth began walking up Oakland Avenue in what she hoped was the direction of her own house.

ELeven

6 days before Thanksgiving

Perry Martin had just had one helluva week.

It was Friday. He was behind the mobile podium in the gymnasium looking out over five hundred bored and sleepy faces, behind which five hundred disengaged brains barely registered what he was saying. He knew that was the case, but it didn't bother him much. Not at this point in his career. The end-of-week, full-school assembly was an Amber Hill High tradition, and by gum, he meant to maintain that tradition until he retired or gave up the ghost. Whichever came first.

'...and we wish them the very best of luck in tonight's game,' he said, skimming his notes. 'I'm sure you'll all be along to show your support, as usual. Go Trojans!'

He half-heartedly raised a fist. Three or four misguided Ninth Graders in the front row did the same, then quickly lowered them.

'I'd also like to remind everyone here to lend their support to the Thanksgiving festival next week, particularly for the members of our faculty who're contributing their time and expertise on the day.'

Someone near the back groaned, sending ripples of sniggering through the crowd.

Little bastards.

'Excuse me,' said Perry, squinting towards the source. 'Enough of that.'

The laughter petered out.

'As I was saying, come along on Wednesday and show your support. I'm told there will be' - He read from his notes - 'a variety of jams, preserves and cakes for sale, all of which have been made by the Life Skills class, and the proceeds of which will go towards charity, and the drama club will perform a Thanksgiving skit during the presentation portion of the event. I've also been asked to remind everyone that the fireworks display has been brought forward to eight-thirty, right after the presentation, so make sure you're there for that.

'Which brings me to my next announcement, one I'm sure you'll have heard already. I'm pleased to say that one of our very own faculty members is set to receive an award this year from Mayor Thomas in recognition of her considerable fundraising efforts over the last number of years. Miss Sparrow...'

Perry gestured flamboyantly behind him, to where the teachers sat in two rows.

'...will be given the People's Hero award for this year, and I know you'll all agree that no-one deserves it more. Round of applause, please.'

The gymnasium shook as hundreds of pairs of hands clapped enthusiastically. Miss Sparrow, front and center among the smiling teachers, raised a hand in humble acknowledgement, blushing.

'Well done, Miss Sparrow,' said Perry. Like the other staff members he was smiling from ear to ear; inside, his thoughts had already turned irresistibly back to events of the last few days.

Helluva week.

Ever since that woman - Jennings, or whatever or name was - had walked into the school on Monday and caused no small commotion in the English department, he'd been well off his game: an important budget meeting with the school board had been a bust; he'd had kids sent to his office for bad behavior and hadn't gotten so much as a bleat of remorse out of them; and the Thanksgiving festival, which normally went off without a hitch, seemed to have consumed far more of his time than was necessary. He wasn't even part of the damn planning team, for pity's sake. All because Beverley hadn't stopped that woman at reception.

He wasn't even sure why the whole thing bothered him so much. Sure, she'd said some stuff in his office that'd really got his back up (*talking about Margaret as though she knew her - that'd really set him off, hadn't it?*) and the whole scenario was just plain *weird* when you really came down to it. Imagine, claiming you were actually a teacher in the school, and that someone else had taken your place while you'd been off sick. What sort of spectacularly-unhinged bullshit was that?

And not just *anyone's* place, either, but a teacher who'd been at the school for the better part of a decade, who everyone loved, students and staff members alike, who'd supported *him* so much since Margaret's passing three years ago. Imagine choosing *her*, of all people.

But it went deeper than that, and he knew it. That woman, for all her crazed notions about imposters and identity theft, had thrown him off-kilter all week because, somewhere far back in the reaches of his mind, he thought he knew her. Not just recognized her, either - that would have certainly been possible, even likely, in a town as small as Amber Hill. He could have passed her in the street or supermarket on more than one occasion, or even spoken to her at a school event at some stage. No, it wasn't just facial recognition. He was so unsettled about it because he thought he actually *knew* her, and that idea infuriated him; her name - her very identity - was on the tip of his tongue, and he knew it, but it remained agonizingly beyond his reach.

Maybe he was just losing his mind. He was getting old, after all.

And now, this.

'I'm also sad to report that Rick Anderson, who most of you know, is still missing.' A number of faces that'd turned back to studying the floor came up at that - he thought that might happen. 'He hasn't been seen since Wednesday and his family are extremely concerned, as you can imagine. If anyone, and I mean *anyone*, has any information they can share about Mr Anderson's whereabouts, please divulge it to your teacher or myself right away. We want to see Rick back among us as soon as possible.'

Eyes peeled for the witch.

Perry cleared his throat. 'That's all for today. Now, everyone please stand for the Pledge of Allegiance.'

As students and teachers alike stood and faced towards the star-spangled banner in the corner, Evelyn Sparrow smiled. She'd been smiling before Perry's announcement about her "award" (she didn't care about that, of course), and she'd just about suppressed her smile during his "sad" report about Rick Anderson. Now, she beamed heartily and pledged her allegiance to the flag with everyone else. She was happy and glad. The final seed had been planted, and soon it would bear fruit, and her work would enter its final stage.

'...with liberty and justice for all,' she declared with a passion that verged on sincerity.

'Are you feeling ok, hon?'

Judy looked at him over a raspberry jam-slathered slice of toast held aloft in her left hand; she had the pages of a paperback pinned open with her right.

'Yeah, why?'

She regarded him suspiciously. It was the kind of suspicious lens through which a mother studies her son when she'd already decided he's lying, and wants to know why, and what about.

'You look awful pale.'

Jason took a clean bowl and spoon from the drainer by the sink and joined her at the table. The kitchen linoleum was cold under the soles of his socks.

'Guess I didn't sleep well,' he said, tipping cereal into his bowl. The TV in the next room was still on, playing through some sitcom rerun.

'Is your nose hurtin'?'

'Not so much anymore.'

'Come here.'

Judy Rennor pressed a palm to his forehead, held it there for two seconds, then went back to her book.

'You feel fine to me,' she said. 'If you'd picked up that flu that's going around, you'd know about it.'

'It's not the flu.'

'What, then? You said you didn't sleep well?' Judy crunched into her toast.

'Not really,' Jason replied, gathering Corn Flakes onto his spoon. 'Had some... bad dreams.'

'Mmm.' Judy was slipping back into her book, hardly listening now.

Jason scooped cereal into his mouth and swallowed. 'Mom, did you hear anything last night?'

'Mmm?'

'Mom.'

'Hear what, hon?'

'I dunno. Something upstairs, while you were out on the porch. Did you hear anyone talking? Or... laughing?'

Judy took another bite of lukewarm toast and chewed thoughtfully. She was becoming suspicious again.

'What do you mean? Who would I have heard?'

'Just, did you hear anyone upstairs? Someone who wasn't me?'

'Did you *have* someone upstairs, Jason?'

'No, Mom -'

'And you weren't *watching* anything in your room, were you?'

'Mom! That's not -'

'Because I'll take that laptop away again.'

'No, Mom,' Jason snapped, pushing back his chair. 'Forget it.'

'Where're you going? You need to eat.'

'I'm not hungry.'

'Jason!'

Judy watched as he left the kitchen and listened to him stomp up the stairs. She looked at her slice of toast, now cold, then dropped it back on the plate.

'...with liberty and justice for all.'

'Enjoy your Friday,' Principal Martin said, and the gymnasium began to empty.

Jason had watched Miss Sparrow from the back of the room while the rest of the school clapped, stamped their feet and, in some cases, whistled in appreciation of her. He'd watched her wave bashfully and nod her head at the teachers who leaned across to congratulate her, perfectly white teeth flashing while she sat beautiful and resplendent among the other dowdy staff members. Jason may have been the only person in the room who didn't join in with the applause.

She didn't see him during the assembly, he was pretty sure, though she must have known he was there. He made a quick exit and headed straight for class, pausing briefly at his locker to collect his books. He didn't want to talk to anyone that morning. And yet, equally, he didn't want to be alone.

That Friday passed without incident, right up until the end of the school day. Jason attended each of his classes - History, Biology, Geography, Social Studies and Shop - and paid a great deal more attention than usual, making sure he arrived at and left each room with the rest of his classmates. No messengers came to the doors to summon him; no-one pulled him aside in the hallway. He faded into the background, was lost in the crowd, and went back to simply being Jason Rennor, the guy-who-you-knew-but-didn't-really-notice. No-one special.

Jason was just fine with that. There was safety in numbers.

He stuck by his nerdy friends during break, chipping in to that day's debate (why no horror movies made in the last decade have been remotely scary), and sought out Joe and Ste again during lunch. Ste was planning a little road trip to the city that weekend "to purchase some *good* weed" and wondered if they wanted to come along. Jason said he might.

And all day long, there was no sign of Miss Sparrow.

Jason kept an eye out constantly after assembly that morning but hadn't seen her once since leaving the gymnasium. He was frightened now, right to his very bones, and he did an admirable job of hiding it, but anyone who knew him really well (if there *had* been anyone like that in the school) would have noticed how he spent the whole day glancing over his shoulder, or how he jumped when someone spoke to him, especially if it was from behind. Only a particularly close friend would have noticed how the rings under his eyes were darker than ever, and even then, would most likely have attributed their color to his still-broken nose. Jason hadn't slept for more than a few minutes on Thursday night; he hadn't turned the lights off, either.

And yet, that rage he'd felt just before flinging open his bedroom door was still there, deep inside, mingled in with the fear. The last thing he wanted was to bump into Miss Sparrow that day and have her scrutinize him with her blue-gray eyes, looking right past his nothing-to-see-here mask, right into his soul. He knew she could do that, somehow. But if he *did* come across her in the hallway, and if she *did* meet his gaze, he planned to stare right back into those eyes and shoot a big cheesy grin her way and say 'Good afternoon, Miss Sparrow', and see if she had the balls to do much of anything about it.

Unless he was alone, of course. Then *he* might not have the balls.

But he didn't see her, not once, and by the time Shop rolled around at the end of the day, he was feeling downright defiant.

Come at me, Miss Sparrow. Let's dance.

'That's a fine job, boys,' said Mr Mansford, hands behind his back, circling the now-painted stage like a vulture on the Serengeti. 'A fine job, indeed.'

He wasn't lying, either. Mr Mansford - Eric, to his friends - was mightily pleased with how the Thanksgiving festival stage had turned out in the end. Putting it squarely in the hands of high school seniors (and one gifted junior) wasn't a traditional approach - it had, in reality, been somewhat of a leap of faith on his part. The stage was key to the whole event, the center-piece, as it were, and with so little time to spare before Wednesday, it could have all gone belly-up if these three teenagers looking to score some extra credit (or dodge more mundane Shop assignments) had screwed the pooch. But they hadn't, and Eric Mansford knew why.

'You're a natural, Mr Rennor,' he chuckled. 'You should have been an artist.'

'Thanks, sir,' Jason replied, sweeping his paintbrush along the lower edge of the stage, completing the first coat. His dark hair was unkempt and overlong, and there were paint streaks on his forehead where he'd absent-mindedly brushed it away from his eyes.

Mansford smiled. He liked the Rennor kid, had done since he was a freshman. Woodcraft and metalwork came naturally to him, much more so than it did to Ste Summer and Isaac Gonzalez, capable as they were. And apparently, he wasn't too shabby at painting, either. Mansford could see Summer and Gonzalez becoming decent contractors when they graduated, but he knew Rennor had more in him; Rennor would be a genuine *carpenter* someday. He'd bet his house on that.

The final bell sounded and the rest of the students in the cavernous Shop room began filtering out. Summer and Gonzalez were gone in a flash but Rennor, Mansford saw, had already gathered their brushes and taken them to the sink.

'Leave it, Jason,' he called over. 'I'll sort those out.'

Rennor looked his way. He'd taken off his hoodie and his bare arms, still skinny but beginning to gain some muscle, were speckled with brown paint.

'You sure, sir?'

'I'm sure. Go home - you can help with the second coat on Monday.'

The boy seemed to consider that for a moment. Even from across the room, Mansford saw his eyes take on a far-away look, as though he was somewhere else. Then he snapped back and said, 'Monday - sure. No problem.'

Mansford nodded, but he kept one eye on the boy as he went to grab his things. What was that look that'd been on his face, just for a second? He couldn't say for sure, but he didn't think he'd seen it before. Not on Jason Rennor.

'Have a good weekend, Mr Mansford.'

'You too, Jason.'

He left the room, the last student to go. Eric Mansford, still puzzling over it (and uncertain as to why it was troubling him so much), set about shutting down the machines around the room.

Jason had been in good spirits throughout Shop class. Once the paintbrush was in his hand, he'd been able to tune out Ste and Isaac's usual trash talk, and the other students in the room fumbling around with their various projects had faded into the background. As always, Shop was a period of happy disconnection from whatever else was going on in his life; it was a time when his hands took over and his mind settled back to enjoy the show.

So when Mr Mansford unintentionally reminded him that he'd have to come back to school on Monday, that his reprieve from Miss Sparrow was finite and that he'd have to face her all over again, his brain had briefly attempted to nudge him back to the somber reality of his situation. But Jason's hands, fresh from completing a solid couple of hours of cathartic labor, had still been in charge, and as such, he hadn't fully registered what his teacher had said, or what his reply to him had been.

He wasn't aware, either, that after he'd left Shop he'd stopped by the bathrooms to wash the paint off his arms and face (he got most of it) while the Amber Hill Trojans jogged past outside the door on their way to after-school practice, and the rest of the school rapidly emptied of students and staff eager to start their respective weekends. Ste Summer had persuaded Isaac and Joe to join his crusade to find some good weed in the city, and the three of them had rushed home to pack their bags and spin their lies to their parents, who collectively believed their sons were traveling upstate to attend a concert put on by some band they'd never heard of, and consented without any further thought.

Jason, largely alone in the school by the time he'd finished drying off his arms with paper towels from the dispenser, had tugged his hoodie back on, left the bathroom and drifted through the empty hallways to his locker in a sort of blissful daze, one that he'd later attribute to some supernatural force that "guided him along like a puppet on strings" while his mind was elsewhere. If he'd been thinking clearly at the time, as he had been earlier in the school day, he'd have gotten out of there fast.

It wasn't until after he'd swapped books between his bag and locker and grabbed his jacket that he began to come out of that lethargic haze, and when he slammed the locker door shut again, the sound of it jolted him back to the moment, and he realized for the first time that it was almost three-thirty, and he was alone in the school.

'Oh shit,' he breathed.

The fear-rage concoction rushed back into his veins, energizing him, amphetamine-like, and he started up the corridor from the central hall, almost trembling with fight-or-flight readiness. His earlier bravado had melted away; Amber Hill High was now silent and empty, and he wanted to leave right away.

The doors to the reception area were just up ahead and warm light glowed through their glass panes, illuminating a portion of the central hall, which was now bathed in shadow. It was still light outside but not much of it was getting in through the small, high-placed windows near the ceiling. Faintly, Jason could hear the last stragglers laughing as they crossed the school grounds towards the entrance gates, and he imagined he could hear Coach Denvar's whistle out on the football field as his players went through their warm-up routine.

He reached the reception doors, took hold of the handle, and stopped.

Slowly, he turned and looked down the languages corridor, vaguely thinking *My head's on a string*, and saw two people at the far end of it, deep in conversation.

Mr Doyle and Miss Sparrow.

Their voices floated towards him, ghost-like in the gloom. He couldn't make out what they were saying but the tone was cordial. They were side-on to the central hall and hadn't noticed him by the reception doors.

Leave. Go now. The voice begged him. Implored him. *Get out of the school.*

But he couldn't. Wouldn't.

Mr Doyle laughed then and started to back away. Miss Sparrow returned the laugh, smiling pleasantly. She had some book clutched under one arm. Jason didn't have to see it clearly to know exactly what it was.

Instinctively, he stepped back a few paces, out of the light from the reception doors. Mr Doyle was coming down the Languages corridor now, his shoes clocking on the floor.

Jason remained in the shadows by the door, but he knew Mr Doyle would see him when he left. He couldn't miss him. *And so what?* Jason thought. *Other teachers are probably still in the school, grading papers before going home. Mr Orville's probably emptying trash cans somewhere, and Mr Mansford could still be in the Shop room. Some kids could even be in detention. Who cares if I'm seen now?*

Mr Doyle strode into the central hall with his jacket over one arm. Jason watched him approach. He didn't speak or move, but all Mr Doyle had to do was turn his gaze marginally to his left and he'd be looking right at him.

And then, Mr Doyle *did* look his way, looking straight at him... and looked right *through* him, as though he wasn't there. He didn't smile or flinch or give any indication he'd seen Jason at all, even though he couldn't possibly have missed him. It was as though he was invisible, or Mr Doyle had been struck blind in that very instant.

Humming tunelessly, the English teacher pulled open the reception door and passed out of the central hall. Jason heard him call 'Have a good weekend, Beverley' before the door swung shut.

Trembling now, and not knowing why, Jason stepped forward out of the shadows and looked up the languages corridor again, just in time to see Miss Sparrow turn the corner into the English hallway.

RUN! the voice screamed. *Open the door and fucking RUN!*

Instead, Jason started up the Languages corridor.

He placed each foot carefully in front of the other, moving with soundless deliberation up the hallway. He passed the Spanish classrooms, and then the French classrooms. He walked by the bathroom he'd detoured into just yesterday when Sophie Wentworth had summoned him to Miss Sparrow's room. There was no stopping this time, however. There was no more delaying of the inevitable. His limbs were on strings now, and he was going.

He turned left into the English hallway. Mr Doyle's door was closed. Miss Sparrow's was wide open and the light was still on.

Jason walked to her room. He made no sound. He was aware of nothing else now, not the colorful posters on the walls emblazoned with famous quotations from literary masters (*Do not go gentle into that good night / Rage, rage against the dying of the light*), not the electric whine of the ceiling lights blinking off one by one as he passed beneath them, not the prickle of spectral fingers on his skin as the temperature began to notch upwards. Even the voice - that screaming, desperate voice - had become nothing more than a hiss of white static.

He came to her door and hesitated. He knew exactly what he was doing, even if every atom in his body was slewing the other way. The strings had brought him here, but now they were dropping off. He *could* leave if he wanted. He could turn around and leave right now, and that would be the end of that.

But he had to know now, didn't he? He'd come this far.

Jason craned his neck around the threshold of Miss Sparrow's doorway and looked.

The room was empty. Each desk was in its proper place with its corresponding chair pushed neatly under it. The ceiling lights blazed and the curtains were open. Outside, the afternoon sky was a deep blue, shading into purple.

Jason leaned in further and saw that her desk was unoccupied too. Where was she?

He hesitated just a second longer, then stepped into her room and looked around.

Miss Sparrow was gone.

His eyes trailed over the student desks and notice boards, darted to the corners of the ceiling (half-expecting to see her hanging there upside-down), and across to the board behind her desk, which was blank. Then they dropped back to the desk itself and settled on the notebook.

It was closed, but a pencil was sticking out from between the pages, marking a place.

Jason walked towards it, his school bag slung over one shoulder. The further he went from the door, the stiffer his hackles became. He was ready to bolt at the first hint of any movement in the room. He didn't care if she saw him now. He wouldn't waste time with excuses. He'd just run.

His mouth had gone dry and he licked his lips. Reaching out a sweaty, trembling hand, he slipped his fingers between the pages into the space marked by the pencil and flipped the notebook open, and he looked.

Later, if you'd asked Jason Rennor what had been scrawled on those pages, he might have told you he didn't quite remember. He might have grinned and shrugged his skinny shoulders, and you might well have believed him. But the truth was, he did remember. He would always remember, until his dying day, what Evie Sparrow had scribbled on those sheaves of paper in her delicate hand, what she'd been sketching during their detentions that week while they'd sat facing her across the room, oblivious, helpless. He would never forget.

Jason retracted his hand from the page. With some effort, he wrenched his gaze away from the obscenity and gritted his teeth hard against the scream boiling up in his throat. He knew if he opened his mouth, that scream would explode out of him and might never stop. He also knew there was a strong chance he'd wet himself if he succumbed to it now.

His heart was beating so hard he felt like he might collapse. Forcing his feet to move, he started to turn back to the door. And then he saw it, out of the corner of his eye, and he understood.

Miss Sparrow's store room door, to the right of the board, was ajar.

She was in there.

He was light-headed by that stage and worried he might faint at any moment. But he'd seen it now, and he knew for sure. He knew what she was doing. He knew - or thought he knew - what she was.

rage, rage against the dying of the light

Jason went to the store room door. It was hot in the classroom now, impossibly hot, like the place was on fire. Cold rivulets of sweat trickled down his back under his t-shirt, seeping into his underwear. He leaned towards the gap between the door and the threshold - it was no wider than an inch.

A bare lightbulb hung from the store room ceiling, casting a sickly yellow glow over the books and binders stacked on the shelves within. In truth, it was just a glorified closet, and there was barely enough space inside for one person to stand comfortably.

Miss Sparrow had her back to him. The smooth curve of her white neck ran all the way up to her hairline, just below where the bun started - from this close,

Jason could see pale freckles and tiny hairs on her skin and he could smell her flowery perfume, overwhelmingly strong in such a small space.

She was holding something, working at it. He leaned closer, his face almost touching the door frame. She was whispering to herself.

'...been a hard day at the office, huh? Not for you.'

She laughed then, and Jason recognized it instantly as the same child-like giggle he'd heard on the other side of his bedroom door the night before.

RUN! The voice was back. *Run, you moronic fucking idiot, run!*

'You've had it easy in here. Yes you have.'

Another tittering of laughter. Then she set whatever she'd been holding on the shelf. Jason's heart pinballed around inside his chest cavity.

'No rest for the wicked,' Miss Sparrow sighed. She stepped out of view.

Jason stared at what was on the shelf.

It was a head. A human head, severed just below the jaw. Bloodied flaps of loose flesh splayed out beneath it, providing balance, like the feet of a Christmas tree. The mouth was wide open, frozen by rigamortis in a shriek of agony and terror. The hair was snow-white and stood on end. There were no eyeballs in the dark, empty sockets, and it took Jason another second to realize they'd been stuffed into the mouth. He could see one of the optic nerves wrapped around the tongue like a slimy gray eel.

He stepped away and turned towards the classroom door. She mustn't have heard him because the storeroom door didn't move. All the rage had left him - now there was only fear. Pure, undiluted, maddening fear.

When Jason was nine years old, he'd been confronted by a very large, very angry dog in the park. It bared its teeth and snarled, slobbering and ferocious, arching its back the way predators do when they're about to attack. Jason had been in Elementary School at the time, a skinny, gawky kid who was yet to experience his catch-up growth spurt, and he'd never found himself face-to-face with anything like that dog before. But he didn't freeze up, and he didn't run. He didn't even cry out. He just turned, slowly, calmly, and walked away. The dog had continued to growl and gnash its teeth, but it had remained where it was. Jason had just walked and walked until the danger had passed and he was safe again.

He did the same then, walking straight out of the English classroom without looking back. He hadn't stared down a feral dog this time, though the fear was equivalent. When he saw Rick's eyeless, petrified head on the store room shelf, he simply walked away. His brain took a back seat and his feet did what was needed.

He walked down the English corridor, bag still over one shoulder, taking care to place the soles of his boots to the floor tiles in silence. The hallway was mostly dark now - the ceiling lights were off and very little light came in through the windows. He couldn't hear the football team anymore. All he could hear was his own ragged breathing.

He reached the end of the English hallway and turned right, facing down the Languages corridor. The central hallway was straight ahead. The lights were still on in reception.

Jason looked back the way he'd come.

Miss Sparrow was standing in the hallway outside her door. Her arms were by her sides. She was a black shadow, almost hidden, but when she cocked her head to one side and grinned, Jason saw it.

She was the feral dog in the park.

He ran.

'JAAASSSOOONNN!'

It wasn't the voice of a woman that came from down the hall. It was something else, something deep and alien and jarring to the ears. The sound of it propelled Jason forward like an invisible hand shoving him in the back. He sprinted down the Languages hallway, passing empty classrooms, the rubber soles of his boots smacking and squeaking on the floor. His bag swung wildly in his right hand where he gripped it by the strap.

'NO RUNNING IN THE HALL MR RENNOR!'

She sounded like she was right behind him. He was almost at the central hall now. He stole a glance back over his shoulder and his breath caught in his chest.

Miss Sparrow was on the ceiling, crawling on all fours.

Her hair, now free of the bun, was a crazy mane hanging below her head, creating the impression of an upside-down beard. Her eyes were completely white and bulged from her face like ping-pong balls. She scrambled across the ceiling tiles after him, keeping pace and cackling maniacally, throwing crazy shadows over the walls as she rounded the flickering light fixtures.

'STOP RUNNING JASON YOU LITTLE SHIT!'

He tripped, stumbled, almost fell, and then was in the central hall. He crossed it in seconds. The reception doors were right in front of him.

This was his dream. He was in it now.

Behind him - far too close - he heard her drop to the floor. She couldn't be more than a few feet away.

The doors. They're not going to open.

I'm going to bounce off them again.

'JASON!' she shrieked, right by his ear.

The doors...

...open inwards.

He grabbed the handle and pulled. The reception door swung open easily and he launched himself through it into the light.

His foot caught on the mat on the reception floor and he fell, turning as he went, to land on his shoulder. His bag flew out of his hands and skidded away.

Jason rolled onto his back. He caught the briefest glimpse of a membranous gray wing before the interior reception doors swung shut with a bang that rocked them on their hinges. He heard her roar in fury on the other side and slam into them again. The doors shuddered perilously. He saw her shadow on the other side of the glass panes.

Surely he only had seconds before -

'What on earth are you doing?'

Beverley was at the little partition between the school office and the reception area, staring down at him incredulously.

'You could've broken that door, boy,' she said, pointing at him, and then at the door.

Jason followed her finger, panting. He waited, still sprawled on the floor, for the doors to swing open and Miss Sparrow to burst through and grab him by the ankles. Beverley would get a front-row seat as he was dragged off into the darkness, where he'd become the next trophy on Miss Sparrow's storeroom shelf.

'Did you hear me?' Beverley demanded. 'What do you think you're doing?'

The doors didn't open; there was no sound from the central hall on the other side of them.

Why had she stopped?

Jason scrambled to his feet, oblivious to the pain in his right shoulder where he'd hit the floor. He stooped to grab his bag, then backed away quickly, feeling behind him for the glass entrance doors.

'Did you... did you hear?' he stammered, his eyes on the inner doors. 'Did you see?'

'See what?' said Beverley. She leaned out through the office window and frowned at the door. 'See *what?*'

Jason's fingers connected with the glass entrance door behind him. Beverley was still looking from him to the inner doors, which remained closed. Jason leaned against the glass.

'If this is some sort of prank...' Beverley started.

At that moment, the entrance door Jason was pushing into swung open and he staggered out through it. Someone was there - a man - but Jason didn't have time to register his face before he fell backwards and tumbled down the steps at the school entrance, rolling end over end; his elbow banged off concrete and he skinned his hand painfully before coming to a stop, dazed, at the bottom.

Boots thumped down the steps. A hand slipped under his arm and yanked him to his knees.

'Get up,' the man snapped, his fingers digging into Jason's flesh. 'Get up, now.'

Jason got to his feet, still dazed (and now winded for good measure), and looked the man in the face. He was black, with an untidy, graying beard and bloodshot eyes; his forehead creased with wrinkles as his eyebrows went up, and Jason made a quick guess that he was in his fifties.

'Who - ' Jason started, but the man was already dragging him away from the school.

'There's no time,' he said, throwing an anxious look back at the entrance. 'We need to leave.'

'Wait,' said Jason, stumbling as the man pulled him towards the gates. He was strong, and nearly a head taller than Jason, who was tall himself. He tried again, more insistent now: 'Wait!'

The man stopped. He was breathing hard. 'What?'

'Who are you?'

'There's no time - '

'Yeah there is. Who the hell are you?'

Cars zipped by on the street and Jason wondered if any of the passengers inside recognized him. The man was still staring back at the school. He hadn't taken his eyes off it since they stopped. Now, he turned those eyes on Jason, and there was terror in them.

'My name's Maurice,' he said. 'And you're Jason Rennor.'

'How do - '

'You're sixteen years old. You live on Penborough Avenue with your mom. You dad walked out on you a long time ago. He lives in Rockford now, with another woman. He's had a kid with her: your half-sister, Nancy. You don't have many friends and you can't wait to leave school because you're good with your hands, and all you want to do is work somewhere where you can use them and fix stuff and make things all day long. You're smarter than you think and you can be more than you aspire to be, but that doesn't matter right now, does it, because *she's* after you, and you know exactly what *she* is, and if we stick around much longer, she's going to kill you. Right, Jason? Isn't that right?'

Maurice had him by the shoulders now. He was shaking him.

'Yes,' Jason said. *What else was there to say?* 'Yes.'

'I'll tell you how I know all this,' said Maurice, 'but not right now. Right now, you need to come with me. If you don't, she'll get you. D'you understand, Jason?'

Jason nodded, still dazed, and looked involuntarily towards the school. Maurice shook him again; he met his gaze.

'You understand? Enough for now, at least?'

'Yes.'

'Good. Then follow me.'

Maurice released him and started running. Jason had no choice but to follow.

They passed through the school gates and turned right. The older man was fast for his age and Jason had to work to keep up. His bag jostled on his shoulder. He desperately wanted to look back, but something told him that if he did, he'd stop dead in his tracks. He had to keep going.

Maurice rounded the corner and Jason followed. There was a car there, a battered old station wagon. Maurice went round to the driver's side; he fumbled keys from his jacket pocket and jammed one in the lock.

'Get in.'

Jason got in and slammed the door, just as the first drops of rain began to fall. Inside, the station wagon was fusty with the smell of stale sweat and cigarette smoke.

Maurice started the engine and gunned it.

'Put your seatbelt on,' he said.

He waited for Jason to do so, then pulled away from the curb and merged with the traffic.

Eric Mansford had been on his way to the school reception area when he saw Jason Rennor dart through the central hall up ahead. The boy had been sprinting with one hand outstretched. He'd looked wild and crazed, in total panic.

'Jason?' Eric had started to say, and then was cut short by a hellish shriek that made his weary old heart skip a beat dangerously. It sounded like some sort of animal.

An animal inside the building?

Jason disappeared from view. Mansford started forward again, hurrying now, panicking himself for no earthly reason he could name. The hallways were dimly-illuminated with emergency lighting that would cut out automatically after five o'clock, and some of the ceiling lights were flickering. Anyone who didn't know the school well might struggle to find their way around.

There can't be an animal inside the school, he thought, and then something fell from the ceiling with a thud, some black thing, and he faltered. It was there, and then it wasn't. He heard the reception door swing open. There was a loud *bang* as something collided with it, followed by what sounded like the furious snarl of a big cat. Then silence.

Puffing for breath and struggling to control his racing heart (now beating painfully in his chest), Eric Mansford reached the central hall. He slowed as he came through the archway from the Arts corridor, his fear rising to fever pitch. If it was an animal, what was he going to do? If it was, he'd just jogged himself into a deathly situation, and he didn't have the energy or fitness to run back out of it.

There was movement by the reception doors. His eyes adjusted, not fast enough, to the glare cast through the glass panes in the door, and he imagined he saw something he couldn't have, some dark creature reaching its talons towards the door handle. He saw wings, like those of a bat, and long, scraggly hair. He saw horns.

He spoke without thinking, without really meaning to, and his voice came out in a weak whimper: 'Hey, who's there?'

The thing by the door started to turn his way

WHAT IN THE BASTARD HELL IS THAT

and then whipped away into the shadows, disappearing from view. Eric heard a shuffling, a flurry of movement, then nothing at all.

His feet began sliding forward across the tiled floor of the central hall. He was sure he wasn't moving them by himself. He didn't even know how he was still standing.

He came near the doors, into the glow cast by the reception area lighting, and a figure stepped out of the shadows. She smiled, fixing her hair. He saw that she was flushed.

'Goodness, Eric,' said Evelyn. 'You startled me there.'

Eric Mansford stared hard at her. She stared back, locking her bright blue eyes onto his, and some internal circuit in his brain cut out. That circuit had been on the verge of completion, and she snapped it just in time.

'Evelyn,' he said, dreamily. 'I... didn't see you there. I thought...'

'No thought, Eric,' she said. Her hand was on his cheek, glacially cold; whatever notion he'd been reaching for slid away into the black. 'No thought at all.'

He continued to stare - good ol' trusting Mr Mansford, who enjoyed playing Words with Friends and sometimes fainted at the sight of blood - and then nodded slowly in agreement, saying, 'No, nothing at all.'

She grinned, baring pointed teeth that Eric didn't notice. He also didn't notice that the voice now emitting from her mouth was really two voices blended together, one sonorous and inhuman, the other sweet and breezy, that of Miss Sparrow the English teacher.

'You go home and have a lovely weekend, ok?'

'I will,' he replied, smiling back at her. 'You too, Evelyn.'

She took her hand away from his face and pulled open the door for him. He walked through, unaware of the abrupt change in light, and the door swung shut behind him.

'Eric!' cried Beverley from behind her partition. 'Was that you on the other side of the door just now?'

'Why, yes it was, Bev,' he said jovially. 'Sorry about the noise. I was checking the durability of the hinges, you know? Might need Frank to look at them on Monday.'

'The Rennor boy - '

'Don't mind him, I think he was just in a rush to get home.' He waved a hand. 'Well, see ya soon!'

Eric Mansford strode out of reception into the cool November air. By the time he reached his car, he'd forgotten everything about the creature in the central hall.

He hadn't, however, forgotten about Jason Rennor. He'd be on the lookout for him.

It had just begun to rain.

Part Three: Maurice Baxter Gets in the Game

TWeLVe

6 days before Thanksgiving

Everyone who grew up in Amber Hill knew about the witch.

It was impossible not to know. If you were born and raised in town, you'd have been told, most likely from a young age, that you had to have "eyes peeled for the witch" at all times, especially if you were anywhere near the woods, and *most* especially at night, when the witch was on the move. After dark was her time, they said. That's when you'd bump into her, if you were in the woods.

Her name was Agnes, or Anne, or some variant of those - it depended very much on who you asked, and on what they'd been told themselves. To some, she was Agnes, a shriveled, hundred-year-old crone with sour-milk breath, a wart-covered nose and eyes as dead as the night, who'd mutter a few garbled words of enchantment and curse you for the rest of your time on Earth, were you to wrong her in some way, intentionally or otherwise; to many others, she was simply Anne, the misunderstood outsider, lonely and forgotten by everyone who'd once loved her, a social pariah in need of pity and compassion, but still a witch, nonetheless.

Agnes or Anne's background wasn't especially interesting to most of Amber Hill's residents (mostly because it was entirely fictionalized) - once a witch, always a witch, and that's all folks. What *was* of interest, however, was what the witch who lived in the woods might *do* to you if you were unfortunate enough to run into her while enjoying the great outdoors in your marvelous ignorance. According to some - and you might hear this while standing in line in the supermarket, or while propped up at the bar on a Friday evening - if old Agnes-Anne crossed your path in the middle of the night under a fat, porcelain moon, she'd turn you into a toad or rat, right then and there, and then she'd scoop you up into her bag and take you back to her little house, and she'd keep you there with all the other toads and rats for what remained of your miserable, shrunken lifespan, just to keep an eye on you. Other more rational townspeople might tell you that the Amber Hill witch would most likely curse you in a more practical way, and within days of your encounter with her you'd discover a lump somewhere on your body that certainly hadn't been there before, and you'd go to the doctor, and the prognosis would come back as "not good, but we'll do all we can", and that'd be that; or, if old Agnes-Anne was feeling more benevolent, she might decide to go after your finances, or your marriage, or your reputation - either way, you'd come off the worse for meeting her.

But of all the wicked things the witch might do to you, none were so bad as those she would do to your children, should she get her gnarled old fingers hooked onto them.

Little Freddy Brockheimer was the first to go; it was just after the Second World War ended, right at the beginning of the Golden Age of Television in America, when families would gather round the tube and watch just one show at a time, performed live somewhere else in the country and beamed straight to their home. Freddy had been on the edge of the woods with his brothers on the evening he disappeared, playing hide and seek among the trees. He was never found, but his younger brother Billy, who couldn't have been more than six at the time, later recalled seeing Freddy walking off into the woods alongside an old woman in a trailing brown cloak, shortly before sunset. His hand had been in hers, and according to Billy, she'd been singing softly to him in another language. Billy still heard that singing long into his seventies, when he eventually died of a pulmonary embolism while watching television late one night, one show at a time.

Freddy was followed by Dorothy "Dot" Pauson some years later, and then by Susan Stinne, whose disappearance Lou Jennings' nurse vividly remembered. By then, the existence of the Amber Hill witch was widely accepted as fact, even among the most straight-shooting, grounded people in town. Vague rumors and stories shared around campfires had become local legend, and over time, that legend had cemented itself in the imagination (and nightmares) of the town's close-knit population: parents used tales of the witch (inspired by the real-life disappearances of Freddy, Dot and Susan) to keep their kids away from the woods when it simply wasn't sensible to be there; an aspiring author who was born, raised and full-grown in Amber Hill before the first child had even vanished wrote a passable work of "non-fiction" detailing the history of the witch (he was the first to refer to her as Agnes) and managed to offload a modest number of copies throughout the county before his clientele realized it was all baloney; certain stores in town even distastefully marketed Amber Hill as "home of the witch", encouraging the few tourist who passed through to visit the woods and Fair Creek "if they dared", which many did, and were by-and-large disappointed to not find it riddled with hanging voodoo dolls and black magic runes carved into trees.

It wasn't until the fourth child disappeared in the summer of 1988 that the entire town collectively decided to abandon all promotion of the Amber Hill witch legend. Stores removed their tourist-oriented signage, and any literature still left in town relating to Agnes or Anne was disposed of; the people of Amber Hill, it seemed, had entered into an unspoken agreement to stop talking about the witch altogether, and from that summer on, no-one did.

The fourth - and, until the week Jason Rennor got detention for the cardinal sin of having his nose broken, final - disappearance of a child left a different taste in the mouths of Amber Hill's residents. By that time, many years had passed since Susan Stinne was "taken", and those most keenly impacted by it had long-since left town, either of their own volition or because the nearest mental institution was all the way across the county. The witch, who'd become a sort of folksy myth in the intervening period since Dot Pauson's family lost her in the dense woodlands north of Fair Creek, suddenly became tangible again; she was back, and with her came The Fear, that creeping sense of dread and foreboding that many in town had grown up with and largely forgotten since little Dot vanished.

Overnight, it became tactless and unwise to talk about the witch, even within the confines of one's own home, with one's own family and friends. No-one joked about her at the bar; no-one nudged you good-naturedly with their elbow, winked, and whispered 'Eyes peeled for the witch now, sonny.' No-one was looking for the witch anymore because no-one dared to.

Daniel Berk had been twelve years old. He went into the woods on the twenti-eth of August and was never seen again. As with the other children, hundreds of residents from Amber Hill searched for him for weeks, covering acres and acres of forest, and found no trace of him, not so much as a thread of his sweater caught on a bush. He was simply, and completely, gone. The fourth child.

What shook the town of all, however, had been Daniel's last reported words, spoken briefly to his twin sister Maisie as he'd walked out of their backyard that evening and headed across the field behind their house, towards the woods. Maisie, in her innocence, had relayed those words to her parents later and scarred them for life.

'Where're you going?' Maisie had asked as she'd laced up her roller skates.

'The woods,' Daniel had replied.

'Why?' Maisie had said.

'Because the weird sister wants me to.'

When Rick Anderson disappeared exactly one week before the Thanksgiving festival, something shifted in Amber Hill. That "dark feeling" had returned, unbidden and unwelcome, curling silently around the spines of the townspeople who'd lived through the previous unexplained vanishings, unraveling the fragile walls of repression they'd built around their nightmares with one swift and decisive tug of thread. Lou's nameless nurse had been right, more right than she could possibly have known, when she proclaimed that "something evil" was back in Amber Hill that hadn't been there for a long time.

Of course, the nurse was also quite mistaken. There *was* evil there and it hadn't been there for a long time, certainly not in the lifetimes of even the oldest residents in town, but it wasn't the witch. Truthfully, there *was* no witch, and never had been. The four children - her supposed victims - had simply gotten lost in the woods and never found their way out again. But evil had come to Amber Hill nevertheless, a *real* evil, and Rick Anderson fell prey to it first.

Maurice Baxter could taste it the moment he entered town.

He arrived on the Saturday morning of Ben Jennings' soccer game, around the time Lou was waving across the parking lot at her good friend Julie Heller, who by then no longer recognized her. The air crackled with that typical weekend buzz of excitement, when kids are briefly free from the tyranny of school (and didn't the weekend seem so much *longer* when you were a kid?) and parents could, for a time, forget about their work problems. They could wait til Monday - they'd still be there then.

Maurice didn't feel any of that, though. That sense of hopefulness had long since departed from him - it would be an alien feeling now, were he to experience it again. When he passed the *Welcome to Amber Hill - Drive Safely!* sign as he swung in off the freeway, and as enormous, gaudy billboards advertising various local businesses flashed by on his right (*'Grab a coffee at Doreen's, the Home of Homemade!'* declared a top hat-wearing cartoon muffin, aiming a big thumbs-up towards the road), Maurice felt only one thing, a sensation that always came when he entered the vicinity of the object of his pursuit, a dark death knell heralding his arrival into her territory, as sure as lightning precedes thunder and the end of the day ushers in the night.

Fear. Exhilarating, electric fear.

It was a sure sign she wasn't far away.

He arrived in Amber Hill behind the wheel of an old Mercury Sable and drove straight to the nearest motel, one called the *Purple Rose*, right on the edge of town. As he'd done dozens of times before, he checked in under a false name, paid in cash for a two-night stay, went to his allocated room and fell asleep within minutes of his weary body hitting the mattress. He'd been on the road almost five hours and he was exhausted.

When he awoke it was after lunch time and his stomach was rumbling impatiently. He rolled out of bed, grimacing at the loud cracking of his joints, and went to the bathroom, where he urinated like a racehorse and then took a shower. It was one of those over-the-tub situations, which he didn't like - he'd always imagined himself tripping on the edge of the bath when stepping out and cracking his head off the sink on the way to meet the tiles. Well, that's something he *used* to be afraid of, anyway.

Freshly showered, he pulled clothes from the bundle in his suitcase and got dressed, then left the motel in search of food; he found it in a diner a couple of miles down the road, where he ate an enormous plate of eggs and bacon, guzzling three refills-worth of black coffee in the process. The place was busy, typical for a Saturday. Maurice read a newspaper someone had left in his booth and paid no attention to the other diners around him. He knew she wasn't there - if she had been, that Fear would have dialed all the way up and his heart would have jacked right out of his chest. He was in tune with her now.

After eating, his strength returned, and he began scouting out the town. He'd already familiarized himself with its general layout using the maps app on his phone, but nothing beat seeing the place in person in order to get a real feel for it.

He cruised the streets in the Sable, listening to one of the local radio stations, just keeping it casual, a tourist in a new town hundreds of miles from home. He watched the people on the sidewalks: parents with kids in tow, laughing their way from store to store; couples strolling arm-in-arm, holding to-go coffee cups, enjoying an easy day off. No-one afforded him so much as a second glance, except maybe to cast a critical eye over his filthy, dented vehicle. They were oblivious, blissfully ignorant of what was in their midst.

But it was more than that, Maurice knew. The residents of Amber Hill weren't simply unaware of their situation - they were *lost* in it, consumed by it. They were like fish in a bowl, instantly forgetting how confined and fraudulent their world was by the time they'd reached the other side of their plastiglass enclosure.

He'd seen this all before. Contented, peaceful townspeople unwittingly circling a black hole, held in place by her gravitational pull. Puppets on her strings.

But they didn't matter. They weren't the ones in real danger, for the most part. She was only really interested in one of them, after all.

Maurice had seen her in his dreams. She was pretty, if not especially striking, and she looked younger than she was. She had a husband, a man with a beard, and they had two kids. A boy and a little girl.

It was always worse when children were involved. It hit them hardest once it was all over.

He knew she was a teacher. He'd dreamt about her in a classroom, standing by the board, talking to older kids. Teenagers. It'd be a high school.

He found it before long and parked up outside. By now it was early afternoon and the grounds were locked up after the morning's sports activities, but at least he now knew where it was. This was the epicenter for Amber Hill, ground zero. She wouldn't be too far away.

He drove to the outskirts of town, to the edge of the forest where the children had gone missing all those years ago. Maurice didn't know much about Amber Hill's witch or the kids she'd supposedly taken, nor did he care. He was looking for something in particular, something all of these small Midwestern towns seemed to have. Something he needed, if he was to stay below the radar. He was well within the danger zone now and he couldn't stay visible for much longer. She'd have eyes everywhere.

It didn't take him long to find them - a collection of wooden cabins on the bank of the river that ran through the forest and on into town. They were vacation rentals and holiday homes owned by out-of-towners who visited rural Illinois in the summer. Right now, in mid November, they were empty.

Maurice parked a little ways down the road (not much more than a dirt track) and walked to where a metal barrier blocked off the cabin area. It had a *Private Property* sign attached to it. There looked to be about six cabins in a row along a single-lane trail by the river: older buildings, some refurbished. These were not like some of the purpose-built properties he'd guested in over the last few months, though they were well-enough kept, and each had its own little garden and barbecue pit.

He vaulted over the barrier (much less gracefully than he might have ten years ago) and strolled to the cabins, still in his innocent-tourist persona. He walked along the row, stopping to look at each one with his hands jammed in his coat pockets. A passer-by might have called out, 'Hey buddy, those are private, you know', and he would have waved apologetically and strolled back to the barrier. But no-one did, and he didn't.

After studying each cabin, he found the one he was looking for. It was on the end of the row, with the river rushing by just a few yards from the back deck and nothing but woodland beyond. It was the oldest-looking of the six, possibly the first built, and crucially, it had no alarm.

Maurice checked around the back door and was amazed to find a key under a flower pot by the step. *So naive*, he thought, and went inside.

The cabin was small, with just one bedroom, one small bathroom and a combined kitchen-living space. It clearly hadn't been used in months, if the musty smell was anything to go by. It'd do the job nicely.

With the sun setting, he left the cabins and drove back to town, where he grabbed a burger and fries and ate in his car before heading back to the motel. He'd enjoy a night or two of warmth and free Wi-Fi before returning to his parallel life of breaking and entering. He'd earned the brief respite, and he knew he was in the closing stages of it now. The thought of breaking into someone else's property no longer bothered him either, not really. If things worked out, the good he'd do for the world would more than outweigh any damage he'd cause, even if he was the only one who'd know about it. Well, him and that woman, Louise Jennings.

He'd see her in his dreams again tonight, and he'd know what to do next.

That had been Saturday. On Sunday, he did nothing. Not because he was religious and wanted to keep the Sabbath, or something like that. He just knew that not doing anything that particular day was the right thing to do. The dreams had told him so.

On Monday, he checked out of the motel and went back to the school, where he watched Lou Jennings rush inside after being made late by her flat tire. He had some idea what she was about to encounter, though he wouldn't have been able to say for sure how it'd pan out. But he knew it wouldn't be good.

Sure enough, Lou emerged from the school around thirty minutes later and went straight to her car. Maurice was some distance away in his Sable with a pair of binoculars pressed to his eyes. He watched in grim silence as Lou laughed hysterically behind the wheel until tears ran down her face. She was talking to herself, he could see that pretty clearly. She was in a bad way.

'It's started,' Maurice muttered to no-one.

He tailed Lou as far as Debbie's house (the dreams hadn't told him anything about Debbie and they never would) and waited a short distance down the street for her to come back out, scribbling notes on a pad like some sort of private detective. Is that what he was now? No, not that.

He was a hunter. And he was closing in on his prey.

Lou stayed at Debbie's for much longer than she'd been in the school. Maurice started to think about what might happen if *she* suddenly showed up, now that she knew Lou was aware of the game, and thought better of sticking around. He wasn't ready for that, not yet. He started up the Sable and drove off. Lou walked out through Debbie's front door just a few minutes later and went home.

With no more dreams to guide him that day (they'd only taken him as far as the school again), Maurice headed back to the woods, stopping briefly at *Harold's Hardware* on Main Street and at a gas station on the way out of town to stock up on supplies. Once back in the woods, he parked his car in the trees by the road and walked the last hundred or so yards to the Private Property area, then broke back into the cabin he'd visited on Saturday. He was now confident no-one was watching, but still pulled all the drapes before firing up the ancient-looking Coleman lantern he'd found under the sink. He stayed there the rest of the day, and waited.

Tuesday came as Tuesdays always did, and by now Maurice was starting to get anxious. He'd dreamt about the school again on Monday night, only this time he'd been inside the building itself, watching from that blurred, obstructive place one often finds oneself in dreams, a place from which you can neither interact with nor walk away from what's happening right in front of you. Look, but don't touch. This time he saw a kid, some gangly teenage boy with messy hair and a thing on his nose (*a Band-Aid, maybe?*), and he was sitting in an empty classroom (but it didn't *feel* empty) while hosts of other kids streamed by the windows on their way home; he saw the messy-haired kid stand up and point towards a door in the corner of the classroom, and then he abruptly bolted from the room, screaming all the way.

Maurice woke in the darkness, bundled in his sleeping bag in the cabin's larger bedroom, and found that he too was screaming his lungs out. He quickly clapped a hand over his mouth, but no-one heard him.

He drank instant coffee the next morning using still in-date grounds from a pot in the cupboard and water boiled on the gas stove. He had no appetite. Perhaps he'd hoped - maybe even expected - that the dreams would point him straight to Lou's house, as they had in the past with previous Victims. He felt like he was ahead of the curve with this one, closer than ever to achieving his goal, but time was, as always, of the essence, and the clock was running down fast. And now just to compound things further, the focus of the dreams had shifted to some random kid. That had never happened before, not at this late stage. Maurice didn't want to admit it to himself, but as he sat alone in that stranger's cabin sipping black coffee, he had quietly begun to panic.

However, luck would soon be on his side, and not for the first time.

He'd gone back into town later that morning and visited a cafe, as much to use their Wi-Fi as to eat - his appetite still hadn't returned in full but he knew he needed to keep his strength up, so he ordered scrambled eggs with toast and managed to finish half of it before giving up. Using his phone, he scoured the internet for Louise Jennings of Amber Hill but, as expected, found no trace of her. There was, of course, a Miss Sparrow now teaching English at the high school, but beyond brief mentions of her educational background on the school website, there was no way to find her address. Which would soon be Lou's address, if it wasn't already.

Maurice scratched his chin and stared at Evelyn's image on his phone. A few months ago, the sight of her would have sent him into a delirious rage and his phone would have acquainted itself with the cafe wall, but things were different now. *He* was different, wasn't he? That's why it was going to work this time.

He stared at Evelyn's smiling face a moment longer, then set the phone down. She was moving quickly this time - Lou didn't have long.

That lucky break came around later that evening. Frustrated with a lack of guidance from his dreams, he'd decided to drive back into town for a drink (just one, mind you) rather than stay holed up in that fusty cabin all night. The dreams were his yardstick, his compass in the fog that shrouded Evelyn Sparrow's actions, and he couldn't take another step until the next move was revealed to him. When it came, it would be clear as day, so he'd just wait. This was no time for a leap of faith - that sort of thing had almost gotten him killed before.

The rain was coming down hard by the time he walked out of *O'Hare's* Irish bar and climbed back into his car. He was a little buzzed but not tipsy, and certainly not drunk. He'd made a half-hearted attempt to strike up some conversation with the man next to him at the bar, a wrinkled old bastard by the name of Frank, but he wasn't having any of it. He'd had a "shitfire" day, apparently, and he wasn't in the mood for talking.

Nothing like that small town hospitality, eh?

Maurice wasn't especially tired when he got behind the wheel of the Sable and decided to take another drive round town before heading back to the cabin. Couldn't hurt, could it? Might clear his head, if anything.

It was during that drive that he passed by the school again and happened to spot Lou standing at the padlocked front gates with her face pressed to the bars.

Even in her workout clothes with the rain falling around her in sheets, he recognised her immediately. He slowed as he went by, then drove on up the street and swung a uey, coming back just as she got into her own car. He tailed her again, just as he'd done the day before, and this time she led him straight back to her house. When her blinker came on and she pulled into her driveway, he eased to a stop a few houses down; he watched as she got out and walked (not ran, strangely) to her front door before disappearing inside.

He had her home address now. That was something.

More than something, actually. Was it a sign? Were the dreams directing his path during his waking hours now, too?

That night, he dreamt about the kid again, and this time, they exchanged words.

'Are you Jason Rennor?' his dream-self asked. They were in the school again. It was dark, but he could make out the scared look on the boy's face.

'Yes,' the kid replied.

'Tell me more,' he said.

When the boy - Jason - spoke again, what he had to say came out at a hundred miles an hour with no pauses for breath: 'I'm sixteen, I live on Penborough Avenue in Amber Hill East, it's just me and my mom, my dad left us years ago and he lives in Rockford now with some woman, they have a daughter called Nancy, I don't have many friends here and I want to leave and get a job fixing things because I'm good at fixing things and that's what I want to do but I'm scared I might die here in this school because *she's* coming and - '

'She's coming,' Maurice said, looking up the hallway at the flailing black thing heading their way. 'You better run, Jason.'

Jason ran, and Maurice woke up screaming again.

He went back to Lou's house on Wednesday morning. He'd just gone to scout it out, just to have a look. Instead, for the first time in as long as he could remember, he did something rash.

When he got there, no-one was home. Lou's Corolla, the one he'd followed back there last night, was still in the drive, but there were no lights on in the house. It was a gloomy, overcast morning in November, so unless she was still asleep or was some eco-warrior trying to save on electricity, no lights meant no occupants.

Just to be sure, Maurice walked up to the front door and ran the bell. He waited with his hands clasped behind his back and his head bowed, like a doctor about to deliver bad news. He had no idea what he'd say if she actually opened the door.

Oh, sorry lady, wrong house. I'm looking for the monster trying to steal your life - is she in?

He waited twenty seconds, rang the bell again, waited again. No-one came to the door.

Keeping one eye on the neighbor's house, he walked casually around the back of the Jennings place like he'd been there a hundred times before. The house was well-kept, and the backyard was bigger than he'd expected. He didn't know what the father did for a living, but it must be alright. No teacher's salary was paying the mortgage on this place.

Maurice went to the back door, hesitated, and tried the handle. It was unlocked, and the door swung open.

He went inside, closing the door carefully behind him. The kitchen was neat and homely; breakfast dishes were stacked by the sink, ready for washing. There was coffee in the pot.

Wherever she was, she wouldn't be gone for long.

He went through the house, hands still clasped behind his back, inspecting anything that might be helpful: the kids' drawings taped to the fridge; the photos on the mantle; the one row of paperbacks on the shelf above two rows of DVDs (wasn't she an English teacher?); Derek's record collection, which wasn't to his taste. Lou's laptop was on the coffee table, but he didn't open it, as useful as it might have been. He'd come to look, not touch.

He did, however, take a photo of Lou on his phone, the one of her and Derek on their wedding day. He had a hunch that might come in handy later.

At the foot of the stairs, he cleared his throat and called 'Excuse me', but there was no answering cry of alarm from above. She was definitely gone.

He went upstairs, noting how several creaked under his weighty steps. Turning right at the top, he went into the kids' bedrooms, but didn't linger long. He hated when children were involved in these things. Kids always made it worse.

He crossed the landing and eased open the master bedroom door. The room still held the stale odor of sleep, one that would diminish once the blinds were undrawn and the windows opened wide. It was a scent that had been familiar to him once. Lou's teacher outfit, which she'd worn for a grand total of twenty minutes that morning, was still strewn over the bed after her hurried switch into running gear. Maurice glanced into the en suite bathroom, saw nothing of interest, then went to the bedroom window and parted the blinds, just enough to glimpse the street below. It was still empty. Most people were probably at work by now, or at least on their way -

A key turned in the front door.

Maurice let go of the blinds and stepped back. Below him, the front door opened.

Stay calm.

Battling to keep his breathing measured, he stepped across the room as silently as his large frame would allow and got to the door just as Lou started up the stairs. He had no time to think. He went behind the door.

Lou breezed into the room a second later. She was muttering to herself and didn't clock the fact that the door was wide open when she'd left it barely ajar before. She started to strip out of her running gear. Behind the door, Maurice closed his eyes and held his breath.

He hoped against hope that she'd hop in the shower, giving him a chance to slip out when the water was running, but she didn't. He listened as she sprayed on deodorant, fumbled into her home sweats and padded into the en suite; the sink faucet squeaked and water splashed, but it was over in seconds. He could hear her tugging the towel back onto the rail.

Oh man, oh buddy, what've you done?

Lou came back into the bedroom, still muttering to herself. He heard her say the words 'how do I tell', but that was all he got. She kicked her gym gear towards the laundry hamper, then walked back out to the hall and pulled the door closed behind her. Had she glanced behind it, she'd have seen a tall black man in a gray overcoat, staring back at her with wide, panicked eyes.

But she didn't.

Maurice stayed right where he was until she'd gone back downstairs. He stayed there while she poured herself a coffee in the kitchen, and he still didn't move when her chair scraped across the linoleum and she went through to the living room below.

Lou was on her laptop now, meticulously checking every single online account in her possession for signs of Evelyn's interference. Maurice watched the digital clock on her bedside table across the room as the minutes ticked by: ten, fifteen, twenty. He became increasingly aware of the two cups of morning coffee resting in his bladder; he fidgeted, rolled his head on his neck, cracking the once-verile muscles there. He considered the window, but the drop to the garden was too far and he'd be seen straight away, either by a neighbor or by Lou herself. And a black man climbing out of an upstairs window in the suburbs? *Forget it.*

No, he was trapped right where he was until she left the living room. If she went back to the kitchen, or another room downstairs, he might be able to slip out. Even if she turned on the TV or played one of those lame records, it'd give him a chance. He wouldn't have long, though, and he couldn't actually hear her anymore. Was she there at all? Maybe she'd fallen asleep - did people do that after exercise these days?

He had to at least try. Maybe, if he could get the door open, he might see a way out.

Lifting one foot, he placed it carefully on the floor, a step away from his position behind the door, and leaned towards it. There was no sound. Down below, Lou was now texting Debbie.

Maurice took another step and swiveled to face the door. He reached for the handle. He didn't remember the door making a noise when he'd opened it before -

Beneath his left foot, the floorboard creaked.

He stopped dead. His breath caught in his throat.

In the living room below, there was silence. Then, her voice: 'Who's there?'

Maurice waited. It was all he could do.

'Who's there?' she called again. The fear in her tone was unmistakable. 'I'll call the cops.'

Would she? he thought, standing by her bedroom door, afraid to move a muscle. *Would she call them right away, or will she check first? She'll want to see for herself, won't she? No sense in calling the police to report a creaky floorboard.*

He still couldn't hear anything from downstairs - no sound, no movement. What was she doing?

He had to push her towards an action, one way or the other. If she picked up the phone and called the police, it'd force him to react, too. He couldn't just stand there all day until Amber Hill's finest or her husband arrived.

Should he reveal himself? Tell her who he was?

No, it wasn't time. He'd know when it was time for that.

Downstairs, she made a move. Probably going for the phone.

Do something.

He took a breath, turned, and walked a few paces across the room, deliberately putting weight into his steps.

Silence again downstairs. She'd stopped whatever she was doing.

Just leave! Get out of your house and drive away to safety!

She didn't leave. And suddenly, he knew exactly where she was.

He heard the stair creak, the one near the bottom he'd stood on earlier. She was on her way up.

He knew more of them would creak as she ascended and, using the noise to disguise his own steps, crossed to the far side of the bed.

A louder creak. She was at the top of the stairs.

Maurice lowered himself to the floor. Both his knees cracked, surely loud enough for her to hear. He used the edge of the mattress for balance and almost toppled over sideways when it gave beneath his weight. The thing was a glorified sponge under his hand.

He got himself flat on the carpet and slid awkwardly under the bed, as far as he could go. His tailbone banged off the wooden bed frame and he had to bite his lip to keep from crying out. Mercifully, the frame itself was fairly tall, otherwise he'd have been screwed right then and there.

'If you're up here, just come out.'

She was right outside the door. He could barely fit under the bed. She was going to see him.

'Evelyn,' she said.

Hearing someone else use her name made him freeze up at the worst possible time. He still had one big leg out in the open for all to see.

Evelyn.

Summoning a final surge of determination, he hauled his leg under the bed and lay still, just as the door swung open.

His cheek was flat to the dust-covered carpet under the bed and he had a clear view of everything below her knees as she came into the room. She wore sweatpants and thick, woolen socks. He held his breath again.

Lou walked cautiously towards the bed. He could hear her breathing - quick, sharp inhalations. Each of her steps was cat-like and noiseless. He dug his fingers into the carpet and tried to think what he would do if she crouched down and looked under the bed.

How in the hell have I gotten myself in this mess?

She was by the bed now, standing just a couple of feet away from his arm. If he wanted, he could reach out and grab her ankle. Wouldn't that be fun? The neighbors would hear her screams from the end of the street and he'd be on his way to prison.

She stood there by the bed for what felt like an age. And then, to Maurice's relief, she swiveled on the carpet and crossed to the en suite bathroom. She moved out of his eyeline for a few seconds before appearing again by the wardrobes. He watched, still barely breathing, as she opened each door and closed it again. She sighed, and the metal tip of something appeared by her leg. He frowned, unable to decipher what it was. But then it didn't matter, because she was leaving the room.

He waited under the bed, listening and trying not to sneeze as she searched the family bathroom. He heard the shower curtain being drawn back. Then she was in the hall again.

'Last chance,' she called.

She walked away down the hall towards the kids' bedrooms. It was now or never.

He slid himself from under the bed, coming out on the other side of it now, right in front of the open door. If she decided to come back for another look (or heard him in his clumsiness), there'd be nowhere to hide.

She was in the first bedroom now, the one belonging to the little girl, searching for intruders. For Evelyn.

He moved to the bedroom door and peered around the threshold. Just as he did so, she came out of the little girl's bedroom. She would have seen him if she hadn't turned immediately to her left and walked to the boy's bedroom. She had her back to him, and there was a wet umbrella in her hand.

She's plucky, anyway.

He could go now, creep straight to the top of the stairs and make his way down. If she lingered in the boy's room for thirty seconds, he might make it. But the stairs creaked, didn't they?

He had to take the chance.

Come on, Maurice.

He stepped out of the bedroom, and behind him, the phone rang.

This time, he didn't freeze. He took two big steps towards the family bathroom and got through the door a half second before Lou appeared at the far end of the hall. He pressed himself into the corner as she passed the doorway and went back into the master bedroom. The ringing stopped.

'Hello? Mom. Yes, it's me. Are you ok?'

And now you're stuck in the bathroom, you dumb old bastard.

'I, uh, felt a little sick again today.'

Trembling with adrenaline, Maurice looked around the door frame and saw Lou sit down on the bed. She was facing the window and once again had her back to him. Her dark hair was tied up in a ponytail. She looked to be shorter than he imagined from the photos.

'Yeah, it's not good,' she said, with the phone to her ear. 'I got over it pretty quick, though. How is Aunt Jane, anyway?'

As she talked, Maurice slipped out of the bathroom and moved beyond her line of sight. Taking enormous care with his steps, he descended the stairs, avoiding most of the creaks along the way, and moved quickly through the house to the back door. Lou, who was being fed every available shred of news about her mother's social circle in Mount Vernon, didn't hear a thing.

Maurice left through the back door, strode around the side of the house, turned right when he reached the sidewalk, and returned to his car. If Lou had been standing by the window instead of sitting on the bed, she'd have had a perfect view of him walking down the driveway, but she wasn't, and she didn't.

Providence.

That night, Lou fell down the stairs. She broke two ribs and sprained her wrist, and her head smacked off the wall at the bottom, giving her a concussion. Evie watched the whole thing happen from the landing, grinning and invisible. Neither she nor Lou ever found out that Maurice had been in the Jennings household earlier that day.

On the far side of town in someone else's cabin, Maurice saw Lou go down the stairs and crumple in a heap at the bottom. He saw Derek scramble down after her, screaming her name while Ben and Ruth stared horror-struck from the landing with Evie's spectral hands on their heads. He saw the paramedics hoist Lou into the back of the ambulance and watched its blue lights swirl down the street and disappear into the night.

Then he saw the boy again, Jason, back in the school. He was running now, legs pumping, straining for the exit. Lights were going off as he passed under them with a rhythmic *whump whump whump* sound, plunging the hallway behind him into thick blackness. He was desperate and terrified, and that dark screeching entity was right on his tail (right on the *ceiling*, actually), gaining ground by the second. Maurice knew he wasn't going to make it, and even if he somehow reached the doors, they weren't going to open. It would grab him by the shoulders and drag him backwards, faster and faster, into the darkness. He would scream and thrash, but it wouldn't make a difference. It would take him away into the black and rip him apart.

Maurice woke with a start and found he'd been sobbing into his pillow. He sat up in his sleeping bag, fully-clothed and not yet aware of how cold the interior of the cabin was, and covered his face with his hands.

The boy. The boy was key. He was part of it now, for whatever reason.

She was going to try to kill him.

On Thursday morning, Maurice remained in the cabin and deliberated over what to do next. Lou was still alive and in hospital - he was sure of that. He didn't know how badly she'd been injured in the fall, but she wasn't dead, so there was still hope. Maybe, just maybe, the time had come to approach her directly. Actually talk to her.

'You were hidin' under her bed,' he said aloud, sitting at the kitchen table in the cabin. 'How much more direct do you need to get?'

He chuckled to himself, but it quickly died out. Had he missed his chance? He'd gone to her home and broken inside (*stupid, reckless old fool*) and had ultimately gained nothing from it, beyond confirmation that Lou knew about Evie, on some level.

I should have talked to her. I should have made myself known.

'Yes, you should have,' he said.

So what now?

He had to see her, to find out more. He needed to know how badly she'd been hurt. Maybe she'd broken her neck or back, and now she was paralyzed. If that was the case, Evie had already won.

He'd go to the hospital and see for himself.

But first, the boy.

'Jason Rennor.' He drummed his fingers on the table, twice.

The kid was important somehow. He was an ace in the hole for him, and by default, for Lou. And if he was their trump card in all this, it meant he was a problem for Evelyn. He could only hope she didn't already know more than he did about why.

He went by the school that afternoon, just as the final bell sounded. Kids streamed out of the building and dispersed in all directions once they reached the street, talking, laughing, almost all glued to their phones. No-one saw Maurice Baxter parked opposite the school gates in his station wagon.

He knew what he was going to do this time. It would be another foolhardy act of recklessness, yes, but he feared time was running out for Jason, and probably for himself. He needed to speak to him.

He waited, watching the school as the remaining stragglers came out of the main entrance and trudged towards the street. There was still no sign of Jason.

Maurice shifted in his seat. Had he gone out via another exit? He didn't know the building at all. There could be - most likely was, in fact - another way out.

He unbuckled his seat belt.

'What're you doing, Maurice?' he muttered under his breath. 'This is a bad idea.'

He opened the car door and put one foot on the asphalt, and stopped.

A girl was watching him from across the street.

He stared back at her. She was blonde, with a purple backpack slung over one shoulder; she wore a checkered gray coat and flared jeans, neither of which flattered her rounded figure. Her eyes were bright green and fixed on him.

Slowly, as if fearing a sudden movement might cause her to rush across the road at him, Maurice eased himself back into the Sable and closed the door. He re-buckled his belt, started the engine and drove off down the street without looking back. The girl watched him go until the car was out of sight, then turned and started home. Later that evening, she would walk all the way to Sixty-Four Oakland Avenue and report what she'd seen, and then immediately forget how she'd gotten there.

Maurice went to Amber Hill General later that day. He bought flowers at the gift shop and asked for Louise Jennings at reception. He was a close family friend and had heard about her accident the night before. Evening visiting hours were almost over, the lady told him, but she directed him to Lou's room anyway.

He took the elevator up to her floor and walked to her room with the flowers in his hand. A couple of nurses shot him a glance but said nothing. He knew he didn't look great but that hardly mattered now.

He passed an old woman and two kids at the vending machines just round the corner from Lou's hallway.

'Get that one,' the little girl was saying, pointing at a candy bar near the middle. 'Mom likes those.'

'She does not,' said the boy, but by then Maurice was already around the corner and didn't hear the rest. He knew who they were. He was close.

When he arrived at Lou's room, he heard Derek speaking within and sat down in a plastic chair by the door. The hallway was for private rooms only, and apart from another man seated at the far end, he was alone.

'Get me?' Inside the room, Derek laughed humorlessly. 'Shit, Lou. I need to talk to this woman. I need to talk to Perry. You just fell down the stairs and almost broke your neck. You're lucky it wasn't anything more serious. I'm going to find out what's going on.'

She's ok, Maurice thought. He studied the bouquet in his hands.

'Just look after the kids, ok?' he heard Lou say.

'Yeah.'

'I mean it, Derek. Watch them. Don't let them go anywhere alone. And get Mom to pick them up from school tomorrow, not Debbie.'

Debbie?

'You think - '

'I don't know, but I don't want to take the chance. If she calls you, just make up some excuse. Mom's visiting for the week so she can do it - it's not even a lie. Just keep them all safe until I get home.'

'I will. Don't worry.'

Voices further down the hallway. The old woman and the kids were on their way back. Maurice rose to his feet.

'Get some rest, hon, ok?' Lou said.

'Count on it.'

'If anything happens, anything at all - '

'I'll call you first.'

'Right.' The kids were coming around the corner. 'Tell me about your day. I need to hear something normal.'

Maurice placed the flowers on the chair and walked away from the room. He didn't make eye contact with Carol or the kids as they passed. Only Ruth looked over her shoulder at the tall black man as he turned the corner. None of them noticed the flowers.

Maurice drove straight to the Jennings' house from the hospital and parked a hundred yards down the street. He watched as Carol and the kids arrived home and the lights came on. Derek followed not long afterwards in Lou's Corolla. He walked up to the front door with his head down and disappeared inside.

At nine-fifty, Derek came back out, got into his own car and backed out of the drive.

Where are you going? Maurice wondered, starting up the Sable. He pulled away from the curb and followed the Corolla down the street at a safe distance.

Derek drove to a gas station roughly two minutes away from the house and pulled into a parking bay outside it. Maurice arrived ten seconds later; he dropped the Sable into neutral and coasted across the forecourt into an empty bay next to the store entrance. Some Michael Jackson song he couldn't quite place blared out from the external speakers. He killed the engine and watched Derek in his rear view mirror as he climbed out of the Corolla and walked under the canopy towards the doors with his hands stuffed in his pockets.

Maurice ducked his head as Derek passed, but of course, the other man wouldn't have recognized him anyway. It was just instinct now, one of many habits borne from months of amateur surveillance, of... let's call it what it is... stalking people.

Detective Baxter, reporting for duty.

The gas station doors slid open and Derek went inside. Maurice got out of the Sable and followed. Behind him, the forecourt canopy lights flickered.

The same Michael Jackson song that'd been playing outside also reverberated around the interior of the store. It was bright inside - too bright - and Maurice had to pause to rub his eyes. Three short aisles ran to the back of the store, separated by two rows of sparsely-stocked shelving. Maurice glimpsed Derek pass up the right-hand aisle towards the medication section, massaging his temple as he went. That explained the late trip to the gas station, anyway.

Ignoring the kid behind the counter (who was pretty much ignoring him right back), Maurice moved near the end of the central aisle and began shuffling through the DVDs in the Bargain Bin, trying to watch what Derek was doing. He needed him to stay put for a few seconds, just long enough to get to him. If he could reach him, out here in public, he might have a chance. One conversation, that was all. It could be enough.

He let the faded two-dollar copy of *Turner and Hooch* he'd been holding drop back into the basket and stepped out into the aisle. In the same moment, Derek moved into it halfway up the store. Maurice stayed where he was for a second too long, conspicuous in the middle of the aisle, before his brain kicked back into gear and he moved to the end of the aisle Derek had just vacated; Derek had glanced his way as he turned towards the refrigerators at the back of the store, then stopped abruptly by the hair products.

He knew he was being watched.

Nice going, Detective. You're going to scare him off before you have a chance to...

An ice chill ran down Maurice's spine. The store doors had slid open behind him and someone had breezed inside, passing by the counter and out of sight up the left-hand aisle. Suddenly, Maurice found he couldn't move. His heart, which had until that moment been content to beat calmly in his chest, even while he closed in on Derek, was now trying to pound its way free of his body and bounce out of the store. He'd begun to sweat and shiver uncontrollably, like an addict going through withdrawals. All in the space of a few seconds.

She was here. *She was in the same motherfucking room as him.*

His knees weakened and he grabbed the nearest shelf for support. From the back of the store, he heard Derek's voice: 'Oh, sorry!'

And then, another he recognized all too well.

'No no, my fault.'

Maurice tasted bile in the back of his throat. The room began to spin.

She got there first.

The greasy-haired kid behind the counter was looking at him over his phone. At the back of the store, they were laughing now.

'I'm such a klutz,' she was saying. 'I bump into someone at least once every time I'm out in public. Seriously, every time.'

'No, don't worry,' Derek replied. 'We've all done it.'

I have to get him away from her. It's too soon. It can't happen yet.

Still gripping the shelf for support, Maurice staggered back to the end of the central aisle. He must have appeared drunk - the store clerk was staring at him now with clear concern.

He heard her laugh and the sound of it almost propelled the bile into his mouth. He couldn't throw up here, not now. If she saw him, he was dead. He hadn't come all this way, for all this time, just to die in a gas station because he was too much of a pussy to control himself.

But the Fear was real; it implored him to run.

'Do I know you?' he heard Derek say.

He looked up the aisle, to where the other man stood by the refrigerators with a bottle of Gatorade in his hand. He was swaying on the spot, like he'd slept-walked his way there. Maurice couldn't see her, but her voice carried to him over the music coming from the speakers above his head, clear as day.

'Sure you do. We've known each other for a long time, haven't we, Derek?'

Oh shit, this is it.

He lurched towards the sunglasses display stand.

'Do you want me to come home with you, Derek?'

Maurice grabbed the stand and threw it to the floor with a crash. The store clerk was on his feet behind the counter.

'Hey!' he cried.

Without a glance back, Maurice bolted out through the doors, pulling the hood of his coat up as he went.

'Mister! You can't just...'

He fumbled his car keys out of his pocket and yanked the door open. His heart was beating so hard and so fast he thought he might collapse. From inside the store, he heard the kid yell 'Jerk-off!', and then he slammed the car door shut.

'Come on, come on,' he stammered, sticking the key in the ignition with sweat-soaked fingers. He twisted it and the Sable rumbled to life.

Throwing the car into reverse, he swung out of the parking bay, just as the gas station doors slid open and she stepped outside. Her head turned towards the car and for one horrifying (and exhilarating) split-second, their eyes met, but the Sable's rusted frame was in the way and it wasn't a clean connection. He wrenched his eyes away, shifted into drive and accelerated out of the forecourt onto the empty road.

He drove like a maniac back to the cabin, keeping an eye on his rear-view mirror the whole time. He refused to look at the passenger seat. When he got back inside the cabin, he locked and bolted the door, then dropped to the floor on his knees, first laughing, then sobbing.

That night, after smoking half a pack of cigarettes and downing most of a bottle of whiskey he'd stumbled across at the back of a cupboard in the kitchen, he fell into a deep sleep and dreamt about the kid, the boy Jason, who was key to the whole thing. He saw him in the school again, running for the reception doors. Light pulsed under and around the doors as Jason drew closer; they seemed to expand in the middle and pull back, expand and pull back, like a pair of wooden lungs, and the light pulsed brighter with every outward throb until it seemed as though the doors might burst off their hinges. A high-pitched whine had filled the air and it grew louder as Jason stretched out his hands towards the doors, towards freedom and escape and life, and the black creature at his heels reached out too, talons flexing, jaws wide and slathering.

In the dream, Maurice reached the other side of the door and pulled it open. He saw Jason running towards him and reached for him, straining every sinew, agonizingly close to grabbing the terrified teenager's outstretched hand. Behind him, the creature reached out as well, enraged now to the point of madness at the notion its prey was about to escape.

In the dream, Maurice's hand closed around Jason's, just as the creature's claws snagged on his ankle. The boy screamed, and then Maurice was awake, lying on his side next to the couch; he'd rolled off it onto the floor and been jolted back to consciousness. The interior of the cabin was freezing and so was he - he'd drunk himself to sleep and hadn't wrapped up warm for the night. Shivering, he staggered in the dark to the bathroom. He got within a foot of the toilet before vomiting everywhere, retching hard until his throat was dry and aching and his stomach was drained.

He would never dream about Jason or Lou again.

The next day was Friday, and he knew the time had come from the moment he woke up again, this time tucked into the sleeping bag with two layers of clothes on.

He waited until mid afternoon before driving to Amber Hill High. The school day ended at three o'clock (he'd deduced that much over the last few days); he arrived ten minutes before the final bell was due to go, did one pass by the school gates, then parked around the corner. He didn't want the blonde girl seeing him this time - he had a feeling she'd be there again, looking out for him.

Does Evelyn know? he wondered, lighting up a Marlboro. He took a drag and exhaled through his nostrils, watching the school entrance through the metal fencing from his new side-on vantage point. It wasn't ideal, but it was safer, for him and the boy. He knew the time had come for him to get involved, *really* involved, do more than just linger in the background and perhaps tip over a sunglasses display carousel.

Does she know? he thought again. He took another drag and cracked the window an inch. A chill breeze instantly swept into the car, and the sound of a bell drifted to him across the school grounds.

Kids began filtering out a minute later, and ten minutes after that, the school grounds and the streets beyond them were swarming with teenagers. Some hurried to the yellow buses drawing up to the curb, others trudged to their parents' cars with heads down, somewhat embarrassed to be seen with them (they were often the younger students, who weren't yet trusted to make their own way home), and many more slunk off together in pairs or small groups, talking and laughing in the cold, darkening November afternoon. The weekend had begun.

Maurice squinted at the school entrance, watching for Jason. He knew what the boy looked like purely from his dreams - if he came out with his hood up or simply had his back turned to him, he might miss him entirely. But he knew, somehow, that wouldn't happen. He had a part to play in Jason's exit from school today and he was going to play it, quite possibly at the cost of his own life.

By three-thirty, the grounds had emptied. On the far side of the school, the Trojans were being put through their paces by Coach Denvar ahead of the game that night, running drills over the partially frozen football field; in reception,

Beverley was starting to pack up for the week, tunelessly humming the theme to her favorite soap opera, which she'd force her husband to watch with her over dinner. In English Room 2, Jason was opening Evelyn Sparrow's notebook.

Maurice waited as long as he could bear, then stepped out of the car. He turned the corner and walked to the front of the school, hands deep in his pockets, cigarette stub between his teeth. He paused at the school gates, staring up the drive at the entrance. Warm light spilled out from the reception area; there were very few other lights on inside the building.

'Let's see, now,' said Maurice. He took a final drag and flicked the Marlboro away. 'Let's see.'

He began walking up the drive towards the front of the school. His boots clapped on the asphalt and bone-dry leaves skittered out of his path. A whistle sounded from the football field and someone cheered.

He reached the foot of the entrance steps. Through the small window looking out from the school office, he saw Beverley stacking files, her frizzy hair bobbing as she hummed to herself. Her head was down and she didn't see him.

Maurice took his left hand from his pocket and pushed back the sleeve. His watch, once a surprise birthday gift, had a hairline crack across its face, but it still told the time perfectly well. It was three thirty-seven.

From inside the school, there was a bang.

Maurice looked up at the glass doors, just in time to see Jason Rennor fall to the floor in reception. Beverley spun away from the little exterior window. Even from the foot of the steps, Maurice saw the internal reception doors shake as they were slammed-into from the other side.

Now Beverley was at the glass partition, pointing incredulously at the doors. Maurice watched as Jason scrambled to his feet.

This is it. He started up the steps.

Jason was saying something to Beverley. He backed towards the glass, away from Beverley's accusing glare. Maurice reached for the handle just as Jason leaned back against the door.

'Let's see now,' he said.

He pulled the door open and Jason tumbled out. He'd underestimated how hard the boy had been leaning against the door, and his momentum carried him backwards down the steps before Maurice could stop him. He landed in a heap at the bottom.

From inside, Beverley squawked, 'Who are you?'

Maurice ignored her and let go of the door handle, hurrying down the steps. He grabbed Jason by the arm (*he's skinny as a rake, this one*) and hauled him up. He got as far as his knees.

'Get up,' Maurice demanded. 'Get up, now.'

The boy got unsteadily to his feet and looked him in the face. For a split second, Maurice was stunned by how young he looked and wondered if he had the right kid. But he saw the Band-Aid on his nose and the black rings under his eyes, and he knew this was Jason.

'Who -'

'There's no time.' Maurice started away from the entrance, dragging Jason with him. He saw Beverley at the window. 'We need to leave.'

'Wait. Wait!'

He didn't have time to wait. He told Jason what he knew about him, what the dreams had told him, and it was enough. The boy followed.

They got back to the Sable just as it started to rain. Maurice unlocked the doors, looking back towards the school. The receptionist might have called the principal, or even the police. That might complicate things.

'Get in,' he said.

The boy got in and Maurice followed, slamming his door harder than was necessary.

He pulled the station wagon out from the curb and drove away from the school.

They got to within a half mile of the woods before Jason spoke.

'Let me out.'

'No,' Maurice replied.

Jason reached for the door handle and Maurice hit the lock button on his side. The kid pulled the handle anyway.

What, you're just going to jump out and roll onto the shoulder?

'Seriously, man, let me out. I can walk from here.'

'Can't do that, Jason.'

'Why not?' He could see him out of the corner of his eye, staring at him now. His face was set. 'How do you know me?'

Maurice's throat was dry and he swallowed. 'I'll explain everything real soon.'

'Explain now.'

'I can't, Jason, not 'til - '

'Then let me out. This is abduction, or something.'

'It's not.'

'Yeah, it is.' The kid moved to unbuckle his seatbelt.

'Fine.'

Maurice slammed his foot down on the brake pedal and the kid lurched forward in his seat. If his belt had actually been unbuckled, his face would've been in the dash. The driver behind them lay on the horn and flashed his lights.

'The hell - ' Jason wheezed as Maurice guided the Sable off the road. The car following veered around the bulky end of the station wagon and the driver gave them a good look at his middle finger.

Maurice brought the car to a stop on the shoulder. Beyond the passenger-side door was a steel traffic barrier, and beyond that, a shrubby slope ran down to where the woods began.

'Look, kid,' he said, turning towards Jason. The boy's face was flushed with anger and shock. 'You know I'm not abducting you. I just saved your life back there from someone... some*thing*... that would've killed you without a second's hesitation. If she'd got you, you'd probably be dead right now. You know that, right?'

Jason didn't reply, but he also didn't try for the door again.

'Right.' Maurice sniffed, and ran a hand down his face - he was sweating. 'I'll tell you everything you need to know, absolutely everything, but not here. Not on the road. We're not safe anymore.'

The boy looked at him and he saw it in his eyes. He understood, to some extent, anyway.

'I can't explain how I knew to be there today, at that exact time, at your school. Least, I can't explain it in a way that'll make a whole lotta rational sense, you know? Because it isn't rational, and even if it was, I'm not the kind've man who could lay it all out in a way you'd understand. Hell, *I* can't even understand it, and I've been in it a lot longer than you, I expect. But if you want to go - '

He pressed the lock button again and the pin on Jason's door popped up.

' - then go. It's your choice - I won't stop you.'

Jason's eyes went to the door. And then to Maurice's surprise, he actually unbuckled his seatbelt and reached for the handle. But just as his fingers found it, he stopped. Maurice held his breath, waited, prayed. Finally, Jason's hand dropped away from the door and with a sigh of resignation, he turned back towards him.

'I'll hear you out,' he said, and right then, he appeared to Maurice much older than he was. 'But then I'm gone.'

Maurice held his gaze for a moment, then nodded, once.

'So, go. Explain it all.'

Maurice broke his gaze and glanced out through the rain-splattered windscreen as a car sped by, then looked back at the boy, who was now staring at his hands with wide, faraway eyes, drifting off again. He knew he was still in shock, even if he was able to respond to conversation.

'I can't explain it all,' Maurice said, measuring his tone. 'What I *can* tell you is this: you're not alone now. Not anymore. That may not be of much comfort, I know, but it's the truth. Whether you like it or not, you've got me now, and I'm the only other person in this lil' town of yours who knows. I *know*, Jason - you understand? I know about *her*.'

The kid's shoulders started trembling.

Don't stop now. This is it.

'We both know about her now. And actually, there's one other person who does, too. Someone more important, and in more danger, than either of us, if you can believe that.'

He pulled out his phone and opened the image gallery. Jason watched him carefully. His shoulders continued to tremble.

'I'm going to show you a picture of someone,' Maurice said, quietly relieved the image was still there and hadn't magically disappeared like so many others. 'And I'm going to be honest - it'll screw with your brain when you see it, ok?'

'What d'you mean?'

Maurice regarded the photo of Lou in her wedding dress and imagined she would have been quite beautiful on the day it was taken. Her dark hair had been grown out especially for it and flowed lustrously around her shoulders. She appeared youthful and happy. Maurice knew someone else was probably in that photo by now, smiling at Derek's side.

'This is a picture,' he said, 'of Lou Jennings.'

He paused for the expected response, and smiled morosely when it came.

'Who?'

'Lou Jennings is the English teacher at your school, Amber Hill High. She's taught there for over six years.'

He waited patiently. Jason stared back at him; rain pattered softly on the roof of the car.

'Um... Mr Doyle was my English teacher. I've never heard - '

'Lou Jennings has taught at your school the whole time you've been there, until last week, when her place was taken by Evelyn Sparrow.'

Jason was frowning now.

'She was... replaced?'

'No,' said Maurice. The phone almost slipped from his sweaty hand and he gripped it tighter. 'Let me be very clear about this, Jason. She was not replaced - her place was *taken*. Ok?'

'I don't really understand.'

'I know, and I wouldn't expect you to. Not yet. But before I show you this photo - and I'm warning you again, it'll fuck with your head when you see it - tell me what you know about Evelyn Sparrow.'

Now the frown on Jason's face dissolved into stricken fear as her image swam back into his mind's eye.

'She... she, um...'

'It's ok, Jason,' Maurice said. Inside, his old heart began to jig again.

'She's not... human,' the boy finally managed, and Maurice could tell the admission came as a relief of sorts. The expression of fright that had settled back into his face loosened slightly. 'I saw her in detention the other day, just for a second. I don't know what she was, or is, but she's not a woman.'

Maurice nodded and said nothing. *Let him get it out.*

'I think she's controlling some people in the school,' Jason continued. 'I don't know how, but I think that's what's happening. She sent Sophie Wentworth to get me and she tried to... I dunno... hypnotize me, or something. But it didn't work.'

But why didn't it work?

'I followed her to her room today after everyone was gone.' His voice began to rise in pitch. 'I saw what was in her notebook. I saw *her*, in her storeroom, and she had...'

His eyes took on that faraway look again.

'She killed him. She killed Rick.' He was starting to hyperventilate. 'And she saw me. I ran, but she chased me, like in my dream. She was... some creature, with wings. She was *on the fucking ceiling*.'

Maurice wanted to put a hand on his shoulder, to reassure him, but he resisted. This was the moment of truth for Jason - it had to happen now. *Don't stop.*

'She almost had me. She would've killed me too.' Jason met his gaze again and his eyes welled with tears. 'Why is she trying to kill me?'

'Because you *know*, Jason,' Maurice said firmly. 'You know, and she's aware of it now. I'm not sure how you know, but you do, and that's all that matters to her. She won't stop until you're dead. Just like she won't stop with me, either.'

'But - '

'Evelyn Sparrow - whatever the hell she is - took Lou Jennings' place in your school, and no-one but you and I know about it. You, me, and Lou herself.'

He held the phone screen up for Jason to see.

'This is Lou.'

Jason looked at the photo and abruptly stopped breathing. His mouth dropped open and his eyes bulged wider than Maurice could have imagined. When he started speaking again, it was gibberish.

'Wha wha wha what is is who who who who...'

He started to shake all over, like he was having a seizure.

'It's Mrs Jennings, Jason. You know who she is. You've known this whole time.'

The boy turned away from the phone and bent forward. He was about to vomit.

Oh shit, this is a mistake.

'Jason? Jason, listen to me.'

It's too much.

'Jason - '

The kid threw open the car door and staggered out into the rain.

'Jason! Wait!'

Maurice fumbled off his seatbelt and pushed open his door. Another approaching car had to swerve to avoid it and the driver furiously blared his horn. Maurice got out and ran around the back of the car.

Jason was bent over the steel barrier, hurling his guts out. The back of his jacket was already soaked.

'Boy, are you alright?' Maurice said. He threw a glance up the road but apart from the car that'd just passed by, the lanes were clear. Maurice reached out and placed a hand on Jason's shoulder. 'Jason.'

The kid looked round. His face was deathly pale; there was yellow vomit on his chin.

'Mrs Jennings,' he said. 'I... I...'

Jason's eyes rolled back in his head. Maurice dived forward and caught hold of him, just before he hit the asphalt.

THIRTEEN

4 days before Thanksgiving

A faint shuffling sound.

Damp, tasted rather than smelt.

Orange light, dim at first, glowing stronger out of the darkness.

Something under his head. Too firm to be a pillow.

A cushion.

Jason turned his face into it and recoiled sharply as it pressed against his still-broken nose, stabbing pain through his skull. The sudden burst of discomfort drew him back to full consciousness. He lifted his head (which was easier said than done) and looked first at where he lay, and then at his surroundings.

He was on a couch, and his head had indeed been propped against a cushion. The couch and its cushions were faded blue, almost like denim. A patterned quilt had been thrown over him, but it wasn't long enough to cover the entirety of his lanky frame - his feet stuck out at the end. He suspected (though he couldn't be sure because of his nose) that both the couch and the quilt didn't smell daisy-fresh.

His eyes went from the old quilt to his sock-covered feet at the end of the couch, and then to the wall beyond them. It was wood... no, more than that... it was made from *logs*, running horizontally from one end of the room to the other.

The ceiling was also made from logs, packed tight together above thick, angular beams. He was in a real, bona fide log cabin.

His neck hurt when he twisted his head to look around the rest of the room. There wasn't much to see: a stone fireplace set against one wall was as cold as the November wind outside of the cabin - the orange glow came from a small, gas-powered heater placed in front of it; a faded, once-ornate rug dominated the center of the room, and what little furniture the cabin contained had been arranged around it - Jason's couch sat at one end with a couple of matching armchairs at the other; a glass-topped coffee table stacked with magazines rested between them, and an enormous television set from the nineties stood dormant against the wall opposite the fireplace. This, Jason supposed, was the living room.

He looked past the armchairs to the open-plan kitchen and saw the man seated there, cradling a mug in his hands. There were playing cards spread out on the table in front of him.

Jason cautiously eased his stiff body into a sitting position. Without looking his way, the man (*his name... something beginning with M, was it?*) reached out and flipped a card over. He studied it for a moment, then set it aside.

'You're up,' he observed.

Jason rubbed the side of his head. His whole body ached.

'Where is this?' he said, watching the stranger.

'Somewhere safe,' said the man. 'For now, anyway.'

In the weak orangey light from the heater, Jason got his first good look at the guy. He'd seen him already, outside the school and in the car, but his perception had been muddied by shock and fear. Now, he had a chance to look at him properly.

When he'd first seen him, he'd guessed he was in his mid-fifties, but now he thought he might have shot too low. The guy's face was wrinkled; he had a wiry beard, mostly gray, and fleshy bags under his eyes that spoke of someone who rarely got as much sleep as their age required. He reminded Jason of a blood-hound. And he was big, though perhaps not overweight. He looked as though he'd lifted weights when he was younger, or maybe even boxed.

Has this guy kidnapped me? he thought. The back door of the cabin was on the right-hand wall of the kitchen. The front door must be somewhere behind him.

'How d'you feel, kid?'

'Um, alright.'

'You took a fall on those school steps. Nothing hurtin' now?'

Everything's hurting.

'No.'

'That's good.' The stranger flipped over another card. He raised the mug to his mouth, then paused before taking a sip. 'You want some coffee?'

'Um, no,' Jason replied, looking over his shoulder. The front door was there, just a few feet away. The chain was on. 'Listen, I don't - '

'I'm Maurice. You might've forgotten that, in the moment. We were in a rush.' He took a swig of whatever was in his mug and shifted in his chair to face him. 'And like I said in the car, you're free to go any time you want. This isn't an abduction. You know that.'

I don't know that. Jason was creeping towards being fully awake; he was starting to read the guy now, and he didn't exactly believe what he was saying. He hadn't turned in his chair in order to make conversion easier - he was getting ready to cut off his escape, if necessary.

The man, Maurice, sighed. He looked as though he was about to stand and then changed his mind.

'I know how this must look,' he said, 'and I'm sorry it went this way, but it couldn't be helped, not really. You've just woken up in some place with some stranger and you don't even know what day it is. You must be shittin' your pants right now.'

He paused again, waiting for Jason to respond. When he didn't speak, or try to run, he went on.

'I'll answer every question you want to ask, I swear. But please, before you leave, *ask* them. I want to help you, Jason - '

'Ok then,' Jason said. 'Let's start with the obvious one: how do you know who I am?'

Maurice grimaced, as though this was the one question he'd rather not have started with, but he answered anyway. 'I saw you in a dream. A few dreams, actually.'

No shit.

'In the dreams, you told me your name, where you're from... things like that. Not much, just enough. That's usually how it works. The dreams showed me where you went to school, and that's how I knew to be there on Friday, at the

257

exact right moment. I've learned to trust them because... well, because of things like that. The dreams save lives. At least, they've started to, it seems.'

If Jason hadn't had such insanely vivid, seemingly-prescient dreams himself over the last week, he'd have walked out the door already. He stayed where he was, but he was perched on the edge of the couch now, just one wrong word from Maurice away from leaving.

Maurice appeared to know that, and continued his explanation carefully.

'I've been having these dreams for a long time now, about the guts of a year. They've been guiding me, drawing me on. Until now, they've always been just a little too late, but this time - '

'Wait,' Jason interjected, picking up on something Maurice had said. 'What do you mean, "on Friday"? What day is it now?'

He looked at the drawn curtains. Maurice followed his gaze and grimaced again.

'It's Sunday.'

'*Sunday!*'

'Yes. You've been asleep since Friday afternoon. You came out of it briefly last night, but I don't think you were fully awake. You were babbling about someone called Rick.'

Jason's mind, dulled with lethargy, took longer than usual to work the problem.

'My mom,' he said, suddenly aghast. 'She doesn't know where I am. She must be - '

Maurice held up a big hand.

'Easy. It's all ok.'

'What d'you mean? How?'

The older man considered what he was about to say, then replied, 'I've taken care of it. I sent her a couple of messages from your phone, told her you were going away for the weekend with your friend, um... Ste, or something. Saw he'd sent you some messages recently. Anyway, it worked.'

Jason stared for a moment, processing. 'You took my phone?'

'Easy,' Maurice said again, but Jason was on his feet now.

'You can't do that, man,' Jason said, pointing across the room at him. 'That's my phone, my information. You can't go through my stuff like that.'

'Jason, it had to be done.'

'The hell it did!'

'It was necessary, to protect your mother. Trust me, if she went looking for you now, it'd only lead - '

'*Trust* you?' Jason exclaimed. 'Why should I trust you? I don't even know who you are! What gives you the right - '

'Enough!'

Maurice stood up and his chair toppled backwards, clattering onto the floorboards. Jason, who'd been on the verge of flipping the coffee table out of his way, took a step back.

'Enough of this.' Maurice's hands were balled into fists. 'You don't know what you're talking about, boy. You don't know, and yet you presume to yell at me, the one who saved your life. Do you understand that? Has your teenage brain comprehended it yet? You would be *dead* right now if it wasn't for me. You get that? Dead, or worse.'

Jason remained standing, squared off against the bigger man across the room. But he didn't make a move towards him, or towards the door. Right now, staying put seemed like the best option. This guy, Maurice, might just as easily decide to hurt him as he had chosen to rescue him back at the school. He was old and Jason knew he could probably outmaneuver him if it came to it, but he didn't fancy his chances if the guy got a hold of him.

Maurice didn't speak for a moment. He just stared at Jason, waiting for something. But that something never came, or it passed. Maurice wiped the back of his hand across his mouth, then gestured towards the couch.

'Sit,' he said. 'Please.'

Jason thought about it, weighing his options. Then he lowered himself back onto the couch. As soon as he did, his head started to swim. He'd stood up too quickly and now felt faint. He hadn't been aware of it right away.

Maurice picked up the overturned chair and set it back on its feet at the table, then sat down with a tired sigh.

'I'll tell you what you want to know,' he said. 'But first, I need to ask you one thing, and it's important that you answer honestly. Ok?'

'Depends what it is,' Jason replied.

Maurice pondered that for a second, then went on.

'When we were in the car, before you passed out,' he said, 'I showed you a photo on my phone. Do you remember that?'

259

I remember spewing my guts out.

'Yeah.'

'Do you remember her name? The one I told you?'

'Yeah. Lou... Jennings. She teaches English at the school.'

The old man's face brightened. 'You know that now?'

'It's what you told me.' Maurice's smile began to melt away before Jason added: 'But I *did* recognize her. And then when I really thought about it, I started to... remember her. But not so much remember like I'd forgotten her. It was more like I'd always known, like it was obvious, and when I saw the photo and you told me her name, something just... I don't know... clicked back into place.'

'Yes,' said Maurice, nodding eagerly. 'Like a broken fuse had been repaired.'

'Sure.' Jason frowned, and Maurice inched forward in his chair. 'You going to be sick again?' he asked.

'How the hell should I know?' Jason replied. But he could taste bile at the back of his throat - there was an association now, something about the photo of that woman. Maybe he was going to vomit again. 'Got any water?'

'Water. Yes.'

Maurice stood and went to a cupboard next to the sink. He took out a glass tumbler, filled it with icy cold water from the faucet and came across the room.

'Forest fresh,' he said, attempting a smile as he handed over the tumbler. Jason took it and gulped the water down. He hadn't realized how dry and raw his throat was until then. He probably hadn't drank anything since Friday.

Maurice sat again. Jason drained the rest of the glass and set it on the coffee table. Some idle notion about coasters flitted into his mind, and was gone.

'I remember her,' he said finally. 'Mrs Jennings. She was the English teacher. She never taught me, though.'

Maurice nodded.

'And I know now. Or at least, I think I do. Miss... Sparrow... isn't supposed to be there, is she?'

'No.'

'But everyone thinks she is, right? They all think she's been there the whole time?'

'For as long as Lou's been there, yes.'

'And they don't remember Mrs Jennings?'

'It's like you said,' Maurice replied. 'They know, and they've always known, but it just isn't clicking. The fuse has been broken. I think when you made the connection again, it overwhelmed you. That's why you reacted like you did.'

'It was too much,' Jason said, scratching his temple vacuously. 'It felt like a bad trip, you know?'

'I do,' Maurice said, grinning lop-sidedly. 'Do *you* know what a bad trip's like?'

'Sure.' *Screw you, man.* 'So I was out cold for, like, two days?'

'Almost. Had a hell of a time carrying you here from the lane. You're not as scrawny as you look. And then you turned cold as a corpse. Thought you were a goner on Friday night.'

'You shouldn't taken me to the hospital.'

'If I had, she'd have found you. And then you *would* be a goner.'

Jason lowered his gaze and allowed the stillness to settle again. A few feet away, the gas heater ticked dutifully, and beyond the wooden walls of the cabin, a chill November breeze whistled. Maurice watched him, cradling his mug in one hand.

'So who exactly are you?' Jason said.

'Maurice Baxter. I'm fifty-seven years old and I'm from Seattle. Or I was, once. Probably can't go back there now.'

This time, it was Jason's turn to wait. Maurice studied the contents of his mug, swirling it a little, before continuing. 'I worked a desk job for the Postal Service most of my life - nothin' special, but I liked it well enough. I was married for thirty-three years. My wife died two years ago. Brain aneurysm. We had one daughter, Melanie, who was studying to be a veterinarian. She loved animals, always had. Workin' with them was all she'd ever wanted to do.'

Maurice paused, and this time, it went on for so long Jason wasn't sure he was going to continue. He was about to speak when Maurice cleared his throat.

'She was in her final year at college, workin' hard like she always did. Cynthia - that's her mother - had always been so proud of her. So was I. She stuck at it, even after Cynthia passed. Tough kid. Stronger than me, I think.

'She was coming to the end of her education. Had a job lined up and everything. It was all laid out in front of her, like a clear highway stretchin' off into the distance, you know?'

Jason nodded. He didn't really know, but it seemed like a good time to nod.

'Anyway, that's when Evelyn found her. Mel turned up at class one morning after Christmas break and she was just there, sittin' where she'd always sat, like

261

she'd been there forever. Mel went to take another seat and her professor asked who she was, said she might be in the wrong room. That professor had known her for years, maybe the whole time she'd been at college. Mel was so confused by it all. She argued with the professor, right there in front of everyone, and they kicked her out of the room. She went straight to the Dean's office and demanded to see her, and when she got to talkin', the Dean of the college acted like she'd never seen her before. But she knew Evie, of course. According to her, Evie Sparrow had been there for years. And she was a top student, like Mel had been. Funny, that.

'So Mel calls me up, in hysterics. She told me everything and I didn't believe her. Not right away. How could I? It sounded crazy, even to me. I just didn't understand, but I don't think anyone can until... they're in it, you know?'

'Yeah,' said Jason.

'So I drove down to see her, and as soon as I walked into her room, she grabs me by the arms - ' Maurice mimed the movement as he spoke, shaking an invisible body in front of him. ' - and she says, "Dad! Dad, do you know me? Do you know my face?", and of course I told her I did, even though I was convinced she was on drugs or something by that point. And when I said I knew her, why wouldn't I know her, she just started cryin', sobbin' into my shoulder. And that's when she told me about her boyfriend.'

'He didn't remember her?'

'No.' Maurice took up his mug again, staring into it like he expected its contents to reveal the future. 'She'd gone to him first, naturally, and he'd acted like he'd never met her before. She thought she was losing her mind, as anyone would. But of course, that's not what was happening, not at all. It was just that Evie had gotten to them first, while she'd been away. Her friends, her teachers, her boyfriend... all of them. She'd been with that boy for a couple of years by that point, too. Evie took them all from her.'

Maurice became quiet and vacant again. Jason shifted on the couch, watching the old man's expression. There was no emotion there - he'd buried it, or it'd burned out long ago.

'What about you?' he asked, not just to break the silence. 'Did you still know her?'

'Yes,' said Maurice slowly. 'I did. For a while. I took her home with me, to recover. There wasn't anything else to do, no-one recognized her there anymore. But the people at home, the people that'd been around her when she was young, they still knew her. We went to see her doctor and he prescribed plenty of medication, and it calmed her down. He had to give her sleeping pills too because she kept having nightmares about someone being in her room. I started to have them too, after a while.

'She was home for about a week when Evie showed up at the post office. She just walked in, all timid and mousey, like she is at first, and started talking to me from the other side of the glass. I'd wanted to go back up to Mel's college to find her, see if I could get to the bottom of the whole thing, but I couldn't afford to take time off work. We were real busy, you see. And with Mel being home, there was more pressure. I just couldn't afford the time.

'So when she came to the front of the line and started talking to me, I had no idea who she was. If I'd known, I'd have had it out with her right there. Probably would've called the police, or something. But I didn't know. And after that conversation, it started.'

'What did?' said Jason, listening intently now.

'It starts off slow, like a candle burning down. When I was around Mel after that, I'd have these little moments, passages of time, where I'd look at her and couldn't for the life of me remember her name. Then I'd get it back, and it'd be ok again. I thought it was just old age, or maybe the first signs of somethin' more. I didn't say anything then, and I regret that. Lord forgive me, I do.

'It got worse real fast. Mel would come into the room and I'd just stare at her like she was some stranger. I think once I even asked how she'd gotten into the house. She had to shake me back to myself a couple of times. That really frightened her. She could tell I was slipping away. She took me to see the doctor but he couldn't find anything wrong with me. I didn't know it at the time, but the doc wasn't entirely sure who Mel was by then, either.

'I fell in and out of it for about a week before I was gone. I don't remember exactly what happened, but I think I might have yelled at her. Maybe even pushed her away, when she was trying to shake me. There could have been more than that. But she disappeared around that time and I didn't see her again. Not until I opened the newspaper one morning in work and saw her photo next to a picture of the tree they'd found her hanging from. When I saw that, the same thing happened to me as happened to you in the car. I had a breakdown, right there in the post office, and they sent me home. There wasn't even a name under her photo, either, because no-one knew who she was anymore. They'd taken it from one of those photobooth pictures they found in her purse - there'd been friends in those pictures before then, but they'd vanished, of course. The caption just said "The unidentified woman".

Jason swallowed. His mouth had gone dry now.

'I remembered her after that. I remembered everything. As soon as I was able, I went to the store and bought a shotgun, and I headed for the house I knew she was livin' in. Not her house, of course, just one she'd taken, like she does. But on the way, I got into an accident. It was raining and I crashed. They had to put me into a coma for three months.'

Abruptly, Maurice stood up. He walked over to the sink and set his mug into it. Jason waited.

'By the time I got out of hospital, I'd lost everything. My job, my home. My only girl. Thought about killin' myself plenty of times in those days, for sure. But I was angry, and that anger kept me alive. It burns through your soul. If it hadn't been for that rage, I'd have gone to Mel's tree and followed her lead. Would've been happy to do it. But the rage kept me going.

'The only good thing that came out of the crash was the fact that Evie thought I'd died in it. Maybe I had, at some point, and maybe that broke the connection, whatever hold she had on me. Maybe the coma did it. But either way, she didn't come after me again. And that's when I started having the dreams I told you about.'

'The dreams that guided you,' Jason said.

'That's right.' Maurice came back to the table. 'Thought they were just night-mares at first. Real bad ones, the kind you think you won't ever wake from. They were so vivid I was convinced they were really happening. You know the kind?'

'Yeah.' Jason recalled the image of the black creature chasing him through the school (before he'd *actually* been chased by Evelyn) and shivered.

'They were dreams about other people, folks I'd never met, and they almost always ended with them dying in nasty-ass ways. And they were so *vivid* and clear that I started thinking maybe they were more than just dreams, after everything that'd happened with Mel, and I started writin' them down after I woke up, as detailed as possible. I ended up with a notebook full of random facts about total strangers all across the country: their names, places they lived, who their spouses were, where they worked. More besides.

'After a while - this was a few weeks after I came out of the coma and was livin' by myself again in some fleabag apartment - I realized there was a pattern in the dreams. Well, in the locations, anyway. They were all pretty spread out, coverin' dozens of towns and cities in different states, but they were always moving' roughly in one direction - east - and each place was within a few hundred miles of the last, matchin' the order of the dreams. It was a pattern, a trail.'

'Her trail,' Jason said.

'Exactly that,' Maurice replied, tapping the table. 'I started my research and found out that each of the places in my dreams had suffered a tragedy in recent times. Obviously that was harder to pinpoint in the bigger places - too many tragedies - but in the smaller towns, they were easy to spot. I'd find them on the websites of local papers, or in online groups, that sort've thing. And they were almost always the same.'

Jason didn't want to say it, but he found he couldn't help himself - he and Maurice had slipped into a pattern of their own now.

'Suicides.'

Maurice nodded grimly. 'Most of them, yeah. Some were just people who'd lost their minds and usually ended up in the nearest asylum after doing something crazy in public. One fella in Wyoming ran up and down the town mall screamin' his lungs out, even took off all his clothes and threw his underwear at a security guard before they stopped him. None of them ever came back from that, either. They were committed and then abandoned. Lost causes. But like you say, most of them were suicides, like my Mel.'

Maurice paused again, and this time, Jason felt a genuine stab of pity for the guy. He was a stranger who'd snatched him from town, taken him off to some remote place, gone through his personal belongings, and who knew what else? But he couldn't deny the fact that he'd also saved his life. And what's more, he believed his story.

'After a while,' Maurice continued, 'I upped sticks and started following the trail. In the first few places on the list, I tried approachin' the families of those it'd happened to, but I soon learned that was a bad idea. I'm not the shiniest penny in the jar, but when the bereaved husband heads for the gun cabinet, you know it's time you were goin', you know?

'Anyway, I started skipping places, tryin' to catch up with her. Because I knew now what it was, and I knew she was at the other end of it, doin' just what she'd done to Mel to some other poor soul. I say "soul" because it wasn't always the woman she took the place of, neither. Sometimes it was a man, and in those cases, a woman who'd never displayed the slightest inclination towards her own gender was suddenly convinced she'd always been so, even if she had kids. I've no idea how Evie explained those ones away, or even why she bothered to do it, but she always got away with it. And in the end, the families of the one she chose were left in pieces.'

'How *does* she choose?'

'Beats me, there never seems to be any rhyme or reason to it. I'm sure in her own twisted way she chooses them specifically. I don't know how. But I think it makes her stronger, taking them. That's why she has to keep doing it. When her victim dies or goes mad, the spell breaks and she has to move on to the next one, to start again. She feeds off them.'

Feeds off them, Jason repeated internally.

'What is she?'

'Evil,' said Maurice. 'Evil made flesh.'

Neither of them spoke for a moment. Outside, the wind was picking up.

'She was in my house,' Jason said, trying not to remember the sensation of someone standing behind him, but remembering it nonetheless. 'I dreamt about her, and then I heard her. She banged on my bedroom door and I heard her voice. She... what?'

Maurice was shaking his head. 'It's not her, in those moments. She's not really there - she just appears to be. It's how she screws with you. She did it to me and I know she's done it to others. But it definitely *feels* real.'

'It did.'

'Always does. But I'm pretty sure she can only be in one place at one time, which is why I'm pretty certain she can be killed.' Maurice drew one of the playing cards towards him on the table. Jason couldn't see what it was.

'You're going to try to kill her?' he said.

'I mean to,' Maurice replied. He flipped over the card, smirked, flipped it back. 'That's why I've followed her all the way here. It's taken months. I've... failed plenty of times along the way, too. There were plenty of good folks I might've been able to save if I'd acted faster, been smarter. But this time, it's different. I know it is. I've never gotten this far before. It's never been like this.'

'Why?'

'Because her victim - Lou - is still alive, even after all this time. Normally the whole thing only lasts about a week, but something's changed. And I think you have something to do with that, kid. You're the spanner in the works.'

Jason was about to ask why and then disagree with whatever explanation Maurice had for him, but before he could, the older man stood up again.

'Listen, Jason, I've got to go.'

'What?' Jason said, louder than he'd intended. The prospect of being alone in the cabin, somewhere in the woods where kids went missing, didn't appeal to him at all.

Maurice had already lifted his heavy-looking coat from where it'd been draped over one of the kitchen chairs and was pulling it on.

'I haven't left this place since we got here, 'cept to grab something from the car. I have to go check on Lou, at the hospital.'

'She's in hospital?' Jason replied, standing now. Memories of Mrs Jennings (or rather, more simply, the awareness of her existence) flooded back to him faster with each passing minute. 'What happened to her?'

'I'll explain later,' said Maurice. He patted the pockets of his coat, located his keys and tugged them out. 'I won't be long. Just stay put and get some rest. There's some food in that coolbox. If you need to heat water for coffee or to wash up, you can use the stove - it's gas. The electric's been switched off.'

'Wait, how do I get in contact with you, if something happens?'

'My phone's out of juice,' Maurice said, going to the door behind Jason's couch. 'I'll charge it at the hospital if I can find an outlet. But you'll be fine, don't worry. No-one knows you're here. *She* doesn't know you're here.'

'But - '

'Just stay,' said Maurice, looking him in the eye. He said it with authority and Jason decided not to push back again. Not right now. 'Don't try walking back to town or anything either, you hear me? It'd be a long way to go on foot and it's cold out. You're not a prisoner here, kid - we're just pretty far away and I don't want you getting eaten by a bear, or getting hypothermia, or something. Ok?'

'Ok,' Jason said.

'Eaten by a bear. Wouldn't that be a kicker.'

Maurice looked at him for a moment, car keys in hand.

'Don't open that door for anyone other than me, alright? She could have anyone keeping watch now, even those closest to you. Maybe especially them.'

He unlocked the door and opened it. A blast of cold air shot inside through the gap, ruffling the curtains.

'If anything does happen,' Maurice added, 'there's a double-barrelled shotgun under the bed in the next room. Use it, if you have to. Just in case. And bolt this door after I go.'

He went outside and closed the door behind him. Jason stared at it stupidly, then crossed quickly to it and shot the bolt closed. He turned the key in the lock and stepped back, as if the door might suddenly explode inwards off its hinges and flatten him.

Use it, if you have to.

He'd never fired a gun in his life.

Jason went through to the bedroom, a space about half the size of the living area. It was dominated by a double bed that shouldn't, by all logical accounts, have been able to fit through the doorway. The duvet was smooth and as musty as the rest of the cabin - the bed hadn't been slept in for some time.

Where had Maurice slept the last two nights?

But no sooner had the thought occurred to him than the answer came along in its wake. Of course - Maurice hadn't slept at all, at least not in a bed. He'd surely seated himself in one of the armchairs or at the kitchen table and kept watch throughout the night, just in case.

There was that wonderful phrase again: *just in case*. A three-word disclaimer papering over a multitude of horrible outcomes.

Just in case Evelyn Sparrow shows up at your door with murder in her eyes and you have to blow her head clean off her shoulders. That was the just in case, right?

Jason pulled the gun out from under the bed. It was a monster, almost four feet long from butt to muzzle. He cradled it in both hands, down on his knees by the bed like he was praying, testing the weight of the weapon. It felt too heavy for him, but he supposed it'd be just fine for a bigger guy like Maurice. He broke it open and was slightly alarmed to see two slugs already loaded into the chamber. Snapping it shut again, he slid the gun back under the bed and returned to the living space.

'If I had to, I could,' he said aloud.

After a moment's hesitation he pulled the bedroom door closed behind him, then stood for what felt like the longest time he'd ever stood in one spot without moving. He listened to the whistle of wind around the cabin and the audible swaying of trees; he could also hear the rush of fast-moving water and wondered if he might be near a river. Wasn't there a big river flowing through the woods and into town? Yes, he thought, there was - it came down into Fair Creek as little more than a brook and broadened during the descent to Amber Hill, splitting into two less-impressive rivers (one of which was man-made) that ran near the outskirts of the town. How many times had he walked along the banks of those rivers, kicking pebbles into the water while listening to music, usually by himself? And here he was, right next to the parent river that fed them both, deep in the woods.

Where the witch lived.

That simple knowledge sent a wave of gooseflesh racing down his spine. The feeling was so abrupt and so powerful, in fact, that his legs, already weak from a day and a half of almost complete immobility, began to give way, and he was forced to return to the couch. He sat there, still enveloped in the silence of the cabin's interior, listening to the sounds of the forest outside. Finally, and very gradually at first, his mind began to turn the situation over.

Am I a prisoner?

No, he thought, not at all. Unless this Maurice guy was playing some sick game with him, and was perhaps hiding in the bushes outside waiting to see what he'd do, he could simply open the cabin door and walk away, any time he liked. Sure, he'd be in the middle of the woods all by himself (the woods where kids go missing) and it'd take quite some time to get back home on foot, but he was free to do that if he liked, wasn't he? And why not? What was keeping him there, now that Maurice was gone?

He looked over his shoulder at the front door, and shivered again. No, right now he didn't want to go anywhere by himself, even in broad daylight. He'd seen enough for one day... enough for one lifetime, actually. If he went anywhere now, it'd be with the guy who seemed to understand exactly what was going on, and had use of a fully-loaded, double-barrelled shotgun for good measure.

Which led to the second question: *had the guy abducted him?*

He supposed he had, on some level. He was just a kid, after all, and the other guy was a total stranger with a gun who'd taken him to an unfamiliar location while he'd been unconscious. And he *had* looked like he'd try to stop him leaving earlier, but that was before Jason had heard his side of the story. Maybe that was all he'd needed him to do - hear him out, and then decide on his own course of action. He'd offered him several opportunities to leave since getting into the station wagon (which Jason had done of his own accord), and the clearest opportunity yet was right there on a plate, ready to be taken. So yes, he'd been abducted, but no, he wasn't a prisoner. In fact, if everything Maurice had told him was true, hadn't he saved him from probable death back at the school?

He owed his life to the old man, he guessed. Still, he didn't like the fact that he'd gone into his phone and made some decisions on his behalf. That wasn't cool.

Where is my phone?

Jason stood again and found his legs had regained some strength. He performed a quick search of the living area and discovered his school backpack leaning against the other side of the old television unit, where it'd been out of his field of vision. Its contents appeared untouched, but his phone wasn't among them. Maurice had taken it.

'Bastard,' Jason muttered, going to the kitchen.

He'd said his own phone was out of charge, so he'd taken it to the hospital to top it up while checking on Mrs Jennings. *Maybe he's doing the same with mine*, Jason reasoned, opening the coolbox on the counter; inside, he found a half-empty carton of milk, a packet of processed chicken slices, and a wedge of cheddar. *Not exactly a feast.*

He closed the coolbox and rummaged through a couple of plastic bags next to them, coming away with a bag of potato chips and some Hershey's peanut-butter cups. He pulled out Maurice's chair, sat down, and began to eat.

It was possible Maurice was charging his phone for him, assuming his device was compatible. However, he knew that wasn't the most likely motivation he'd have for bringing it along with him. He'd taken a sixteen-year-old kid to an empty cabin in the woods - one he'd broken into, no doubt - while he was passed out in his car, and rather than call his mother or the authorities, he'd watched over him by himself while fabricating a cover story, one that would unravel quickly if anyone contacted Ste (who might happily go along with it if it kept his drugs trip under wraps, and Jason knew Ste was the kind of stand-up guy whose sense of self-preservation usually took priority over anything else).

Maurice had taken Jason's phone because he didn't yet trust him not to call for help, an action that would certainly lead to his arrest.

Jason munched on the potato chips, flipping over some of Maurice's cards. He had no idea what game he was playing, and he didn't much care. His nose was starting to ache again, too.

'Cards,' he muttered. 'Game for suckers.'

By the time he'd finished the bag of chips and most of the chocolate, he'd decided to forgive Maurice for "kidnapping" him. The guy had been through hell by the sounds of it. Jason also decided he could even forgive him for invading his privacy and for cutting off his communication with the outside world by taking his phone. He'd forgive him for those things, for the time being at least, because it was abundantly clear they were in the same boat right now, and until they were safe, it was probably best to stick together. Safety in numbers.

But the question was, just how long would Maurice be gone? And what exactly was Jason going to do if, for whatever reason, the guy just didn't come back?

How long should he wait before trying to get home?

Leaving the empty potato chip and chocolate wrappers on the table, he went through to the cabin's little bathroom and used the toilet. When he flushed it, the aging pipes running beneath the cabin made *donking* sounds as they ushered the waste water out to the septic tank, which would be somewhere adjacent to the building. Mr Mansford had a cabin (or *had* a cabin, at one time) and on more than one occasion in Shop had grimly recounted a time when he'd had to go in through the access riser and unblock a clogged output baffle pipe.

'Clogged with what, sir?' Jason remembered someone asking.

'Hardened shit,' Mr Mansford had responded, matter-of-factly.

Jason didn't suppose the cabin's septic tank had been cleaned out in quite some time, and when the hour came for either the owners or the sewage disposal company tasked with handling it to open those access caps and stick their head in for a look-see, the smell would be horrendous.

He washed his face, taking care not to touch his nose, which was now the deep purple-black color of healing bruises. He was also careful not to look in the little mirror nailed above the sink, just in case. He hadn't really looked in a mirror since Thursday evening.

There was a small can of deodorant on the window sill, probably Maurice's. He sprayed thoroughly under each armpit and went back into the living area again. Outside, the wind seemed to have died down a little.

He needed some fresh air.

Don't open that door for anyone other than me.

Jason hesitated, then crossed to the end of the couch and picked up his boots. Maurice must have unlaced them when he was unconscious. He'd taken off his boots, laid him on the couch and tucked him in with a patterned quilt.

'Creepy as hell,' Jason muttered, tying his laces.

He was still wearing the same clothes he'd dressed himself in on Friday morning, which seemed like a month ago now, so at least Maurice hadn't gone any further in his quest to make him comfortable. He hadn't even removed his jacket - probably wise given how cold it is in here, Jason thought.

Unlocking the door, he listened for a moment, unsure of what he expected to hear. There was still nothing out there but the whistling wind, the creaking of trees, and the rush of flowing water.

Taking a deep breath, Jason opened the door and stepped out onto the porch.

It was a chilly November morning but the sun was out, angling rays of warmth over scudding clouds and in between trees swayed lazily above the cabin. The wind - really no more than a breeze now - swept dry leaves and pine needles across the ground and gathered them into crinkling mounds of orange, yellow and brown at the edge of the parking area out front. Friday's heavy rainfall had given way to a cold, dry Saturday, and only a handful of muddy puddles now remained. A red-breasted robin flitted around a puddle to Jason's right, dipping his beak into the water, flitting again, dipping again. There were many more birds in the trees, singing and cawing.

Jason looked up the track from the cabin and saw another similar building about twenty or thirty yards away, all shuttered up for the winter. It was easily twice the size of the one Maurice had chosen and must have been at least a decade younger. Modern enough to have an alarm system, no doubt.

It was clear from where he stood that a river flowed right behind the cabin - he didn't need to look; the sound of fast-flowing water mingled with that of the breeze and the constantly-moving forest, which extended in every direction around him. On any other day, that Sunday morning in the woods might have seemed tranquil to Jason. He may even have welcomed it as a change from the never-quite-peaceful suburbs of Amber Hill, where a car always motored down the street or a dog barked to get back inside. Today, however, the ordinarily placating sounds of nature, alive and exuberant in late Fall, only made him more keenly aware of his isolation. He was far from anyone, unable to reach out meaningfully for help, at the mercy of a stranger who may not return for a long time, or at all.

'Screw this,' he said, and turned back to the door.

As he did, a memory hit him so hard and with such clarity that it stopped him in his tracks, poised at the threshold of the cabin door with the sun on his back.

It was a memory from seven years ago. He was in his backyard at home, having just come out of the house. His dad was over by the fence that separated their yard from the Marshe family next door. His back, sweaty beneath his *Led Zeppelin* t-shirt, faced Jason as he approached; he was hunched over, muttering to himself, working at something.

Jason stood nearby, unnoticed for a solid minute, before breaking the mid-summer afternoon silence. 'What're you doing, Dad?'

His father jerked, startled by the high, pre-teen voice at his shoulder.

'Holy shit, Jase! You scared me.'

He straightened up and turned to look at him. Alec Rennor was a tall man, and at thirty-five was almost painfully skinny, with sinewy limbs and dark, unkempt hair. His son would inherit those particular genetic traits over the course of the coming years, whether he liked it or not.

'Sorry. I was just asking.'

'I know,' said Alec, 'it's ok.' He pushed greasy hair away from his forehead and almost stabbed himself in the eye with the screwdriver he was holding. 'Shit on a brick, that was close!'

'You need to be careful, Dad.'

'Says who?' replied Alec, noting that the boy had sounded unnervingly like his mother just then. But he grinned down at him, and after a second or two, Jason returned it. 'Where's your Mom?'

'Out, I think.'

'Out where?'

'I dunno.'

I'll bet she told you where and you didn't listen, right?'

Jason shrugged and Alec turned back to the fence.

'What're you doing?' Jason asked again, coming round to see now.

Alec squatted down and gestured towards the wooden post he'd been working at. Like the others, it was badly in need of painting, and starting to rot.

'Just taking a few of these old screws out, you know? They're all rusted. Your mom was... asked me to do it, and I kept forgetting.'

Jason looked at the screwdriver in his dad's hand, and back at the screw. It was the last one still lodged in the post - the others were scattered in the grass at its base. The Rennor family toolbox sat open a few feet away, drinking in a rare dose of fresh air.

'Is it not coming out?'

'Nope.' Alec went back to it again; somewhere down the street, a child shrieked, then laughed heartily. 'This one's jammed in there and rusted to shit, unfortunately.'

Alec gritted his teeth and leaned into the post, trying to make the tip of the screwdriver bite into the brown-orange drive of the screw, but it wouldn't catch. Each time he twisted the screwdriver, it chewed further into the screw, stripping away the drive, and each time that happened, Alec Rennor got a little angrier than he'd been before.

Jason, shielding his eyes against the bright summer sunshine, watched this play out for five more failed attempts before venturing what he'd really come to ask.

'Dad, are you and Mom getting divorced?'

Alec stopped twisting the screwdriver. Jason saw his shoulders sag and knew he'd been waiting for the question. It hung uncomfortably between them and nine-year-old Jason suddenly wished he could snatch it back again, but it was too late for that. You couldn't put the toothpaste back in the tube.

'Who told you that?' his father asked, still squatted down on his haunches, not looking at his son. 'Did your mom tell you that?'

'No, she didn't,' Jason replied, eyes on the grass at his feet. It had wilted during another hot and dry June, and was now just barely tinged with green. 'I heard you last week, when you were talking in the kitchen. Well, you were shouting. That's what woke me up.'

'I wasn't... *we* weren't shouting,' said Alec, catching himself. He sighed. 'We were just talking about it, that's all.'

'So you're not getting divorced?'

'I didn't say that, Jase.'

'So you *are*?'

'Jason!' It left his mouth far too sharply and he regretted it right away. The boy had recoiled at it, as though he'd swung a hand. It wasn't the first time he'd seen that happen.

Alec shifted his feet to face him. His long legs were beginning to ache from crouching for so long but he didn't want to stand again - each time he did, he felt a little faint. The curse of being tall.

'Look,' he said, choosing his words as carefully as his simmering temper would allow. 'We just talked about it, that's all. It's something we've talked about for a while, actually. It doesn't mean anything's decided yet, ok? You don't need to worry about it. Not one bit.'

Jason looked into his father's eyes and knew that wasn't true, and he reached for the conclusion that seemed to fit best with his untainted, child logic.

'So you don't love Mom anymore?'

'Of *course* I do,' Alec said, almost affronted. 'I'll always love your Mom. It's just that... things change over time, you know? Love can change, even.'

Jason felt the soles of his feet set a little firmer in the grass.

'No it can't,' he said.

'What can't?'

'Love. It doesn't change. If it does, then it was never really love in the first place.'

Alec chewed on that for a second, and then chose the wrong response, one that Jason had perhaps been expecting and already had an answer for. 'Trust me, it can. It's not something you can understand now, but when you're older, it'll make sense. Trust me, Jase.'

'So does that mean you won't always love me?'

'Of course I will,' Alec replied. He could feel that simmering temper, the one that had gotten him into trouble so many times in the past, the one that was effectively bringing his tenuous marriage to a close, starting to bubble up. 'You know I always will, no matter what.'

'But you *just said* love can change.'

Jason's hands were balled into fists now and his voice was rising. Alec glanced across the yard, towards the Falpert house next door; he wondered if the Marshe family were in theirs now behind him.

'Jason -'

'That's what you said.'

Alec turned back to the fence post and jabbed at the screw. His hand was shaking and he missed it the first time.

'We'll talk about this later, ok? When your mom gets back.' The screwdriver found its target; he twisted it and it didn't bite, shredding the drive further. A volcanic surge of anger leapt upwards in his chest and he smothered it. 'Not out here.'

'You could at least be honest about it, Dad.'

'Seriously, Jase, I -'

The tip of the screwdriver slipped free of the screw. He'd been leaning hard against the post and his momentum carried his hand into it. The ball of his thumb banged painfully off the wood and he cursed, dropping the screwdriver in the grass.

'Shit-damn, Jason,' he spat. 'Will you just *leave* it? That hurt like -'

'Oh for FUCK SAKE DAD!'

Jason stomped across to the toolbox. Alec, who'd never heard his son swear like that before, stared open-mouthed as the boy grabbed the hammer and came towards him. For one delirious second, he thought he was going to swing it at his skull, and wouldn't the Falperts and Marshes have something to talk about then? Instead, Jason flipped it round to the clawed end and, in one fluid motion, rammed it over the end of the screw.

'Watch out,' Jason said.

Alec stood up much too quickly. His head swam as blood rushed downwards through his body and he had to grip the top of the fence for support. Suddenly, the wooden board beneath his hand began to shake violently as Jason pulled on the hammer, bringing it towards him with both hands, again and again, tugging at the stripped and rusted screw. The rotted wood around it split, then splintered, then finally gave way.

With one final grunt of effort, Jason yanked the screw free of the post, taking a generous shard of wood with it. He straightened up, pulled the screw out of the hammer claw and handed it to his dad. His face was flushed and he was shaking, as much from the physical exertion as the adrenaline rush he'd got from swearing at his father.

Alec took the screw from him. Jason held his gaze for a moment, then went back to the toolbox and replaced the hammer.

'Sometimes you just have to pull them out,' he said. 'It's harder, but it works.'

He'd walked back to the house after that without another word. Just a few months later, his parents were divorced.

Jason opened the cabin door and went back inside, locking it behind him.

Maurice came back after dark. The wind had died down completely by then; the only sounds coming from outside the cabin walls had been the steady but muted rush of river water and the occasional gekkering of foxes somewhere nearby. Inside, the cabin had been almost oppressively silent, and Jason had practically jumped out of his skin when the double-knock came on the door.

He went to the window and squinted round the edge of the curtain, but it was too dark to tell who - if anyone - was outside. He was about to head for the bedroom to retrieve the gun when Maurice rapped on the door again, harder this time, and said, 'Let me in, kid.'

Relieved, Jason unlocked the door. Maurice came inside with his hood up and a bag in each hand. One was a plastic carrier Jason recognized from *Al's Convenience Store*; the other was a brown paper bag with grease spots around the bottom. He couldn't quite smell the fried food inside it, but the sight of the familiar bag emblazoned with a yellow *M* was enough to start his empty stomach doing loop-the-loops.

He locked the door again. It had only been open for a matter of seconds, but it'd been enough to drag the temperature inside the room down a notch.

'Where the hell've you been?' he said, his relief at Maurice's return now melting back into frustration at being left alone in the woods since that morning.

'Sorry,' said Maurice, dropping the bags on the dining table. 'Took longer than I thought.'

'You've been gone all day,' Jason snapped, and instantly imagined he must sound absurdly like a bored housewife scolding her husband.

'Like I said, it took longer than I thought it would.' Maurice pushed back his hood and began unzipping his overcoat.

'Have you got my phone?'

'Yes.'

'Well can I have it?'

'Come and eat this food before it gets any colder.'

'Phone first.'

'Boy, I swear.' With a scowl of exasperation, Maurice fished the phone from his pocket and came just short of slamming it down on the table. 'Come and get it, and maybe eat some food while you're over here.'

277

Biting his tongue, Jason drifted towards the kitchen. He picked up his phone but found he was suddenly ravenous. He slipped it into the pocket of his jeans and sat down.

'Why'd it take so long, anyway?' he asked, hoping the change of subject might go some way to placating the other man, who was clearly pissed at him.

Maurice draped his coat over the back of a chair, then ran a hand over his face. In the weak light emitted by the gas heater, he appeared dreadfully drained and ragged.

'She had people watching the hospital,' he said, lowering himself into the chair as Jason removed burgers and fries from the bag. 'I didn't even realize until I was walking from the parking lot to the front entrance. If I hadn't looked up when I did, they'd have seen me for sure.'

'Who?'

'An old woman by the doors. She was standin' there in her robe and slippers with one of those zimmer frames, out there in the wind, just staring around her like she was high or whatever. I'll bet she'd been out there for hours, standin' in that same spot, guarding the doors. Probably has pneumonia by now. Not that *she'll* care.'

'That's wild,' said Jason. He had the burger box cupped in both hands; Maurice noticed and waved a dismissive hand, saying, 'Eat.' Jason obeyed.

'There was another one - a delivery driver. I always know them when I see them. He was sat in his van within sight of the entrance, just staring around like the old woman. No coffee or newspaper, no phone. Just turnin' his head this way n'that, like one of them bobble-head dolls people stick on their dash. Him and the old woman were watching' to see if we'd try gettin' to her.'

'We?' Jason replied through a mouthful of burger.

Maurice nodded, pulling one of the bags of fries towards him. 'Reckon she knows I'm around by now, or she suspects at least. And she's bound to know you didn't go home on Friday. This is how it goes. Once she gets... settled... in a place, she sets up protection all around her, just to make sure no-one interferes until she's done. Lou's still alive - alive and well, seemingly - so she's far from done yet.'

'You saw her? Mrs Jennings?'

'Yup.' Maurice stuffed fries in his mouth and chewed for a moment. 'Had to wait a couple of hours before an orderly noticed the old woman and took her back inside. Practically dragged her, too. Then the place started gettin' busier and the delivery driver had to move on. That's when I managed to get inside.

'Thought there'd be someone guardin' her room, but there wasn't. Maybe there had been and they'd left to do somethin' else. Who knows. Either way, I was able to walk right in there and sit with her awhile. It was after lunch by then, I think, and she'd fallen back to sleep. She never knew I was there.'

'How'd she look?' Jason said.

'Thin, tired. Not much like the picture I showed you. The whole thing's taking its toll on her now, as it always does. I don't know this for sure, but I think the longer Evie's around, the more her victim suffers. It's like she's slowly tappin' the life out of her, one drop at a time, and soon there'll be nothin' left to take. But she's alive, so that's something. And the bandage is off her head too, so they must be gettin' ready to give her the boot. When that happens, I'm not sure what - '

Jason swallowed and said, 'We need to get her.'

'How's that?'

'You said she's looking tired and drained but her injuries are getting better, right? So she'll leave the hospital soon, and then where will she go?'

Maurice took a bite of his burger. 'Home, I guess.'

'Right, so we have to get to her first. If she goes home, Miss Sparrow... Evie... will just, I dunno... finish her off. And if she's gone and there's nothing left to take, Evie'll just move on to the next person and we'll lose her. And that'll be our chance gone.'

Maurice eyed him thoughtfully. 'So it's *our* chance now?'

'Damn right it is. I'm in this now, too. And there's part of me that would be happy to just let her leave and hope things go back to normal, after a while. I don't know how much I care what she does in the next place she goes to, or who she hurts. I wish I could say I did, but it'd just be a lie - no-one's helped this place, until you came along at least, so the next town will just have to help themselves. Maybe they'll have better luck and she'll try to take the place of someone who's a professional assassin, or something. Selfish, I know, but whatever.'

'Harsh, kid.'

'Yeah, but *you're* not here on some righteous mission either, are you? You just want to kill her because of what she did to your daughter. To Melanie.'

Maurice lowered his burger and sat back in his chair. 'I suppose that's about right.'

'Ok. So like I said, part of me wants to just ride it out and wait for her to leave - that's the shit-scared, cowardly part of me, I'll admit that - but the other part of me's thinking like you now. I want to stop her. Not just for myself, or for Mrs Jennings, or for any of the people she's hurt along the way. I didn't like Rick but she killed him and there're probably others, and it's still not *just* for any of them - I want to stop her from getting *away* with it. Because you're right - she's evil, pure and simple, and I don't like seeing evil people, or whatever the fuck she is, getting away with it, consequence-free. Again. I want to stop her because she deserves to be stopped.'

Maurice grinned, and Jason thought it might have been the first time he'd seen him do it.

'Good enough for me, boy,' he said. 'First thing tomorrow, let's start planning how we make that happen.'

Watch out, now.

He's here.

He's come all the way from the West, sniffing along after me with his nose in the dirt, like I'm his bitch in heat. I thought he was dead, but the wrinkled old bastard survived somehow.

Somehow.

Watch out.

Keep your eyes peeled, children.

We're so close to the end now. The final chapter in our little story. And then we'll close the book and I'll mosey along to my next watering hole. Time's a-wastin', now.

There's no rest for The Wicked.

But there's the small matter of the boy, isn't there?

Oh yes.

THE BOY.

The skinny little rat slithered through my fingers, didn't he? Right when I almost had him. Golly-gosh, I would have enjoyed that one, alright. Oh, how he'd have screamed.

I fear he might have gotten to him, the sly old bastard. That was unexpected, but it's not the end of the world. It's too late, now.

Still, watch out.

And if we should fail?

WE FAIL?

We won't fail, my children. Stick with me and I'll see us through. Learn your lines, play your parts. Dance on your strings. Dance, dance, dance.

And if you have to, kill.

Fourteen

3 days before Thanksgiving

Monday.

Jason woke to the sound of birdsong and Maurice snoring in the next room. When he yawned, his breath came out in a white puff. Yesterday morning, the interior of the cabin had been chilly - today, it was freezing.

'Maurice,' he called, sitting up on the couch. His back ached and he groaned, pressing into the small of it with his fist. *What the hell's it going to be like when I'm older?* 'Mr Baxter!'

In the bedroom, the old man emitted a final sleep-snort, and fell silent.

'Mr Bax - '

'I'm awake,' came the groggy reply. Jason heard movement on the bed.

He swung his legs off the couch, stood and stretched, wincing as every muscle in his still-growing teenage body cracked and snapped in protest. Beyond the cabin walls, the river flowed unceasingly through the forest, ushering countless gallons of ice-cold water down the gradual wooded slope into Amber Hill.

Where she *is, right now.*

After they'd eaten yesterday evening's nutritious dinner, the stress of the day's events (and the other days that preceded it) had hit Maurice hard, and he'd retired to bed. He'd planned to sleep in one of the two armchairs in the living area, as he'd done on Friday and Saturday night, but Jason insisted he take the bed and volunteered to stay awake for a while longer, "to keep watch", just in case. He sensed that on any other night Maurice would have refused (the man was stubborn as a mule), but he'd had no energy to resist and had lumbered to the darkness of the bedroom, following the torch light on his recently-charged phone.

Jason's phone had also been charged - Maurice had availed of a free outlet in Lou's hospital room - but he quickly discovered he had no service out here in the woods and couldn't do much with it. There might have been signal outside the cabin, but he sure as shit wasn't going out there in the dark by himself.

His mother hadn't messaged him since Saturday, when she'd simply texted 'Are you ok?', to which Maurice had, somehow, succinctly replied on his behalf with 'Yes.'

Jason knew his mom well, and had never been bothered by her poor communication before - he supposed she trusted him by now, or she just didn't have the time or inclination to track his every move, especially when *he* was usually so bad at letting her know where he was. Standard procedure for a sixteen-year-old, right? But even the enigmatic Judy Rennor, poor as she was at texting, would have contacted him by now.

Had Miss Sparrow gotten to her? Would his mom now no longer recognize his face if he walked into the room?

Or was that only the case with people who knew Mrs Jennings?

Or was all of this just one big nightmarish mess of paranoia and delusion?

Either way, he hoped his mom was ok, even if she didn't seem to give a flying fart-rag about him.

Jason pulled on his boots and went to the kitchen. He filled the pot and set it on the gas stove, parting the curtains to peer outside while the water heated up. It was still mostly dark, but light had begun to break through the trees and glance off the river, glimmering in the dawn gloom.

Maurice ambled out of the bedroom just as Jason took the pot off the stove.

'You want coffee?'

Maurice grunted a reply and sat down at the table.

'How d'you take it?'

'Black. Nothin' else.'

Jason made coffee and poured two cups, handing one to Maurice. He cradled it in one hand, staring wearily into space while Jason took the half-empty milk carton out of the cool box. Maurice had bought a box of Cheerios at some point but still hadn't opened them.

What does this guy eat, besides fast food?

'You sleep?' Maurice croaked, drawing his coffee mug towards him.

'Yeah, for a bit,' said Jason. 'It's hard to these days.'

'Yup.' Maurice agreed. 'Been takin' pills to help me get over for a long time now. Puts me into a real deep slumber. Usually deals with the dreams, too. I only stop takin' them when I need to get back on her trail.' He took a wet slurp of coffee, sucking rather than sipping it, the way older people sometimes do. 'Can get you some too, if you need 'em.'

'No thanks,' said Jason. 'Not yet, anyway.'

'Fair enough.'

Jason retrieved a plastic camping bowl from one of the kitchen cupboards and joined Maurice at the table; once again, the strangeness of the whole situation impressed itself upon him. He opened the box of cereal.

'So what's the plan?' he asked.

Maurice perused the contents of his mug for a moment.

'Think it's time we went to get her,' he said. 'Lou, I mean. It's been long enough. Thought about tryin' to bring her here yesterday but that hospital was so damn *quiet* inside, it gave me the heebie jeebies. Felt like the place was just waitin' for me to try it, and if I had done, there'd have been a whole squad of doctors and nurses - *her* spies - ready to grab me when I stepped off the elevator.'

'So you think the whole town's under her... spell, or whatever?'

'Not everyone, no. Only the ones she's been in regular contact with. Just enough to keep an eye out, 'til she's done.'

'Then how do we get her out?' Jason said, tipping Cheerios into the bowl.

'Think one of us will have to do it,' said Maurice, 'while the other one creates a distraction. You know, like in the movies.'

'Sure,' replied Jason, opening the milk carton. 'I'll blow something up outside and you sneak in when no-one's looking.' He poured milk into the bowl and the Cheerios bobbed to the surface.

'Maybe not as dramatic as that,' Maurice said, grinning sardonically. 'As long as it gets their attention, it'll... hey, wait.'

Jason looked up, a spoonful of Cheerios halfway to his open mouth.

'That milk,' Maurice said. 'You don't smell it?'

'What d'you mean?'

'It's off.' Maurice reached over the table and took the carton. He brought it to his nose, sniffed, and recoiled with a grimace. 'Holy shit, it's definitely off. The ice packs in that box must have warmed up. Put the lid back on that, quick.'

He pushed the carton back across the table. Jason sniffed the opening but got no more than a faint hint of sourness. He screwed the lid back on.

'You couldn't smell that? Geez, it stinks.'

'No,' said Jason, frowning down at his bowl. 'I couldn't. My nose got broke last week and I still can't smell properly.'

Why's that important?

Something was trying to connect in his brain but couldn't quite get there. Two pieces of a jigsaw puzzle, based on some information he'd absorbed along the way, almost aligned. Then it was gone again.

'Sorry kid, you'll have to eat somethin' else,' said Maurice. 'Then we'll get to planning how we break our friend Louise out of that hospital.'

'Wasn't that hungry anyway,' lied Jason, pushing the bowl away.

It started to rain shortly before noon.

They waited in the cabin all day, playing cards, drinking coffee. Maurice said it'd be best to go to the hospital later in the day, when it'd likely be quieter. Jason agreed. According to Maurice, visiting hours were after six during the week, so it would make sense to try and get to her in the window between dinner and anyone showing up with fresh flowers, though he suspected there was very little chance of that happening. Jason agreed with that, too.

They left the cabin at five and drove to town. By then, it was full dark and the trees lining the road were nothing but ominous black shapes against a sprawling starfield above. It was the first time Jason had left the cabin since Maurice brought him there.

'I won't use it unless I have to,' Maurice said, squinting at the road ahead between the swishing wiper blades. He was referring to the shotgun, which he'd lain across the back seat under the patterned quilt from the cabin. 'I don't plan on killin' anyone. The shells in that gun are reserved for *her*.'

Jason had noticed Maurice seemed to avoid using Evelyn's name unless he had to, and he'd soon acquired the habit himself. It was as if saying it too many times would summon her, like the Candyman. The last thing either of them wanted was for her to suddenly appear in the back seat of the Sable, grinning sweetly while she leveled the shotgun at their headrests.

'So you'll shoot her if you get the chance?' Jason asked.

'Yessir. I would've gone to her house and tried it already if I knew exactly where she lived.'

'And that'll do it? Shooting her, I mean?'

Maurice chewed on that for a hundred yards of road. The rain was coming down hard now, far heavier than it had been in the woods a few miles back. Puddles were already forming along the curbs.

'I hope so,' he said at last. 'Damn well worth a try, anyway.'

'Take her head off if you can,' Jason said, only mildly surprised to hear the words come out of his mouth. 'If she's still going after that, well... we'll cross that bridge.'

She can't survive a direct shot to the head, right?

In truth, he didn't know what she could take. He didn't even know what she *was*.

They were in town now, driving along East Main. Every store window was decorated for Turkey Day: turkeys, pumpkins, pilgrims, the works. Amber Hill's Thanksgiving celebration was just two days away.

There was a good deal of traffic - most people were getting out of work around now - and they made slow progress through town to the hospital. Maurice gripped the wheel with one hand and patted his knee nervously with the other. His eyes darted back and forth across the traffic and wet sidewalks ahead of them, constantly scouting. Jason knew what he was looking out for, and he was fairly sure he wouldn't find them, not in this weather in a town this small. He was searching for cops.

They turned left at the intersection and the traffic calmed noticeably, though they still weren't exactly flying. Jason leaned his head against the passenger-side window and watched the sidewalk go by. He saw a woman running to her car with her bag above her head; she was dragging a little girl in a yellow slicker by the hand, and the kid was doing her best to jump in every puddle they encountered along the way. Jason wondered if either of them had been caught up in Miss Sparrow's sphere of influence, which seemed to expand and intensify with each passing day, and if they had, were they now her spies as well, like the old woman and delivery driver Maurice had seen?

Were he and Maurice the only ones left now?

'Lou'll have to take the bed.'

'What?'

'We'll have to give her the bed,' Maurice repeated, 'in the cabin. She's the lady, after all.'

'Right.' They drew alongside the woman and the little girl on the rain-soaked sidewalk, and then they were gone. 'You can have the couch.'

'You keep it,' said Maurice. 'I can sleep in one of the armchairs, or on the floor. Wouldn't be the first time I've had to do it.'

'No seriously, you should take it. I mean, you're... you know...'

Maurice looked at him. 'Boy, just how old do you think I am?'

'Didn't you say - '

'I'm kiddin', son.' He grinned and went back to scanning the street. 'I said I was near sixty, and that was no lie. Feel every day of it, too. But I'm not too old to sleep in an armchair.'

'Your call,' said Jason. Then: 'How long are we going to stay in that cabin, once we have her? There isn't much food.'

Maurice's smile fell away. 'I know.'

'And she'll be looking for her, won't she? As soon as she knows she's gone?'

'Yes.'

'So what the hell are we doing after this, Maurice?'

'Honestly,' replied the old man. 'I can't say for sure.'

It was after five-thirty by the time they reached Amber Hill General. It was an ugly white-washed building with a modern, glass-fronted entrance; a single-lane marked PICK UP AND SET DOWN ONLY curved up to the entrance area, branching off from the main drive. Maurice took the Sable up as far as the signs marking the parking lot turn-off and stopped.

'Alright,' said Maurice, leaning towards the windshield. 'See anything?'

Jason peered towards the hospital building. Most of the windows were lit up, but the place still looked dreary in the rain. A car pulled up to the entrance and deposited a nurse under the shelter of the canopy, then drove off. There was no-one else outside.

'Looks clear,' he said.

'Yeah,' Maurice agreed. 'Don't like that.'

DAVID MCILROY

They watched the hospital for another minute. The rain fell in sheets, turning the lights illuminating the front of the building into a yellow haze along the bottom of the windshield. The wipers continued to *whump* across the glass, but they were fighting a losing battle.

'Ok,' said Maurice. 'You set?'

'Yeah.'

'You know which room is hers?'

'Yeah.'

'Tell me.'

'Room sixteen, fourth floor. Private.'

'Good. Call me right away if something's wrong, and then get the hell out of there.'

'Will do.'

Jason unbuckled his seat belt and stepped out of the car. He slammed the door and tugged up his hood, but his head was already wet. Holding the rim of the hood to stop it blowing back in the breeze, he jogged up the drive towards the hospital entrance, glancing back just once to see Maurice turn off towards the parking lot.

It couldn't have taken him more than thirty seconds to reach the entrance and get under the canopy, but by the time he did, his clothes felt soaked through. He pushed back his hood and walked to the doors, half expecting them to sense it was *him* and remain closed. Instead, they slid apart automatically and he walked into the building, hands deep in his jacket pockets.

The hospital lobby was warm and bright. It was also completely empty.

Glancing around and fully aware of how suspicious he must look, Jason crossed to the elevators. He looked towards the reception desk and saw it was unmanned, though a steaming mug of coffee and tented paperback were next to the computer. Whoever had been there would be back momentarily.

He reached the elevators and punched the call button. The red digits above the doors counted down from six, too slowly for his liking. He realized his heart was thumping.

Why is no-one here? he thought, looking around the empty lobby area. The nurse who'd just come inside was gone. *This is a hospital. When are hospitals ever empty?*

288

He remembered sitting in one of the faded blue chairs opposite the reception desk when he was little, around seven years old, when he'd twisted his ankle badly after dropping out of a tree playing commandos with Bill and Josh Bennet, who lived on his street. More recently, he remembered sitting on one of those chairs after Curtis Lawrence's flailing arm had smashed his nose. His mom has sat next to him on both occasions, and both times she'd told him he "should be more careful, he was getting too old for this sort of thing", before slipping outside for a smoke.

The elevator *dinged* and the doors opened. A man in a suit stepped out, glanced at the messy-haired teenager with the thing on his nose standing nearby, and strode off towards the exit without a word.

At least someone's here.

Jason stepped into the elevator and pressed the button for the fourth floor. The doors closed and the car began to rise.

After much discussion earlier that day, Maurice had eventually agreed to let him go for Lou. Jason had rightly pointed out that she actually *knew* him from school and might be more inclined to listen to his story. Plus, Maurice had already been spotted in town more than once, so Miss Sparrow's little spies would be on the lookout for him specifically. She may not even think he was alive after the scare she'd given him on Friday.

He'd saved Maurice's cell phone number in case of emergency, and together they'd agreed a very simple plan for that evening: Jason would go into the hospital and get Lou while Maurice kept watch nearby; if either of them spotted any signs of trouble, they'd call the other one and get out right away. The *how* of the whole thing wasn't especially important, just as long as they both escaped.

And it was imperative that they make that escape with Mrs Jennings.

Ding. Fourth floor.

The elevator doors opened and Jason stepped off. As he did, the doors of the other elevator to his left closed. He was now at the end of a short hallway which split to the left and right at the far end. He walked along it quickly, approaching a sign with arrows pointing both directions. The arrow pointing right read PRIVATE ROOMS and he followed it, passing a couple of vending machines on the way.

There was no-one in the private hallway. No nurses, no doctors. Not even an orderly.

Jason walked along it as fast as possible, his wet boots clocking on the floor as he read the numbers on the doors. Most were open, revealing patients lying or sitting in bed. Those who were awake were watching TV or reading, waiting for their families to arrive for their daily visit. A few of them glanced hopefully his way as he passed.

He came to room sixteen. The door was closed.

Taking a breath, he gripped the handle in one sweaty hand and turned it. The door was unlocked; he opened it and stepped into Lou's room.

It was empty.

'Shit,' he said.

The bed was unmade and looked as though it had been slept in recently. An empty tumbler and half-full water jug were on the nightstand next to a vinyl-covered hospital chair, occupied solely by a folded newspaper. If any of Lou's belongings had been in the room before, they weren't now.

'Shit, shit,' said Jason again.

He checked the bathroom, then checked round the other side of the bed, and then *under* the bed for good measure. Mrs Jennings was gone.

Almost trembling with adrenaline, Jason pulled his phone from his pocket and hit Maurice's number. It rang twice before he picked up.

'Jason, what is it?'

'She's not here.'

'What?'

Jason went to the door, casting a final glance around the room, as if he'd expected Mrs Jennings to pop out from behind the curtain. 'She's gone. She's not in her room.'

'You're in the right room?'

'Yes.'

'Room sixteen, on the fourth floor?'

'Yes!' he snapped back, going out the door. 'I'm in the right room. I think she was here recently, but she's - '

He stopped just outside Lou's room, facing down the hall towards the elevators.

'Jason?' Maurice's voice came through the speaker, tinny and far-off as Jason lowered the phone from his ear. 'Kid, what's happening? Jason...'

Jason ended the call and slipped the phone back in his jacket pocket.

'Mr Rennor,' said the man standing in the hallway, one room down from Lou's. 'What're you doing here?'

He was a doctor (complete with white coat and stethoscope around his neck) with gray-white hair and a finely-trimmed white beard. He had a metal chart tucked under one arm; he looked at Jason over the rim of his spectacles and cocked an eyebrow.

'Weekday visiting hours don't start until six, son. Are you here to see someone?'

'I, um...'

where are all the other doctors and nurses and orderlies shouldn't there be more people here right now

'... I must have come too early, sorry - '

'I'd say so,' said the doctor, smiling now. Jason recognized him then - he was the doctor who'd examined his freshly-broken nose exactly one week ago - and he thought that smile should have been warm and pleasant, but it wasn't. His eyes went to the name tag pinned to the doctor's breast pocket: Randal.

'How's that nose of yours?'

'It's fine.'

'Healing nicely?'

'I think so.'

'And who did you come to visit, Mr Rennor?'

how did he remember my name when he only saw me for

'Um, just a friend,' replied Jason. He took a step away from the door and felt a stab of alarm when Dr Randal mirrored his movement, side-stepping to block his path.

'A friend?'

'Yes, sir.'

Randal smiled again, and this time Jason saw a flash of something else on his face. Something like... internal acknowledgement. Or triumph.

Shit.

'Jason Rennor,' he said, still planted there in the middle of the hallway. He must have been in his late fifties or early sixties, older than Maurice, but he was well-built and wouldn't be easy to get past.

Had he taken Mrs Jennings?

'I have to say I'm surprised to see you back here,' said the doctor, studying him with that fixed smile on his wrinkled face. Behind the spectacles, Jason saw his eyes were glazed, as though... what, exactly?

As though he's not the only one looking through them right now.

'We thought you were long gone.'

A door banged shut somewhere down the hall behind Jason. He started to turn towards the sound, then stopped. Randal had begun to step forward when he'd moved.

'Who did you come to visit, Jason?' he asked again, and now he was inching closer. 'Who were you here to see?'

When Jason didn't reply, the smile on Doctor Randal's face turned down at the corners, twisting instead into an ugly sneer.

'Were you trying to *save* her, Jason?' he hissed. The sudden change in his voice made Jason's heart leap into his throat. He shifted further to his right, and once again, Randal mimicked the movement. 'You know you can't. It's too late for that now. Far too late indeed. Everything's in place, the pieces are set. We are all *her children.*'

At that, a pair of invisible icy hands trailed down Jason's back and he began trembling uncontrollably. The doctor saw it and his sneer widened into an expression that was very nearly comical.

'She'll have you soon, too,' he said. 'She knows where you are now, and - '

'I'm sorry, Doc,' Jason interrupted, 'but what're you talking about?'

Randal's clown grin faltered. It reminded Jason of the look on Miss Sparrow's face in detention, when he'd briefly seen her true form.

'Mr Rennor, don't try - '

'I just came to see a friend,' Jason continued, his mind racing. He forced confusion onto his face and managed to hold it there. 'His name's Joe Carabine. He broke his arm on Saturday. Fell off his bike.'

Dr Randal stared at him. For a handful of terrifying seconds, Jason thought he was going to dismiss it and lunge at him. Then, finally, the older man's sinister expression dissolved into bewilderment.

'Carabine?' he said, taking the chart out from under his arm. 'I'm not sure I remember that one.' He dropped his eyes from Jason's for the first time, flipping open the chart's metal cover.

Jason had been waiting for that. The second Randal opened the chart, he darted forward, ducking as he went. The doctor must have heard him coming and started to look up, but before he could react meaningfully, Jason had reached him; he rammed the chart upwards into Randal's face with both hands, slamming it against his nose. There was a satisfyingly moist *crack* and the old man staggered backwards with a cry of pain. The chart came away from his face doused in blood and he dropped it, grabbing at his now-broken nose and burst bottom lip, which he'd bitten clean through. His glasses hung askew off one ear.

Jason shoved him aside and bolted down the hallway. From behind, he heard Randal howl in pain and anger. He sounded like an animal.

Rounding the corner past the vending machines, Jason sprinted for the elevators. Randal was yelling something back down the corridor.

There'll be others, Jason thought with a weird thrill of panic.

He reached the elevator and punched the call button. The numbers began to tick up from one, transitioning with painful sluggishness.

Dr Randal was coming now. Jason could hear his footfalls echoing off the corridor walls, getting louder.

'Jason!' he shouted, still in that animal way. 'Don't be stupid, Jason!'

He was coming quickly.

The elevator reached the third floor; the number three dropped down, replaced with the four.

'Mr Rennor!'

Randal appeared at the end of the hallway. His beard was stained red with blood from his nose and mouth.

Ding.

The elevator doors slid apart and Jason backed inside.

'Stay there, boy,' Randal barked, pointing at him as though he'd obey. He started to run towards him. 'Don't you understand? It's too late! Just stay right there!'

Jason pressed the Ground Floor button. The doors began to close.

'BOY!'

With a gasp, Jason staggered backwards in the elevator car as Dr Randal reached the doors, right before they closed fully. The old man, crazed and bloodied, got both hands between them and, to Jason's amazement and horror, began to pry them apart.

He was going to open them again.

'Jason,' he hissed, spitting blood. One of his teeth flew out and tinkled across the elevator floor. 'Come with me. I'll take you to her. You can be her child, too.'

Jason Rennor hesitated for a fraction of a second, then did something he'd never done in his life - he punched Dr Randal in the face. He put everything into it, and when his fist connected with the doctor's broken nose, it squashed it flat into his skull.

Randal screamed in agony and released the doors, stumbling backwards. Jason saw him tumble to the floor, spurting blood over the wall next to him, glasses spilling off his face, and then the doors were closed.

The elevator began to descend.

Heaving breaths in and out of his lungs, Jason pulled out his phone. There were three missed calls from Maurice on his screen; he called him back.

'Jason!' came Maurice's voice from the other end of the line. 'Are you ok?'

'Yeah, I am -'

'What the hell happened?'

'It was one of the doctors here, Dr Randal. He's been... I dunno, turned. He tried to -'

'But you're ok?' Maurice interrupted.

'Yeah, I'm coming now.' The elevator reached the ground floor.

'Good, I'm outside. Come right now.'

There was unmistakable urgency in Maurice's voice. Jason came out into the lobby and was relieved to see it was still largely empty, though the receptionist was back behind her desk. She looked up as he ran across the room towards the doors with the phone to his ear.

'What's happened?' Jason said, but Maurice had already hung up. Jason could see the Sable idling under the entrance canopy.

'Is everything ok?' called the receptionist, starting to rise as Jason passed. He ignored her and ran outside as the glass doors slid apart. Maurice was hunched over the wheel, watching him approach. Jason jumped inside the station wagon and slammed the door.

'What's happened?' he repeated, panting.

Maurice gave him one look, saw he wasn't injured, and pulled away from the hospital entrance. Rain instantly began hammering on the car windshield again.

'It's her,' he said.

'What?' said Jason, buckling his belt. '*Her*, her?'

'No, not Evie,' Maurice replied, accelerating down the drive towards the hospital gates. 'Lou. I saw her.'

'When?'

'About a minute after you called. I'd brought the car back up to get you. She came out the doors there and got into a taxi. Almost didn't recognize her. Don't know how you didn't run into her coming the other way.'

Jason ran a hand down his face. 'She must have been in the other elevator. Holy shit.' He looked back over his shoulder at Amber Hill General as they swung back out onto the road. 'Was she alone?'

'Yeah.'

'Maurice, the doctor in there - '

'Don't worry, it doesn't matter now.'

Jason swallowed hard, suddenly on the brink of tearing up. His nose (and now his right hand, with which he'd socked Dr Randal in the face) ached dully. He shook his head and the welled-up emotion dissipated.

'So she's out?'

'Yeah, she's out.'

'Where do you think she's going?'

'Only place she can go, I reckon,' said Maurice, eyes wide and bright with readiness. 'Home. She's goin' home.'

They reached the Jennings house just as Lou went through the front door. The taxi had passed them in the street, going the other way.

Maurice pulled over to the curb one house down but didn't switch off the engine. The wipers continued to battle valiantly against the rain as it splattered on the windshield.

'What do we do now?' said Jason.

'Don't know,' Maurice replied, watching Lou's front door intently. 'Wait, I guess.'

'How long?'

'Don't know.'

They sat there for several minutes, staring at the house. A couple of cars drove by and sprayed the Sable with rain water, but other than that the street was quiet, like the hospital had been. Jason didn't like it one bit.

'We should go get her,' he croaked, discovering his throat had run dry. When Maurice didn't respond, he started to say it again.

'Yeah,' said the older man. 'Yeah, I think so.'

He popped his seatbelt and turned to reach into the back for the shotgun.

'Hang on,' said Jason.

Maurice swiveled back again and looked at the house. A car was turning into the driveway, its blinker flashing.

'Who's that?' Jason asked.

The car went up the drive and disappeared around the far side of the house. It was a Toyota Corolla, one Maurice recognized.

Lou's car, driven by her husband Derek. And there'd been a woman in the passenger seat next to him.

'Shit,' he said.

'Was that - '

'Yes.'

'Oh man. They're going to find her there. *She'll* find her.'

Maurice ground his teeth behind his lips. He realized he was still gripping the steering wheel with one sweaty hand but found he couldn't let go.

'We have to help her,' Jason said, reaching for his seatbelt. 'We should...'

He trailed off as two figures came around the side of the house and approached the front door. They were half-running in the way people often did in the rain. Jason watched them with a kind of cold dread. The man came first, wrestling with a set of keys, clearly laughing even from this distance; the woman came after him, also laughing, moving swiftly and elegantly to the front porch in bright red heels and a tight red dress. Her auburn hair, damp from the rain, fell about her shoulders; she leaned into the man while he fumbled the door open, clinging to his arm, and Jason may not have been sure it was her at all if he hadn't heard Maurice's sharp intake of breath next to him. His eyes widened, and that cold dread running through him turned to ice.

The man and woman went into the house and closed the door. A light came on in the hall.

Jason swallowed. 'She looks... different.'

'It's how it goes,' said Maurice. He couldn't keep the resignation from his voice.

They watched and waited. Jason expected the front door to suddenly fly open and Lou to come screaming out into the night with Miss Sparrow at her heels, but she didn't. In fact, nothing happened at all.

After ten minutes, Maurice started to reach for the gun again.

'What're you doing?' said Jason. 'You can't go in now.'

'Have to.'

'No, man. It's too dangerous now. You could kill someone.'

'That's the plan.' Maurice threw the coat off the gun; the barrels gleamed in the streetlight.

'Maurice...'

'I have to, kid,' he said. 'This is it.'

'Maurice,' Jason said again.

Something in his tone made Maurice stop. He turned around in his seat.

An elderly woman was standing under one of the lights on the opposite side of the street. She wore a knee-length raincoat, but the hood was down and her white hair was soaked flat against her head. Water ran down her wrinkled face in rivulets. She clutched a leash in one hand, attached to the collar of a small dachshund dog, which was also dressed in a raincoat.

She was staring right at them.

'Umm...' Jason murmured.

The old woman's eyes were huge and unblinking. Her mouth was ajar and working soundlessly. At her feet, the little dog whined and strained on the leash.

'Umm, Maurice?'

Maurice closed one hand around the shotgun, keeping his eyes on the old woman.

'Don't make me do it,' he muttered.

She stared at them, unwavering, seemingly oblivious to the rain that must be soaking through her clothes by now. Then she dropped the leash and stepped off the sidewalk into the road. The dachshund hesitated, then turned and trotted off in the other direction, disappearing into the nearest garden.

'Maurice?' Jason said. There was an odd tremor in his voice that he couldn't control.

'One of Evie's,' said Maurice.

The old woman waddled towards them, arms by her sides, her mouth still working. Jason noticed for the first time that she was wearing fluffy pink slippers.

'Go,' Jason said. Maurice was lifting the gun off the back seat, still staring at the woman. Jason grabbed his arm. 'Go, now.'

Maurice seemed to snap back at the touch. He released the gun and reached instead for the handbrake. The old woman was just a few feet from Jason's door now. She lifted one arm, reaching towards the handle.

'Maurice!' Jason cried.

Maurice shifted into drive and accelerated away from the curb, just as the old woman's fingertips brushed the passenger-side door. Jason watched her in the wing mirror, swaying in the rain, arm still outstretched.

Then they were passing the Jennings house, and as they drove by, another car signaled towards the driveway. Jason caught a glimpse of an older woman behind the wheel and a little girl in the back seat. The kid made eye contact with him as they passed.

Maurice took the Sable to the end of the street and swung a uey, spraying puddled water over someone's mailbox. He started back towards the Jennings house, taking it slow.

'Those were her kids, right?' said Jason. 'In the other car?'

'Think so.' Maurice's voice was thick.

'They're all there now,' Jason observed.

'Yup.'

Maurice slowed further as they neared the house again. Beyond it, the old woman had wandered back to the sidewalk and seemed to be searching for her dog.

'Look,' said Jason, pointing.

A figure had emerged from the front door of the Jennings house. She walked to the end of the garden, turning to look back. Something flashed in her hand.

The Sable was crawling now, almost stationary. Jason and Maurice watched in silence. There was nothing more to say.

Lou stared at the house for a moment. The front windows were lit now, casting a warm glow out across the sodden grass. The thing in her hand caught the light and flashed again. She looked down at it, then dropped it on the sidewalk and started walking away.

Maurice cleared his throat but didn't speak. He followed after her, keeping about fifty yards between them. As they passed the house, Jason looked down at the sidewalk and saw the knife Lou had been holding, wet and glinting in the rain. He didn't look up at the window.

They trundled along after her for a minute or so. She walked with her head down, stumbling occasionally. If she was aware of their presence, she gave no indication of it. The old woman who'd been walking her dog in her slippers had disappeared.

As they neared the end of the street, where the road entered an intersection, Maurice said, 'It's time' and accelerated, closing the gap. Jason swallowed again. His heart thumped steadily, but a conviction of sorts was overtaking him, a kind of surety. Maurice was right - it was time. Finally.

They drew up alongside her and Jason lowered his window. Rain immediately sprayed against his cheek, but he didn't care. He leaned out into it so she could hear him.

'Mrs Jennings?'

She didn't react right away. He tried again.

'Lou.'

She stopped then, and Maurice did too. Jason stayed put, head and right arm out the window, cold rain striking his skin.

Lou turned and looked at him. Her face was ghostly white beneath her dark hair, made heavy with rain water. She met his gaze, not really seeing him straight away. Then she frowned.

'Jason?' she said. Her voice was weak and distant. 'Jason... Rennor?'

He saw what was about to happen and threw open his door. Her eyes rolled back in her head and she toppled, but he got there just in time, gathering her into his arms.

FIFTEEN

2 days before Thanksgiving

The river ran by just beyond their feet, diamond bright and glacially cold in the late November morning. Lou watched, transfixed in the stillness, as an orange-brown oak leaf spiraled down from the boughs overhanging the water, flitting above the surface for a second or two before settling into the flow; it drifted off downstream like a helpless little ship on the high sea before disappearing into the sheen of sunlight.

Maurice had a twig in his hands. He rolled it back and forth between his thick fingers, studying the bark. He'd decided he didn't want to speak until she did. He'd give her the space, like he'd done for the boy. The day after was always the hardest.

He glanced her way. She was in the same clothes she'd worn yesterday and wrapped in a moth-eaten blanket they'd found in a drawer in the cabin bedroom. She'd been able to wash her hair in the sink that morning once Maurice had boiled enough water - it was bunched over her right shoulder, wavy and clean and jet black, framing her pale features.

He was struck by how beautiful she was then, and found himself wondering when someone had last told her so.

She caught his eye and smiled, just a little.

'It's lovely out here.'

'Sure is,' Maurice agreed.

'I don't remember the last time I was in these woods.'

There didn't seem to be anything else to say right away, so neither of them did. Maurice waited a full minute before posing the question he really wanted to ask.

'D'you mind if I smoke?'

'Not at all.'

He took the pack of Marlboros from his breast pocket, knocked one out and stuck it between his lips, then held the pack out to her. She shook her head.

'Sensible,' he said, pocketing them again. He lit up and took a drag, blowing the smoke low and away from her. 'My wife always wanted me to give these things up. I did, for a while.'

Another brief silence passed between them. Off to their left, a bird trilled; another answered from the far side of the river.

Lou shifted on the log they'd chosen as their seat and looked back at the cabin.

'Was he still asleep when you came out?'

'Yup.'

'Boys,' she said. She smiled again, sadly this time. 'They'll sleep forever if you let them.'

Maurice nodded. 'Girls, too.'

'You mentioned last night that you have one?'

He took a long drag on his cigarette and blew the smoke downwards again. 'I did.'

Lou was looking at him now. He could see her in his peripheral vision - her eyes were green as emeralds.

'Was it her?' Lou asked quietly. 'Evelyn?'

Her name rang inside his head for a moment, then he nodded.

And all at once, a memory flooded back to him, clear and visceral. He was sitting by the water, like he was now, but this time there was sand beneath him rather than a moss-covered log, and instead of a fast-flowing river, he was looking out at the sea. It'd been evening then too, and he'd been on the beach at Golden Gardens Park, gazing out across Puget Sound; the sky had been crimson above the jagged peaks of the Olympic Mountains on the other side of the water. Melanie had been next to him, hugging her knees, not quite as old as Jason at that point. He remembered looking at her and wondering how she'd gotten to be so grown-up, and how much like her mother she was becoming. Beautiful, like

Cynthia. She'd looked back and smiled, and he'd thought then, as he did now, that no sunset in the world could ever quite compare with his daughter. His little girl.

'Her name was Mel,' he said. 'Evie did to her what she's doin' to you. Happened just as quick. Everyone forgot her, me included. She ended up taking her own life with a rope. That sort've thing changes a man, you know? Don't suppose I've ever been the same and never will be again. That's where all this rage comes from. It's what's drivin' me now. The need for vengeance. Justice.'

He took another drag.

'My wife, Cynthia, she wouldn't like seeing me like this. Wouldn't *approve* of it, I reckon. She was a God-fearin' woman, always had been, and she'd have thrown a Bible verse my way. Know exactly which one she'd have used, too - it's in Romans twelve: "Never avenge yourselves, but leave it to the wrath of God, for it is written, "Vengeance is mine, I will repay, says the Lord". Read that one a few times since Mel's passing, even ended up memorizing it by accident. Have to admit it sounds good, but I couldn't quite wrap my head round it properly. Much as I'd like to leave it to the Lord to stop Evie, and much as I believe He'd prefer to, think there comes a time when a man has to step up and play a part in that wrath, you know? Can't just sit around forever and wait for God to do it all for you.

'Cynthia might have wanted me to choose the path of forgiveness, and I thought long and hard about that one, and I even tried to at one point because I was just so damn *tired* of chasin' after her, but I just couldn't do it in the end. Think when the Lord was callin' us to forgive others, He meant other *people*, and Evie ain't close to being human. She's something else, from some*where* else, and she doesn't deserve human forgiveness. There's only one place for creatures like her, and I intend to send her there, or die tryin' to.'

'The abyss,' said Lou. She sounded far away. 'Eternal damnation.'

'That's it,' Maurice said.

Tears welled in his eyes, and for the first time in a while, he didn't immediately brush them away. He glanced at Lou, perched there on that rotting log, and saw she was looking at him with silent compassion, and he found himself marveling at it. Because it was hard to comprehend, wasn't it? How could a woman who'd been through - no, who was *going* through - so much shit in her own life right now, have the time or inclination to care about him, a stranger, and one she'd only known for a few hours?

And yet, even as he thought it, she reached across and placed a hand on his arm. 'I'm sorry,' she said, 'about Mel. I'm sorry that happened to you.'

The tears were flowing now. He squeezed his eyes shut and let them run hot down his face and into his beard. After a moment, he wiped at them with one hand, sniffed, and opened his eyes again. He knew Lou was still looking at him in that wordless, understanding way. He kept his gaze on the river until the tears were done and his composure had returned.

'So you're a teacher?' he said, bringing the cigarette to his mouth again. They were done talking about him for now.

'Yes. English.'

'I would've been able to tell, even if I hadn't already known. You've got that teachery way about you.'

'Teachery way,' she repeated, grinning. 'I like that. It's a great job - I love the school, the kids.' She twisted a strand of dark hair around her finger. 'I miss it.'

'You'll be back there soon. Once she's gone, you can go back.'

'Are you sure?' She looked at him again, and now her eyes also sparkled with tears. 'Is that how it works?'

'Honestly, ma'am, I don't know for sure. But I think it might.'

'Ma'am?' she snorted a laugh. A single tear rolled down each cheek. 'I'm no ma'am, Mr Baxter.'

He smiled. 'Was always taught to be polite, ma-... Mrs Jennings.'

'Lou,' she corrected.

She'd been in a real state when he and Jason had brought her back to the cabin last night. They'd practically had to carry her inside after she collapsed in the street and was only semi-awake when they reached the woods. She'd been soaked to the skin. They'd wrapped her in blankets and made her sit by the gas heater until she stopped shivering. Jason had been the one who'd talked her out of her daze (though it was really more akin to shock). He was good at it. Maurice thought it'd been like drawing a coma patient back to full consciousness after several years in medically-induced hibernation. It was hours before she really started to take in what they were saying, and longer still until she was able to contribute to their discussion on what to do about Evie. But when she'd started sharing, the pieces had quickly begun to fall into place.

It was Jason who made the all-important connection.

Maurice had handed Lou a mug of coffee and apologized for the milk being a little off, saying he hoped the sugar would balance out any sourness. That's when the kid jumped up and cried 'The milk!' and Maurice almost spilled it into Lou's lap.

'Boy, have you lost your mind?' he said. Lou was looking at him with wide, startled eyes.

'The milk,' Jason repeated, pointing first at the mug of coffee, then at the carton on the kitchen table. 'Does the milk still smell?'

'Sure it does, you know it - '

'I *can't* smell it,' Jason said excitedly. 'My nose is broken and I can't smell it. I haven't been able to smell anything for a week.'

'Ok, so...'

'So I think that's the reason,' he went on, pacing between them now, back and forth across the living room. 'It has to be.'

'The reason for what?' Lou asked.

'Why I was able to see her - Miss Sparrow - when we were in detention. I was able to see her as she *really* is. It was just for a second, but it was enough. But even before that, something was never quite right. I was just as fooled as everyone else for the first week, during the time you were off sick, Mrs Jennings. But after I broke my nose' - He pointed at it, as if they didn't know where it was - 'I couldn't smell anything, and that's when I started seeing her properly. That's when her spell, or whatever it is, stopped working on me. It's all to do with *smell*.'

Maurice scratched his beard, puzzled, but it was Lou who spoke first.

'What do you mean exactly, Jason?' she said. 'Explain it to us.'

The kid sat down in one of the armchairs. His eyes darted back and forth as he considered what to say next.

'It's something animals produce in nature,' he said, gesturing as he spoke. 'I think people do, too. Mr Albee taught us about it in biology class. Some hormone that's secreted into the air, that other animals of that species pick up on.' He snapped his fingers. 'Pheromones. That's what they are. Pheromones.'

Maurice frowned, but Lou was nodding.

'Pheromones,' she said. 'You think that's what Evelyn produces?'

'Yeah.'

'And they, what... have an effect on everyone around her?'

'Yeah, I think so,' Jason said. 'I think she pumps those suckers out everywhere she goes, all around her in a big cloud, probably filling every room she walks into. And when people smell it, they aren't aware of it at all, but it does something to their brains. Causes, like, a chemical imbalance, one that makes them think she's someone else. Or at least, it makes it *possible* for her to manipulate them into thinking that. Like they've been drugged, and they're susceptible. Open to suggestion, you know?'

'Shit, kid,' said Maurice. 'That's clever.'

'I'm smarter than I look, old man,' grinned Jason.

'Wouldn't go that far.'

'But it *is* clever,' said Lou. 'And it does make sense, on some level. All three of us managed to dodge her spell for different reasons: you were in that car crash, Maurice, and your coma probably broke the connection; I'm Evelyn's target this time, so I'm the one she's... umm...'

'Feeding off,' Jason said.

'Ok, but let's never say that again. So it's better for her if I'm alive for as long as possible, until I crack and she moves on. And you, Jason - you've managed to evade her because you can't smell anything right now and so, if your theory's right, you're not picking up on the pheromones she's producing. The three of us are immune to her.'

'And we're probably the only three in town who are,' said Jason.

'Unless someone else has a problem with their sense of smell,' added Maurice. 'Or is in a coma.'

'I'd say she's only been manipulating the people in my social circle,' said Lou. 'There'd be no need to do it to people who don't know me. Just my friends, my co-workers. My family.' She stared at the floor. 'My husband.'

Suddenly, she jumped up and ran to the bathroom. Jason and Maurice listened uncomfortably as she wretched into the toilet before returning to the living area, drying her mouth.

'Sorry,' she said, lowering herself shakily onto the couch again.

'No sweat,' said Jason.

'The thought of it just... turns my stomach.' She reached for her mug on the coffee table with her good hand - her left wrist was still strapped up tight. 'I don't know how I'll... but it's not his fault. He doesn't know.' She sipped the water, not looking at them.

'So,' Maurice said, directing his question at Jason. 'Pheromones?'

'Yeah,' Jason replied. 'I think that's how she's doing it.'

'So how do we use that information, kid? What do we do with it?'

Jason frowned, turning it over in his head. Maurice smiled to himself, watching the boy work. He'd meant what he said - he was smarter than he looked, or made himself out to be, at least.

'If we could block the smell,' he said at last, 'that might break her hold on everyone.'

'Sure,' Maurice said. 'I'll head to town now and start crackin' noses.'

Jason flipped him the bird.

'Could we, I don't know, cover her in something?' Lou said. 'Throw something over her?'

'Pig blood, maybe?' Jason said, with a crooked smile. '*Carrie* her ass?'

'Might not be strong enough,' said Maurice, perhaps missing the reference. 'And I don't think we can run up to her with a bucket of somethin' and just chuck it over her. And what good would that do, unless she's around a lot've people?'

'Like on a stage?' Jason said.

'Well, yeah, but -'

'She's getting an award at the Thanksgiving festival tomorrow.' Jason's eyes were bright. 'Principal Martin mentioned it in assembly on Friday. People's Hero, or something...'

'Hey!' Lou said indignantly, 'I didn't know I was in the running for that.'

'Maybe *you* weren't,' suggested Jason. 'But I guess if you can control whoever you want, you can win whatever you want.'

Lou sighed. 'Still.'

'So she'll be on the stage?' asked Maurice.

'Yeah.'

'In front of everyone?'

'Probably most of the town, yeah.'

'And we can cover her in something that'll mask the smell?' said Lou.

'Is there a way to drop it from above?' Maurice asked, rubbing his bearded chin again. 'You know... *carry* her ass, or whatever you said?'

'I don't think so,' said Jason, but his eyes remained alive with excitement. 'But we could do it the other way round.'

'What d'you mean, kid?'

'I'll explain later,' Jason said, looking around the cabin. 'It won't matter if we don't have something to cover her with, something that'll mask the smell long enough to break her hold on everyone who's watching.'

'But what do we have here?' said Lou. 'Is there anything in the cabin that would...'

She trailed off, and as one, they all turned to look towards the bathroom.

Maurice grinned. 'That oughta do it.'

'Man, that'll be rough,' said Jason.

'There's one more thing, though,' said Maurice, his grin fading. 'It's all well n' good if we break her spell, or whatever it is. But what then? She's just goin' to run, and we don't know where. If she escapes, she'll just do it all again in the next place. I don't know about you young'uns, but I don't have much energy left to keep chasin' her. Not when we're so close now.'

'She won't escape,' said Lou coldly. 'I know where she lives.'

'You do?' Jason said.

'Yes. My friend Debbie texted me her address. It's in my phone, but I memorized it just in case it disappeared, like a lot of other stuff has. She lives at 64 Oakland Avenue. If that shotgun of yours doesn't do the trick, Mr Baxter,' she said, looking him in the eye with steel, 'I'll burn that house to the ground with her inside it.'

That had been last night. Now, in the light of a new day, and after a great deal more discussion, they were almost ready to start putting their plan into action.

Maurice took a final drag of his cigarette and dropped it on the ground. Lou watched as he stubbed it out with his boot heel.

'D'you think it'll work?' she asked.

'Can't say for certain, Lou,' he replied, 'but we'll sure as shit give it a try.'

'Evie, you've positively outdone yourself this time.'

George Albee raised his wine glass and the others followed suit.

'To Evie.'

'Evie!' they chanted happily, clinking their glasses together. George found it to be a merry sound.

She blushed, waving away their praise.

'Don't be silly,' she laughed. 'You're all too kind. This was all Derek's doing, honestly - he's the star of the show.'

'You *would* say that,' giggled Julie Heller, the wine in her glass slopping perilously close to the rim. It was Julie's third drink and she was already barrelling towards inebriation. 'You're far too *modest*, Evie. Isn't she too modest, Ken?'

'Too modest,' agreed her husband Kenneth. Ken Heller didn't really know much about Evelyn Sparrow, whether she was particularly modest or not, but he *did* know it was better to agree with his wife's assertions when she'd thrown back a few at dinner.

'Where *is* Derek, anyway?' asked Lisa Doyle, wife of Alain Doyle the English teacher, who'd escorted Lou away from her own classroom just over a week ago. Alain was seated to her right and was deep in conversation with Faith Logan, who taught Social Studies at Amber Hill High. It was her first year at the school and Alain was determined to make her feel welcome, and it showed. Lisa threw him a look for about the twentieth time since dinner began, and for the twentieth time, Alain missed it.

'He's upstairs,' Evie replied, 'just putting Ruth down again.'

'Oh gosh,' said Julie. 'I hope we didn't wake her?'

'She hasn't been sleeping well lately,' said Evie, eyes flicking to the ceiling and back again. 'I don't know why. But she'll be fine, it'll pass.'

'Just one of those phases,' Lisa agreed knowingly, before throwing Alain another look.

In truth, Evie knew exactly why the little girl hadn't been sleeping well. She'd been having bad dreams every night since Lou fell down the stairs, and even though she no longer consciously remembered her real mother, the dreams were hard to shake. Especially this one. Except now, she dreamed it was Evie tumbling down that staircase, and it was Evie smacking her head off the wall at the bottom, leaving a mark. She'd wet the bed twice over the weekend.

The boy had also been dreaming, but more disturbingly, he'd also started picking up on things his father was missing. Just little things, like how Derek suddenly started putting mushrooms into his chili even though no-one liked them (except Evie, and that's all that mattered); how Evie wasn't reading Ruth bedtime stories anymore, not after the first one when the little brat told her she was going too fast, and Derek had to do it now; how Evie hadn't known what he was talking about when he mentioned some other kid called Ralph Nowak, who was apparently now one of his best friends, for whatever tedious reason.

Children were always problematic. Oh, how she *detested* them.

'Has everyone finished their starters?' she asked sweetly.

A chorus of satisfied affirmatives. George looked like he was about to toast her again.

'Perfect,' she said, starting to rise. 'I'll just clear those plates, then.'

'No, no, Evie!' cried Julie, getting quickly to her feet. 'We can do it, can't we Ken?'

'Oh, yes.'

'You've done enough, just stay where you are.'

'Are you sure?' Evie said, already sitting again. Julie was quite the lapdog, so eager to please. She'd given her no trouble at all.

'Of course! Ken, stack those plates.'

'Yes, dear.'

'That crab dip was delicious,' Perry Martin commented from the far end of the table. 'I've never had that at Thanksgiving before. Oysters, maybe. But not crab.'

'Well it's not Thanksgiving quite yet, Perry,' said Mary Albee, George's prissy (and incredibly boring) wife. 'There's still time, you know.'

'Uh, yes, I suppose there is.'

Her guests fell into conversation again, giving Evie some brief respite. She sat back in her chair, surveying the room like a mother hen observing her helpless little chicks. Fluffy, yellow, baby birds. Yes, that's what they were. She could crush each of them in one hand, if she wanted. She'd listen as their hollow, matchstick bones snapped and their tiny organs burst open - that'd sure make her smile. Better yet, she could have them do it to each other. Wouldn't that be fun?

Maybe later.

In the kitchen, Julie and Ken clattered around with the dirty dishes. The mouth-watering scent of roasted meat wafted into the living room.

Evie brushed a lock of auburn hair behind her ear, exposing one of the pearl earrings Derek had bought her yesterday, "just because". She was full and sleek now, no longer the skinny, pallid creature she'd been on that first day when she'd looked Beverley the receptionist in the eye and asked which room belonged to Lou Jennings, and after only a moment's hesitation, Beverley had told her it was

Room 2 in the English hallway, and had then begun discussing some television show they apparently both watched.

Beverley had been the first.

Yes, she was quite different now. Her decidedly more curvaceous frame was packed into a tight pink dress that made her ample bosom even more prominent than usual (Jeff Clarke hadn't been able to take his eyes off it all night, the filthy little pervert), and when she walked between the kitchen and the living room, where they'd set up the extended dining table for tonight's celebratory meal, her toned alabaster legs drew inaudible gasps of admiration, ones only she could hear.

It was the most complete she'd been in a long time. Her skin was practically shimmering with iridescence. She could feel every single pump of blood in the room.

She was *alive* with it, and not only that, but as they all sat there around the table with flames crackling agreeably in the fireplace nearby and Elton John's *Don't Shoot Me I'm Only The Piano Player* spinning on the platter, she was content.

There it is, ladies and gentlemen. Right now, I'm content in this backwater shithole town, miles and miles from any place fun. Can you even believe it?

She was almost completely content.

But not quite. One of her guests was troubling her. He'd been largely silent since dinner began, smiling amiably while the others joked and laughed and chugged the cheap store-bought swill she had them believing was an extravagant French pinot noir. She looked his way now, piercing him with her electric-blue eyes. She could feel his heart-rate bump up a notch or two.

'Are you ok, Eric?'

He looked up from his glass, startled. His mind had been elsewhere. She didn't like that.

'Oh,' he said, 'yes, of course.'

'Are you sure?'

'Sure,' he nodded, smiling.

She regarded him with cold precision, as a snake might scrutinize a rat before swallowing it. That coolness rippled out from her into the others at the table; one by one, their conversations petered out until they, like her, were all staring at Eric Mansford.

The old man glanced about the table, apprehension clearly visible on his face now. She *did* like *that*.

'You're having a good time, right Eric?' said Perry.

'Yes, yes of course - '

'This is a celebration, Eric,' added Jeff Clarke tonelessly. He wasn't smiling. 'We're celebrating tonight.'

'I know, yes.'

He was sweating now, and Evie grinned. His heart was pounding, his panic rising. Wasn't it just *delicious*?

'We're celebrating Evie,' continued Jeff. He gestured towards her and knocked over his wine glass, spilling red onto the white table cloth, where it immediately soaked through. Jeff didn't notice; none of them did, apart from Eric, who appeared too stunned to say anything about it.

'Yes. Evie,' added Faith.

'Evie's award, from the mayor,' finished Alain, his head bobbing.

'Where's your wife, Eric?' asked Lisa mildly. Unlike the others, she *was* smiling, and that was somehow much, much worse.

'I told you,' Eric said, his face shiny with sweat. 'She wasn't feeling well earlier. Her stomach... was a little upset. She gets that way sometimes.'

'Does she?' said Evie, taking a sip of the dark red liquid in her glass.

Eric cleared his throat. 'Yes, Evelyn, she does.'

She knew he'd seen her in the school on Friday, when she'd been after the Rennor boy. It'd just been for a second, but that was sometimes enough. She had him, of course - she had them all - but once those flickers of doubt started to take root, they were hard to eradicate. Ben Jennings had the beginnings of them, and she was sure Eric did too. It may not matter, of course, especially if Lou finished herself off soon. She thought that might have happened already, but for some reason she was still alive, and she didn't know where she'd gone. Not yet, at least.

No matter. She'd enjoy it while she could. After all, she hadn't felt so hellishly *alive* in such a long time, had she?

But this insolence from the old Shop teacher...

'Eric - ' she began, and then the living room door opened.

'There he is!' exclaimed Julie, who had appeared at the kitchen door with a dish towel draped over one arm.

Derek grinned behind his copper beard as he came into the room.

'Sorry about that, guys,' he said. 'Took a few minutes to get her down.'

'Is she ok?' Evie asked, not caring. Across the table, Eric was staring hard at the glass in his hand, which was trembling.

'She'll be fine.' He leaned down and kissed her once on her full, succulent lips.

Julie giggled again in an uncomfortably childish way. 'Save it for the bedroom, you too.' Derek chuckled, reddening a little, and straightened up.

'You'll have to tell us how you made that crab dip, Derek,' said Perry. 'I've never had crab at Thanksgiving before. Oysters, maybe...'

'A magician never reveals his secrets,' winked Derek. Then, to Evie: 'Are we all set for the main course?'

'Debs?' Evie called.

A pale, gaunt woman appeared at the kitchen door. Her dark hair, normally clean and gathered into a neat braid, stuck out untidily in all directions, slick with grease and graying in places. There were deep, black bags under her bleary eyes.

'Yes, Evie?' she replied. It was little more than a murmur and barely audible over the music.

'How's dinner coming along, sweetie?'

Debbie looked back over her shoulder. The oven mitt she wore on her right hand was stained reddish-brown.

'Almost done,' she said. 'I might need some help - '

'Derek, be a dear,' said Evie.

'Of course, honey,' Derek replied, walking obediently to the kitchen. Debbie shrank out of sight.

'Such a wonderful meal,' declared George exuberantly. 'And we've barely begun!'

'That crab dip - ' Perry started.

'All Derek's doing,' Evie said again. 'He's been slaving over that stove all day.'

'So much to do all by himself,' commented Lisa, downing her drink. 'He must be exhausted already.'

'Are you excited for tomorrow, Evie?' asked Julie, now seated again.

'Oh, I suppose so. It's not a big deal...'

'Not a big deal?' Julie exclaimed shrilly. Evie winced - Julie was becoming tiresome. 'Of course it's a big deal! It's the People's Hero award, for crying out loud. They don't give that out every day.'

'Just once every year,' added Ken, unhelpfully.

'It's a real honor,' said Jeff, once again staring at Evie's breasts. 'A *huge* honor.'

'You should be proud,' Julie beamed.

'I am proud.'

'But you should be *so* proud. I mean - '

'Go to sleep, Julie,' said Evie.

Julie Heller instantly face-planted onto the table cloth, causing her cutlery to bounce. Next to her, Ken took another sip of wine. Eric gawked open-mouthed at Julie, who was completely unconscious. The others didn't seem to notice.

'It *is* an honor, of course,' said Evie. 'And I am proud. It's a wonderful *meaningless* award, and I'll be glad to receive it. And you'll all be there, right?'

They nodded vigorously. Eric continued to stare at Julie, but even he nodded. He was on the same string as the rest of them.

'Lovely,' Evie said.

Maybe I'll stay here a while longer, she thought. *Maybe I should settle down for a while. It could be just what the doctor ordered. A little rest, for now.*

Julie snorted in her sleep, drooling into the table cloth.

'Here we are,' announced Derek, sweeping back into the room. He was wearing an apron now.

There were *oohs* and *aahs* as he placed steaming bowls of potatoes and yams on the table; Debbie followed with green beans, corn, an enormous gravy boat, and a veritable mountain of stuffing. She went out and came back in with a stack of warmed plates.

'Julie,' said Evie.

Julie sat up with a start, a strand of hair stuck to the side of her face. Debbie passed out the plates and returned to the kitchen.

'This all looks fabulous,' said George.

'Evie, you've outdone yourself,' added Mary.

'Our actual Thanksgiving dinner isn't going to top this,' grinned Alain, glancing at Lisa, who flushed pink.

'And now,' said Derek, coming back into the room with a covered stainless steel platter in his hands, 'for the pièce de résistance.'

'Fabulous,' repeated George.

Derek set the platter at the end of the table and lifted off the lid.

'Oh, beautiful!' exclaimed Lisa.

'Cooked to perfection,' said Jeff.

'Well done, dear,' purred Evie.

Eric Mansford was on his feet. His chair clattered back against the bookcase behind him. His face had gone completely white.

'What is this?' he stammered, pointing at the platter. 'What *is* this?'

'It's dinner, Eric,' said Evie, smiling.

'Sit down, man,' instructed Perry.

'What the FUCK IS THIS?' Eric cried, hands on his head.

Evie decided to let him have his moment.

'What's the matter, Eric?' she cooed. 'What's up, chuck?'

Derek removed a pair of carving knives from his apron pocket and scraped them together, grinning happily. From the corner, Elton's voice blared from the record player.

Oh, lawdy mama those Friday nights, when Suzie wore her dresses tight, crocodile rocking was out of sight...

Derek leaned over the platter and put the knives to the meat.

'Who wants the breast?' he asked.

'Ooh, me please!' said Lisa.

'Save some for me, too,' Alain said, rubbing his palms together.

Derek began to carve, slicing into the meat. Juices flowed onto the platter, hot and clear.

Eric made a low moaning sound, rocking on his heels, clutching at his face. Then he stopped. His eyes rolled back in his skull and he folded to the floor. He cracked the side of his head off the hearth as he went down and blood spurted across the tiles. His body spasmed a few times in front of the fire, right behind Jeff's seat. None of them paid any attention - they were all staring at the roast, their mouths watering. Only Evie looked towards where Eric lay; she grinned toothily, briefly exposing her real teeth.

'Eat up,' she said, 'before it gets cold.'

They obeyed, passing around the creamed potatoes and gravy, scooping vegetables onto their plates, laughing and joking and drinking more cheap wine as Derek carved slices off Rick Anderson's perfectly-cooked upper torso and stacked them neatly next to the platter.

Rick's eyes, which had leered at Evelyn Sparrow in detention not so long ago, bobbed in the gravy like shallot onions.

sixteen

The day before Thanksgiving

Perry rubbed the back of his neck and looked at the crowd gathered on the lawn. He couldn't quite believe this day had finally arrived; it'd felt like the longest month of his life, at least since Margaret's passing, and that had been absolute hell. He couldn't wait for it to be over at last.

The festival had, in fairness to its various organizers and contributors, largely gone off without a hitch. None of the colorful lights strung around the town center lawn - which was more of a small park, really - had blown this time (that had happened before) and the sound system hadn't come close to short-circuiting; none of the hyperactive children running between the vendor stalls lining the lawn had been lost in the crowd or knocked anything important over, and none of their parents had shown up drunk (that had *also* happened before); the local folk band providing the music had actually sounded pretty good, and even the Amber Middle School choir had dialed down their cringe-factor this year by sticking to the classics and avoiding any more Miley Cyrus songs (that had been the longest five minutes of the whole event last time round). The weather had held up as well, drawing a sizable portion of Amber Hill's residents to the festivities, all wrapped up in coats, scarves and winter hats. The atmosphere was nothing short of jovial, and that wasn't always a given at this thing.

All in all, Perry was relieved. He'd arrived about an hour in, mingled expertly with parents and students and fellow staff members, purchased a token jar of blackberry jam from one of the stalls, commented several times on the decorations ("Yes, I believe the lanterns *are* bigger this year, and don't those leaves looks *real*?"), and nailed his brief introductory address, which had drawn some polite applause from the crowd.

Yes, he was relieved his part in the whole performance was done; he'd be even more relieved, however, when he was able to get down from the stage and slip off home during the concluding fireworks display, as was his custom, because dammit if his stomach hadn't been giving him grief all day. He must have eaten far too much at Evie's dinner party the night before, though for some reason, he couldn't remember an awful lot of it now. Too much of that good wine, maybe.

They'd gathered at the Jennings house at Derek's invitation to celebrate Evie receiving her award. It was a fairly trivial accolade in the grand scheme of things, but not if you were a resident of Amber Hill. The People's Hero award meant you were popular, and not just with parents of school children - every adult in town was eligible to vote for the person they believed had earned the right to wear the crown (metaphorically speaking, thankfully - they no longer had to wear a physical crown); the winner was often someone who did a lot for charity, usually voluntarily, or who went out of their way to help those around them, beyond the regular call of duty. Evie did both, had done for a while now, and was finally getting the recognition she deserved. Even if it was just a trivial thing.

Perry Martin had been the one who nominated her this year. He'd pushed for her, pressing his fellow town council officials, and had been delighted when they selected her from a shortlist of five. The others had all been chumps, really.

There was only Evie.

He spotted Derek and the kids in the crowd, just a few rows from the front. The little girl, Ruth, was on her father's shoulders. Derek caught Perry's eye and raised a hand; Perry winked back.

'And now,' said Mayor Thomas, leaning into the mic, 'for the final award of the evening.'

Applause rippled through the gathering crowd. Someone whooped, producing a smattering of good-natured laughter near the back.

'Each year, the People's Hero award goes to the person who best exemplifies what Amber Hill is all about, in my opinion.' Mayor Thomas read from his notes, gripping the edges of the podium with gloved hands; his bald spot was bright orange in the glow of the lights strung above the stage. 'Someone who puts others before themselves, someone who's kind and passionate about their community, who leads by example, and does so with humility.'

'He didn't write this,' muttered Tracey Calvin, head of the town council. She was seated to Perry's right in the short row of elected officials. 'I know for a fact he didn't write this.'

'This person is chosen by you - the people,' continued Mayor Thomas, with a grandiose sweep of the hand over the crowd. 'And this year, I'm delighted to present the award to Mrs Evelyn Jennings of Amber Hill High.'

He turned, clapping, and the crowd joined in. There were cheers as Evelyn came up the steps onto the stage. She wore a red winter coat with a fur-lined collar and black boots; her auburn hair fell about her shoulders, unmoved by the breeze. She glanced at Perry as she passed, and he was struck once again by the beauty in those pure blue eyes. Her cheeks were rosy but took nothing away from her scarlet lips and thick, dark eyelashes, which batted playfully at Mayor Thomas as she approached the podium. Perry was amused to see the podgy mayor of Amber Hill look a little flustered at that, and he didn't blame him one bit. Evie Jennings was a knockout.

The crowd continued to applaud as Evie dipped her head and Thomas draped the ribbon around her neck. Perry was sure the dirty old fart had taken a big whiff of her hair as she leaned towards him.

Evie raised her head, smiling at Thomas, who blushed like a schoolboy and stepped back. As she moved to the podium, the cheers and applause intensified, reverberating off the municipal buildings lining the town square. Perry looked towards the Jennings family again and saw the little girl waving her arms ecstatically on Derek's shoulders. The boy, however, wasn't doing the same. He stared up at the stage with his hands in his pockets, his expression blank.

That's odd, Perry thought, but then the crowd hushed and the moment passed. He lowered himself into his chair again alongside the other council members. He didn't recall standing up.

'Thank you, *so* much,' said Evie into the mic. 'Honestly, I never expected this in a million years. I really don't think I deserve it at all.'

'You do!' someone shouted, and there was laughter again. Evie joined in with her breathless, sing-song chuckle. *Even her laugh's beautiful*, Perry thought.

'Well, it's a real honor,' she continued, looking down at the gold-colored medal, nestled between her breasts on the end of the ribbon. 'Truly, it is. The past few years have been hard work, I'll admit - ' She held up her hands to emphasize the admission and someone in the crowd giggled; Perry thought it sounded like Julie Heller. '- but it was totally worth it, because I love my job, and I love this town.'

More applause. More cheering.

'And of course, I couldn't have done any of it without my wonderful husband Derek and our two children, Ben and Ruth.'

She gestured in their direction. Those nearby slapped Derek on the back and tousled Ben's hair. Derek beamed; the boy didn't react.

'Honestly,' Evie said, 'those three down there are my joy, my rock. Everything I do, I do for my family. They're why I get up in the morning, why I go to work with a smile on my face. They're why I...'

Perry had been watching Derek and the kids, again wondering why Ben wasn't smiling like the rest of them. He shifted his eyes back to Evie as she trailed off.

'They're, um... they're why I...'

She was looking into the crowd, staring at something. Perry heard murmurings of confusion from below. He tried to follow Evie's gaze, to see what she'd seen. When he looked back at her, she was smiling again, but it was different now.

'They're why I do what I do,' Evie said. Her voice had changed and her grin was widening. 'They're my delight. My inspiration. And they're *mine*.' She raised a hand and pointed into the crowd. 'And if someone down there doesn't grab that black-haired bitch right now, I'll - '

She never finished her sentence.

Perry watched in astonishment as Evelyn simply dropped out of sight, disappearing into the floor of the stage. The crowd gasped as one. Perry saw her arms flail for just a second, pinwheeling in the air, and then she was gone. There was a hollow splash sound - almost more of a slap, like someone jumping into a shallow bathtub - and a splurge of dark liquid slopped up onto the stage from the space Evelyn had dropped into. Someone in the crowd screamed.

Then her head and shoulders appeared again, drenched in the black stuff. Her lustrous hair was now a goopy, tangled mess clinging to her head.

'Help her!' someone shrieked.

Mayor Thomas, who'd been gaping at the spot Evie had occupied just seconds before, stumbled towards the hole in the stage floor, reaching for her. Others were doing the same. Tracey Calvin was already on her knees, grabbing at Evie's arm, her round ass stuck unflatteringly in the air.

Perry stood up.

There was Derek, glasses askew, scrambling Ruth off his shoulders.

There was Julie Heller, muscling her way through the crowd, shrieking 'EVIE! EVIE!' like a crazed fan at a concert.

They were pulling her out of the hole now, hauling her up by the arms. He started towards her in a daze, reaching past the others to grab her.

And then the smell hit him.

It stung his nostrils and seemed to suck the breath from his lungs. Tracey Calvin caught it at the same time and recoiled, releasing the arm of Evie's sodden coat. Mayor Thomas actually leapt to his feet and staggered backwards like a drunk man, both hands covering his mouth and nose.

'What the hell *is* that?' someone cried.

Tracey was gagging now. She looked like she might throw up.

Perry had smelt something like it before when he was young. He'd been messing around with his friends one hot summer afternoon and, for reasons he could no longer fathom, they'd decided to pry open a manhole cover on their street and stick their heads inside. The smell had been horrendous, so putrid it had clung to his hair and his mother later asked just where the hell he'd been that day. The stench now saturating Evie's entire body was just like it.

'It... it's shit,' Tracey gasped. 'It smells like *shit*.' Then she vomited on the stage at Perry's feet, splattering her lunch all over his polished leather wingtips.

Evie had her arms on either side of the hole now. Perry held his breath and took hold of her right sleeve. She grabbed at his arm, staring up at him through the black liquid caked to her face.

'Thank you, Perry,' she said in a weird shuddering voice. 'Help me out of this thing.'

He pulled, vaguely surprised at how bony her arm was under the thick coat. She got her upper torso out of the hole (*it's a trap door, isn't it?*) and flopped onto the stage floor, panting. The crowd stared at her, horror-struck, but those nearest the front were already backing away, covering their noses. She was completely covered in the stuff. The smell was overwhelming, even in the open air.

She still clung to his arm. 'Thank you,' she breathed. 'Help me up.'

He began to pull her up. And then it happened.

He was looking down at her, still holding her by the arm, and he suddenly didn't know exactly who she was. At first, it was like he'd bumped into someone from his childhood and couldn't recall their name (that had happened to him plenty of times in recent years), but then the feeling suddenly became more visceral. He felt as though he'd just woken from a deep slumber after sleep-walking his way through the house, and he'd caught himself doing something he had no recollection of starting. He was looking at her, gripping her arm, and he hadn't the slightest idea who she was.

'Perry, help me up,' she said.

He let go of her arm and stepped back. His foot planted in Tracey Calvin's vomit.

'Perry,' the woman said again, frowning at him. 'What're you doing? *Help* me.'

He stared hard. The others on the stage were doing the same now, backing slowly away from her.

The woman rose shakily to her feet beside the trap door and looked back at them. Her red coat clung to her body; her hair was matted to her face. Blue eyes, wild with fear and fury, glared out from the black and brown goop dripping off her face. It had already begun to pool around her feet.

'What're you doing?' she demanded, turning in a circle. The stench came off her in waves. 'Why're you all just standing there?'

Perry's vision began to swim. He pressed his palm against his temple.

What's happening here? he thought. *What's happening to me?*

Instead of retreating, the crowd now pressed towards the stage for a better look, forcing those nearest the front closer to the stench.

'What's the matter with you people?' the woman cried, but there was panic in her voice now, making it quiver. Cursing, she began struggling out of her coat. Her fingers fumbled uselessly at the buttons, which were smeared in the slippery, fetid liquid. The People's Hero medal got in the way and she yanked it off with a shriek of frustration. Perry flinched at the sound.

Mayor Thomas had been edging towards her while she tried to get the coat off, extending his hand defensively like she was on fire and he was trying to determine just how hot she was before getting too close.

'Miss,' he said shakily. 'Miss, are you alright -'

'Of course I'm not alright!' she snapped, wheeling towards him. He drew back, and for a split second, Perry saw a flicker of gratification in her expression; it was replaced almost immediately with uncertainty and unease.

'Why're you calling me "Miss"?' she asked.

'I'm sorry, um... madam, but - '

'Why did you call me *Miss*?' she spat. The medal was still in her hand, the stained ribbon flapping in the breeze. A thick, stunned silence had settled over the crowd.

'It's just...' Thomas said, and Perry could see that the other man's head was spinning too, right on the precipice of madness. 'It's just that... I'm not sure who you are, Miss.'

The woman's eyes widened - no, Perry thought, they *bulged* - and her mouth fell open. She stared back at Thomas, disbelieving, then swept her gaze across the other officials on the stage. Finally, the blue eyes found him.

'Perry,' she said.

He looked at her for a long time before responding - his mind wasn't working right, he knew that, but it was so much more - and when he did speak, he almost didn't recognize his own voice. It came out in a whisper.

'Who are you?'

Her expression crumpled, collapsing in on itself, and then her face began to change. Something was coming out of it. Perry took a step back. His foot skidded through Tracey's vomit and he almost lost his balance.

'Who am I?' the woman cried, incredulous. She hurled the medal at his feet; it bounced away across the stage floor. 'WHO AM I?'

She's going to kill me, he thought. *Oh dear, I'm going to die.*

'Evelyn.'

The woman's face froze in a manic, rictus grin. She wasn't beautiful now; in fact, Perry thought with dull horror, she didn't even look like a woman anymore.

She turned and looked towards the crowd. He followed her gaze.

Another woman was standing a few feet away from the stage, just below them. Those nearby, frightened now, quickly drew back, leaving a semi-circle of empty, trodden grass around her.

She had jet black hair tied back from her face and her eyes were emerald green. There was a cut on her forehead, just below the hairline, and her left wrist was strapped in a bandage.

'Hi, Evelyn,' she said. 'Remember me?'

Perry didn't see what happened next. A moment after he laid eyes on Lou Jennings, something snapped in his brain. It was as if a lightbulb that hadn't been switched on in a long time suddenly flared to life, and then exploded.

Darkness closed in around the edges of his vision. He saw Lou Jennings smile, and he heard Evelyn Sparrow shriek in fury, and then he blacked out.

Maurice was behind the stage when the crowd began clapping and cheering, crammed uncomfortably into a large rhododendron bush. He'd been there since the awards portion of the Thanksgiving festival began, crouched in the dark among the leaves like an old jungle cat, and his back was now throbbing.

'Come on,' he muttered. 'Hurry up.'

The bush serving as his hideout was right on the edge of the town square, at the point where the grass ended and the paved area in front of the town hall began. The hall itself was sparsely decorated for Thanksgiving, and he'd noticed, when doing his sweep of the perimeter just before the festival started, that unlit Christmas lights had already been strung across its upper facades. During his sweep (thinking of it in those terms really took him back), he'd walked with his head down and hood pulled up, a not-unusual thing to do for a man of his age on a chilly November afternoon; it'd taken him less than ten minutes to complete a full loop of the square, strolling along the sidewalk at the back end of the vendor stalls with his hands in his pockets, avoiding eye contact with anyone who could very well be an Evie spy. He estimated about a thousand people could fit on the grass at a push, but imagined there'd be fewer that evening.

He was right, but only just. He'd parked the Sable across the street from the square just after five o'clock and, along with Lou and Jason, had watched in amazement as a steady stream of people flooded the center of Amber Hill throughout the following couple of hours. They just kept coming and coming: couples, families, the young, the old. By six, every parking space around the square was occupied; by seven, the grass within the square itself was no longer visible.

'Is it always this busy?' Jason had asked from the back seat, watching a kid go by with a pink, foot-long candy floss in his hand. 'I don't remember it ever being like this before.'

'No, it's never been like this,' Lou had replied. 'It's like a carnival.'

'Evie,' Maurice had muttered. 'They're here for her.'

The awards were due to be handed out at eight o'clock, just after the musical numbers put on by the schools. At ten before eight, they'd left the car and slipped into the crowd. Jason stayed near the sidewalk to keep an eye on their escape route while Maurice took up his position at the rear of the stage. Lou told them she wanted to get close, just in case something went wrong. She said she'd throw Evelyn into the barrel of shit concealed under the trap door by herself, if it came to it.

Getting the barrel into town had been no mean feat, and wasn't something Maurice wanted to repeat ever again. They'd found it outside one of the neighboring cabins and, as per Jason's plan, had managed to fill it with waste liquid from the septic tank using a pump. The smell was revolting and had almost overpowered them, but somehow, they'd gotten it done. Fortunately, the barrel came with a cover that sealed it air-tight, otherwise there was no way Maurice would have been able to get it from the woods to the center of town without hurling all over the inside of the car.

They brought it down in the middle of the night and set it up under the stage. He and Jason had to dig a hole in the grass to make it fit with enough room for the trap door to swing open, and even then, it didn't go all the way. It would spill her into the barrel at an angle, but it would hopefully be enough. They all knew it was a big gamble, especially if the mechanism Jason had rigged to the door didn't work exactly right.

Thankfully, the kid was a genius with his hands, and he was the one who'd repaired the stage door long before all this even started. While Maurice had worked at the frost-hardened ground with a spade (it was the most difficult thing he'd done in a long time, and having to do it in the dark didn't help), Jason had worked at the trap door. He removed the wooden struts he'd attached in Shop class under Mr Mansford's direction and replaced the lock with a pin, which when pulled out, allowed the door to fall open. Amazingly, the boy had been able to salvage everything he needed from the cabins, including tools they'd discovered in a container behind the one farthest down the row.

It'd taken them over an hour to dig the hole, place the barrel, rig the door with a pin and cable twine, and drag the stage back to its original position, all under cover of darkness while Lou acted as lookout from the car. She was to honk the horn at the first sign of trouble, but trouble never came. The town center was completely dead, and apart from a curious tabby cat watching them from the sidewalk, they were undisturbed throughout it all.

And now, here was Maurice Baxter, hiding in a bush with the other end of the cable twine in his hands and his fifty-seven year-old back on fire. One firm tug of the cable would simultaneously pop the trap door pin and knock the cover off the barrel. They'd tested it several times after shifting the stage back into position - Jason wouldn't let them leave until he was completely satisfied that it worked. Now, all they could do was cross their fingers and pray.

The stage backdrop, really nothing more than a black curtain over a metal frame, obscured Maurice's vision of the proceedings on the other side, but he heard Mayor Thomas's voice booming loud and clear from the speakers.

'This person is chosen by you - the people - and this year, I'm delighted to present the award to Mrs Evelyn Jennings of Amber Hill High.'

The applause swelled. From his position, Maurice heard the stage creak as the council officials rose to their feet. He had the impression of a figure moving across it from the right and felt a chill creep through his bones.

When she spoke, he almost yanked on the cable right away.

'Thank you, *so* much,' he heard her say. 'Honestly, I never expected this in a million years. I really don't think I deserve it at all.'

He listened with gritted teeth as she gushed her thanks and the crowd gleefully lapped it up, hanging on her every word. He didn't need to see them to know it was happening. The atmosphere had completely shifted the moment she stepped onto the stage. There was a sort of reverence in the air now. An awe.

He could feel the weight of the shotgun leaning against his leg.

'Everything I do, I do for my family,' she was saying. 'They're why I get up in the morning, why I go to work with a smile on my face. They're why I... they're, um...'

Maurice frowned. He tightened his grip on the cable, tensing.

'They're why I do what I do. They're my delight. My inspiration. And they're *mine.*'

Mine. He heard it and set himself, drawing in a deep breath.

'And if someone down there doesn't grab that black-haired bitch right now - '

Maurice yanked the cable as hard as he could. The pin shot out of the lock and the cover flew off the top of the barrel. There was a bang as the trap door hit the rim, followed by a thick splash and a scream from the crowd. The stomach-turning stench of rotten human waste hit him immediately.

Some cried 'Help her!' from the crowd. There was a commotion on the stage. People were yelling, scrambling over the wooden boards.

Maurice dropped the cable and grabbed the shotgun. As the town council members did their best to drag Evelyn out of the barrel and a good portion of the crowd descended into hysterics, he wrestled himself free of the rhododendron bush and headed for the sidewalk, tucking the gun into his coat as he went.

Jason almost couldn't believe what he was seeing.

He stood beneath one of the birch trees that lined the perimeter of the town square, leaning against the ashen-colored trunk; above his head, orange and yellow lights glowed from its branches. Every tree in the square was adorned in the same way. Jason thought it made them look like they were on fire.

He'd watched the whole thing from his position on the edge of the crowd, first from the shadows of a depleted vendor stall, then, when he was confident no-one recognized him, by the tree, where he had a clear view of the stage. He'd initially been worried some passer-by would notice him standing there and strike up a conversation ("Great festival this year, huh? Weren't those choir kids just *angelic*?"), but none did. There was no sign of his mother, either. If anyone *did* recognize him - and plenty of people looked him square in the face as they passed - they didn't show it. He'd gone back to being Jason Rennor, that kid in the school hallway whose name you couldn't quite place and instantly forgot about once he was out of sight.

Right now, Jason was ok with that, although he was pretty sure he could have danced naked on top of one of the stalls and no-one would have given him more than a fleeting glance. Every man, woman and child in the square that evening was a glorified sleepwalker, treading a familiar path through the usual festival motions, barely aware they were there at all.

Maurice was right - they were only here for Miss Sparrow.

Jason had suffered through the town awards, which this year included the new and apparently controversial 'Best Spot for Coffee' trophy (someone actually muttered 'What the fuck?' when *Doreen's* was announced as the winner), until Mayor Thomas finally began his gushing preamble to the big People's Hero reveal and every head in the crowd immediately snapped in his direction. He had their full attention then, alright.

Miss Sparrow walked onto the stage and a ripple of excitement went through the crowd like an electric current. Jason felt it, too. He tried to resist it, but it washed over him all the same, pumping adrenaline into his veins. His heart began to pound.

She went to the podium and shook the Mayor's hand; when she turned to her audience, they responded as one, pressing towards her. Jason thought she was impossibly, unnaturally beautiful.

He could feel it now, pulsing through those gathered on the lawn. The crowd hung on her every word as she accepted the accolade, enraptured by her, *adoring* her. This was Evelyn, after all, wasn't it? Beautiful and charming Evelyn. This was the People's Hero, the pride of Amber Hill, and oh how they *loved* her. That intoxicating, pulsing sensation went out from them, electrifying the atmosphere. It crackled with it, made it like the air before a thunderstorm. Jason knew what that sensation was, knew exactly what Evelyn was making them feel in that moment - it was pure, unfettered *desire*.

Her speech faltered and he came out of the trance, just enough. He saw Lou - the back of her head, anyway - at the front, just below the stage he'd helped build.

Miss Sparrow pointed at her, said something, and Jason saw some members of the crowd move towards Lou. Then Maurice sprung the trap door and Evie dropped out of sight with a cry of surprise. There were gasps all around him. Someone even screamed, and that woke Jason completely. He craned his neck, trying to see what was happening on the stage.

It worked! he thought with a thrill. *Holy shit, it worked!*

He didn't see Principal Martin and the other town council officials pulling Evie out of the hole. He couldn't smell the septic waste now clinging to every part of her clothes and body, wouldn't have been able to even if he'd been right there beside her. But when she staggered to the edge of the stage, wild with rage and caked in black stuff, her imperceptible scent now masked under a new, vomit-inducing stench, Jason saw the crowd fall.

It was as if some giant, invisible hand had just swept across them, starting with those nearest the stage. It rippled out from the front and they went down like dominoes, toppling backwards, crumpling to the ground. Jason watched, open-mouthed, as the entire crowd collapsed onto the grass. As soon as they hit the ground they began convulsing, jerking spasmodically where they were, moaning like mummies from a 1930s horror movie. A woman dropped near Jason's feet and began foaming at the mouth, her eyes turned back in their sockets, and he realized with some shock that it was Beverley from the school reception, who'd yelled at him just last week for slamming the door.

Jason tore his eyes from her and looked back towards the stage. Only Lou remained standing in front of it, an island surrounded by a sea of writhing bodies under the festival lights. It was a jarring image and it rooted Jason to the spot. His legs had become dead weights under him.

Evie shrieked, a horrific, piercing sound in the evening air. Jason saw her tense, preparing to spring. Her hands were up, fingers bent into claws. The blue was gone from her eyes.

Lou didn't move. She remained where she was, arms by her sides, just a few feet away from the creature that had taken her life.

Evie's jaw elongated. Her tongue unfurled. Her shriek deepened into a gutural snarl.

Jason found his voice and yelled, 'Lou!'

The podium to Evie's right exploded. Shards of splintered wood shot out in all directions, embedding themselves in the stage backdrop and the council officials sprawled nearby. Evie dived away from the blast with a scream, arms shielding her face. Below the stage, Lou tumbled backwards and landed on top of a spasming person in the crowd.

Maurice stood by the corner of the stage with the shotgun in his hands, the barrels still smoking. He was already reloading.

Jason saw Evie leap from the far side of the stage and bolt off into the shadows. A second later, life returned to his legs and he started stumbling across the square towards Lou, hop-scotching over fallen townspeople. He stamped on someone's fingers on the way and grimaced, but there was no time to stop and see who it was.

He reached Lou and grabbed her arm, helping her up.

'She's getting away,' he said earnestly. 'We have to go.'

'No,' she gasped, still dazed by the shotgun blast. For a heart-stopping second, Jason wondered if she'd been hit, but there was no sign of blood on her.

'We can't let her get away.'

'We won't.'

She was on her feet now, turning on the spot. Maurice was coming towards them.

Suddenly, Lou uttered a little choked cry and darted off.

'Where're you...' Jason started, and then he saw.

He'd never met Derek Jennings before, but he recognised him from the wedding day photo Maurice had shown him on Friday, even with his much-thinned hair and glasses, now hanging off one ear. He was on his back a few yards away, head to one side, white foam in his copper beard. The little girl was face-down on his chest.

'Derek!' Lou cried, throwing herself on her husband. 'Ruth! Ruthie!'

Jason watched as Lou gathered the girl into her arms. She was unconscious, with drool around her mouth.

'Ruth! Wake up!' Lou patted the child's face, smoothing her blonde hair back with her other hand. Tears rolled down her cheeks. 'Ruth! It's me, baby. It's your mom.'

Maurice was suddenly there. 'She won't wake up. Not yet.'

Lou looked at him with wide, desperate eyes. Maurice shook his head.

'She'll be ok,' he said. 'But she won't wake up just yet. Not for a while. None of them will.'

'It happened to me, too,' agreed Jason, standing over Lou and her unconscious family. 'I was out for two days. But I came back.'

'We have to go,' said Maurice.

'I can't just leave them here!' Lou snapped. She was crouched protectively over Derek like an animal, holding Ruth's limp body against her own. She glared at them, ready to attack if they or anything else came closer. Jason noticed Ben for the first time, curled in the fetal position by Derek's left arm.

'You *have* to,' Maurice insisted. 'They'll come out of this and they'll be fine, but if *she* gets away, none of us are safe. If I could shoot for shit she'd be dead now. But I can't, and she ain't, so we have to go. We have to finish it.'

Lou wrenched her eyes back to Derek. She continued to hold the little girl tight to her body. Her tears flowed freely now.

'I... I can't leave them,' she managed, trembling. 'Not now...'

'Ma'am - '

'Go,' Jason said to Maurice, crouching beside Lou. 'I'll stay with her. We'll come soon.'

Maurice looked down at them, his mouth working behind his beard. The shotgun looked enormously heavy in his hands. He looked from Jason to Lou, and back to the kid again.

'You know where to go?'

'Yeah.'

'How'll you get there?'

'We'll take someone's car.'

Maurice hesitated.

'Don't be long,' he said gruffly. 'I don't know if I can take her myself.'

With that, he turned and jogged off across the square in the direction of the Sable.

'Oh baby, you've done it now. You've done it now, haven't you? Yes, you have.'

She hurried along the sidewalk, keeping to the shadows. The streets were almost completely empty. Most people in town had been at the Thanksgiving Festival, or had stayed at home by the fire. It was November, after all. Only those she'd wanted at the festival had been there, and each of them had dragged along a dozen or so of their friends and family for good measure.

Why not? It was *her* moment.

'You were greedy, baby, weren't you? Yes, you were. Greedy, greedy, greedy.'

She *had* been greedy. For the first time in a long while, she'd gotten sucked into her own illusion. It was a powerful thing. Potent, intoxicating. Feeding off this town, off the network of people connected to Louise Jennings. It'd rejuvenated her like never before. Sometimes things just fell into place like that. Sometimes she just got lucky with her prey.

Her left arm was bleeding where the shot from Maurice's gun had caught her and she left a trail of blood-like splodges in her wake. He'd missed, of course, the doddering old codger. But some of it had gotten her anyway, right through the sleeve of her favorite coat.

It was ruined now. It was *all ruined*.

'Should've been gone already, babycakes. What were you thinking?'

One of her heels snagged on the sidewalk and she stumbled, grabbing hold of a lamppost for balance. Anyone who'd seen her then under that streetlight would have been shocked, especially if they'd known how she normally looked, when her illusion was ripest: she was a tangled, black mess, sodden with the foul-smelling liquid Maurice had dumped her into, wild-eyed and breathing hard in the November chill.

She kicked off the heels and continued down the street barefoot.

'I'll take that gun,' she panted, 'and shove it up his fat ass. Yes I will. The old fuck won't be so clever then, will he? None of them will. Oh baby, no.'

She uttered that high, tittering laugh of hers. It echoed off the storefronts along the street, sending a nearby tomcat scurrying for cover. Animals hated her - the illusion didn't work on them at all.

Her laugh petered out. The corners of her mouth turned down into a scowl. How had she missed them? The rat-faced brat had just barely escaped her clutches on Friday and then had promptly disappeared. She was sure he'd go straight to his deadbeat mother and spill the beans, and she'd have no choice but to send her darling boy to the nuthouse, and that would be that string all tied up. Who would believe a kid, anyway? The disgusting little creatures were all liars, and if they weren't liars, they were just frightened idiots too scared and stupid to be a threat. Most of the children whose beds she'd slithered out from under over the years were now deranged.

The boy should have been that way by now. She'd have gotten to him eventually. But then the old man stepped in, stuck his nose where it didn't belong, and here they were.

And just what the hell was this stuff?

'Home,' she whispered to the night. 'Home is safe and clean. Yes it is.'

She'd love nothing more than to throw off her tired human rags - skin and all - and rush back there right away, where she could recover in peace and then slip out of town, but part of her knew it was no longer a safe option, or maybe not even possible at all. Something had changed when they'd dragged her out of that barrel. She felt weaker now, far *too* weak, and couldn't risk any more of them seeing her for what she really was. Weakness was a feeling she wasn't accustomed to, and it made her uneasy. Frightened, even.

The network had been broken; the strings had been severed. Lou - that simpering, unimpressive creature - was back in the frame, and unless Evie removed her from it all over again, her hold on Amber Hill was lost.

But she still had a few of them. Oh yes, she did. It wasn't over just yet. Not by a long shot.

And she liked this town.

Yes, she did.

Maybe she wasn't ready to leave it just yet.

Lou cupped her husband's face in her hands as she'd done a thousand times before and tried to make him see her. All around them, residents of Amber Hill lay motionless on the cold grass. They'd convulsed at first, some even fitfully, but it had passed. Now, the town square was still.

She'd laid Ruth down next to her father. The little girl breathed steadily into his shoulder. On his other side, Ben appeared almost peaceful, curled into himself as though he was tucked up in bed.

'Derek,' she whispered. Her tears had stopped flowing but her eyes were still full of them; she saw him through a blurred veil. 'Honey, it's me. It's Lou.'

He continued to stare up at the night sky, glazed and expressionless. She'd replaced his glasses on the bridge of his nose, knowing they'd be the first thing he'd check on when he woke up. The thought of him doing so almost made her cry again and she swallowed hard against the lump rising in her throat.

'It's ok, honey,' she said, running her thumbs through his beard, feeling the warmth of it. 'It wasn't your fault. It's all ok now.'

Jason was still on his haunches next to her, darting his gaze anxiously around the square. She could sense his restrained disquietude. Maurice had left them several minutes ago, roaring off in his battered old station wagon, taking the shotgun with him.

What if she came back now?

'She won't come back,' Lou said aloud.

Jason cleared his throat: 'What?'

'I said, she won't come back.' Lou's hands slid down to Derek's chest. She could feel his heart beating beneath his coat, and when she spoke again, it was addressed to him. 'We won't let her come back.'

Jason rose, a little ungainly, continuing to scan their surroundings. The stench from the waste-filled barrel still hung in the air, but Lou knew he couldn't smell it. She still couldn't quite believe it had worked, and so powerfully, too. But there was no time for that now.

What if she comes back?

'I have to go,' she said, still to Derek. Jason seemed to understand that she wasn't speaking to him and moved off, stepping carefully over bodies as he went. She thought there was something perversely comical about the way he had his arms stuck out for balance, doing his best to avoid tramping on anyone's extremities. She watched him for a moment, then leaned close to Derek's ear.

'I'm going, baby, but I'll be back,' she whispered, trembling all over as she said it. 'I just have something to do. It won't take long, I promise. And I'll be here when you and the kids wake up, and we'll go home, and everything will be ok again. I *promise* you that.'

She reached over and kissed Ben's cheek, surprised at its warmth, and then did the same to Ruth. They both could have been asleep in bed, and the simple surety that they would be again soon brought a glimmer of a smile to her face. She leaned over Derek and kissed him gently on the lips, ignoring the stab of pain in her ribs as she did so.

As she drew back, she heard it, barely audible in the night air.

'Lou...'

Her heart rate quickened. She took his face in her hands again and stared deep into his eyes, willing him to see her. For a fraction of a second, she thought she saw something in them. His lips moved again, soundlessly this time, but it had been enough before, whether she'd imagined it or not.

'See you soon, honey,' she whispered.

She kissed his cheek, then gently tilted his head to one side, facing Ben. She hoped it would be enough to stop him choking if he started convulsing again. There wasn't time to reposition him properly.

As if to reiterate the point, Jason appeared at her side again. He took her by the arm as she stood up, and she was glad he did. Her legs had turned to rubber.

'Are you ok?' he asked.

He was pale and sweating, hair matted to his forehead. She saw then, not for the first or last time, just how young he really was.

Just a kid, scared out of his mind. He's been through the ringer and he's still here.

'Yes, I'm fine,' she replied, forcing a smile, thinking it was an insane thing to say when you were standing next to the unconscious forms of your husband and children.

You're still here, too, she told herself. *So make it count.*

'I found this.' Jason held up a handgun.

'Where'd you get that?'

He motioned with his head. 'There's a cop over there. This was in his holster. Pretty sure it's a Glock 22.'

'Do you know how to use it?'

Jason looked at the gun thoughtfully for a moment, then slipped it into his jeans pocket.

'I think so,' he said; then, when he saw her dubious expression, he added, 'The safety's on. Don't worry.'

'I'm not,' said Lou. 'Use it, if you have to.'

'I will. The cop also had these on him.' He held up a set of car keys. 'His cruiser's parked just over there.'

Lou took a breath. 'Then let's get going.'

She took the keys and started across the square. She didn't allow herself to look back at where her family lay on the grass.

It was the only way to keep her feet moving.

Maurice turned onto Oakland Avenue. He could taste metal, the byproduct of too much adrenaline in his system.

They'd scouted out the house the night before, timing how long it took to get from it to the town square in the event they'd have to pursue her. Lou's friend had given her the address and it'd been spot-on, confirmed by the red mailbox with 'Sparrow' emblazoned on it. Maurice hadn't been remotely surprised by how neat and picturesque the place was, either, right down to the still-blooming begonias lining the garden path and the honeysuckle clambering lazily around the front door. He'd encountered one of Evie's "homes" in a Wyoming town she'd decimated some months back, but it'd been after she'd abandoned it and moved on to the next place. Before Amber Hill, she'd always been just ahead of the curve.

It was why, Maurice thought, stopping her this time was so imperative.

The drive from the center of town to Oakland Avenue took roughly ten minutes, without traffic. There was hardly anyone on the road that night and Maurice made it there in good time, bouncing the Sable unceremoniously onto the curb a couple of houses down from sixty-four. He grabbed the shotgun from the passenger side, paused as a wave of deja-vu washed over him, and got out of the car.

The air was still, but the cold nipped at his face anyway. His boots clumped on the sidewalk as he approached Evie's house. Somewhere far off, an engine revved, then dropped off again.

'Walk to the door,' he said, 'knock on the door, wait for it to open.'

Curtains were pulled across the windows of neighboring houses, but he could see light behind some of them. At least a few of Amber Hill's residents hadn't gone to the Thanksgiving festival, then.

What does that mean for them? he wondered.

He came to the foot of Evie's garden and paused to look at the house. Like those on either side of it, the curtains were pulled across the windows and the lights were all off. The place looked deserted, but he knew better than to trust his own eyes at this point. She'd more than likely got here first and was already waiting for him inside. She may be watching him from between the drapes right now.

A sense of dread began to wash over him, as though he was pressing into some unseen barrier, and he was sure that sensation was coming directly from the house itself, pulsing in waves. He'd felt the presence of evil in a place before, but nothing quite like this. The air was thick with it. He could practically smell it.

'Walk to the door,' Maurice commanded himself, and started towards the house.

He hadn't taken more than three steps when a figure emerged from the shadows and drifted in front of him, blocking his path. He immediately stopped where he was, gun held protectively across his chest, peering into the darkness. It was difficult to make out who the figure was, but judging by their frame, it wasn't Evie.

He swallowed and found his throat had run dry. 'Who's there?'

The person standing in the darkness didn't reply.

'Who are you?' Maurice said, before adding, 'I don't want to hurt you.'

Again, no response. Maurice hesitated, then took a step forward,

As he did so, the person in the shadows bent down and lifted something from the flower bed next to the porch. Maurice couldn't make out what it was. He maneuvered the gun into a forward-facing position, pointing the barrels at the ground.

'Please,' he said. 'Go home. It ain't safe here tonight.'

He took another step forward, halfway up the walk now, and this time, the figure responded in kind. She came out of the shadows into the weak glow cast by the streetlight on the sidewalk, and Maurice saw two things things right away: first of all, the figure was the girl he'd seen outside the school last week, the plump blonde who'd been staring right at him until he drove off; second of all, she had a large round stone in her hand.

'Miss, you should go,' he said. The shotgun seemed to gain ten pounds in his hands. *She's just a kid*, he thought. *I can't shoot a kid.* 'Please, just go.'

Her eyes were wide and unseeing. When she spoke, her voice was dreamy, almost sing-song in its tone. 'Hello, Maurice.'

He shivered. Suddenly, he became consumed with the urge to turn and look back towards the street, sure another of Evie's puppets was sneaking up behind him. He fought it, standing his ground. If he turned away, that stone would fly right at his head. His heart battered against the inside of his chest.

'Where're you going, Maurice?' asked the girl, grinning. The stone was about the size of a grapefruit and she held it in her palm. It was certainly big enough to knock him out, maybe even kill him. He doubted she'd pass up the chance to smash in his skull, especially if she managed to daze him with a blow to the head first. 'What're you here for, Maurice *Baxter*?'

He heard Evie's voice coming from her mouth then and he cursed her for it. She'd put a kid between them, using her as a shield. She was going to try and make him kill a kid to get to her.

'C'mere, Mo,' said the girl, taking another step towards him, grinning like a maniac now. 'Let me whisper in your ear.'

Damn you, Evie. Damn you for this.

'Please, kid,' he pleaded, raising the gun. 'Please don't make me do this.'

'But you've already done it, Mo,' she said. 'So go ahead. Blow my brains out.'

'Please, don't -'

'What're you waiting for, Mo?' she shrieked.

She came at him. He saw the stone go up.

Lord, forgive me.

He pulled the trigger.

The report was like a bomb going off in the still night. The barrel jerked up, smoking, and the stock dug into his armpit. He hadn't set himself properly and had to take a step back to keep from falling.

He saw the girl spin away as if a cord attached to her shoulder had been wrenched violently from behind. The stone clunked off the path and rolled onto the grass.

Maurice lowered the gun. His body had become weak, languid. A dog started barking further down the street, startled by the gunshot. Out of the corner of his eye, he saw a porch light turn on.

He walked to where she lay, willing his legs to move. She was face-down in the grass next to a bed of yellow chrysanthemums.

'What've you done?' he whispered.

He crouched next to her, leaning on the gun. Placing one big hand on her shoulder, he rolled her over onto her back.

The girl's eyes were closed. Her head rolled on her neck as she flopped over on the lawn and she groaned, long and slow. The shot had caught her on the side, barely clipping her wide frame, and Maurice could already see where the slug had dug a divot into the grass just behind her. There was blood on her sweater, soaking into the wool, but she was alive. She'd been stunned by the blast, certainly injured by it, but not fatally-so.

'You're a fuckin' crappy shot, Maurice,' he muttered, hauling himself back to his feet.

More lights had come on along the street. The dog was still barking, scared and insistent.

Maurice left the girl on the grass and walked to the front porch of Evie's house. He paused there long enough to load another shell into the gun, then knocked twice on the door. When nothing happened, he tried the handle, and wasn't the least bit surprised when it turned freely in his hand.

Smiling, and not knowing why, he pushed open the door and went inside.

At the exact moment Maurice Baxter went inside number sixty-four Oakland Avenue, Frank Orville stepped out of *O'Hare's* bar on Second Street, spat a wad into the gutter, and started towards the center of town.

He'd been drinking on and off since six o'clock, propped up on the bar, regaling John O'Hare himself with every shitfire story he could think of from the past week. He was a regular at *O'Hare's* and John was accustomed to this routine. Normally Frank reserved his inebriated expositions for the weekend, but it was Thanksgiving tomorrow and he had the day off, a whole *day* off, so here he was, preparing to make the most of it.

Patrons had come and gone throughout the evening while Frank filled John in on the events of the last few days between gulps of beer: he told him about the kids smoking joints behind the dumpster and how he'd almost caught them red-handed, but they'd slipped away at the last second, the little bastards; he told him all about the Thanksgiving festival, and about the mess kids had been leaving behind them all week preparing for it, and explained why it wasn't his job to pick up after them every second of every day in that little fucking school, no sir; Frank even told John about the unsettling incident at the geography room last Wednesday, though he omitted the part about being too scared to open the door, and about his hastened exit from the school that afternoon. No, he'd keep that one to himself for now.

John took it all in, nodding when he should nod, offering to refill Frank's glass each time he reached the bottom. He didn't mind the incessant grumbling, foul-mouthed as it usually was. Frank had been his regular customer for years and he aimed to keep it that way. Besides, he knew the old man was good for his tab. Frank was nothing if not reliable, and he always settled up eventually.

At eight-thirty, Frank finally had his fill and bid John a slurred good-night - he'd been at *O'Hare's* since just after five, and he was getting hungry. He headed up the street in the direction of his car (that's where he'd parked it, right?), muttering to himself as he went. Even by his own standards, he'd managed to put an admirable number away tonight. The sidewalk ahead of him tilted and swayed as though he was walking the deck of a boat, sloshing the beer in his belly. He knew he'd throw up at least some of it later, but that was for then. Right now, he needed to find his car, and then he needed to eat.

Had Frank not been drunk, or even been *less* drunk, he might have noticed sooner how quiet Second Street was that night. Storefronts were lit up and decorated for Thanksgiving (here was Billy Struth's barber shop with an enormous cardboard cutout turkey in the window and a sagging pumpkin by the door) and there were plenty of cars still parked along the curb, but Frank didn't pass a single person after leaving the bar, and no-one drove by in either direction. He knew the festival should still be on and folks should be coming and going from it, but there was no-one about. Not a dicky-bird.

'Where the hell's the car?' he said. He looked back the way he'd come in case he'd missed it, but he was sure it'd been further down, nearer the town square. Or had he parked at the square itself?

Frank sighed and continued on, trudging now. His mind went back to his conversation with John. He remembered telling him about what happened in the school last week and the memory seemed to sober him up a little. He squinted down the street, shielding his eyes from the glare of the streetlight above. Why couldn't he hear the festival? There'd be a crowd, full of noisy, disrespectful kids and their pansy-ass parents, all too afraid to take the belt to them when the time came. This fucking generation. Frank didn't like kids, never had. He'd never wanted any of his own and had made damn-well sure over the years that he didn't make one by accident. His wife, long-gone now, might have wanted them, but Frank didn't know one way or the other. He hadn't asked, and that wasn't his problem anymore.

He tried and failed to push the memory of the geography room out of his wizened old head. That'd been real fear that day, hadn't it? He wasn't sure if he'd *ever* felt that sort of thing before, now that he thought about it. He'd practically tasted it. Whatever was on the other side of that door that afternoon, whatever was moving around the room, had been giving it off like a bad stink. And it'd left its mark on him. Frank supposed it might be something like shell-shock, the sort of thing army vets experience after coming back from some overseas war. Frank couldn't say for sure - he'd managed to avoid going, even when most of his peers had saddled up and shipped out to make Uncle Sam proud. Fighting in some foreign country for some phony-baloney reason, that hadn't been for him. It was just another thing that hadn't been his problem.

If he couldn't forget what happened in the school, he'd just drink some more. There wasn't much that couldn't be solved with another drink.

Frank came to the end of Second Street and stopped.

He was across from the town square, leaning on a lamp post for support. He could see the orange and yellow lights strung from the trees, and he could see the top of the stage above the vendor stalls, but he couldn't hear anything. No music, no voices. Nothing at all.

He stuck a finger in his ear and twisted it. Had he gone deaf? Had he drunk so much he'd lost his hearing?

'What the hell,' he muttered, starting across the road. He looked both ways. The street here was swaying too, but there were no cars on the road. Plenty parked along it, but none on the road.

Frank crossed the street, approaching the edge of the park. A breath of wind dragged some dry leaves over the sidewalk. He heard them, alright, but nothing else. Still no voices.

Was the thing over already? All that time, all that panic, and the thing was over before nine. What a bust.

Frank entered the square, coming in under a banner reading 'Welcome to the Amber Hill Thanksgiving Festival!', straining to hear something, anything. The beer sloshed in his stomach. He suddenly needed to pee really bad. He was either going to pee or throw up.

He passed between two vendor stalls and walked onto the grass. And stopped again.

'Shitfire,' he said.

Frank stared dully at the bodies spread across the lawn. The entire square was covered in them, all the way from the stage at one end to the stalls at the back. He saw men and women and children, all flat on the cold grass, unmoving in the glow of the festival lights. His eyes went to a mother a few feet away, face-down next to her baby's stroller. Just beyond her, he saw a kid curled up on his side, still clutching a stick of his candy floss. There were hundreds of them, some piled on top of each other in places, filling the square. And they were all dead.

Shaking, Frank walked further across the grass. He saw a big man slumped over the counter of his stall in a puddle of hot chocolate. The family he'd been serving were in a bundle in front of the stall. Static crackled from a speaker mounted nearby. Up on the stage, he thought he could see someone who might be Perry Martin, crumpled near an open trapdoor.

Shot, Frank thought, in a detached sort of way, like he was watching it all on his TV screen at home. *They've all been shot and killed. It's a terrorist attack*.

But as he bent next to a teenage boy (one he perhaps recognized from the school), he saw that wasn't true. There were no bullet holes on anyone, no blood. Some of them had white stuff around their mouths, but that was it. And what's more, they weren't even dead. He could see the boy's chest rise and fall beneath his jacket. The kid was unconscious, but he was alive, alright.

Frank got unsteadily back to his feet. His head was spinning now and he was closer than ever to throwing up. But not here. He wasn't sticking around to find out what had poisoned all these people. If he wasn't careful, he'd be next. He could even smell something in the air, couldn't he? Some rancid stench, like something you might pick up in a hospital.

No way, no sir. He was going home, even if he had to walk all the way there. The police would be along soon to sort this mess out, he was sure of it. His car could wait until tomorrow, wherever the hell it was. None of this was his problem anyway, was it?

Frank Orville turned on his heel and walked out of the town square.

He made it about half a mile before decorating the sidewalk with the contents of his stomach, and walked on.

'That's his car,' Jason said, pointing.

Lou slowed as they passed the Sable, craning her neck to peer through the window. Maurice wasn't inside.

'Where is he?'

'He's gone in already,' she replied.

She angled the police cruiser onto the curb in front of Maurice's car, wincing at the pain in her sprained wrist. The Tylenol she'd swallowed several hours ago was wearing off and she wasn't accustomed to maneuvering the larger car. She killed the engine.

Jason was halfway out the door when she grabbed his arm.

'Hang on.' He stopped where he was, one foot on the sidewalk. 'What's the plan? We expected to do this as a three, right? And with a shotgun.'

Jason looked at the gun in his hand, then back to her. There was doubt written on his face, but not in his eyes. The eyes were sure.

'I'll shoot her,' he said, as though they were discussing the grocery shop. 'And I'll keep shooting her until I run out of bullets.'

Lou looked back at him, long and hard, then nodded. 'Good enough for me.'

She opened her door and got out. A dog barked rhythmically a few houses down. There were lights on in some windows but no-one had come outside, even at the sight of the police cruiser on the sidewalk. But she was certain they were being watched.

Jason was already at the foot of Evelyn's garden, the gun hanging by his side. Lou drew up next to him and saw what he was staring at.

'Who is that?' she asked, keeping her voice level.

The girl was over by the bushes. Even from distance, she could see blood soaked into her sweater.

'I don't know,' replied Jason, starting forward. 'No, wait. Shit, it's Sophie.'

'Sophie who?' said Lou, and then she saw. It was Sophie Wentworth, sweet and kind Sophie Wentworth, flat on her back on the cold grass. She'd been shot. Lou covered her mouth. 'Oh no, oh no.'

Jason went to Sophie and knelt by her. Lou followed but stayed on the garden path. She suddenly felt sick.

Did Maurice do this?

Jason stood up again. He was paler than ever.

'She's alive,' he said. 'I don't think she's badly hurt. But she needs to go to the hospital.'

'You have your phone?'

'Yeah.'

He took it out and dialed.

Lou turned to look at the house. She heard Jason say 'I need an ambulance' but his voice sounded muffled, like he was on the other side of a door. She looked at the flower-patterned curtains pulled over the windows, at the honeysuckle snaking around the porch, at the brass six and four fixed next to the door. The whole thing was so surreal, so detached from anything that had gone before, that for the briefest moment she actually thought she might be dreaming the whole thing. Wouldn't that be nice, to wake up in her bed next to Derek and realize none of it -

'They're on their way,' Jason said.

She blinked at him.

'Ok, then we don't have long.' She looked at Sophie, lying motionless on the grass, then turned back to the house. 'Come on.'

She went up the path. The dog was still barking further down the street, on and on.

She stopped at the door, keenly aware of how weaponless she was.

'I'll go first,' said Jason, reaching for the handle.

'No,' she said, grabbing it before he could. 'You keep both hands on that gun.'

She turned the handle. The door clicked open easily and she pushed it wide. Beyond it was an empty hallway and a set of stairs leading up to the second floor. A pink mat on the floor informed them that *Home Is Where The Heart Is.*

I can feel it, she thought, her heart racing. *I can feel her in here.*

Lou stepped over the threshold. She could hear Jason breathing heavily just behind her.

There were three doors in the hall that she could see. One to the right at the foot of the stairs was closed; another at the end of the hall was ajar, and through the gap she could see a kitchen, illuminated by moonlight through the window. A third door to their left was also closed, but light emitted from beneath it.

Lou looked back at Jason as he eased the front door closed. She thought of telling him that was a bad idea, that they should keep their escape route clear, but talking aloud suddenly seemed like the last thing they should do.

They were inside *Evelyn Sparrow's house.*

A familiar scent reached her nostrils. It was comforting, memory-inducing, and after a second she realized what it was. Cinnamon. The smell of Christmas.

Her house smelled like Christmas.

I can feel her.

In the darkness of the hallway, she barely saw Jason motioning towards the door with the gun. She put a hand on his skinny forearm, acknowledging that she'd seen him, and opened the door.

They squinted into the light. Lou saw a living room, neat and tidy, with little decoration beyond a standing lamp in one corner, a TV in another, a green plant by the window, and a few framed photos of what appeared to be famous national landmarks hung on the rose-print walls. Above the fireplace, four American presidents gazed out from the face of Mount Rushmore. The fire was lit, spilling warm light over the deep red carpet. A couch and two armchairs were arranged in front of it.

'Lou,' said Jason softly. 'The fire.'

She followed his gaze to the flames, and for a moment didn't see what he was talking about. When she did, she swore under her breath: what remained of Evie's fur-lined coat was among the logs, burned black. Her other clothes could have been in there, too.

'She took it off,' said Jason, 'to get rid of the smell - '

A door on the wall opposite them swung open. Jason jerked the gun towards it.

'Wait!' Lou cried.

She stared in disbelief and the woman in the doorway stared back. She wore a rose-printed apron and held a rolling pin in both hands. There was a dusting of flour on her front.

'Debbie?' Lou said, gasping her name. 'What the hell are you doing here?'

'Lou - ' Jason started.

'Lou!' Debbie beamed. Her face was flushed and happy. 'It's great to see you.'

Her friend took a step into the room and Lou matched it without thinking. She hadn't seen Debbie since...since...

'Lou,' Jason said again. There was something in his tone that stopped her from moving any closer. She stood near the couch, watching Debbie, thinking: *She looks good. She's never looked better.*

'Are you ok?' she asked.

Debbie's smile widened. She brushed her hair back, smearing flour on her temple.

'I'm fine,' she said. 'I was just doing a little baking, you know? Cookies. Chocolate chip. Your favorite, right? They're hot from the oven.'

Lou tried to process what she was saying. She barely noticed Debbie inching further into the room, the rolling pin still in both hands. Something about the way she was holding it jarred in Lou's mind. She was holding it like -

'Why don't you take a seat and I'll bring in a plate?' said Debbie. 'You too, Jason.'

In response, Jason leveled the gun at her.

'NO!' Lou screamed, reaching for his arm. Across the room, Debbie shifted the flour-covered rolling pin towards them.

Lou was struck from the side and went down behind the couch. There was a flash of light and an ear-splitting boom. Glass shattered. She hit the carpet and Jason landed on top of her. From the other side of the living room, she heard Debbie shriek in fury.

Jason tumbled off her and she rolled onto her front. Stars swelled and popped behind her eyes. Her wrist was on fire - she'd landed on it and the carpet had done nothing to cushion her fall.

The carpet.

Lou stared, dazed, at the dust-covered floorboards beneath her palms. She smelled mildew and rot. The cinnamon aroma was gone.

Jason moved next to her. She heard his boots scuff on the floor, and then there was another bang, sharper than the first. Debbie shrieked again. There was a thump as she hit the floor.

Lou scrambled onto her knees and looked around. The rose-print wallpaper was gone. The green plant was gone. The TV and the stack of DVDs were gone.

The room they were now in was bare, damp and derelict. There was no carpet on the floor, and the couch shielding them was a stained, stinking thing, chewed apart by mice. Flames continued to flicker in the fireplace, licking up the last of Evie's clothes. Jason dropped down next to her again, panting.

'You didn't see it?' he gasped. 'You didn't see the shotgun?'

'No,' Lou said. Suddenly, she understood. 'I saw something else.'

'It's the illusion,' Jason said. 'She's here.'

'I know.' Lou pointed at the open door. 'Go, find her. Help Maurice.'

'I can't leave you here.'

'You can,' she hissed, looking him in the eye. 'I'll deal with Debbie. We don't have much time. Go, quickly!'

Jason hesitated for a fraction longer, then, keeping low, darted to the door, swinging it closed behind him. It wobbled on its hinges.

Shit, what now? Lou thought.

She turned to look behind her and broken glass tinkled from her hair and clothes. The window was boarded up and there was a fresh hole in the wood, right behind where she'd been standing seconds before. The glass inside of the boards had shattered, spraying the living room with cutting shards. Wintry air gusted through the hole, causing the fireplace flames to thrash shadows against the wall.

'Lou.'

Debbie's voice drifted across to her. She sounded weak. Injured.

'Lou?'

She swallowed and called back, 'I'm here, Debs.'

Silence.

'Debbie?'

Lou adjusted her position behind the moldy couch, getting onto her haunches. The pain in her wrist was growing steadily and her middle throbbed. She heard Jason move off down the hallway.

'Debbie,' she said, trying to sound calm. 'It's me. It's Lou. You know me.'

'Lou.' A croak this time.

'Yeah. Debs, can we talk?' She glanced towards the wall separating the living room and hallway. Had she heard a door creak? Best to keep Debbie distracted. 'Debs, what happened to you? What did she do to you?'

Silence again.

Lou's heart thudded hard, pounding blood past her ears, which still rang from the report of the shotgun blast. She had to get through to Debbie somehow, to at least pinpoint where she was in the room.

If she was even still in the room at all.

She cleared her throat. 'Debbie, I'm coming out.'

Slowly, painfully, she stood. Another shock of cold air came through the hole in the boards behind her, sending a shiver up her back. She peered across the room, momentarily disoriented by the flickering light from the fire. She saw that the hearth below the fireplace had been smashed long ago - sharp chunks of tile were scattered across it. The two armchairs, equally as molded as the couch, faced her like dank sentinels. The door to the kitchen was wide open.

Lou came around the couch, running her hand along the top of it, ignoring any sense of repulsion. She stopped in front of the fireplace. Her eyes went from the open door to the shadowy corner of the room beyond the armchairs, and back to the door again. Did she leave? The adjacent door from the kitchen to the hallway had been ajar when they arrived. She could have easily gotten from the living room to that other door without them noticing, while the shotgun blast had still reverberated. She could have met Jason in the hallway, in the darkness, where he wouldn't have seen her coming.

'Oh no,' Lou whispered, looking to the door Jason had exited through. She took a step towards it.

Debbie came out from behind one of the armchairs and sprang at her. Lou just had time to register what was happening before her friend fell upon her, screaming in animal fury. Debbie wasn't any bigger than her but she'd caught her by surprise and managed to knock her back onto the couch. Then she was on top of her, shrieking and clawing and gnashing her teeth.

Lou attempted to push her off, but it was like trying to wrestle a large, ferocious dog. She yelled in pain as Debbie yanked out a fistful of her hair. Then she actually went for her throat, straining to bite into Lou's jugular, snapping at the air an inch from her flesh with yellowed teeth.

Holy shit, she's lost her mind, Lou thought, and swung her uninjured fist at Debbie's head. The connection was good and Debbie cried out, rolling to one side. Lou used the momentum to scramble on top of her. Beneath them, a spring in the couch snapped with a *boing* sound. She grabbed hold of Debbie's wrists as best she could and pinned her with her knees. Debbie kicked and thrashed and spat obscenities at her, but Lou held on.

'Debbie!' she yelled. Tears ran down her face, as much from the pain in her wrist and ribs as the shock of having to fight her best friend. 'Debbie, stop! Listen to me!'

Debbie did look at her then, and what Lou saw sent a lightning bolt of despair into her heart. Debbie, her closest friend in Amber Hill, strong and confident Debbie Lathem, stared up at her with eyes that bulged from a sallow, cadaverous face; her lips were cracked and broken, and her hair was a wild tangle on her head. She was dreadfully frail and, Lou noticed with anguished disgust, she reeked of pungent body odor. It was clear Debbie hadn't bathed in a long time.

'Debs,' Lou said, tears dripping off her chin onto Debbie's sweater. 'Look what she's done to you.'

Debbie gaped up at her. She was no longer thrashing, but her expression was blank.

'Let me help you,' Lou said, nodding, trying to encourage understanding from her friend. 'I can help you, we all can. You'll be ok. We won't let Evelyn - '

At the name, Debbie's face dissolved into rage again and she lunged at Lou, very nearly taking a bite out of her cheek. Her teeth actually clacked together near Lou's ear. It was all she could do to hold her down. Debbie fought to break free from her grasp for a few moments then collapsed into the couch again, exhausted. Lou wondered when she'd last eaten anything.

'There's an ambulance coming,' she said, trying to hold eye contact. 'They'll be here soon. We'll get you some help, ok?' Then, something else occurred to her, something she should have thought of long before now. 'Debbie, where's Sarah?'

Debbie became still. For a few seconds, she stared off into space, her face blank again. Then her mouth started working, straining to form words.

'Sss... Sssaa...'

'Debs, where is she?'

'Sss... Sarah.' Debbie met her gaze then and her eyes welled with tears. Lou saw a glimmer of awareness, of sanity returning. 'Sarah. *Sarah!*'

Lou felt Debbie's body relax under her. Or rather, it went limp. She loosened her grip on her friend's wrists.

'Do you know where she is?' Lou asked.

'Sarah... Sarah...'

'Where is Sarah, Debbie? Where's your girl?'

Debbie's expression was no longer blank. A mixture of dawning horror and panic flooded into her face.

'Sarah! Oh, oh...'

'Does she have her?' Lou said. She shifted her legs off Debbie's. 'Does Evelyn have - '

She realized her mistake too late. Debbie's eyes went wide and she roared, propelling herself into Lou. She hadn't been ready for it and toppled backwards. Debbie came with her and they hit the floorboards hard, sending plumes of dust into the air. The breath was instantly knocked from Lou's lungs and her broken ribs screamed in protest under Debbie's weight. Dizzying pain rocketed through her system and into her brain.

'EVIE!' Debbie shrieked. 'Evie! Evie! Evie!'

She backhanded Lou across the face. Her vision clouded, filling with stars. Debbie's hand came back the other way and she raked Lou's cheek with her nails. Lou heard a sound like tearing paper.

'There is only Evie!' Debbie cried manically. 'Evie my friend! Evie my FRIEND!'

Lou tried to wrestle her off, but Debbie seemed to have gained new strength. She grabbed Lou's throat with both hands and squeezed, digging her fingers into her neck. Lou gasped as her windpipe closed over. She tried to pull Debbie's hands away but couldn't break her grip. Debbie bared gritted teeth, straining. Saliva dribbled down her chin.

Darkness began to creep into the fringes of Lou's vision. She felt her arms weaken. Debbie was a dead weight on her torso, immobilizing her, pressing her lungs flat with one knee. She squeezed harder, her nails digging into Lou's skin, drawing blood. Lou felt her mind loosening.

I came so far. The thought seemed far-off, like it wasn't hers. *I came all this way. Now I'm going to die here, in this old house.*

Debbie was throttling her now, shaking her like a rag doll. The back of Lou's head banged off the floorboards and her arms fell away limp. Her vision was almost black.

I'll never see Derek or the kids again, she thought, almost serenely. *I hope they'll be ok without me.*

Her head went to the side, facing the dying fire. She saw the smoldering logs, the last shreds of Evie's coat. She saw the hearth, the pieces of tile. Her hand was next to one.

'Evie is my friend,' Debbie seethed, her face a white contortion of madness.

Lou reached.

'Evie is my BEST FRIEND!'

Lou's hand closed around the chunk of tile. It was cold beneath her fingers. She swung it at Debbie's head.

The tile buried into Debbie's temple with a moist *thunk* and her grip instantly relaxed. Lou's arm, finally spent of strength, dropped back to the floor. She stared up at Debbie, sitting statuesque on top of her with a wedge of broken tile sticking out of her skull and a trickle of blood coming out of her left nostril. Then, as if it was happening in slow motion, she toppled to one side and thumped to the floor.

Breath rushed back into Lou's lungs and she uttered a long, wheezing gasp. She put her hands to her midriff, sucking in lungfuls of stale, dust-filled air, then rolled towards the fireplace and coughed violently. Her throat was raw and every intake of oxygen was agony. A foot from her face, the fire smoldered down to embers.

Once she was breathing steadily again, she pulled herself into a sitting position and, reluctantly, turned to Debbie. Her friend lay on her side, eyes and mouth open, an expression of surprise etched on her face. The chunk of tile was still lodged in her head, deeper than Lou had thought. How she'd found the strength to do it, she'd never want to know.

No time for this.

It was a cold, hard thought, but it came to her anyway, and it got her moving. She would mourn Debbie later. She would confront what had just happened when there was time to do it. Not now. Only one thing mattered now. After that, she would gladly give herself to the sorrow. Let it consume her then, but not now.

Biting her lip, she swallowed down the misery bubbling up from within and rose shakily to her feet.

It was the squashed pack of Marlboros that helped him find Maurice.

After Jason had slammed the door to the living room shut behind him, he'd stood in the hallway and listened, waiting. The second shotgun blast didn't come. That was enough for now.

He looked down the hall towards the kitchen. The door was still ajar but there was no movement beyond it. There was nothing in there but rotting countertops and rusted faucets, all bathed in moonlight shafting between criss-crossing boards nailed over the window. There'd be a back door, of course, but Evie wouldn't have rushed all the way here just to escape again. She'd have known they were coming. Jason knew she was here - he could feel it, somehow.

Voices from the living room. He heard Lou call out, but her voice was muffled. It wasn't the density or integrity of the walls doing the muffling, either. Something had thickened the atmosphere inside number sixty-four Oakland Avenue. Jason couldn't smell it, if there was a smell at all, but he wasn't entirely certain he couldn't *taste* it.

He went to the stairs. They were falling apart and he didn't fancy his chances of reaching the second floor. Even if the warped steps held under his weight, the landing was blocked off by what looked to be either a wardrobe or dresser turned on its side. It was flush to the wall with no room to squeeze past, and there was no way Maurice could have hauled himself over it. He wasn't up there.

So where the hell was he?

Voices from the living room again.

I have to go back.

Jason turned to the door, made to reach for the handle. Then something halfway down the hall caught his eye. Something small and white against the damp-darkened floorboards. A pack of cigarettes.

Maurice's pack.

His eyes traveled from the pack to the door next to them, one he hadn't noticed before because he hadn't been looking for it. It was narrower than the other doorways in the hall and set directly under where the second floor landing would be.

The basement.

Of course.

Jason went to the door and tried the handle. It opened easily and he went through, easing the door most of the way closed behind him. He was at the top of another rotted flight of stairs, running down into darkness (but was there a glow down there?); the sliver of light coming through from the kitchen was enough to see by. Trailing a hand along the wall, and trying to pretend he couldn't feel dozens of ancient cobwebs snagging on his fingers as he did so, he started down the stairs. The gun, now in his weaker hand, felt heavier and more cumbersome than he'd have liked.

The moonlight from the kitchen quickly disappeared, but his eyes were already adjusting to the gloom. About halfway down, with the steps groaning under him, the cobweb-strewn concrete wall gave way to a rickety wooden handrail. The staircase was right in the center of the basement, with open space on either side of it. Jason became aware that the temperature had dropped a degree as he neared the floor. Suddenly, he felt completely exposed. If Evie - or anyone else - was down here, he wouldn't see them coming.

But there was that glow, wasn't there?

He came to the foot of the staircase and stepped onto a rough, earthen floor. The basement wall was directly ahead of him, just a few feet from the bottom of the stairs. He supposed he was now standing right under the front entrance of the house. Sophie Wentworth would still be lying up there, bleeding into the grass. Jason strained to hear ambulance sirens, but there were none. Were they coming at all? Maybe it was already too late for Sophie. For all of them.

He did hear *something*, though. It came from behind him, further back in the basement.

He moved around the end of the staircase, using the handrail post as a pivot in the dim light. The walls, barely visible, were green with mildew. He could imagine what it must smell like down here in this damp, rotting place. That foul taste in the air was more potent down here. It laced the back of his throat like bile.

The sound again. A murmuring.

Jason faced towards the back of the basement. He could see the glow now but its source was blocked off by some bulky thing positioned next to the staircase. He moved towards it, switching the gun to his right hand, reaching out with his left. His fingers connected with the thing near the staircase and he recoiled. It was a stack of moldy cardboard boxes, all damp and sagging into one another. His fingertips had sunk an inch into one before he realized what they were, and when he pulled them back, a tired puff of putrefied air wheezed out after them.

Repulsed, he stepped around the boxes.

He saw it all at once, completely.

The basement, like the rest of the house above it, was mostly empty and seemed to be in the latter stages of degradation. The walls were brick and laced with more dead cobwebs and black mold - in sections, plants had broken through cracks in the mortar and starved in the darkness. Two narrow windows just below the ceiling were thick with grime; to the left of them, at the top of a short flight of concrete steps, was a set of double cellar doors, sealed with a rusted padlock. The steps met the floor next to an almost-bare wall on the left side of the room, from which a handful of variously-sized, corroded pipes protruded. There was a raised block section under the pipes, and Jason guessed there'd once been a boiler positioned on top of them.

The wall opposite the boiler area, on the right-hand side of the basement, was stacked with more molding cardboard boxes and the remains of an old, tireless bicycle. In the corner, an oil-fired lantern proved to be the source of the light; its flickering yellow glow created moving fingers of shadow on the walls and ceiling. There was a workbench along the wall at the back of the room, and just beneath the obscured window panes, a set of barely-hanging-on wooden shelves displayed a collection of random, long-forgotten items.

Jason's eyes scanned over all of this and came to rest on Maurice, standing at the far end of the basement, facing away from him. He'd removed his overcoat and Jason could see the bulges of his once-muscular back moving beneath his shirt. His head was ducked down; only the nape of his neck was clearly visible in the lantern light. Jason could hear him muttering softly, and at first he didn't notice the pair of white hands on Maurice's lower back.

He took a step forward, squeezing the grip of the gun tighter, staring hard at those neat little hands gripping Maurice's shirt. He heard the other man say, in a voice that was uncharacteristically thick with emotion, 'Where've you been, honey?', and then there was a crash from upstairs.

Jason looked up towards the sound, thought *Shit, that's the living room*, and looked down in time to see Maurice turn in his direction.

'Kid,' he said, blinking at him through tears. Then he uttered a choked laugh and grinned, big and broad. 'Look who it is.'

Jason looked, and his blood became ice.

Evie stood there in Maurice's arms, her hands on his waist, smiling. Her hair was slick and wet in the moving glow from the lantern, and her skin was bone white. She wore Maurice's overcoat; it was much too large for her, trailing around her feet. When Maurice turned, the coat fell part way open at the front and Jason saw she was naked underneath it.

Maurice had one arm around her shoulders, hugging her side-on. Tears continued to roll down his cheeks.

'Look who it is,' he said again. 'Look.'

Evie's smile widened. Her eyes were as blank and white as her skin. In fact, Jason thought, her skin wasn't just white - it was almost *translucent*, as if it was pulled thin over something else, some dark thing that moved and shifted beneath.

And she was no longer covered in the barrel waste.

Jason couldn't smell her either way, but Maurice could. He was right next to her, breathing in her scent. That's what was thickening the air throughout the whole house.

Her scent.

'What's wrong, Jason?' she said, and her voice was no longer that of Evelyn Sparrow. It wasn't even the voice of a woman anymore. 'Aren't you glad to see me?'

She's shed her skin, he realized with burgeoning horror. *Like a snake. She's gotten rid of her clothes and her skin, and the smell's gone now.*

'Maurice,' he said, forcing himself not to look at her. 'Whatever she's making you think, it's not true. That's her. That's *Evie*.'

A frown creased Maurice's brow. He seemed to hug Evie tighter to himself.

'What're you talkin' about it, boy?' he said. 'This is my girl. My Mel. She's come back, after all this time. I thought she was gone, but she's come back.'

Jason felt dizzy. He kept his legs straight, straining against their sudden weakness.

'That's... that's not Melanie,' he said. The basement walls were beginning to waver around him now, as though he was underwater. 'That's not her, Maurice. I swear it's not.'

Maurice's frown deepened. His smile was gone now.

'Kid,' he said slowly. 'I understand you've never met her, but I know my own daughter when I - '

'That's not her! That's...

jaaasssooonnn

...Evie. You know it is. She murdered Mel and we're here to kill her for it, Maurice. You have to let her go.'

Maurice's eyebrows went up. 'Kill her?'

For the first time, he became aware of the gun in Jason's hand. He let go of Evie's shoulders and moved in front of her.

'Kid,' he said, even slower than before. 'You gotta give me that thing, ok?'

'Maurice...'

'Jason.' He held up his palm: stop. 'You give it to me, alright? I'll take it.'

Jason saw Evie smile with teeth and he thought *Fuck, he'll kill me if he gets it.*

'Come on, boy,' said Maurice, taking a step towards him. His eyes were huge, desperate, ready. 'You don't know how to use it anyway. Give me the gun.'

'Come on, Jase,' Evie giggled behind him, clasping her hands together. 'Come on, now.'

Jason pointed the gun at her.

'NO!' Maurice screamed.

He was faster than he looked, much faster. Jason had the trigger halfway pulled when Maurice slammed into him, throwing him back onto the floor. The gun sailed out of his hand and disappeared into the shadows. Evie tossed her head back and howled with laughter.

Jason started to get up, but then Maurice was on him. He saw rage on the older man's face, burning in his eyes. There was madness there.

'No,' Jason managed.

Then Maurice's fist connected with his mouth. A bright flash of red pain exploded in Jason's skull. Two of his teeth popped free and skittered across the floor, followed by a spurt of blood from his split lips. He grabbed for Maurice's neck but was too slow; Maurice's big, powerful hand closed around his wrist and bent his arm back, pinning it to the dirt floor. He hit Jason again in exactly the same place, harder this time. Jason heard a dull *crack* as his cheekbone shattered.

After that, he remembered little else. Maurice sat on his chest and whaled on him, punching him rhythmically and efficiently with both fists, snapping his head back and forth like it was made of rubber. His nose was broken afresh; his mouth became a bloody, swollen mass. Both of his eyes closed over, blackened beyond recognition.

Maurice did it all without pause, devoid of awareness, consumed with weariless fury.

As he pummeled Jason into the floor, Evie danced giddily in circles behind him, twirling in Maurice's overcoat, laughing with delight.

Lou left Debbie's body behind in the living room and went into the hall. She did so in a haze, like she was sleep-walking, barely registering the movement of her feet or how the grimy door handle felt against her skin. Her mind was gradually slipping away, drawn by something more than cold shock or grief. She wasn't entirely sure where she was, but a countdown somewhere at the back of her consciousness was ticking down, *tick tick tick*, and she knew she didn't have long left.

She looked to her right, towards where Evie's front door should be, and was only mildly surprised to see that it was now a set of double elevator doors. The digital readout above the elevator rolled from zero to zero in a constant loop. She imagined she could hear voices on the other side of the doors, faint and earnest.

She looked to her left, and instead of Evie's hallway there was now a long, white corridor with doors along one side. The doors were all open. She was back in Amber Hill General.

The voices from the elevator grew louder and she started walking down the corridor. She wasn't afraid - the force driving her along wasn't a fearful one, no - but she knew that Fear was coming, probably soon. She also knew that she couldn't possibly be back inside the hospital right now, but that didn't seem to matter a great deal. She was simply in the moment.

She passed the first open doorway. Jason Rennor was sitting on the edge of the bed, staring blankly ahead of him. A woman with a cigarette between her fingers stood behind him on the other side of the bed, gazing out the window; tobacco smoke filled the room like big city smog.

A doctor with white hair and thick glasses was examining Jason's scalp. As Lou walked by the room, she heard him say, 'I'm afraid there's nothing else for it - the head has to come off.'

'But doc, it's just my nose,' Jason replied in a voice that was dreamy and without inflection.

'Still,' said Dr Randal.

Lou saw him produce a big red Pulaski from somewhere behind Jason and hold the blade up to the light, and then her feet carried her on.

She saw Maurice in the next room. He was in bed, bandaged up like a mummy, with a breathing tube jammed down his throat. A guy in a Seahawks baseball cap stood over him, tapping him repeatedly on the shoulder.

'Hey, buddy,' said the guy. 'You can't park here, man.'

Lou went on.

She knew what she'd see in the final room before reaching it, but it still came as a surprise. There she was, also lying in bed, with her mother seated in the chair next to her. Carol held a dog-eared paperback in one hand and talked abnormally fast without pauses for breath, oblivious to her daughter's unconsciousness.

'...and the Reverend you remember him although I suppose he would've been a lot younger the last time you saw him anyway HE told me that Josephine volunteered to help with the raffle but where was Josephine when I went looking for her I'll tell you where she was avoiding me HIDING from me anything to get out of lifting a blasted finger to help when she'd VOLUNTEERED to do it and you know the Reverend wouldn't lie you remember the Reverend don't you although I suppose he would've been...'

And then she was gone, and Lou found herself at the end of the hallway. There was a door on the right, one she hadn't seen from further back. A sign above it read *Fire. Escape.* It was slightly ajar. Lou pulled it all the way open and sent a small object at her feet skittering across the floor. It came to rest against the far wall and she saw it was a flattened pack of cigarettes.

'Maurice,' she said aloud, and went through the door.

It slammed shut behind her and she was back on the second floor landing of her house, right at the top of the staircase. The nightlight they'd bought for Ruth flicked on, illuminating the topmost stairs. The bottom steps vanished into darkness.

Lou teetered there for a moment, resisting a sudden, powerful tug of vertigo (*just throw yourself down the stairs and get it the hell over with*) before grabbing hold of the banister. She wobbled at the top step, almost went, then steadied herself. A spasm of pain jolted through her ribs, as if to remind her what had happened the last time she'd been at the top of this particular staircase.

But she wasn't *really* there now, was she?

'It's the illusion,' she said. 'It's her.'

Something cold brushed across the back of her neck. A breath. A finger. Every hair on her body stood on end.

Lou cleared her throat and said rather than called, 'Jason? Maurice?'

Nothing. The darkness yawned below her.

'Screw it,' she said.

She went down the stairs, one hand on the banister, the other on the wall. Each step creaked beneath her feet. She moved slowly, carefully, watching where her sneakers went. The banister was ice cold against her skin. She was certain the wall was wet, but she kept her eyes on where her feet were going. She didn't want to stumble, nor did she want to acknowledge the images that now hung in frames on the wall. They were all of Evie, and they were all obscene.

The pull of vertigo began to ease halfway down, but the sensation that something was right behind her grew steadily stronger. Gooseflesh rippled up and down her back under her clothes. The cold tickle on her neck, which was surely breathing now, came rhythmically.

'Forget it,' Lou said, with a little gasp as the step behind her creaked. She was almost at the bottom, beyond the reach of the nightlight. 'I'm not stopping now. I'm coming for you. I'm taking back - '

A whisper in her right ear: 'Naughty, naughty.'

Lou uttered a choked cry and leapt down the final two steps. She hit the floor, stumbled, ran into a wall obscured by darkness. There was a door on the left. She grabbed the handle and pushed it open, bundling herself through. As the door swung shut behind her, she heard Evie's tittering laugh from the foot of the stairs.

'Fuck you!' Lou yelled back.

Her voice echoed around and away from her. She looked at where she was now, and wasn't especially surprised to find herself in the Languages hallway of Amber Hill High School. It was dark and empty.

'Of course,' she said. *It's all part of the game, isn't it? She's messing with me, trying to put me off. She's trying to scare me into leaving.* 'Sorry, Evie - I'm still here.'

There was no response. The school remained silent.

She started walking. Her sneakers squeaked on the tiled floor. She flexed the fingers of her good right hand, wishing she'd had the presence of mind to grab the shotgun from the living room before coming down here. That would've been helpful, wouldn't it? Even if it'd been empty, she could've used it as a club to bash in Evie's skull.

I'll do it with my bare hands, she thought.

She passed the bathroom where Jason had killed some time before visiting Miss Sparrow, back when she was doped up in hospital and Maurice was roaming around town by himself, still waiting for his dreams to show him the way. Lou knew some of what had happened to Jason and Maurice over the past week, but not all of it. There were some things they didn't share. Some things were better left alone.

She came to the end of the hallway and turned left, and stopped. Her breath caught in her throat.

A boy stood there. He had unkempt black hair and green eyes. His arms were by his sides and he smiled when he saw her.

'Mom,' said Ben.

Her knees almost buckled. He was right there, just a few feet away.

'Ben,' she gasped, and his smile broadened. She took a step towards him, and then her feet planted and she couldn't go any further. It wasn't a supernatural force stopping her this time, though. She just couldn't bring herself to touch him. It would only confirm what she knew - that he wasn't really there.

'Where're you going, Mom?' Ben asked.

She swallowed. Her throat still ached where Debbie's hands had been not so long ago.

'I'm going to see her,' she said. Her eyes went past his shoulder. The English hallway behind him was empty, but there was light back there.

'No you're not,' said Ben, snapping her attention back. 'You're not going to see her. You're going to *kill* her.'

It wasn't a question.

'Yes,' Lou replied. 'If I can.' *Why didn't I grab that shotgun?*

Ben's smile dropped away. When he spoke again, his voice was tinged with sadness. Almost regretful. 'I wish you wouldn't.'

'I have to.'

'But you don't,' he said, and took a step towards her. He looked so small then, so young, and her heart burned. *My boy. My beautiful boy.* 'You don't have to go on. I need you. So does Ruth, and Dad, and Grandma. We all need you, Mom.'

Tears welled up in her eyes. She gritted her teeth behind her lips.

Ben was right in front of her now, gazing up into her face.

He's tall for his age.

'You can come back to us,' he said softly.

The tears welled over and trickled down her cheeks.

'I... I don't know if I can,' she whispered.

Ben nodded. 'You can,' he said. 'All you have to do is turn around and go back the way you came. Back up the stairs and out the door. And then come find us. We'll all be awake soon.'

Lou's hand went unbidden to her son's face. She drew it back with some effort. 'You will?'

'Yes. You can come find us and we'll all be ok again. It'll all be over. You just have to leave here.'

She stared into his green eyes, long and deep. She desperately wanted to believe him. Maybe part of her did. She was sure, somehow, that this wasn't Evie's doing, not right now. Ben was here of his own volition and he was trying to pull her away for himself, for his dad and his sister. For their family. This was her son, asking his mom to come home.

'Please,' he said, and took her hand. She felt his touch. It was warm and real to her. 'Please come back, Mom.'

She squeezed his fingers. He was right, wasn't he? She *could* go back. She could just turn around and walk out of here. Leave the illusion behind, leave Evie's house. Just go back to the town square and find her family, and it'd all be over. She knew that much was true - Evie was done with her now. She'd served her purpose, sustained her for a while, but it was time for her to move on. And she would. She'd leave Amber Hill and never come back.

But that was the problem, wasn't it? She'd just go on to the next town, and this would happen all over again. She'd take someone else's life and bleed them dry, and it would just roll on and on forever.

And she was weak now, Lou could feel that. Jason's plan had worked. Evelyn was weak and on the defensive. And she was afraid.

She'd come this far. And she wasn't about to leave Maurice and Jason, wherever they were. They'd saved her life. It was her turn, now.

Ben held her gaze without wavering, even when she let go of his hand. It was the hardest thing she'd ever had to do.

'I have to keep going,' she said. 'I have to do this.'

'You don't,' replied Ben, shaking his head.

She smiled then and marveled at her son. Her boy.

'You're right, I don't,' she said. 'But I'm going to.'

Ben looked at her for a moment longer, then nodded. 'Ok. I better be going, then.' He walked past her soundlessly; his arm brushed against hers as she turned to watch him.

'Where're you going?' she asked.

He went around the corner as he replied: 'I have to go wake the others.' Then he was gone.

Lou stared at the empty hallway for a second, then wiped a hand across her eyes and turned back. She half expected to see Ruth or Derek standing there and was relieved that they weren't. She wasn't sure if she could have resisted much longer.

She started walking again. Up ahead, she could see light pooling from under a door on the right. It was a door she knew very well, and she knew this was the end.

She came to it and paused to read the words printed at head height. The last time she was here (*really here*) they'd been 'Welcome to English!' and 'Room 2, Miss Sparrow'; now, they simply read 'LOU JENNINGS RIP' in scrawling black letters.

She turned the handle and pushed open the door.

It was as she'd expected. Who knows, maybe she was becoming incapable of surprise at this point. Maybe the rolling tides of trauma thundering over her had finally numbed whatever semblance of hope and rationality she had left. She'd been slammed into the ocean floor enough times now - all of the shock had been pulverized out of her.

She was back in her classroom in Amber Hill High and the kids were there. All of them. Every kid from every class she'd ever taught, all packed into the room. And yet the room remained the same size. Smaller, even. It was impossible, but it didn't matter, did it?

The kids watched her in stony silence. Some were seated behind desks with their actual textbooks open in front of them and pencils in their hands, as though she was once again their teacher. Others crowded into the remaining space, leaning against the walls, the cupboards, the window sills, and against each other. Hundreds of them, rows upon rows of them, all inside her classroom, all with their mouths shut and their eyes fixed squarely on her.

The classroom door closed. She looked back and saw Perry Martin take one hand away from the handle, and then clasp both of them together in polite expectation. He was dressed in a suit she'd seen him wear a thousand times, and even now, here in this unreal place, it still didn't fit him right. Like the kids, he simply watched her, and waited. Like the kids, he didn't speak, and he didn't smile.

It was hot in the room, airless. She became aware of something on her shoulder and reached up to touch it - a strap, slung casually where it hadn't been slung a moment ago. It was her teaching pack, the one she'd taken to work the last time she'd been here. She could smell the coffee that'd spilled on it.

There were other teachers in the room now, too. She saw Alain Doyle over by the window, and George Albee in the corner, leaning on the computer station. Julie Heller, her once-best-friend at work, was among the kids, staring. More of them, muddled in with their students. A wall of eyes, all for her.

'What do you want?' she heard herself say. 'What do you expect?'

Instantly, every eye shifted an inch to her right, just past her shoulder. She turned and looked.

There was her desk, the one she'd been sitting behind when the first suggestions of flu had begun manifesting inside her. It was empty now except for a notebook, which lay open and face-down in the middle.

There was her chair, the one that creaked in protest every single time she sat on it.

There was her whiteboard behind it. The words KILL CUT SPILL were written on it in blood. It dripped in little streams down the board and plopped to the floor, puddling there. The room was growing hotter by the second and the blood stank.

She turned back again to find the students and teachers had parted like the Red Sea, leaving a space through the center of the room. At the back, beneath the motivational posters she'd tacked to the wall ('*It's not about being the best, it's about being better than you were yesterday!*') sat Evie, gazing at her with gray, unblinking eyes. Gone were the red winter coat and black boots. She'd tied her mousy hair into a bun again, and she was in the same clothes Lou had first seen her wear: a beige sweater, long gray skirt, and sensible flats. She was seated on one of the classroom chairs with her hands in her lap and Maurice stood next to her, pressing the stolen police handgun to her temple.

'Lou,' he croaked, 'I've got her.'

Evie appeared tiny next to him. She tried flinching away from the gun but Maurice kept it against her head. His face was haggard and drawn, but his expression was triumphant.

'Come here,' he said. 'Hurry.'

'How?' Lou asked. Her feet were moving, carrying her through the crowd. They continued to stare at her as she passed. She could feel sweat running down her back in the oppressive heat.

'I got her,' Maurice repeated. His eyes flashed and a grin curled the edges of his mouth. 'She ain't gettin' away this time.'

'Lou,' Evie said in a small voice. 'Please...'

Maurice cocked the gun and Evie yelped.

'Don't give her a chance to talk,' he said.

Lou reached them. She stood in front of Evie, regarding her cooly. The other woman didn't meet her gaze. Lou was disgusted to see she was trembling.

She dumped the backpack onto the floor. Evie jumped at the sound.

'Look at me,' Lou said.

Evie raised her eyes to Lou's. They were gray and swimming.

'I'm... I'm sorry,' she moaned. 'I... I...'

Lou looked to Maurice and said, 'Do it.'

Maurice grinned. Then he shook his head.

'No. You do it. It should be you.'

He took the gun away from Evie's head and held it out to Lou. She stared at it for a moment, then took it. The grip was slippery with Maurice's sweat.

'P-p-please,' stammered Evie, visibly shaking now. 'M-m-mercy.'

Lou paused, watching her cower, then put the muzzle to her forehead. Evie became still and Maurice's grin grew wider. The room was an inferno.

'Mercy?' Lou breathed. The crowd pressed in. 'Sorry. I'm fresh out of that.'

Kill the pig.

Evie closed her eyes. Lou clenched her teeth, gripping the gun hard.

Cut her throat. Spill her blood.

'Do it,' Maurice urged. 'Do it now.'

Lou's head was heavy on her neck. The gun was light as tissue paper in her hand. It felt like a toy.

'Shoot her and be done with it,' said Maurice.

Evie's lips were moving. Lou watched them, thought she understood the words.

'Fucking do it!' Maurice cried, 'or I'll do it my - '

Lou pointed the gun at Maurice's head and pulled the trigger. The *bang* it produced stung her ears and warm blood sprayed up her arm. Maurice jerked backwards and crashed to the floor.

The crowd of students and teachers vanished as the illusion dissolved. Lou stepped back and the gun dropped from her hand. The bright light of the classroom became the gloom of the basement. Her eyes took a moment to adjust. When they did, she saw Evie sprawled on the floor. She lay on her side in Maurice's overcoat, one pale white leg stuck out like an iceberg on a dark sea. Blood pooled around her head, soaking into the dirt floor.

Lou's eyes swept the room, going from Evie's still form to the lantern hung in the corner, to the shelves along the back wall above the work bench. On one of the shelves sat Rick Anderson's eyeless, tongueless head, already sagged and gray with decomposition. Lou barely registered it, however. It wasn't the only horrific thing displayed on those shelves, and if she'd taken just a few seconds longer to acknowledge what some of them were, she might have lost her mind.

Instead, she looked at Maurice - the *real* Maurice. He was on his knees in the place Evie had projected herself only moments before, staring at her with a look of stricken shock on his face. His lips continued to move, as they'd done in the illusion, mouthing 'Cynthia' over and over. Lou remembered how fondly Maurice had talked about his late wife back at the cabin.

She'd come so close to shooting him in the head.

'Maurice,' she said, reaching for him. 'It's alright. It's over.'

As soon as her hand settled on his shoulder, he crumpled to the floor, releasing a low moan from deep inside him as he went down. She half caught him, but he was a big man and he fell to her left, against her injured wrist. She grimaced in pain as she eased him the rest of the way down.

'It's ok,' she said again. 'She's gone. She's dead.'

Maurice continued to moan. There were words mingled in there and it took her a moment to work out what they were. 'The kid,' he said, covering his face. 'Oh hell, the kid. I killed the kid.'

'What?' said Lou, leaning close to his head, trying to make him out. 'Maurice, where's Jason? What happened to him?'

He took his hands away and gazed at her in abject despair. She'd never seen such a look of total devastation on someone's face before and it snapped her fully back from the lingering haze of the illusion.

'Where's Jason, Maurice?'

His eyes grew wide. Then he was looking over her shoulder, and she felt his body go rigid beneath her hand, and in a voice that was unnaturally high with fright, he screamed:'BEHIND YOU!'

Lou became aware of something in her hair, scrambling for purchase, and thought *Evie's fingers*, and then her head was wrenched back painfully. She'd been in a crouch next to Maurice and tried to stand, but the tug on her hair caused her to overbalance and she fell back, toppling like a redwood tree. She shut her eyes, waiting for the impact that would knock the breath from her lungs and break her fragile ribs all over again, but it never came. Instead, she continued to fall, further and further, beyond where she knew the floor must be. Her insides leapt upwards, as though she was plummeting towards earth in the front car of a roller coaster.

She opened her eyes in time to see the basement pull away from wherever she was now, actually *pull away* like the opening at the end of a long tunnel, and then it was gone altogether, and she was in total darkness.

For a moment, she thought she was dead. The black silence surrounding her was so complete that the presence of breathable air seemed impossible. And the darkness wasn't just *around* her, either - it inhabited every molecule of space beyond her own body, leaving no room for anything else. She was *in* it; it was *in* her.

Where am I? she thought wildly. She stretched out her arms, saw her hands extend into the black. *Where the hell am I? What is this place?*

'Where am I?' she said aloud. Her voice came out clear as crystal but there was no echo, no reverb of any kind. It was as if a thick curtain had been pulled around her, absorbing the sound.

She took a step, then looked down. There was definitely a solid floor beneath her and her step had moved her forward, but she couldn't see what it was she was standing on. Her feet were set on the black and nothing else. For all she knew, there was a limitless expanse beneath her, one she could fall into at any moment, down and down and -

'What do you think?'

She jumped. Evie was right in front of her, just a few feet away. She wore the same white nightdress Lou had seen her in when she'd appeared beside her bed, the night she'd fallen down the stairs. Her hair draped her bony shoulders; her skin was so white it seemed to shimmer. The bullet wound on her head was gone.

Evie grinned and spread her hands. 'Like what I've done with the place?'

Lou could hear her own heart thumping and thought, *at least I'm alive.*

'Where is this?'

Evie looked around, arms still out, still grinning.

'It doesn't have a name,' she said. 'I didn't feel the need to name it. I'm usually the only one here. Well, apart from *them.*'

Something moved at the edge of Lou's vision. She turned and saw a man standing a short distance away with his hands in his pockets. He was old and tired-looking, and he had a cigarette stub between his lips. She recognised him but couldn't place his name. Evie did it for her.

'Old Bert here's been keeping me company,' she said, and giggled. 'Not much of a conversationalist, though. Right, Bert? Got anything to say, you old wrinklebag?'

Bert lowered his head sadly and shuffled away. As he did, Lou saw someone else standing just beyond him, someone else she recognized, whose name she *did* know. Her heart sank into her belly.

'Oh, no. Please, no.'

'Ah, you know this one, too?' Evie said casually.

Sarah Lanthem stood with her arms by her sides, staring at Lou. She wore a denim dress and pink sneakers, and her hair was in a ponytail. Ruth had begged for pink sneakers after seeing Sarah's at kindergarten. Little Sarah Lanthem.

Lou felt some part of her mind start to slip. Her breathing was coming in short, panicked bursts now. She took a step towards the little girl, her daughter's best friend, trapped in this dark, empty place with Evelyn Sparrow.

'Sarah - '

'Don't bother,' said Evie. 'She can't hear you. Not really.'

Lou clenched her fists. She was trembling.

'Is she...?'

'Oh, yes. Very much so.' Evie twirled a strand of hair around her finger. 'Debbie was kind enough to bring her to me. I doubt she could have gotten here all by herself. Children are just so *helpless*, aren't they?'

Lou tore her eyes from Sarah. She had the impression she and Robert Thornberg disappeared the moment she stopped looking at them. She didn't want to look again anyway.

'There are others here, too,' said Evie, 'but I don't think you know them, so let's not waste time.' She snapped her fingers. '"You're only wasting your own time" - that's something you teachers say, isn't it? What a line.'

Lou gritted her teeth. 'Who are you?'

Evie sighed. 'Are we still on that? You know exactly who I am, Lou-Lou. I'm Evelyn, your old pal, your sista from anotha mista. I'm Lou two-point-o, if that tickles you in all the right places. I'm you, only better. Only *fun*.'

'Why me? Why did you choose me?'

'Well that's a silly question, isn't it?'

'You could have chosen anyone - '

'Of course I could have,' Evie said. 'But I chose you, didn't I? That wasn't by chance, my darling, my sweet one. That was fate, providence, serendipity. I chose you because I was destined to choose you. You were in exactly the right place at exactly the right time. Or rather, you *weren't* in the right place, and I just filled the void. That's what I do, you see. When the spot's vacated, I step in and save the day. Hold your applause, please.'

Evie's eyes were huge and white. Lou felt light-headed looking at them. *Don't you dare faint*, she thought. *Not here. Don't give her the satisfaction.*

'You take what's mine,' she said sluggishly, 'and it makes you stronger.'

Evie grinned. 'If that's what makes sense to you, sure. Stronger. I prefer to think of it as more complete. As your life reduces, mine fills out, like sand falling from the top to the bottom of an hourglass. Eventually, the top half empties and the bottom's all full.'

'So what then?' Lou said. The numbing sluggishness was gradually giving way to anger, simmering into rage. 'You just... move on to the next person?'

Evie shrugged. 'I suppose so. I take a little break in between, when I'm all full and fleshed-out. There's no need to chase after anyone then, you see. And when I sense that starting to wind down, I keep an eye out for the next lucky gal. Or guy, depending on how things go. It always works out. Guess I'm just lucky that way -'

'What the *fuck* are you?' Lou spat, shaking where she stood.

'Ah, but that's not important, is it?' Evie replied, wagging a finger. 'People have been asking that question for a long time, trying to put me in a box for years now. Decades, even. Before that, they just accepted that I *was* without concerning themselves with *what* I was. People were easier back then. Everything was just black and white. The good ol' days, Lou-Lou-Bell.

'Lately, though, folks have been trying to name me, to *define* me. "What is she?" they ask. People like your buddy Maurice and that little shit Jason Rennor. They were so very annoying, weren't they? It would have been *delicious* to watch you blow old Mo's brains out, right there in my basement, but you're not so easily fooled, are you my dear? No you're not. Such a shame - I really thought you had it in you, too. The way you popped Debbie up there in the living room - that was the *real* Lou, wasn't it? I could've gotten on board with a best friend-murdering psychopath like her. But no, I'll just have to get my kicks some other way. And I *will* get them, I promise you that.

'And let me tell you this, Louise: all those people trying to put me in a box found out pretty quickly and painfully that I can't be defined with ease. Not by Maurice, or Jason, or by anyone else on this slimy little planet of yours. There's no-one like me in all the world. I am what I am, and I do what I please, and that's the end of it.'

She cocked her head, cupping a hand behind her ear.

'Hear that?' she said. 'That's the sound of the school bell. Our lesson's over.'

'No,' said Lou.

'Oh, but yes.'

And suddenly, Evie lunged at her. Lou had no time to react. In a flash, she was knocked flat and Evie had both hands on her face, her nails digging into the sides of her neck.

'I'll be off now,' she whispered, an inch from Lou's nose. This close up, she was horrific; Lou felt her legs turn to rubber. 'There's still a lot to do, isn't there? Yes there is. I think I'm done with this shithole town after all, but I've decided it deserves a parting gift. One in honor of you, Mrs Jennings, for all the trouble you've caused me tonight. You dumped me in a barrel of *shit*, you little bitch. That was *totally gross*.'

'Please,' Lou gasped, winded by the fall. 'Please, just go. No more - '

Evie wrenched Lou's head from side to side like it was some plaything. Lou heard her neck muscles crack. The pain was excruciating.

'No, no, no,' Evie said almost to herself, still wrenching Lou's head. 'No more favors, no more mercy. After all, you came here to do me the way you did Debbie, didn't you? Fancy thinking I was something you could hunt and kill!

'I'll swing by your house - well, *our* house - one last time, and give Derek and Ben and Ruth one for the road. And I won't bring them here afterwards, either. No, you can mind the place for me. I'm leaving you here, without them. For a *long* time.'

'No,' Lou said again, seizing Evie's wrists. Her own sprained wrist screamed back.

'Yes,' hissed the thing holding her face. 'Discussion over. Toodaloo, Lou.'

She let go and started to pull away but Lou held on, burying her nails in the cold flesh of Evie's wrists. It was like trying to keep hold of a dead eel. Evie's upward momentum pulled her back onto her knees. She almost lost her grip but somehow, in spite of everything, managed to hold on.

Evie was briefly taken aback. Lou caught the surprised look on her face and her strength was renewed. She planted one foot on the nothing-floor and pulled back. Her sprained wrist had gone numb,

'Let go,' Evie said. When Lou didn't, she swiped her across the face; Lou managed to duck partially out of the way and Evie's talons sliced open her cheek instead of her eye. She bit back a cry of pain and held on. Hot blood dribbled down her face.

Evie made a sound that was part exasperation, part predatory snarl. She tried to pull away again, directly upwards, but Lou kept her head down and didn't let go. Even when she heard Evie's wings unfold like bedsheets flapping in the breeze, she didn't let go.

'Why're you doing this?' Evie asked. Her voice was changing; it was no longer feminine, barely human. 'What's the plan? Keep me here with you, forever and ever? That seems like

FOLLYYYYY

to me, Lou. Not one of your better ideas.' Evie's fingers went in her hair again. 'There isn't anyone to help you, Lou. There's only me. And I'm the Beast.'

Evie rammed her talons into Lou's scalp and she screamed.

Across town, Ben Jennings sat up. He was wide awake and he'd been having the weirdest dream ever.

It was cold and it was nighttime. He looked around, trying to take in his surroundings.

There were people everywhere, lying on the ground. Orange and yellow lights swayed in the branches of nearby trees. About twenty yards away, a tabby cat perched contentedly on a large woman's back, cleaning its paw.

'Hello?' Ben said. No-one answered.

He dropped his disoriented gaze and saw his father lying next to him, flat on his back. His head was turned towards him and his eyes were closed. Ruth lay on the other side of him, breathing softly.

'Dad?' said Ben. He shook him. 'Dad, wake up.'

Derek Jennings did wake. He came out of it slowly, staring at his son, his consciousness knitting itself back together.

'Ben?' he mumbled. 'What's happened? Are you alright?'

'Yeah,' Ben replied, but he wasn't looking at his father anymore. He sat on the grass and watched as people began to wake up all around them. Most of them did as he'd done, hauling themselves upright, as if they'd just woken from an overlong sleep. Murmurings went around the town square. Someone was crying, a feeble sound in the still night air.

Derek had gathered Ruth into his arms and was patting her cheek gently. Her nose wrinkled and her eyelids began to flutter.

'Is she ok?' Ben asked. An image floated behind his mind's eye, just out of reach. Some place, dark and empty.

'I think so,' Derek said. Ruth smacked her lips and said 'Milkshake', and he stroked her hair. 'Ben,' he said, 'your mother. She was here. Where is she now?'

'Not here.'

'Then where... what're you doing?'

Ben was on his feet, wobbling a little. Derek grabbed his leg.

'Ben,' he said, looking up at his son. The orangey-yellow hue from the Thanksgiving lights framed Ben's head as he gazed across the square. 'Son, where's your Mom?'

'Away,' Ben replied.

He began to move off and Derek tightened his grip on his calf.

'Away where?' he asked. 'Ben, away where?'

'It doesn't matter right now.' Ben looked down at him, and something in his face made Derek let go. 'We have to wake up the others.'

'What? What others? Ben - '

'Not everyone's awake,' said Ben. He started to walk away. 'They all have to be awake. I have to bring them all back.'

'Ben!' Derek cried, trying to twist on the spot to see where his son was going. 'Ben, what're you doing?'

Ben was already crouched down beside someone, shaking them by the shoulders.

369

Evie let go of Lou's head. Freshets of blood ran down her face, trying to get into her eyes. She gasped, agonized, and looked up.

The thing that had once looked like a woman stood over her, flexing its claws. Folds of loose, gray skin hung limp below its jaw, which had fallen open to the brink of complete detachment; its head, skull-like and now devoid of any womanly features, was tilted upwards, and what hair it had left clung to it like rotting seaweed at low tide. Its wings were huge and black and punctuated with holes.

Lou could smell it now, a pungent, nauseating stench that reminded her of spoiled meat and urine. It was the smell of decay.

Evie looked down at Lou's hands still gripping her skeletal wrists. Her hanging jaw had elongated to the length of her head and a slippery gray thing that must be a tongue flopped out. When she spoke again, Lou heard the words entirely in her head, and what she sensed in them was unmistakable.

Fear.

Release me. Release me now!

She held on as the wings began to beat. Evie pulled her back to her feet as she tried fruitlessly to escape, but it was all she could manage.

She's weak now, Lou thought, and her face broke into a grin. *I don't know why, but she's weak.* The blood running down from her scalp stung her eyes, but she kept them open. She was going to watch this.

Release me!

'No chance,' Lou panted. 'If I'm staying, so are you.'

Evie began to scream. Lou heard it in her head - a piercing, alien sound from beyond the world. The thing jerked and thrashed and tried to rise away from her, but she gripped tighter, straining every muscle against it. The black expanse around them began to shift and move, falling away. She had the impression of people there, watching from distance, watching Evie flail and scream in terror.

Let me go!

She kicked out at Lou, catching her in the chest. Her taloned feet cut into Lou's shoulder and the fresh pain caused her to lose her grip with her injured left hand. Evie momentarily rose into the air, then tilted to one side. Lou still had a hold of her with her good hand. She wrapped the fingers of her sprained hand around her right wrist and leaned back, pulling Evie down.

Nooooo! Release meeeee!

'Take me back or die here!' Lou yelled.

Evie screamed again and the darkness rushed away. Lou felt her stomach drop like a stone. The watching people disappeared. The black nothingness cannoned away and her vision filled with light again. With a gasp, she realized she was standing in the basement once again.

'Lou?' she heard Maurice cry, followed by, 'What the *fuck?*'

She still held on to Evie's wrist, but it was barely more than a bone now. Her skin hung off her in loose rags, actually dropping off in places in gray globules that splattered on the floor. Her eyeballs bulged out of their sockets, quivering like overfilled water balloons. Both wings had snapped free from her back and folded to the floor behind her.

Lou released her grip and her palm came away with a layer of dead skin stuck to it. Evie's tongue flapped against her fleshless chest cavity like a suffocating fish on the deck of a trawler. She staggered where she stood, filling the room, decaying on the spot.

Maurice was yelling something but Lou couldn't hear him. Evie's dying scream filled her head, growing higher and louder by the second, making her dizzy. One of Evie's eyeballs popped out of her skull and burst on the floor.

Lou saw Maurice reach for her. She half turned towards him, extending her hand.

Evie screamed and sprang forwards. She shoved Maurice back and he stumbled into the bench, hitting it with his pelvis with a grunt of pain and surprise. In the corner of the room, the lantern fell and smashed on the floor, spilling hot oil. Some of it splashed on the dried-out bench, some on the molded cardboard boxes. Both caught and started to burn.

Lou held up her hands but Evie was already on her, screaming and flailing. She slammed bodily into her, knocking her back. Lou lost her balance and tumbled into the wall by the steps.

Evie shrieked triumphantly. At the same moment, just as Ben Jennings shook another resident of Amber Hill awake across town and the ambulance turned onto Oakland Avenue with sirens blaring, her insides gave way and slopped out . of her onto the floor with a wet *splat*.

She stumbled towards Lou, clawed fingers outstretched, but then Maurice was there. He grabbed her by the shoulders and tossed her back across the room. She crashed against the stack of boxes, spilling them into the pool of burning oil. Flames licked at them hungrily.

Evie regained her balance. She teetered there for a moment, looking from Lou to Maurice with sightless eyes, a rotting corpse in the shifting gloom. And then, with a hellish scream of rage and despair, she lunged towards Lou again.

The gun went off with a *crack*. Evie jerked to one side as the bullet sliced through her shoulder and embedded in the brick wall behind her. She swayed on the spot, just about staying upright. Gurgling black blood, she turned to look.

Crack.

The second shot hit her square in the temple. The other side of her head exploded open and gray liquid sprayed out of it onto the burning workbench. She pitched towards it, almost stayed on her feet, then toppled backwards into the flaming boxes, sending a plume of orange sparks into the air.

Jason's arm dropped back to his side and the police handgun gun fell to the floor. He spat a gob of blood and said, 'That'll do it,' and collapsed.

Maurice saw Evie tumble into the flames. She didn't go as he'd long imagined she would. There was no scream of rage, no final volley of malevolence. She went in silence, a rotting corpse, already mostly gone. A burst of sparks sent her on her way.

He turned to Lou. She was slumped against the wall with both hands on her chest where Evie had shoved her, evidently winded. There was a lot of blood on her face and she looked dazed, but she was alive.

He wasn't so sure about the kid, though.

Jason had crumpled back to the floor after dropping the gun and now lay on his side, facing towards the stairs. He wasn't moving.

The basement was rapidly filling with smoke as the fire took hold of the boxes. Maurice went to Jason, coughing and hobbling where his hip had bashed off the ancient workbench. He crouched down beside him, grimacing at the pain in his joints, and at what he saw when he rolled the boy over.

He'd done a number on the kid's face. His lips were split and swollen, and his nose looked like a squashed plum. Part of his cheekbone was visible where it had broken through the skin. Both of his eyes were mostly closed over.

How the hell did he see to shoot her? Maurice thought.

He hoisted Jason into a sitting position, cringing when he noticed his own split and bleeding knuckles, and cupped the boy's face in one hand.

'Kid,' he said. 'Kid, are you there?'

Jason moaned. His left eye opened part way. He saw Maurice.

'Is she...?' he slurred. He'd bitten through his tongue. 'Is...'

'Yes sir,' said Maurice, grinning humorlessly. 'She is. You got her.'

Jason mumbled something but Maurice couldn't pick it up. It sounded like 'Sucker', or something.

'We've gotta get out of here, kid,' he said, 'before this whole dried-out tinder-box goes up.'

He hauled Jason to his feet, coughing again, and helped him across to the exterior cellar doors. He called to Lou as he went, asking if she was alright, but she didn't answer. Wincing again, he lowered Jason onto the bottom concrete step leading up to the doors. They were sealed with a very old rusted padlock - he was sure it would snap off with a couple of blows. He could hear the faint sound of ambulance sirens above them, coming from the street on the other side of the house.

'Wait here,' he said to Jason, who raised a limp hand in acknowledgement.

He'll never forgive me, Maurice thought, going back to where Lou was. *How could he? I mangled his face. He'll need fuckin' plastic surgery.*

Lou was still slumped against the wall with her hands on her chest. Her legs were flat on the floor and her head was tilted back. In the flickering light from the flames across the room, Maurice could see her mouth moving.

'Time to go, Mrs Jennings,' he said, coughing smoke. *Funny how the stuff bothers me so much when I'm not suckin' it from a stick.* 'Hey, Lou.'

He cupped her cheeks as he'd done Jason's, bringing her head forward. There was so much blood on her face. It looked like she was wearing a red mask.

'Lou,' he said again.

Her green eyes met his. She was breathing heavily.

He dropped his gaze to where her hands were. Slowly, she took them away.

'Oh, shit no,' he said.

The jagged end of a corroded pipe jutted through her sweater, just below her right breast. It was red with blood. She'd been impaled on it.

'Dammit to hell,' he said. 'Come on, let's get you off this. There's an ambulance outside.' He reached for her shoulders, meaning to pull her free from the pipe, but she grabbed his wrist. Her grip was feeble.

'No,' she said. It came out in a wheeze.

'Yes,' he replied, but she shook her head, keeping hold of his wrist. Behind him, the flames crackled and spat as the heat from the fire grew. He looked her in the eyes again and his heart wrenched.

'Please,' he said thickly. 'I can't leave you here. It's ain't right.'

She forced the words out. 'Have to.' Then, tilting her head weakly towards Jason, added, 'Save him.'

Maurice looked at the boy slouched on the step a few feet away, then back at her. He could see she was going fast. There wasn't much time.

'It ain't right,' he repeated, his voice quavering. 'It ain't *fair*.'

Lou nodded, once, slowly. Her eyelids were heavy with blood.

'But... it's done,' she managed. 'Go.'

Maurice held her there, unable to make himself move. Lou let go of his wrist and smiled morosely as her own hand fell limp at her side. Maurice thought, despite everything, and not for the first time, that she was beautiful. Beautiful, and serene.

He swallowed hard, then leaned in and kissed her forehead. When he pulled away, he saw her eyelids were beginning to flicker.

'See you round,' he said, touching her cheek. 'I'll come find you. I swear.'

Her smile remained. He stood up and turned away, going straight to the cellar doors. There was a loose brick on the top step, flush to the wall. He snatched it up and a fat centipede scuttled away from where it had been, disappearing immediately. Bracing himself against the wall, he hit the padlock with as much strength as he could muster. It only took three blows to break it.

He dropped the brick and yanked the smashed lock free. The bolt didn't want to move but he got it sliding anyway. With a grunt, he pushed one of the doors open. A gust of night air swept into the basement and the oxygenated flames whooshed over the workbench.

Maurice descended the steps, coughing in the smoke. He slipped an arm under Jason and pulled him to his feet. The boy was heavier than he looked but still conscious and able to get his legs going up the steps with Maurice's help. Gray smoke billowed past them out through the doors.

They went out into the night.

Lou watched them go. Darkness closed in steadily around the edges of her vision, but she saw them reach the top of the steps and turn out of sight. They'd made it.

She turned her head away from the doors. It felt so heavy on her neck now, like she was wearing a helmet made of stone. The thought came to her coherently. She was surprised by that.

Across the basement, the fire had devoured the boxes and the rusty bicycle, and was now eating into the workbench, spewing smoke. The bottom shelf above it had begun to burn, too. They'd all be up in about a minute, Lou thought.

She could feel the pipe inside her and wondered how she was still alive. She was quite sure it had gone through one of her lungs.

Movement within the flames drew her gaze. She looked towards them, squinting through the smoke, and thought she saw something fall forwards out of them and onto the floor. It lay there, still and smoldering, just beyond her feet. She watched it.

After a few seconds, the burned thing began to crawl. It wasn't much more than a skeleton, fleshless and blackened by the fire. It dragged itself towards the cellar steps, slowly and pitifully, crumbling to ash as it went.

Lou watched it for a moment, then turned away and closed her eyes. She saw Derek and Ruth and Ben, all gathered together on the couch, laughing and content and safe. She smiled, listening to her heart beat down, hearing it more than the sound of the fire filling the basement. She didn't see the crawling thing reach the bottom step, didn't see it desperately extend a gnarled, blackened hand towards the open door.

She didn't see it. She only saw her family.

She went.

THANKSGIVING

Maurice took a long drag on his cigarette. He held the smoke for a few seconds, then blew it out the window in a white puff.

It was Thanksgiving morning. He was in the weed-strewn parking lot of an abandoned diner just off the highway. The diner had once been called 'Betsy's Place' but some letters had dropped off the sign; now it was 'Besy lace' and its "world-famous pancake stack" was no longer on the menu.

Maurice blew another puff out the window. The sun had risen just above the line of trees across the road and their resident birds chorused happily, welcoming in the day. It was unnaturally mild for November.

He'd spent most of the night outside Betsy's, hunched against the driver's side door of the Sable with his arm under his head. It'd given him a hell of a crick in the neck. He knew he'd need a few painkillers or a stiff drink later. Or both, probably.

After leaving the burning basement of sixty-four Oakland Avenue, he'd half-supported, half-carried Jason along a narrow alleyway separating the back-yards of houses on adjacent streets, looping back round to the car further along, well out of sight of the paramedics on the front lawn. He lay Jason down across the back seat and got himself behind the wheel just seconds before the first police cruiser went blaring by. As he turned off Oakland Avenue, a second cruiser passed without slowing. He knew the fire truck wouldn't be far behind.

Jason had been conscious (just about) and was able to tell him where he lived. Maurice drove straight there and helped him up the walk to the front door. There were lights on inside. He bid the boy farewell and hurried back to the car. He waited until the door opened and watched as Judy Rennor came running out and threw her arms around her son's shoulders, sobbing hysterically, and then he drove off. He hadn't stopped driving until he was twenty miles outside of town. By then, Betsy's parking lot had done just fine.

He studied his knuckles in the morning light. They were cracked and raw. He didn't remember doing what he did until the last few seconds; he had one fist raised above the kid's bloodied face and had Mel's name on his lips, and then he understood, and the shock of it made him keel over onto the basement floor. When he came-to again, he was on his knees with a gun to his head and Lou was walking towards him.

He thought about her now. Her wound had been fatal, he knew that. Even if he'd somehow been able to slide her off that rusted pipe and get her to the paramedics out front, she wouldn't have made it. He *knew* it, for sure. Because if she'd thought for even a second she could have survived - could have been with her family again - she would've *made* him take her off that pipe and carry her to the front lawn. And he would have done it, too. He'd have carried her and Jason together, even if it'd killed him.

But she knew. He'd seen it in her eyes when she looked at him.

There'd been a report on the radio just after six. A local station had it. There'd been an "incident" in Amber Hill during the town's annual Thanksgiving festival. Some sort of "mass neurological event", explained the show presenter, who'd never strung those words together in a sentence in his life. No-one could explain what had happened. No-one knew why everyone had been on the ground, or why there was a barrel of stinking toilet waste under the stage. In fact, it seemed no-one could remember anything about the festival after the awards portion of the evening began. The presenter suggested it might have been a gas leak, or perhaps even a terrorist attack.

'Either way,' he'd finished, 'as they say in Amber Hill, keep your eyes peeled for the witch. It's as good an explanation as any, if you ask me.'

Maurice had snorted at that and turned the radio off. He checked his phone sporadically throughout the next hour, drifting in and out of sleep (*shit a brick, had he ever been this tired in his whole life?*) until finally, just before seven, a more detailed report appeared on a county news website. He skimmed the first section about the incident in the town square. It wasn't what he was looking for now.

Then he found it: '*Tragically, the bizarre event at the Thanksgiving festival wasn't the only shocking occurrence in Amber Hill last night. Local media reported that a residential fire in the western part of town had followed a series of shootings in the area. One teenager was found with a non-fatal gunshot wound to the abdomen outside the derelict house on Oakland Avenue where the fire occurred, while two other bodies were recovered from inside. Both were women, the first of whom has since been identified as Deborah Lanthem...*'

He'd skipped past the part about Debbie. She was the one who'd clocked him across the back of the head when he'd gone into the house. She'd taken his gun and left him to Evie.

Two other bodies.

He scrolled down a few lines.

'*...daughter Sarah is still missing. The other victim was found in the basement of the house, where the fire is believed to have originated. Authorities have identified her as Louise Jennings, another local resident and English teacher at Amber Hill High School, survived by her husband and two children. Popular with school students and their families, Louise was also well-known for her charity work, and was to be the recipient of the People's Hero award at...*'

Maurice had stopped there.

'Two bodies,' he'd said aloud. His throat was sandpaper.

He'd wondered at that, but not for long. It didn't unnerve him the way it always had in the past when she'd slipped away. On every previous occasion, she'd left on her own terms, when her work was done and she'd gotten what she needed. She'd left every place full and vivacious and in control. This time, she'd been weak. She'd lost her hold on the town and that had caused a break in the chain, cutting off her lifeblood at the source. And when Lou had died, Maurice suspected, the final chord tethering her to the world had been cut.

He'd seen her brains blown out. He'd watched her burn.

It was enough. He felt it in his heart now, the thing he hadn't felt since before Mel's passing, and it made him sure.

Peace.

Mostly.

He took one last drag on the cigarette and tossed it out the window. There'd been a sign a mile or so back for the next town, some place called Rockmount. He'd stop there for breakfast and then start his long journey west. It was time

378

to go home; he still had enough cash to get there. That, or buy himself another shotgun. Just for some peace of mind.

Maurice turned the key in the ignition and rolled up his window. He pulled out of the parking lot and onto the road, and started driving.

ACKNOWLEDGEMENTS

The idea for *The Substitute* arrived one day, fully-formed, while I was making tea in the kitchen. The kettle was boiling, there was a fresh tea bag in my mug, and Evelyn Sparrow stepped through my doorway. This'll always be my first ever horror novel (I plan to write many more), and it'll always hold a special place in my heart.

That fully-formed idea was sparked by my wife, who spent several years as a substitute teacher waiting patiently by the phone for "the call" from a nearby school. That's where it started, anyway - I have Christine to thank for getting the ball rolling. She was also the first to read the completed manuscript, even though horror ain't her jam (thanks, honey!). I also gladly thank my faithful beta readers, Diane and Margaret, who offered good constructive criticism and helped me refine the story further.

Other thanks go to the patient folks at GetCovers, who designed the cover of the book and graciously tweaked it many times over without complaint, as well as the multitude of generous online creators whose content I consumed and/or shared while bringing this novel to life. The entire process was a major learning curve for me, but I'm proud of how it turned out.

Lastly, I have to thank all the authors, screenwriters and directors who influenced me so heavily over the years with their books, TV shows and movies - you helped establish the endlessly-looping terror reel in my head, from which my worst fears and best stories so often spring.

Evie thanks you, too.

ABOUT THE AUTHOR

David writes from his home in Northern Ireland, where he lives with his beautiful wife Christine and their two dogs, Lupin and Ghost. He loves books, movies, football (he's better at watching than playing), and getting his hiking boots dirty.